THE EDUCATION OF CAROLINE

The Education Series: Book 2

JANE HARVEY-BERRICK

HARVEY
BERRICK
PUBLISHING

Copyright © 2014 Jane Harvey-Berrick
All rights reserved.
ISBN 9780955315084

Harvey Berrick Publishing
www.janeharveyberrick.com

Copyright © Jane A. C. Harvey-Berrick 2014

Cover design by Nicky Stott
Cover photographs by Shutterstock and Justin Bell QGM

Thanks for permission to EMI Music Publishing to reproduce lyrics from 'Martha's Harbour', All About Eve
Acknowledgement to 'How to Avoid Being Killed in a War Zone' by Rosie Garthwaite and 'One Dog at a Time: Saving the Strays of Helmand' by Pen Farthing
'High Flight', John Gillespie Magee, Jr. (1922—1941)

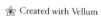 Created with Vellum

DEDICATION

To Lisa Ashmore, for telling me to write this series
To Sheena Lumsden, for her humour and energy and loyalty
To Audrey Orielle, for loving Sebastian so much

Thank you.
JHB

PROLOGUE

WHEN A WOMAN TURNS FORTY SHE IS NO LONGER YOUNG, BUT NOT yet old.

At least, that's what I was told by friends who had reached that milestone some years ahead of me. I wasn't concerned, although perhaps I should have been: my work as a freelance journalist was always uncertain, my mortgage large, my pension minute, with the future unwritten. So, yes, turning forty should have bothered me, or at least sparked my interest a little, but you can't force yourself to feel, can you?

I never dreamed that my past would catch up with me, and that I'd be drawn back into the erotic madness of a decade ago.

But then again, perhaps life is what happens when you least expect it.

CHAPTER ONE

I GAZED AROUND THE TABLE AT THE FACES OF MY FRIENDS, BATHING in the warmth of their love.

Nicole smiled back at me and raised her glass.

"Well, today's the day," she said, winking at me. "The big 4-0! Not that you look it, beotch! Happy Birthday!"

Jenna and Alice lifted their cocktail glasses and clinked across the table.

I smiled wryly.

"Well, some days I certainly feel forty. But not today—it's so great that all you guys made it."

"Are you kidding?" said Nicole. "Of course we made it—and I *never* go to Brooklyn, so you should feel really honored, Venzi!"

"Here we go," muttered Alice, "the 'I never leave Manhattan even to see how the peasants live' speech."

"Yeah, yeah," snorted Nicole.

I laughed, happy to hear their bickering, which was as familiar and innocent as air.

These were my friends, but I thought of them as family. And they had all come to my favorite Italian restaurant in Brooklyn to celebrate with me.

"So, you're leaving us again," sighed Alice. "Up, up and away on your travels."

"It's not exactly a vacation," retorted Nicole.

She would have raised her eyebrows except she'd been for her monthly Botox treatment, and the upper part of her face was currently immobile.

It was true: it wasn't a vacation—I was going away for work. And I was living my dream.

I'd come a long way since arriving in New York ten years ago, penniless and unhappy, fleeing a failed marriage and a doomed affair.

It hadn't been easy, although I doubt that moving to the Big Apple is easy for anyone. But for me, it meant living by myself, by my own efforts, for the first time in my life. I was scared and adrift in a city I didn't understand, where I knew no one.

At first, I'd lived in a horrible, low-rent hostel, before finding a tiny apartment in Brooklyn's Little Italy—a place that became my home for the next eight years. I cleaned people's apartments to earn money for food and rent, while saving what I could to go back to school to study journalism and photography.

I'd been in New York for less than two months when 9/11 happened. The world changed on that day: everyone's lives were different, as if we'd lost our innocence. The smoke and ash had hung in the air for days after, the feeling of shock and despair lasted much longer. And then came the anger—it was so strong, it was like a nightmarish creature that haunted our waking dreams. You couldn't see it, but you could feel it, glimpsed in the faces of people around you —those expressions you caught out of the corner of your eye, that showed the rage was still there.

But there was also a sense of togetherness, maybe of shared experience. It was as if the whole city came together to care for each other. We mourned together, we tried to pick up the pieces together. It was as if we were one big family, living through a crisis together. It was just a different atmosphere. Everyone wanted to help out, everyone had some sort of connection to those buildings.

Somehow, selfishly, it fit in with my own sense of loss: not just the life I'd left behind in California, but also because I'd lost who I was.

A year passed before I opened my eyes, shook myself from my torpor and found a way to live again.

An old acquaintance from San Diego had helped get me some ad hoc work on local newspapers and, from there, I'd managed to begin my freelance writing career. At first, it was just small features: a food festival in Brooklyn, a music festival in Queens, but gradually the scope of my writing became more wide-reaching, adventurous even.

It was shortly after that, when a piece I wrote called 'The New Immigrants' about asylum seekers, had caught the eye of a national newspaper editor and suddenly and unexpectedly, I was on my way. For the past six years I'd been lucky enough to earn my livelihood as a foreign correspondent, working freelance for several major newspapers.

Two years ago, I'd even saved enough to put down a deposit on a tiny, 1920s bungalow in Long Beach. My mortgage was scarily large, but I wanted somewhere of my own: somewhere I could come home to as driver of my own destiny, and queen of my own castle.

I'd loved living in Brooklyn and was sorry to say goodbye to my favorite coffee shops and restaurants. There was a real sense of community in the neighborhood, and the area thrummed with the vibrancy of the constantly changing wave of people that passed through.

By this time, I was working mostly from home—'home' being wherever my laptop was—so the commute into the city didn't bother me, and I was ready for another change. For much of my life I'd lived near the ocean, certainly during the most significant parts, and I loved that sense of space and peace that living by water gave me. Above all things, I loved to walk down to the shoreline when a big swell came and watch the surfers like so many seals, clad in black neoprene, bobbing behind the line-up, then charging down the barreling green waves. Sometimes, in the summer, I'd take my surfboard out and join them. It brought back happy memories and I felt carefree for an hour or so.

My new home in Long Beach was a fascinating and diverse community. I loved the mix of people, and spent many happy hours just watching the world go by, often finding inspiration for new stories. My neighbors included an elderly Jewish lady, Mrs. Levenson, who used to walk side by side with her close friend, Doris, a Hispanic mother of three small children. Then there were the teenage beach bums, quietly smoking pot all day, hanging out on the boardwalk or by the mall, quiet and inoffensive. They all had their presence in the town, all part of the diverse culture, color and life.

In recent years, it had become popular with Manhattanites to come for the weekend, no doubt finding it friendlier and considerably cheaper than a few days in the Hamptons. Long Beach's renewed popularity might have had something to do with the recession, of course, but I liked to think it was for its unique identity and sense of freedom.

My new home was surrounded by delis, bagel shops, and diners. Brunch was my favorite meal of the day, and on weekends, the colorful variety of eateries was packed with people placing orders to go, or waiting for a table to get breakfast. Even on weekdays it could be busy, but I was more likely to be able to get a table to myself and spend an hour or so staring out the window or working on my laptop. An Italian coffee shop on the boardwalk was—for all intents and purposes—my second home, the older members of the family chatting to me in strongly-accented Italian, the younger ones in English, of course.

One of the main commuter rail branches went directly from Long Beach to Manhattan, so it was handy for when I had meetings in the city, which seemed to happen with increasing frequency once I'd quit Brooklyn. Of course.

But the weekends were all about the beach. Even in the winter, when it definitely wasn't lay-out-in-the-sun weather, people still liked to parade. The boardwalk spanned the entire town and every type of person seemed to take a Sunday stroll, although perhaps I was the only one who still enjoyed walking in the rain.

On a nice day, families mingled with the athletic-types taking a break from the overcrowded and sweaty gyms to go for a run or bike ride in the open air. Elderly couples would sit at one the many benches, gazing out toward the water. I liked to fantasize that they were contemplating their youth and memories of earlier days when running and jumping came as naturally as breathing, but perhaps they were just planning what to eat for lunch.

Perhaps they were thinking about their families: children who lived in different states or different countries, long-lost friends, dear, departed parents.

I had been close to my father, but my darling papa had died more than 12 years ago. I was not close to my mother. She did not like her daughter.

I didn't like to look back that often.

My most precious memories were closely guarded secrets and I only looked at them occasionally, taking them out of my Pandora's Box of the past, to treasure and enjoy, then carefully replace and lock away. As the years passed, I looked less and less, because, perhaps, I felt there was more to look forward to. And this was new.

As far as my friends were concerned, I barely had a past. They recognized that I preferred not to talk about it, and they respected my wishes, or else they knew better than to ask.

I'd dropped my married name the moment I'd left my husband, and I'd even hacked my Christian name into small pieces, choosing just one short syllable, a new identity for my new life. Instead of Mrs. Caroline

Wilson, I was now Carolina Venzi—pronounced the Italian way—but known to my new friends as 'Lee'.

And funny enough, it turned out to be very handy: people often made the assumption that 'Lee Venzi' was a man. There was one editor who had bought my freelance features for five months before he'd discovered that it was a woman writing articles about crime in the city. I'm not sure I'd have gotten the commission if he'd known the truth, but by then it was too late and, he had to admit that he'd liked the job I'd done—which was all that mattered, in my opinion.

It amused me, but it suited me very well, too. I was eager to retain a level of anonymity in my work, more particularly, some distance from my past.

And now I was forty. More confident than ever before in my life, believing in my abilities, and comfortable in my skin, I had a career that I enjoyed. True, it was an itinerant lifestyle that could take me away from home for weeks or even months, but it was one that suited me. I'd spent the first thirty years of my life dormant and static, now I liked to be on the move. Besides, there wasn't much to go home to other than a shelf of books, and a closet full of clothes from my old life that I no longer wore.

A few men, very few, had drifted in and out over the years, but there was no significant other, there was no significant anything at all —and I was quite happy to keep it that way. I had the company of my friends, and that was more than enough.

Nicole, in particular, found my casual celibacy hard to understand. She was forever trying to set me up with 'cute guys' that she knew. It became something of a game between us: her vowing that one day I'd meet someone who'd sweep me off my feet, and me promising it would never happen.

What I didn't tell her, what I had no plans for her to know, was that I *had* been swept off my feet once before, and that the trail of devastation I'd left behind me after that event was still too painful to examine. The memories stayed carefully locked away.

My current assignment would take me away for an unknown number of weeks—perhaps as long as two months. I'd been hired by *The New York Times* to write about US servicemen and women being deployed to Afghanistan.

My friends were supportive, but they didn't really understand why I wished to take the risk. It was hard to explain. Perhaps it was about being master of my own destiny and being able to do what the hell I wanted for the first time in my life. Perhaps it was something to do with having arrived in New York with no more than a few hundred dollars, and an ancient and worn out Ford Pinto that died shortly after crossing Verrazano Bridge. Perhaps it was a need to empathize with people who took risks. I couldn't say.

It had taken me years to afford a way of living that many women my age were able to take for granted. Maybe those were the reasons that I seemed drawn to document the lives of those who had significantly less.

My first foreign assignment came about because my agent knew a little of my background—eleven years of living on military bases had certainly given me an insight. I was sent to several camps near Mosul and Baghdad to report on the living quarters of military personnel—and, for once, a woman's point of view was wanted.

So my latest assignment wasn't the first time I'd been paid to go somewhere dangerous, but it was certainly going to be one of the most challenging.

"I'm going to miss you, Lee," said Nicole, sadly. "Who am I going to hang with on the weekends?"

"You'll manage," I smiled, "and I'll be back long before the summer. "Besides, you have the keys to my place, so you can all go and do what you usually do—check out the cute surfer guys."

"Yeah, but it's not the same without you," complained Alice, "even though you never notice any of them."

"Maybe you'll meet a hunky soldier," said Nicole, with a leer. "God, I love men in uniform."

"They're not in them very long around you," snarked Jenna.

Nicole just winked and threw me a challenging look.

I shuddered. My ex-husband had been in the military—I definitely wasn't going down *that* particular route again.

My flight was the following morning, even though the newspaper was still fighting the bureaucrats in DC to get my visa and travel documents approved. An additional set of hurdles had been erected by the Department of Defense, in the form of requiring me to attend a 'hostile environment' training program for journalists, specially put on by the military in Geneva, before traveling on to the Middle East—or South Asia, depending on your point of view or political affiliation.

I'd never been to Switzerland before, although I'd flown over it a number of times. It was something new.

Before dawn, I was ready and waiting at the front of the bungalow for the headlights that would announce my taxi. I'd tucked my passport into my back pocket, packed up my small travel bag, tugged and pushed and pulled at my heavy, wheeled suitcase, and slammed shut the door to my home.

I'd become used to living with the minimum of necessities, and dressy clothes were very low on the list. When on assignment, I lived in jeans and lightweight walking boots, and had a no-frills haircut that required low to zero maintenance—I just pulled it all into a rough ponytail. Makeup? Not really. I had an old lipstick and tube of mascara somewhere in the bottom of my bag, but a fully charged smart phone and laptop were more important, and I never went anywhere, not even to the bathroom, without a small notebook and pencil. I had some of my best ideas in the bathroom. Probably too much information. I'd even perfected the art of making notes to myself in the dark to save the hassle of turning on a light when I woke in the night with an idea —of course, reading my scrawl in daylight was another story.

I did, however, have a set of my own body armor that weighed a ton, and cost me a fortune in excess baggage charges.

My cab driver, who was just finishing his shift, was unusually quiet for which I was grateful. He dropped me off at the international departures terminal, and I began the first leg of my long journey.

~

I rolled over in bed and groaned. The six-hour time difference between New York and Switzerland meant that I was wide awake at four in the morning, and the prospect of sleep seemed slim.

I tried to force my eyes shut, but they soon drifted open of their own accord and I lay staring at the ceiling.

My hotel was one of those nondescript blocks of concrete that you could find in any city, in any country, the world over. But it had a central location, functional rooms, free Wi-Fi, and boasted a tiny swimming pool and gym. I'd stayed in far worse places and probably would again—in fact, as I was headed to Afghanistan sooner rather than later, that was a given.

Feeling gritty-eyed and grumpy, I climbed out of bed and gazed out of the window. My room was just high enough up for me to see Lake Geneva glittering darkly in the distance. I was tempted to go for a walk, to stretch my legs and try to wear myself out enough for sleep to take me again. But wandering the streets of a strange city in the early hours was asking for trouble, even somewhere as safe and well-ordered as Switzerland. I wouldn't have lasted long in my present job taking those sorts of unnecessary risks.

Turning from the window with a sigh, I wondered if the swimming pool or fitness center would be open: it seemed unlikely. Frustrated and sleepless, I pulled out my laptop and spent a couple of hours reading news stories online.

I finally managed to get an hour's sleep before my alarm dragged me awake at 7AM.

The face that stared back at me in the bathroom mirror made me want to shatter the glass with my hairbrush. Today, I looked every one of my forty years. I felt like draping a black cloth over the mirror to blot out the view. Instead, I turned to the shower and contemplated the creamy-white tiles, as my tired brain stuttered into action.

The shower was marvelous, so powerful, it almost pinned me to the back wall. It was like having hundreds of little fingers massaging me, and definitely provided the shot of vigor I needed to face the day ahead. I was very grateful for the deep pockets of my employer in providing for my current comfort.

I pulled on a pair of jeans, not caring that I was woefully underdressed compared to the rest of the hotel's clientele. Hungry, I enjoyed a leisurely breakfast comprising of *zopf*, a rich, white bread baked into the shape of a braid, and served with butter, different jellies, honey, *emmental* cheese and a selection of cold meats. There was muesli, too, of course, but that didn't interest me. Too much like the granola I usually had at home.

I was just contemplating whether or not to order a third coffee when I heard someone calling my name.

"Hey, Lee! Yo, Venzi! What the bloody blue hell are you doing here?"

I looked up and grinned.

Bearing down on me was Liz Ashton, an indomitable British bulldog of a woman in her late fifties. She was rather famous in our field, an English Marie Colvin you might say, having been to every war front since Chad in 1979, every civil unrest since Uganda in the 1980s, and every guerrilla action since El Salvador in 1981. She'd reported on every atrocity from Croatia to the Congo, and was as tough as nails: probably tougher. She didn't take shit from anyone.

Liz was a senior reporter with *The Times* of London. We'd become friends over the course of the last five years when we'd run across each other in a variety of low-rent hotels, pitched together among the testosterone-rich world of the foreign correspondent.

"Hi, Liz! Good to see you!"

She swept me into a hug that almost cracked a rib.

"You, too. So, what's cooking, Venzi?"

"I'm in town for a hostile environment training course," I replied. "I'm supposed to be flying out to Camp Leatherneck in four or five days. You?"

"Hmm, well good luck with that. A little bird told me that your top brass are being tricky customers over non-military personnel visiting their precious Base since that last blue-on-green incident..."

Incidents where our so-called allies attacked US personnel were increasing.

"Who are you with on this one?

"New York Times."

"Well, tell them to kick some arses or you could be stuck here for weeks. My insurers are demanding that I attend some sodding training course for journos, too: how to wipe my bleeding nose in a 'conflict area', that sort of thing. I'm shipping out to Bastion next week, so we'll be neighbors. Just got to jump through the usual hoops first."

Camp Leatherneck was the US Marines' base in Afghanistan, and Bastion was the equivalent for British forces. I wasn't delighted to hear that my travel plans were likely to be disrupted, but Liz's information was invariably accurate: forewarned was forearmed in this job. Liz had spent years, decades even, developing her contacts, and she had fingers on the pulse of the beast that was international news. I made a mental note to contact my editor and see what strings he could pull to get me on my way.

"Is your training at the InterContinental by any chance, Liz? Because if it is, then I'm on the same one."

"Excellent news, Venzi! We can go and get pissed afterwards."

I really didn't think that was a good idea: Liz's drinking sessions were legendary. I definitely wasn't in that league.

"No way! I can't keep up with you. You'd be carrying me home."

"You're such a lightweight, Lee."

"That is true—and I intend to keep it that way, so stop trying to lead me astray."

"Ha! All work and no play makes Jill a dull girl. Come on, let's go and see who they've sent to whip us into shape this time."

Outside, the air was clean and crisp, the faintest whisper of spring penetrating the crystal clear morning. The city felt very European, the architecture reflecting the mix of French, German and Italian influences, and, in the distance, I could see the dominating summit of Mont Blanc, snow lying thick on the top like frosting.

Liz linked her arm through mine and we strolled through the city, behaving like a couple of tourists. I had to drag her away from an upscale chocolate shop where they sold crystallized lemons dipped in dark, milk, and white chocolate. We could have easily spent a week's salary in there and gorged ourselves stupid under the supercilious eye of the sales assistant.

There was a time when the piercing eye of someone like that would have reduced me to a nervous wreck, but not anymore. I wasn't twenty and married to a bullying man; I was forty, myself at last, and doing a job I was passionate about.

Less than a half-mile from the Palais des Nations and its long avenue of national flags, the InterContinental was an ugly, 18-story tower in the center of the diplomatic district. In the distance, the Alps outlined the horizon, reminding me, if I needed it, that I wasn't in Kansas anymore.

The receptionist directed us to a nondescript, beige-colored conference room, where coffee and croissants awaited us.

Liz dug in with gusto and I decided one more cup of black coffee wouldn't go amiss.

I thought about what she'd told me, and the probable delays I'd experience. I suspected this was the old Washington two-step. It had happened five years ago when I'd been trying to get to military bases in Iraq. I was shuffled around between departments, each one denying the delay was anything to do with them. I would try to be stoic, but it wasn't always easy.

For now both Liz and I had to play the game to get where we wanted to be. As we waited, six other journalists from various European nations joined us, a couple that I knew by sight, as well as my friend Marc Lebuin, a freelance writer who sold his stories to French language newspapers.

"*Chère* Lee, and *ma bonne* Liz! This is a most pleasant surprise. How are you, my dear ladies!"

He hugged us warmly and kissed us on both cheeks.

"Keen as mustard, Marc, and as excited as a wet weekend in Wigan. Where are you off to?" asked Liz.

He shrugged. "I do not yet know. I am here waiting for assignment. I think it is to pass the time. Perhaps I will learn some Farsi. I understand there is a language specialist here to train us. It might be useful, who knows? *Ça fait bien.*"

A young-looking British lieutenant entered the room, and looked around him rather nervously.

"New kid on the block," said Liz, grinning. "I think we can have some fun with him."

I groaned inwardly. Liz's idea of 'fun' didn't match mine. But there was no stopping her, not even a Sherman tank could change her mind once it was made up. Her mantra, 'compromise is the sign of a third-rate mind', summed up her general attitude to life.

The young lieutenant disappeared. I wondered idly if he'd noticed Liz's gorgon gaze and gone for backup.

As the scheduled starting time came and went, an irritated muttering rippled through the assembled journalists.

"Damn all this waiting around!" snapped Liz.

I cast an amused glance at my friend—she really didn't do waiting very well—which was ironic, because a good chunk of our work involved sitting around: waiting for the people we needed to talk to, hoping they would acknowledge our presence, waiting for flights, waiting for rides, waiting for visas, and waiting for permission to cross borders into war zones. It was rather similar to the military adage, 'soldiering is 99% boredom and 1% sheer terror'. I didn't mind the boredom.

The room was chilly, overly-air conditioned and similarly soulless. I hunkered down in my chair at the back of the room, and wrapped my long, cashmere scarf twice around my neck so it covered my chin and part of my nose.

Liz, as I said, was made of sterner stuff. She marched to the front of the room and fiddled with the thermostat, while the British lieutenant watched her anxiously. I could tell he was dying to tell her not to touch it, but had quailed beneath her withering gaze. She had that effect on most people—especially men. I wondered if I'd ever acquire that chilling, thousand-yard stare. Probably not.

The lieutenant kept stealing glances at his watch, and it became apparent that he was waiting for someone who was late. I imagined it was probably a journalist who was a no-show. That happened a lot: missed planes, changed schedules, visas refused, or even assignments cancelled at the last minute. As it turned out, I was wrong about that.

Very wrong.

Eventually we were joined by a much older man with the crown insignia of a British Major embroidered onto the epaulettes of his khaki uniform.

His cap badge was the tiny figure of Mercury—winged messenger of the gods—which meant he was from the Royal Signals Corps. I enjoyed the British whimsy embodied by that image.

The Major was a strong-looking man of about 50, with kind, hazel eyes that crinkled when he smiled. He wasn't smiling now. In fact he looked more than a little irritated and as he entered the room, shutting the door behind him, I heard him mutter something that sounded uncannily like "bloody Yanks".

I shifted uneasily in my seat while Liz winked at me.

"Well, good morning, ladies and gentlemen," he began. "My name is Major Mike Parsons and my colleague here is Lieutenant Tom Farley."

He indicated toward the young lieutenant, who was trying to appear relaxed and doing a very poor job of it.

"I apologize for the slight delay in starting, our American colleague has clearly been held up. However, we'll press on and begin with the basics. I'll be talking about prep and planning and what you need to have in your exit plan—primarily how you'll be repatriated in the event of injury or illness. Then I'll hand over to Lieutenant Farley, who will discuss making use of local knowledge and getting around in a dangerous place. In the afternoon sessions we'll cover coping with gunfire, keeping safe in a crowd, and emergency first aid. Tomorrow we'll be covering landmines, IEDs, chemical dangers, and what to do in the event that you are taken hostage. We'll be joined by our colleague from the US Marines for some of the sessions, and for an introduction to Dari and Pashto—the two official languages of Afghanistan." And then he muttered under his breath, "If he bothers to turn up."

Liz nudged me and I felt irritated that my compatriot, whoever the hell he was, was making the US look bad. I had to remind myself that such tardiness was not restricted to press training, after all, it was Washington officials who were deliberately delaying my paperwork.

The Major began his lecture, and although the advice was good, I'd heard it all before and my mind began to drift. I made a few desultory notes for the sake of appearance, but I already knew what to pack in an emergency grab bag for immediate evac (passport, solar-powered phone charger, first aid supplies, dried food, water for a day, flashlight, pocket knife—which I was always having confiscated at airports along with my matches, emergency contact list—known as the 'call sheet'), as well as basic safety messages such as arranging a code word for whoever arrived to pick me up at my destination. Obvious, when you think about it, but a tip that had come in *very* handy on a number of occasions. I'd passed that one to Nicole for when she met her frequent internet dates in unfamiliar places.

The Major went on to remind us about leaving the call sheet and next of kin details with our agency or a trusted third party. That bit always left me feeling sad. My next of kin was my mother, but we hadn't spoken in nearly ten years—not since she'd made it crystal clear what she thought of me when I told her my marriage was over and that I was getting divorced.

I was vaguely aware that she'd moved to a retirement community in Florida, but we weren't in touch. I certainly had no plans to name her in the event of an emergency. My real family were my friends, and I left my important numbers and my Last Will and Testament with my agent in New York.

Major Parsons then reiterated the importance of not having an Israeli stamp on our passports when traveling into Afghanistan or any other Muslim country. Yep, checked that box—we all had.

Then he handed over to the lieutenant who was competent, but far less polished in his delivery. I got the impression that this was the first time he'd delivered his talk.

The Major stayed for a few minutes to make sure his man was going to be okay, and then sidled out of the room. I was a big fan of sidling, and wondered how obvious it would be if I slunk out, too. But I knew the two-day training was compulsory for the newspaper's insurers, and there would be new things to learn after they'd gone through the basics.

I sighed softly and hunkered down a little more.

I woke up slightly when the lieutenant lost his train of thought for a moment, and became aware that someone else had entered the room. I craned my neck, wondering if the Major had come back. But it was someone else entirely.

A man, extraordinarily beautiful with a deeply tanned face, and blue-green eyes the color of the ocean.

A jolt of recognition shocked me. There was no doubt. Ten years older, but still stunning.

Sebastian Hunter.

Oh. My. God.

CHAPTER TWO

MY BREATH CAUGHT IN MY THROAT.

Sebastian: the reason my marriage had ended, the catalyst for my becoming a journalist. The man I'd loved more than any man, before or since. The man I hadn't seen for ten long years. My beautiful boy, my lover, my friend. The man I thought I'd never see again.

Sebastian.

Yes, it was definitely him. He was slightly taller, his shoulders were a little broader and his face a touch more angular, but otherwise he was unchanged. Except his eyes. Yes, they had changed, their sweetness hardened with the years.

Our affair, if you want to call it that, had begun when he was just 17 and I was already 30. As we were living in California at the time, it had been a criminal act. I'd fallen deeply, hopelessly, ridiculously in love. For his part, he'd been infatuated with an older woman, but his zest for life, his enthusiasm, support and belief in me, had opened my eyes to the dismal state of my marriage.

Our secret was discovered and dismembered in the most painful of ways. In a scene that still haunted my nightmares, I'd been forced to leave or face the cruel wrath of his parents. Even though Sebastian had been only months from his eighteenth birthday, my crime was a felony, and his parents had threatened to have me arrested if I ever contacted their son again. And, with California's statute of limitations being three years, I'd been forced to comply.

Since the day I'd walked out of my marriage ten years earlier, I hadn't seen or heard of Sebastian.

I'd thought of him often, wondering what he'd made of his life, where he'd gone, what he'd become, wishing to believe he was fulfilled and happy. And now, here he was, standing in the same room as me again, dressed in the khaki Service Uniform of the US Marine Corps.

I slumped lower in my chair, glad that my face was partially concealed beneath my scarf. My heart was beating so fast I was afraid I might pass out.

Liz nudged me.

"Are you okay?"

I nodded silently. She threw me a puzzled look, but shrugged it off, leaving me to dwell on remembrances of things past.

The door opened again and Major Parsons returned. He waited for the lieutenant to finish his point, throwing an irritated glance at Sebastian, who slouched at the side of the room, a bored expression on his face.

"Thank you, Tom. We'll take a short break now, ladies and gentleman, and meet back here at 1100 hours. Refreshments will be served in Les Nations lounge. And we're very glad to have our colonial colleague Sergeant Hunter to join us. I'm sure his insight will be invaluable."

I doubted I was the only one who heard the note of sarcasm.

The other journalists stood up to go, following our military escort out of the room, but I was incapable of standing, afraid that my legs would give way.

"Ah, the infamous Sergeant Hunter," said Liz, in a stage whisper. "Well, he certainly looks the part. Quite the lady-killer, I hear."

"Excuse me?" I said, faintly.

"The American ... he has something of a reputation. I'm surprised you haven't heard."

"Why would I?" I managed to choke out. "Heard what?"

She gave a conspiratorial chuckle and leaned toward me. If there's one thing journalists the world over have in common, they do love to gossip.

"Oh, I came across our Sergeant Hunter in Paris two years ago, although he was a humble corporal then. Well, not that humble, you understand! Yes, a rather notorious lothario: it was something of an *amour célèbre*. They say he was tupping the wife of his CO, although nothing was made public, and it was all hushed up."

"Surely that's just gossip?" I said, weakly. "I mean—if he had—it would have been a federal felony, a court martial, and then he'd have been thrown out of the Corps."

"I'm just telling you what I heard," said Liz, with a leer. "Suffice to say he was shipped out of Paris PDQ. Whatever the reason, they say he's got an eye for the ladies." She nudged me, a wicked look in her eye. "I imagine you'd be quite his cup of tea, Lee."

"Oh no, I don't feel like joining a harem," I laughed, a little faintly. "I'm sure Sergeant Hunter has a parade of young women following him."

I remembered that feeling *very* well.

If Liz noticed that my tone was off, she politely ignored it.

"Well, perhaps, but I believe his tendencies run in another direction—he's known to like his women older ... more experienced."

I winced.

"They say he's brilliant in the field," she continued, unaware of the impact her words were having on me. "That's why they put up with his behavior off the field. I heard a whisper that he was headhunted by military intelligence, but you know how close-mouthed your lot are about that. I wouldn't be surprised if he were one of those men who's a complete nightmare when he's not doing something dangerous. You know the kind: reckless, a bullet magnet." She tapped me on the arm. "They say he drinks."

Her comment cut through me like a knife. *Oh no. Not like Estelle—not like his mother.*

With some bitterness I remembered her drunken rant the night I'd left San Diego. She'd called me a 'whore' and 'slut' and various other unpleasant names. And she'd slapped me hard enough to make my teeth rattle. She would have hit me again if Sebastian hadn't stopped her.

The memories, long since locked away, came flooding back.

"Do you want to get coffee, Lee?" asked Marc.

"Sorry, what?"

"Coffee, Venzi!" snapped Liz. "Yay or nay?"

"Oh, no, I'm fine. You guys go ahead."

I wrapped my arms around my knees, physically holding myself together, as the intensity of my feelings floored me.

I took deep breaths and tried to keep calm, but my body was swamped by a rush of adrenaline and the desire for fight or flight overtook me. Right now I was favoring flight—except for the inconvenient fact that if I'd tried to stand up I'd have fallen over.

I heard someone return to the room and the blood drained from my face.

"You look a little pale, Lee," said Marc, a hint of concern in his voice. "Are you okay?"

"Yes, I'm fine. Just cold."

He gave me a look that showed he wasn't convinced, but accepted my explanation.

When the others filed back into the room, I hunched over my notes and hid as best I could. I was ashamed of myself. Why on earth couldn't I get up, walk over to him and say 'hi, hello, how are you' like a normal person? I would do it, of course, I told myself: I would do it during the lunch break, when we weren't surrounded by curious eyes.

Liz was the last to return, by which time I'd managed to pull myself together a little more, or, as my father might have said, a horseman galloping by at a hundred yards wouldn't have noticed anything wrong.

"Ready for round two?" Liz whispered loudly.

I could tell that she'd had more than coffee during the ten minute recess. I wasn't surprised—drinking was one of the hazards that beset our way of life.

And then my plans to reintroduce myself to Sebastian with a modicum of privacy and dignity were blasted out of the water.

"Just a quick roll call before we go on," said Major Parsons, "now everyone is here ... so we all know who's who." And he proceeded to call out our names. I was last.

"Lee Venzi?"

I nodded and raised my hand.

I saw Sebastian's eyes flicker across to me, then widen with shock as recognition set in, and, for the briefest of moments, he looked like the 17 year old I had known.

"You're Lee Venzi?" he blurted out.

Everyone turned to stare at me, alerted by the tone of his voice, so I was the only one who saw his expression turn to something darker, almost hateful—before he controlled his features and looked away.

My heart lurched uncomfortably. He looked like he really hated me. I hadn't expected that, although I suppose I couldn't blame him. It must have been a difficult time for him after I'd left. Even so, to have such a residue of dislike after so long ... I began to feel a little sick.

I took a deep breath and tried to focus on my notes.

Marc nudged me to attract my attention.

"You know that guy? Mr. Sullen-but-beautiful?"

"Yes, we've met," I said, dryly.

"Hmm, I think there's a story there, Venzi. Care to share?"

"Some other time."

He eyed me narrowly, but I twitched a small smile and returned my waning attention to the talk.

Unwillingly, I glanced at Sebastian, but he was staring out of the window, a faraway expression on his face. I wondered if he was remembering, as I was, how we'd met, and our brief but stormy summer of love. Or lust. Depending on your point of view.

Even as I tried to beat away the images, they filled my mind. Even now I remembered the intensity of our lovemaking, the way we could never get enough of each other—his hands, his lips, his tongue sweeping across my body.

As the lieutenant continued to lecture us on precautions against carjacking and criminal attacks, shatterproof windows and tracking devices, I was devoured by a series of increasingly erotic images that brought a warm flush of color to my cheeks.

"Because most attacks occur on reaching home," the lieutenant droned on, "always ensure that you can drive right into your garage or compound, and secure the door or gate behind you."

Liz looked bored, utterly clueless as to the helter-skelter of emotions that disturbed the equilibrium of my mind. She began to whisper an amusing tale to me, the gist of which was that she'd ended up ramming her car into the garage wall not once but twice, during a posting in Cairo, doing exactly what the lieutenant was suggesting. Her *sotto voce* comment was more *voce* than *sotto*, and caused several titters among the rest of the journalists.

The young lieutenant looked annoyed at Liz's too-loud interruption to his lecture.

"This is serious, madam. What I tell you today may save your life."

Uh-oh. Wrong thing to say to Miss Ticking-timebomb.

She inflated like the turkey float on the Macy's Thanksgiving Parade.

"Listen, sunshine, you may think you're something special with a weapon of mass destruction dangling between your legs, but let me tell *you* a thing or two: I've been to the frontline of every war since Uganda in 1979, before you were bloody well born." She started ticking them off on her fingers. "Angola, Croatia, Rwanda, Bosnia, Iraq, Kuwait, Afghanistan, and ... bloody hell, places you've never even heard of. And this woman," she pointed her chin at me, "has been in more hot spots than you've had hot dates."

I could have predicted Liz's response, although I didn't agree with her: to me the next assignment was always like the first—and experienced correspondents were just as likely to get hurt as the newbies.

The lieutenant's ears turned red, and he looked flustered. I thought I detected a small smile on Sebastian's lips, but it immediately disappeared, so I couldn't be sure.

Major Parsons stepped in to retrieve the situation and the poor lieutenant was allowed to continue.

Several times, during the rest of the lecture, I felt Sebastian's eyes on me, but every time I looked up, he'd glance away with a sneer on his beautiful face.

By lunchtime, I'd worked up enough courage to speak to him. But Sebastian, it seemed, had other ideas. He disappeared out of the door before I had the chance to utter a single syllable. I sighed. It looked like he wanted to avoid me.

Marc, however, more than usually sensitive to the emotions of others, was on the trail of a story.

"Come on, Lee, spill your beans. How do you know our Sergeant Hunter?"

"And how come you didn't say you know him?" Liz asked, sounding annoyed.

"It was a long time ago," I said, trying to sound casual, and failing miserably.

"And?"

"And nothing," I insisted.

"Oh, come on, Lee!" said Liz, accusingly. "You get me to tell you all the scandal I know about our mysterious Sergeant Hunter, and you don't even mention that you already know him. You're holding out, I can tell."

"Yes, *chérie*," agreed Marc with a smile, "I, too, think you are keeping secrets."

They knew me so well. Plus, they were journalists, which made them the nosiest people on the planet.

"I met him when I lived in California," I said at last. "When I was married."

"Ah," said Liz, knowingly. "Fair enough, Lee."

They both knew I was divorced and didn't like to talk about my marriage. Thankfully, they didn't ask any further questions.

I spent an uncomfortable lunch hour wondering what to say to him. What could I say? *Sorry about that—I hope I didn't ruin your life—how are you?*

In any event, I didn't have to say anything because Sebastian didn't return after lunch. His departure wasn't commented on by his British colleagues, and they stoically ignored his absence.

The afternoon session continued with little to inform or interest those of us who had sat through these lectures several times before. The only part I was really interested in would come on day two and covered questions specific to Kabul and, to a lesser extent, Kandahar.

I wondered why Sebastian hadn't come back. Surely it couldn't have anything to do with me? That would just be ridiculous.

When we were finally dismissed for the day, Liz wandered off to catch up with some sources, or so she said. I suspected these were more sauces—and of the alcoholic type. Marc muttered something about a prior engagement and I was left to my own, tangled thoughts.

Irritated with myself and perplexed by Sebastian's behavior, I spent a dreary evening in my room. I amused myself by writing long emails to Alice and Jenna. I didn't bother writing more than a few words to Nicole because I knew she only read the first and last paragraphs, unless the messages were from a guy.

I thought that I was at least tired enough to manage a reasonable amount of sleep, but my dreams were haunted by a memory of sea-green eyes, golden skin and naked flesh.

I was rudely awoken shortly after dawn, by an orgasm ripping through me. My back arched and my legs were rigid as I rode out the waves of sensation.

I sat up gasping, shocked at the way my body had betrayed me.

What the hell was that? An orgasm in my sleep?! That definitely hadn't happened before.

I staggered into the shower, trying to wash away the memories that continued to torment me.

The second day of the training began much like the first, except Sebastian's continuing coldness toward me became apparent to the others.

"The beautiful Sergeant Hunter is staring at you again, Lee," said Marc, unnecessarily. "He does not look happy with you."

Sadly, I had to agree.

Today, the lectures had started off with how to spot a minefield. Dead animals were a big clue, but it was also looking out for areas avoided by locals, particularly if the surrounding area was turned to agriculture, where anything overgrown stood out. Pieces of waxed packaging were something to look out for, too—explosives often came wrapped in them.

And then, for the language section of our training, we were in

Sebastian's capable hands—something of which I'd once had considerable experience.

"Yes," said Liz, agreeing with Marc's assessment, "young Sergeant Hunter narrows his eyes every time he looks at you."

I sighed and smiled at her. "Maybe my Dari pronunciation is lacking."

I'd been more than a little impressed to find that at some point over the last ten years, Sebastian had become fluent in Dari, a dialect of Afghan Persian, as well as Pashto and Arabic.

He was teaching us how to introduce ourselves and give our name, job title and nationality in the languages we'd need, as well as a useful passage from the Koran for emergencies.

I remembered how quickly his Italian had improved when we'd first started dating. Ugh, 'dating': that seemed such a deeply inadequate word for our tumultuous and passionate affair.

"Perhaps Ms. Venzi can answer that question."

Sebastian's voice cut through my bedraggled thoughts.

"Excuse me? Um, what was the question?" I stammered.

He didn't even bother to answer, but looked away, an expression of disdain on his face.

"Oh, dear! He'll have you staying behind after class," chuckled Liz.

Then he told us that a typical answer to a question an Afghan couldn't answer would be for them to say, 'because the sea is green and the sky is blue'.

"Tell them that and they'll think you're clever," he said, gazing condescendingly at me.

I felt flustered and annoyed—no matter what had happened ten years ago, there was no need for him to be so unpleasant. I decided I'd have it out with him at the first opportunity.

Sebastian's habit was to be the first out of the door as soon as a break was announced, dodging ancillary questions from any of the other journalists: either that or to dodge me. After the morning coffee break, I'd taken a seat near the exit so he wouldn't be able to continue avoiding me as we all left for lunch. And I made sure I paid attention during the rest of the language section so he'd have no reason to pick on me again.

Sure enough, as soon as Major Parsons called a break, Sebastian headed for the door.

"May I have a word, please, Sergeant Hunter?" I said, as he shot past me.

He almost skidded to a halt, but before he turned to look at me, an expression that I couldn't catch flitted across his face.

"I'm rather busy, Ms. Venzi," he snapped.

"Too busy to say 'hello'?" I shot back.

He stared at me for a long second.

"Yes, I'm too busy for that," he replied, then stormed out of the door.

Well, fuck you, too!

Unfortunately, I could see that our little *tête-a-tête* had been far from inconspicuous.

"Bloody hell, Venzi! What did you do to the poor bastard? He looks as pleased to see you as a fart in a teacup."

I shook my head in frustration.

"I have no clue," I lied.

"He is a rude man," concluded Marc. "He is certainly no gentleman."

I had to agree, but the thought saddened me. Ten years ago, Sebastian had been the gentlest of souls. I couldn't help thinking back to his many acts of kindness toward me. That had been a long time ago; it was obvious that he detested me now.

I decided that I'd done as much as I could. If he didn't want to talk to me that was his prerogative. I wouldn't push it. Besides, this wretched training would be over soon, and I hoped to be on my way to Leatherneck within the next two or three days. I'd contacted my editor, and he'd promised to make some calls on my behalf to get things moving.

It seemed my last chance to talk to Sebastian had gone already, because he didn't return after lunch for the end of the training. No comment was made about his absence, but I had the feeling that the British officers were relieved he'd disappeared.

"So, I hope you found the last two days useful, Ms. Venzi," said Major Parsons, as I was packing up my bag.

"Most informative," I said, blandly.

"Glad to hear it," he said, a twinkle in his eye. "Did you actually learn anything new?"

"I have doubled my vocabulary in Dari and Pashto," I replied.

He looked puzzled.

"I didn't know you had spoken any before?" he said.

"I hadn't."

He grinned as he caught the gist of my meaning.

"I see! Well, perhaps I can make up for your lack of progress by buying you a drink tonight?"

Oh. I wasn't expecting that.

"That's very kind of you, Major, but I have some notes to prepare. It has been a pleasure meeting you."

He took my rejection well, returning my handshake with just the right amount of pressure.

"Good luck out there," he said seriously. "Keep your head down. I'd hate to hear that anything had happened to you." He hesitated for a moment. "Perhaps we could meet up—next time you're in Geneva—or in fact anywhere in Switzerland. I'll be in this post for the next six months at least."

"Well, thank you. I don't have any plans to be in the country again, but I'll certainly make a note of that."

At which point he resigned the field, and left with his dignity intact —and my opinion of him rose even higher.

"You are not interested, Lee?" said Marc, a knowing look on his face.

"What's the point?" I sighed. "I won't be in Switzerland again for months, if ever."

"You could just take him for a quick ride—see what his rising trot is like," Liz smirked.

I rolled my eyes. One-night stands had never been my thing, and what I'd said was true: there was no point in starting such a long-distance relationship. Apart from which, I'd have been a fool to get mixed up with another military man after my disastrous marriage.

We headed to the bar and spent the evening with several of the other journalists, swapping tall tales about some of the locations we'd reported from. Liz's tales were by far the tallest—although in her case, I was willing to bet they were all true.

Shortly before midnight, I headed back to my hotel, feeling in a much better mood. I still hadn't heard back from my editor during the day, but I was hopeful I'd be on the move soon.

I threw off my clothes and showered quickly, before checking my emails again. Still no word about my ride to Leatherneck. Annoying— but I wasn't going to worry just yet.

I programmed my cell to wake me in the morning and turned off the light, hoping against hope that I might actually get some sleep.

I was woken abruptly when someone banged on my bedroom door. I scrunched up my eyes and peered at my phone. Jeez! Two in the morning. Who the hell was knocking on my door at this hour?

Grumpily, I switched on the bedside lamp, squinting against the light, and fumbled for my robe.

"Who is it?"

"Let me in, Caro."

No one had called me 'Caro' in years, in fact, only one person had *ever* used that version of my name. And I knew his voice—except the tone was off.

Surprise and shock made my heart rate spike suddenly.

"What do you want, Sebastian?" I called through the door.

"Let me in," he mumbled again. "I need to talk to you."

Now he wanted to talk?

He banged on the door again. "Caro!"

At this rate he'd been waking up the entire hotel. His timing was lousy.

Reluctantly, but curious nonetheless, I pulled the door open.

Sebastian was leaning against the door frame, deliciously rumpled in old jeans, black t-shirt and a brown leather jacket. Irritating *and* gorgeous.

"Caro," he said, a leer on his face.

Oh hell. And also *very* drunk.

"What do you want, Sebastian?"

He didn't answer, but pushed past me into my room.

"What are you doing?" I asked again, my temper rising.

"Catching up with old friends," he smirked

"How did you find me?"

He grinned and tapped the side of his head with one long finger, "Military intelligence."

I closed the door, hoping that no one had seen or heard his noisy entrance into my room. But the hotel corridor was silent.

He fumbled out of his jacket and tossed it toward the chair, missing by a mile. I couldn't help noticing that his t-shirt was snug on his body in a way that brought back too many memories.

He sat down on the bed, and patted the space next to him, suggestively.

"Come and sit with me, Caro," he slurred.

Oh, I really didn't think so.

I folded my arms across my chest and stayed standing. His gaze drifted up and down me in a way that heated my whole body. I hadn't blushed like that in a long time.

"Why are you here, Sebastian? You had your chance to talk to me earlier today, but you preferred to ignore me."

He blinked up at me, his sea-green eyes puzzled. It was strange seeing him so far from the ocean. Then he smiled again.

"You still have a great ass, Caro."

Enough was enough.

"Okay, I think you'd better go now. Whatever you have to say to me can wait until you're sober."

He just sat there smiling at me. I decided to make the hint more obvious. I walked forward to pull him off the bed, but instead he leaned forward, wrapped his arms around me and buried his face in my chest. This was getting ridiculous. Couldn't the man take 'no' for an answer? And I certainly didn't want to be part of any harem.

"Sebastian, stop that," I said forcefully. "I want you to go. Now!"

But he increased his grip, and his shoulders started to shake. With something like horror, I realized he was crying.

"Why didn't you come back?" he sobbed. "I waited and waited for you, like I said I would, but you never came back! Why? Why didn't you come back? I love you I love you I love you."

I was stunned. No. This was not what I'd expected at all. And then I wondered if all his apparent dislike, all the rudeness he'd shown me, was just a wall protecting him from the pain I'd put him through, a rejection that had lasted years. He still loved me?

Oh no.

He couldn't mean it. No, it was the alcohol talking.

"Sebastian..." I began.

He clutched me tighter and started kissing my chest, pulling open my robe and exposing my breasts. He fastened his mouth over my nipple and began to tug gently with his teeth.

I tried to push him away.

"No!"

But he didn't stop. He pulled me onto the bed and pushed himself on top of me, kissing my throat and breasts over and over. He was so strong, I couldn't fight him off, his arms held my wrists and his body was heavy, crushing me into the mattress.

"Get off me!" I yelled at him, dragging my hands free and pushing at his chest with all my strength.

With a long sigh, he rolled onto his back and was still.

I sat up, shocked and afraid. I pulled my robe together and stared at him. He was fast asleep, passed out drunk and snoring softly.

I was shaking from a fear-fueled adrenaline rush.

I shoved him with my hand.

"Sebastian, wake up! Wake up!"

He mumbled something and rolled onto his side.

Shit. Just what I didn't need.

I wondered what the hell to do. If I phoned for help, everyone would just assume we'd slept together. I didn't want to ruin my already dented reputation, and if I reported his assault, he'd be arrested and court-martialed, with the distinct possibility that our illicit past would be uncovered.

No matter how far I traveled, no matter how hard I worked, I was never able to outrun my past. The thought made me cold with fury.

In the end, I decided the simplest thing to do was to leave him as he was. He certainly wasn't going to be making any more passes at me in that condition, and a small but insistent part of me remembered that we'd once been in love.

I wrestled his heavy biker boots off his feet and pulled the duvet over him. I definitely wasn't going to sleep naked like I usually did, so I hunted down a loose t-shirt, pulled on a pair of panties and crawled back into bed.

It felt so strange to have him lying next to me again after all these years. I lay awake for a long time, listening to the sound of his breathing, a flood of memories stirring my brain and warming my flesh.

When my alarm woke me the next morning, for the briefest moment, I couldn't remember what had happened. I froze when I realized I wasn't alone in bed, and then it all came back to me: Sebastian banging on my door, his fumbling kisses, his strange admission—drunken Sebastian passing out in my bed.

I felt his body shift on the mattress and he flexed his hips, lightly pushing his very noticeable morning wood into my back. Some things never changed.

Cautiously, I moved away from him and sat up.

A sleepy blue-green eye blinked up at me. He looked puzzled.

"Caro?"

"You're awake then," I said, sharply.

He looked embarrassed and confused when he realized where he was.

"Did we...?"

"No, we most definitely did not. You woke me up in the middle of the night by banging on my door, and then passed out on my bed."

"Oh, right."

He leaned up on one arm and looked down at the clothes he was still wearing, assessing the truth of my statement. Then he grinned at me.

"Sorry about that. We can make up for it now if you like?"

I couldn't believe him. Who the hell did he think he was?

"Astonishing as this may seem, Sebastian," I said in a cool voice, "your charming offer doesn't thrill me."

His smile slipped and for a moment he looked hurt: I remembered that look. Then his arrogant expression was back.

"Whatever."

He swung his long legs out of the bed and sat up. He didn't seem to be experiencing any hangover effects whatsoever. *God, he was annoying!*

"Where are my boots?" he muttered.

"Under the chair," I said, pointing. "Along with your jacket."

He stood up and I was a little amused to see he had to rearrange his pants. He picked up his jacket and I realized he was leaving. I was surprised to feel a pang of disappointment.

"Why did you come here last night, Sebastian?"

He frowned, then shrugged. "I don't remember."

He strolled toward the door and glanced over his shoulder once.

"See you around, Caro."

And then he was gone.

I sat there for several minutes, trying to process what had just happened. He'd always been so easy to read, but now I didn't have a clue what was going on with him.

I shook my head and made a mental note not to open my door to strange men in the middle of the night, no matter how hot they were or how well they filled a pair of jeans.

After my unusually stimulating wake-up call, the day dragged. My editor had emailed during the night to say that my travel documents had definitely been delayed, but that he was hoping to get hold of someone who could help as soon as possible. The small print was: expect to be stuck in Geneva for at least a few days.

Liz commiserated with me over breakfast.

"Sorry to hear that, Lee. I got my papers couriered over from the Embassy first thing. My flight leaves in a couple of hours. Maybe see you out there."

"Maybe," I said, wearily. "Look after yourself. Keep your head down and watch your back."

"You know me, Lee, I wear brass knickers—utterly indestructible."

We hugged briefly, and she was off again.

I texted Marc to see if he was free. I couldn't face a day wandering around pointlessly by myself. I much preferred pointless wandering with company. I was relieved when Marc said he'd be happy to meet up. We spent a peaceful day examining a photography exhibition in the Sonia Zannettacci gallery, and strolling along the Quai de Seujet toward the lake.

By early evening, I was starting to feel hungry and Marc offered to keep me company over a plate of pasta in a small, family run bistro that I'd discovered just around the corner from my hotel. I was digging into a very tasty *pizzoccheri*, a tagliatelle-type pasta made from buckwheat flour and cooked with asparagus and diced potatoes—a local specialty—when Marc's phone beeped to tell him he had a message.

"I am afraid, *chère* Lee, that I will be leaving you alone after this night. My papers and assignment have come through."

I was pleased for him but a feeling of despondency washed over me. How could the British and French governments expedite visas for their nationals, while my own was so inept?

As we discussed his imminent departure to Fayzabad in the north of Afghanistan, we made vague arrangements to meet up, should we find ourselves within spitting distance.

We'd nearly finished a carafe of house red, when I became aware that someone was hovering over us. To my astonishment, and more than a little dismay, I saw it was Sebastian.

He looked as though he was barely managing to rein in his temper, his eyes blazing.

"We need to talk," he said from between gritted teeth.

Before I could frame a reply, he grabbed my arm to pull me up.

Marc stood immediately. "Let go of her, *m'sieur*, or you and I will have a problem."

Sebastian scowled at him and for a moment I thought I was going to be breaking up a fight, but then he dropped my arm.

I wanted to know what the hell Sebastian was playing at. Whatever his problem, I'd had enough of this game of hide and seek where he was the only one who understood the rules.

"It's okay, Marc," I said, quietly.

He raised his eyebrows, stared at Sebastian, then back at me. "Very well, but I will be phoning your mobile in 15 minutes to check on you, *chérie*."

I smiled and blew him a kiss.

"Who the fuck does he think he is?" snarled Sebastian as I left the bistro with him.

I stared at him in amazement. "A friend! What's it to you?"

He didn't answer.

I trailed along beside him as he marched down the street in furious silence. I didn't know whether to be amused at his petulance, angry at his rudeness, or wary of his apparent temper. All three, probably.

He ducked into a small *bierkeller*, holding open the door for me. Well, that was a small improvement in manners. The barman nodded at him in recognition, and Liz's words came back to me: *they say he drinks.*

He ordered without asking my preference.

"*Deux* whiskies."

He had a damn nerve!

"*Non merci, je préfère du vin rouge, monsieur.*" I'd always preferred red wine to whiskey.

Sebastian looked enraged. *Well, fuck him.*

The barman poured our drinks, then wandered off to serve a couple of tourists at the other end of the bar.

Sebastian tossed the whiskey down his throat, and turned to face me.

"What are you doing here, Caro?" he said, a scowl marring his lovely face.

"That's a good question, Sebastian," I replied calmly. "Right now, I'm wondering why the hell I'm listening to you order me around."

"Oh, for fuck's sake!"

His reply was almost amusing. Almost.

"Seriously, what is it to you?" I asked, genuinely interested in an honest answer.

He ran his hands over his hair, a gesture, I remembered, that expressed extreme frustration.

"It's dangerous out there, Caro. In Afghanistan, I mean. I know that's where you're going—obviously."

What?!

I took a deep breath.

"Sebastian, apart from the fact that I've already had assignments reporting from Iraq and Darfur—which weren't exactly summer camps —*it's none of your business.*"

"It *is* my business!"

He really was unbelievable.

"Based on what?"

He was silent.

"You know, Sebastian," I said, my voice rising with anger, "I spent 11 years being told what to do by my ex-husband—I don't need *you* to do it as well. You of all people should understand that."

He blanched, his expression wounded. It was the first time either of us had referred to the past or what had happened between us.

"Caro, that's not it, I..."

But I'd had enough. If these were the pearls of wisdom that I'd come to hear, thereby screwing up my last evening with Marc, I'd had enough. I stood up to leave.

"Caro! Don't ... don't go."

His expression and voice were pleading.

"Why did you bring me here, Sebastian? And I'd *really* like to know why you assaulted me last night."

He gaped at me.

"Assaulted? I didn't! I'd never..." his words trailed off and he stared at me in anguish, as he saw the anger on my face.

"Actually you did—you were just too drunk to remember it. You're damn lucky I didn't report you. Although I'm fairly sure you can work out the reason why I didn't—why I couldn't. Good night, Sebastian."

I took a step away, then turned and looked back at him. "I hope you have a nice life, I really do. And while you're at it—quit drinking before you really do something stupid. More stupid."

And then I turned on my heel and left.

CHAPTER THREE

I WAS FUMING AS I STRODE BACK TO MY HOTEL. WHETHER IT WAS the chill night air or the memory of his hurt expression as I walked out, my anger began to cool.

And no matter how inappropriate his behavior, I realized it was because he was concerned about my well-being. I shook my head. I really couldn't figure him out. One minute he was either ignoring me or just plain rude, the next trying to sleep with me, then acting like a jealous boyfriend when he found me with Marc. And *how the hell* did he find me in the first place? Twice.

I wished we could have talked like two normal human beings. That seemed unlikely. There was too much history, too much turbulent water under the bridge.

By the time I slid the keycard into the door of my hotel room, my ire had leached away. Instead, I felt restless and irritable. I checked my cell to see if I'd had an email from my editor, but although he'd written to say he was still chasing his contacts in the Defense Department, there was no other news. Worse still, it was beginning to look like the delay would be numbered in weeks, not days.

I threw the phone onto my bed in disgust, and decided a hot shower might relax me. It was a futile hope.

I'd just wrapped myself in a towel when I heard a knock at my door. My instincts told me it wasn't going to be room service.

"Yes?"

"Caro, it's me. Can we talk?"

"I think we've said everything, Sebastian."

"Can I come in? Just to talk."

"Is that a joke? No, you can't."

There was a pause, then his voice became quieter and more strained.

"Caro, please. I won't ... try anything. I just want to talk to you. Please."

His voice sounded so desolate, my resolution began to waver, buckle, and give way entirely.

"Okay," I sighed. "Listen, I'll meet you in the lobby in five minutes. That's my best offer."

"You ... you don't trust me?"

I didn't reply.

"Okay," he said, softly, "I'll be waiting."

I ran a comb through my wet hair and pulled on a pair of jeans, t-shirt and jacket.

I half expected him to be waiting outside my door, but the corridor was silent and empty.

The elevator slid to the ground floor, exhaling with a soft hiss as the doors opened. My eyes scanned the room and I saw him at once. He was sitting on a long, low sofa, his head in his hands.

When he looked up and saw me, his expression cleared, a small smile appearing on his face. He stood up politely as I approached, but my own gaze, I'm sure, was wary.

I sat on a chair next to the sofa, and waited for him to speak.

"You came," he said, quietly.

"Evidently. What do you want now, Sebastian?"

My voice was cool and distant, although inside I felt anything but.

"Would you like a drink?"

I raised my eyebrows. "Is that supposed to be funny?"

"No ... I..."

He looked longingly toward the bar, then dropped his gaze to his hands.

I crossed my arms and waited for him to speak.

"What you said earlier..." He took a deep breath, and that simple action seemed to raise some sort of emotional barricade.

"I didn't really assault you, did I," he said, confidently. "You were just saying that to get back at me."

Is that why he'd begged me to come here? To call me a liar? A fantasist?

"No, Sebastian, you really did," I replied with some heat. "You were drunk ... I couldn't ... couldn't stop you."

I closed my eyes, and shivered at the memory.

"If you hadn't passed out when you did ... you scared me," I said, looking him in the eye. "It reminded me of your..."

I bit my lip to stem the flood of my hasty words, but it was too late. He gasped.

"I reminded you of ... of my father?"

I nodded, and his expression was stricken.

"You were really afraid to let me in your room just now? I scared you that much?"

I didn't reply, leaving an appalled silence hanging in the air.

"Oh God! Caro ... I never ... I couldn't..."

I stared at him doubtfully. The boy I'd known would never have hurt me—but he was long gone. I didn't know who Sebastian was anymore—he was a stranger.

"Fuck, Caro! I'm so sorry."

He dropped his head into his hands again.

I beat back a long-dormant urge to comfort him, to hold him and tell him it would be okay. Instead I continued to stare at him, tracing the memories of ten, long years in the past.

My cell phone rang, which was a very welcome interruption.

"*Chérie!* I have been calling and calling you! Are you all right?"

"Oh, shit! Sorry, Marc. Yes, I'm fine. Really. You don't need to worry."

"Hmm, okay, you are still with him?"

"We're just sitting in the lobby at my hotel. I'm good, really."

"*Bien, ma chère.* If you say so. Call if you need me."

"I won't, but thanks, Marc. Have a safe flight and look after yourself—I wouldn't want anything to happen to you. *Ciao.*"

Sebastian frowned. "Was that your *friend?*"

I rolled my eyes.

"Is he your boyfriend?"

I laughed, but without humor.

"Marc is a good friend. He was just ... being concerned."

"Yeah, right."

"Actually, I think you're more his type."

Sebastian looked surprised. I'd known for years that Marc was gay, but he didn't broadcast the fact—it wouldn't have been good for his career.

"Did you ... tell him about me?" he asked, quietly.

"Which part?" I sighed. "It doesn't matter: the answer is no—it's not anyone's business but mine."

I looked pointedly at my watch.

"Sebastian, it's late and I'm tired. If you've got anything else to say to me, say it quickly. Otherwise I'm going to bed."

He stared at his hands again.

"I'm sorry I've been such a jerk," he said, his voice quiet, almost humble. "It was just ... a shock ... seeing you again."

"For me, too," I said, softly.

He looked suddenly hopeful, and I regretted giving him a reason.

"Let me make it up to you, Caro. Let me take you out tomorrow. I could show you the city. I've been here for months—I know my way around pretty well."

"I don't think so..."

"Caro, come on. I'll be on my best behavior, I promise—I know your travel permit hasn't come through."

I narrowed my eyes. "How do you know that?"

"Well..." He paused. "That was just the impression I had. You'd have been packing otherwise."

Again, there was something off about his tone, but I couldn't put my finger on it. On the other hand, this whole conversation had been more than usually fraught.

"Please, Caro, I know some great Italian restaurants. It'll be like..."

He hesitated, so I finished the sentence for him, "...old times?"

He gave a small smile. "Do you have anything better to do?"

I sighed, giving in. "No, I don't. Fine. But one false move, Hunter, and you'll regret it."

He grinned hugely. "Yes, ma'am!"

I couldn't help smiling back.

I was exhausted by the heated emotions that had been superabundant lately. A glass of wine sounded damn fine. I looked over toward the bar.

Now we'd talked and he'd apologized, I was able to relax a little.

"I think I will have that drink now."

Before I could stand up to go to the bar, he was on his feet.

"I'll get it. A red wine?"

"Yes, thank you."

I slumped in my seat, watching him lean against the bar while waiting to be served. The last time we'd spent time together like this, he hadn't been old enough to buy alcohol.

I was surprised when he returned with two glasses of wine, I'd assumed he'd be hitting the whiskey again. I was very glad to see he wasn't.

"I got you a Barolo."

"Mmm, my favorite."

"I know. I remembered you liked it."

I stared at him in amazement. How on earth did he remember something like that?

"Oh, well ... thank you."

I suddenly felt awkward again, his gaze was too intense. I sighed. It was time to have *that* conversation.

"How was it ... after I left?"

He leaned back on the sofa and closed his eyes, as if in pain. When he opened them again the old wounds were raw.

"Bad."

He swallowed, and I could tell he was trying to find the words.

"Mom and Dad were ... in the end Mitch went to see them—I didn't know what he said at the time but he and Shirley took me to live with them. Later, I found out that Mitch had threatened to go to my dad's CO and tell him that he'd been ... beating up on me."

My hand fluttered to my mouth, trying to block the rising nausea.

"On my eighteenth birthday, I enlisted in the Marines." He looked up. "That's pretty much it."

"And Mitch and Shirley? Ches?"

"Mitch and Shirley were posted to Germany soon after that. Ches was studying at UCSD so when I had leave, I used to hang with him and his college buddies." He smiled briefly. "He's married with two kids now."

"You're kidding me? Really?"

I tried to imagine happy-go-lucky Ches as a responsible father of two. And then I remembered a time when Sebastian and I had thought about having children. An impossible dream.

"Did he enlist?"

"He was going to, but then he met Amy at college and she talked him out of it. He's the manager at La Jolla Country Club now."

I had memories of the country club, the brief few weeks of my membership while Sebastian had worked there as a lifeguard. In particular I remembered one very steamy session of illicit sex in a changing room storage closet, of all places.

From the heat in Sebastian's eyes, he was currently on the same page. I had to look away.

"Are Shirley and Mitch still out in Germany?"

"No. Mitch got sent to Parris Island as an instructor. But last time

I saw them, they were talking about going back to San Diego. I guess they want to be near their grandkids."

"Where did Donna and Johan go?"

An odd expression crossed Sebastian's face. "How did you know they went away?"

I hesitated, wondering if an honest answer was in anyone's best interest after so many years. But, perhaps, after all, it needed to be said.

"I wrote to them."

He leaned forward, staring at me.

"When?"

"Around the time of your 21st birthday, Sebastian. And to Shirley and Mitch. My letters were returned to sender, unopened. I assumed they'd either gone away or..."

I didn't need to finish the sentence. He let out a lungful of air in a long sigh, as if he'd been holding his breath for a very long time.

"So, you did try to contact me?"

"Yes and no. I wanted to believe that you'd gone on with your life and I didn't want to ... disrupt anything. That's why I tried to contact Shirley and Mitch. I wanted to find out if my approach would be a positive thing—or not. When my letter was returned..."

I looked up at him. His expression was skeptical and I felt both hurt and annoyed: he didn't believe me.

"Everyone said I should just forget about you," he said, his voice deep with regret. "As if that was even possible. I tried to find you, Caro, but I didn't know your surname—your unmarried name—and the only person who knew..."

Was my ex-husband.

"I left messages everywhere I could think of," he continued, quietly. "I asked the new tenants at your house, at Shirley and Mitch's, and Donna's—I asked them to forward any mail to me ... I guess that didn't happen. Fuck, Caro, we would have been..."

He couldn't finish, his voice becoming choked and indistinct. I noticed his hands were shaking slightly as he took a long drink of his wine.

"You thought I didn't care."

He shrugged. "I didn't know what to think at first. Later ... yeah, I guess I thought you'd ... moved on."

I sighed. "I did move on, Sebastian. I had to. When those letters came back ... and even before I sent them, I thought you'd be better off without me. I hoped that your life would be ... different. More like

Ches's. I guess that explains why you were so unpleasant the last few days."

He winced and looked apologetic.

"Shit, I'm really sorry about that. It was just such a fucking shock. I didn't know what to think. It sent me into a real tailspin."

"It was a shock for me, too, Sebastian, but I didn't behave like a dick."

He glanced at me, surprised, then gave a small, contrite smile.

"Not your style, Caro."

His smile faded and I could tell he wanted to ask me something, but wasn't sure if he should. I could probably guess...

I leaned back in my chair.

"Just ask me, Sebastian."

He blinked a couple of times, then shook his head slowly, an admiring smile lifting his lips.

"You're so fearless, Caro, I love that about you."

His words caught me by surprise, leaving me speechless. Again.

"I was wondering ... if you were seeing anyone."

Yes, that's what I'd thought he was going to ask.

"No, I'm not."

He seemed to relax one degree. "But you were? I mean ... since..."

"I dated a couple of times, but no, there was nothing serious. Besides, I travel too much to sustain a relationship. And I definitely don't want to get tied down again."

He frowned, but didn't comment.

"What about you? Any significant other?"

He snorted and rolled his eyes. "Fuck, no!"

I raised my eyebrows. "That's not what I heard."

"What? What did you hear?" he said, almost angrily.

I was rather taken aback by his tone, but as we seemed to putting it all out there...

"About your CO's wife—in Paris? Maybe it was just gossip."

He grinned wickedly. "Oh, that. Guy was a first class bastard—he deserved it."

I shook my head in admonishment. "And did she 'deserve' it? His wife?"

"Yes, she did."

I hated to see such an ugly expression on his beautiful face.

"And the possibility of getting court-martialed and thrown out of the Corps ... that didn't matter to you either?"

He shrugged arrogantly. "I don't give a shit."

I didn't like this aggressive, macho-bullshit side to him. I decided I'd done enough strolling down memory lane for one evening.

"Well, I think I'll call it a night now, Sebastian."

His startled expression met my cool one.

"Don't go, Caro! We've only just started talking again. You haven't finished your wine, you..."

"No, I'm tired."

I started to stand but he laid a restraining hand on my thigh.

"Caro, I really want you."

What? He was unbelievable! Why was I even listening to this crap?

"For God's sake, Sebastian! We have one civilized drink together and you think I'm just going to fall into bed with you?"

"You used to."

I felt like I'd been slapped—and I really, really wanted to hit him.

"How dare you!" I hissed.

The realization of what he'd said and how I'd interpreted it sank in, painting his face with disgust. At himself, I hoped.

"I didn't mean it like that," he said, sullenly.

I stood up to leave and he grabbed hold of my hand.

"Caro, wait! Shit! I'm sorry."

I shook him off.

"Sebastian, we can't just roll back the last ten years and pretend it never happened. Too much has happened—too much time has passed."

"Come on, Caro, don't say that."

"Good night, Sebastian."

I didn't bother with the elevator—I needed to burn off some of the angry energy that coursed through me. I couldn't help feeling that his clumsy pass was some sort of attempt to punish me—to add me to his list of conquests so he could reach some closure maybe, seal shut the door to his past.

Just when I'd started to feel...

No. Not going there. Definitely not going there.

To add insult to serious irritation, there was still no news from my editor. I stormed around my hotel room, finding insignificant jobs to do, then hammered out more emails to Jenna and Alice as an attempt at distraction. It was a futile attempt.

I didn't know what the hell was going on with Sebastian. Some moments I could sense the presence of the sweet boy he had been, whose thoughtfulness and kindness had swept me off my feet, as much if not more than his physical presence. But at other times, I saw nothing more than a bitter and predatory manwhore whose aim was to bed as many women as possible, and whose primary weapon was his ridiculous good looks.

I was half expecting him to come knocking on my door again, and I had a few choice phrases on standby, but the corridor was eerily silent.

Annoyed with myself, annoyed with him, I flung myself into bed and spent a sleepless night fighting with the duvet.

Before dawn, I gave up and headed to the hotel's pool, swimming a few dozen laps before other guests arrived to make it unpleasantly crowded.

I staggered out of the pool and wrapped myself in the bathrobe provided by the hotel, before padding back toward my room.

Rounding the corner, I heard his voice before I saw him, his angry tones echoing down the corridor.

"For fuck's sake, Caro! Can we please just talk?"

He thumped on my door again, and then I heard him mutter to himself, "This is fucking crazy."

"That's one of the words," I said quietly, and saw him flinch.

He turned around and had the grace to look ashamed.

"Oh. I thought you weren't talking to me."

"That certainly would have been one of my better ideas."

He sighed, and rubbed the light brown stubble on his chin.

"Look, I'm sorry. I mean it. Around you, I just seem to open my mouth to change feet."

"You can say that again."

"I will if you let me buy you breakfast," he said, raising one eyebrow and grinning at me.

"Are you stalking me, Sebastian? I thought we said everything we had to say to each other last night?"

His face fell and he looked hurt.

"I just want ... can't we be friends?"

"Friends? I was under the impression you wanted to fuck me, out of some sense of revenge."

I glared at him.

"No!"

"Are you sure about that? Because last night you told me that's exactly what you did to your CO's wife. Why should I be any different?"

He stared at me in disbelief.

"Just go," I said, wearily.

I really didn't want to fight with him again, it was too tiring.

He took a deep breath.

"I know I'm saying everything wrong but ... we used to have fun, didn't we? Let's just spend some time together—get to know each other again. You're right—we can't pretend the last ten years never happened. Just ... give me a chance. I'm not the heartless bastard you seem to think I am. I'm still me, Caro."

He was still beautiful, but the same? I didn't think so.

I stared back at him, remembering how two nights ago, he had cried in my arms. Was that the real Sebastian, or was it the cold predator who preyed on women? I desperately wanted to believe that the former was the real man.

He must have seen in my eyes that I was weakening.

"We could start with breakfast," he said, almost hopefully. "Who knows, I might be able to get through a whole meal without making you mad at me."

"It seems unlikely," I replied, a reluctant smile creeping across my face.

He grinned back.

"You gonna wear that robe? Not that I give a shit—you could go naked for all I care. In fact..."

I groaned. "I'm going to take a shower. I'll see you in ten minutes."

"Want me to scrub your back?"

"Sebastian, I thought you were going to try and make it through breakfast before making me mad at you—right now your adolescent flirting is just annoying."

He grinned at me, but held his hands up in a gesture of defeat. "Okay, I get the message. I'll see you downstairs."

He turned on his heel, and strode off toward the stairs, whistling to himself.

God, he was annoying. And cute. But mostly annoying.

I took my time getting ready, I wanted to test his threshold of tolerance. I dressed slowly, checked my messages and took a moment to email my editor—again. It was nearly half an hour before I made it down to the hotel's restaurant for breakfast.

He was gazing out of the window, an untouched cup of black coffee in front of him.

I took a moment to drink in his beauty, which seemed almost otherworldly in the low light of early morning. His eyes were softer than I'd seen them in the last few days and had a faraway expression that suggested he was lost in memories. His short, Marine-style hair was golden blond, no doubt bleached by a foreign sun, and his full, sensual lips were slightly parted. His long legs were stretched out in front of him, his hands relaxed in his lap.

When he saw me, his eyes brightened and he stood up politely.

"You look great," he said.

Yeah, in old jeans and a t-shirt.

I rolled my eyes at him, and his smile slipped a notch.

"Did you order yet?"

"No, just the coffee. I was waiting for you."

"I usually have the continental breakfast."

He waved to the waitress, who was unusually attentive. I had the impression she'd been watching us. Well, watching him.

Plus ça change.

"Was there anything in particular you wanted to see in Geneva?" he said, once the waitress left with our order.

"You have to make it through breakfast without being irritating first," I reminded him.

"Yeah, well, I like a challenge," he said, smiling. "Seriously, anything you want to see?"

"Not really. I saw a lot wandering around yesterday. The Russian Church, maybe? I hear that's pretty amazing."

He fiddled with his napkin, then looked up.

"I had an idea of something we could do—if you like."

"Which is?"

"How about a trip to Chamonix? It's only an hour away—or just a little longer if we take the scenic route through Lausanne. It'll be a really great trip through the Alps." He grinned at me. "I'll have you back before bedtime."

Nope. Still annoying. But I couldn't resist his enthusiasm and playfulness. Plus, I'd heard that the road to Chamonix was particularly stunning, and I liked the idea of getting out of the city.

"And you absolutely *promise* you'll bring me back here by evening? No accidentally running out of gas or getting lost."

"I wouldn't dream of it," he said, with a look on his face that made me doubt every syllable.

"Okay, but I'm serious about getting back. I'm waiting for my travel permits and I can't afford to miss them."

He shifted uncomfortably in his seat. "Caro, I'll get you back here tonight, I promise."

Our breakfast arrived and Sebastian proceeded to chow down on anything that didn't move. Something else that hadn't changed.

"Tell me about Ches's kids," I said, trying for some relaxed conversation, but also genuinely curious.

Sebastian smiled.

"They're great. They call me 'Uncle Seb' ... well, Simone, the youngest one, she calls me 'Zed' because she still gets her words mixed up sometimes. She's nearly three. Ben is four and he's a little surf-rat already. I see them as often as I can, but every time they seem so much more grown up. Jeez, they grow fast."

"What's Amy like?"

"Yeah, she's okay."

I raised my eyebrows—his tone was distinctly lukewarm.

"Let me guess—she doesn't approve of you?"

He looked surprised. "What made you say that?"

"First, because you're single, and married women get nervous that their husband's single friends will lead them astray; second, because, from the sound of it, you've had more women than most men have hot dinners, and *that* will make her nervous because she won't want you reminding Ches of what he's missing out on, and..."

I stopped mid sentence.

"And what?"

"Well, the drinking, Sebastian. She wouldn't want that around her husband and kids."

He grimaced. "Yeah, I guess that about sums it up."

"When did you start drinking?" I said, gently.

"What do you mean? I don't drink that much, not like that bitch mother of mine."

I stared at him. "Well, twice in as many days you've been so drunk you've either passed out or made inappropriate comments to me."

Sebastian's face darkened perceptibly.

"I think my question stands," I said, holding his gaze.

He looked at me, hesitating to reply immediately.

"When I was 21," he said at last. "That's when I started drinking."

And then it hit me, fool that I was. The drinking, the womanizing, the reckless disregard for his career: it had all begun when he was 21. It had all begun because he'd given up—given up hope of love ... of me.

"Sebastian, I'm so sorry. I had no idea."

My words seemed deeply inadequate.

He shrugged and looked away. "Old news, Caro, don't worry about it."

I struggled to think of something neutral to say.

"Do you like living in Geneva?"

Lame, but it was the first thought that came to mind.

"It's okay, but I miss the ocean."

"Ah, no famous Swiss surfing beaches."

He grinned, his equilibrium restored. "I haven't found any yet."

I smiled back.

"Are you done eating?" he asked impatiently. "Let's go."

"I just need to go back to my room and pick up a jacket and, I presume, my passport, but otherwise, yes, I'm good to go."

He frowned. "You're a journalist: you should always have your passport with you. Hell, that was in that fucking tedious lecture that Parsons gave the day before yesterday."

"So you were listening."

He shook his head and smiled.

"Yeah, yeah, just grab a sweater, too—it's going to get cold."

I nodded as I left him at the table, but I was puzzled. It was mid March, it wasn't *that* cold. But when I saw him waiting for me at the front of the building, I understood why he'd told me to dress warm.

"Are you kidding me, Hunter? You expect me to get on that thing?"

Sebastian was standing next to a large, black Japanese motorcycle with French plates, his eyes dancing with amusement.

"Sure! It'll be fun."

I eyed the monster warily. It didn't look like *fun*: it looked dangerous and cold.

"Do you know how to drive it?" I asked suspiciously.

"Caro, I rode it from Paris—I think I can manage 88 kilometers to Chamonix," he said, grinning widely.

"I don't know," I muttered, shifting from foot to foot. "I've never been on the back of a motorcycle before."

He looked surprised. "Really? Because we used to talk about riding from..."

He stopped abruptly.

Was it ever going to get easier to talk about the past?

"Oh, what the hell," I said, shaking my head.

"Such faith in my abilities, Ms. Venzi."

"If I get killed on this thing, I'm going to come back and haunt you!"

"Promise?"

"Oh, you'd better believe it, Hunter!"

He smirked, then passed me a heavy, leather jacket that was obviously one of his. It was old and battered and so enormous that my hands disappeared inside the long sleeves. It had that pleasant musty smell of old leather, and a faint trace of Sebastian's own delicious scent.

He pulled up the zipper for me, and turned back the cuffs so I could free my hands.

"Suits you," he said, raising an eyebrow.

Then he handed me a shiny, black helmet that matched his own. He swung one long, denim-clad leg over the seat and held out his hand to help me mount the machine.

The seat tipped me slightly forward so my thighs automatically gripped his.

"Hold on tight," he said, his voice muffled through the helmet.

I could tell from the tone that he was enjoying himself. I would really have liked to ignore the suggestion, but I was so terrified of falling off, that I wrapped my arms around his waist and hung on tightly. I could feel the hardness of his body beneath the leather and I knew for certain that agreeing to this trip had been a bad, bad idea.

The engine started with a gravelly roar that crescendoed as Sebastian revved the accelerator.

He started forward at a gentle pace, mostly for my benefit I had to assume, and soon we were traveling steadily through Geneva, before taking the lakeside road north-east to Lausanne.

The lake was a steely green-gray and flecked with white. It was serene and timeless and I felt my body start to relax. Irritating as it was to admit, I was beginning to enjoy myself.

Sebastian must have felt the change in my body because he accelerated smoothly, bending forward slightly, weaving his way past the patchwork fields as we continued to circle the lake. I snuggled closer, grateful for the warmth of his body as the cool air flowed past us.

He slowed as we reached Montreux, giving me time to appreciate the chocolate-box prettiness of the old town with chalets and fairytale granite castle, and the contrasting modernity of the concrete and glass buildings, and hotels that looked like chateaux.

"Do you want to get a coffee?" he called over his shoulder.

I nodded enthusiastically, bumping my helmet awkwardly on the back of his, and gave him a thumbs up.

He drew up outside a small café that looked out onto the lake, then kicked down the stand and cut the engine. The sudden silence was very welcome and I gazed out across the water, feeling peaceful, at peace.

Sebastian pulled off his helmet and grinned at me.

"How was that?"

I struggled out of my own helmet and hoped my 'hat hair' wasn't too scary.

"That was ... surprisingly okay!"

He laughed at my bemused expression, then his eyes darkened in a way I remembered. It was a look of lust and need and deep, burning desire. Yes, I remembered.

I scrambled off the bike hastily and rubbed my hands trying to get some warmth back into my fingers.

"Are you cold?"

"Just my hands."

Without saying a word, he took my hands in his and lifted them to his lips, heating them with his warm breath and rubbing them gently.

After a moment, I pulled free.

"That's fine, thank you."

He continued to stare at me, his expression serious. I looked away, confused and ill at ease.

"This café looks good," I said desperately.

I heard his soft sigh, but refused to look at him. Instead, I strode into the café and found a table by the window.

Sebastian followed more slowly, sliding into the chair opposite me.

"*Un espresso et un caffé americano, s'il vous plaît.*"

"You speak French?" I asked curiously.

He shrugged. "Enough to get by. I never studied it."

"And the Dari? The Arabic? How did that come about?"

"My first tour in Iraq. I was playing soccer with some of the local kids who used to hang around the Base. They taught me a few words and I just started picking up some phrases. My sergeant heard me talking to the kids and sent me on a couple of training courses. When we started pulling out of Iraq, they figured I should learn Pashto and Dari so I could be useful in Afghanistan. I found I could just *hear* it, all the different cadences." He sneered. "Finally found something I was good at. Who knew."

I was shocked by his dismissive tone.

"You were always good at lots of things, Sebastian. You picked up Italian really quickly."

"That's because I had an Italian girlfriend," he said.

"Really? When was that?"

He rolled his eyes as if I was missing the obvious.

"Oh, right," I muttered, embarrassed. "And you taught me to surf, don't forget."

He grinned, breaking the tension of his odd outburst.

"Yeah, that was fun. Did you ever keep it up?"

"I go quite often in the summer," I said. "I bought a place in Long Beach and..."

I ground to a halt, worried by his stricken expression.

"Sorry," he said, shaking his head, as if to cast off some grim thought, "It's just ... well, we used to talk about going to Long Beach and checking out the surf spots."

"I didn't have any other plan," I said, quietly. "When I left you ... when I left San Diego, I drove for eight days until I arrived in New York. That old Pinto I had, died crossing Verrazano Bridge. I got an apartment in Little Italy because I didn't know anywhere else and you'd mentioned it once. I lived there for eight years. You were right, I did like it."

He closed his eyes and let his head drop into his hands. He looked so vulnerable. How such ordinary words can hurt us, I thought.

"God, Caro, when I think about how things could have been ... it makes me a little crazy."

"I know what you mean," I said, softly. "But there's no point thinking like that."

The waitress returned with our coffees. I stared into the dark liquid, losing myself in the wisps of steam.

"I'm glad you went there, I'm glad you did the things we said we'd do."

"Not all of them," I amended.

"Fuck, if only..."

"Stop, Sebastian," I said, forcefully. "No 'what ifs': what if we'd never gone to that Sicilian restaurant that night, what if Brenda hadn't seen us, what if she hadn't told your parents ... there's no point thinking like that. Like you said, it'll just make us crazy."

"I know you're right, it's just that..." He ran one hand over his hair in frustration.

"Hey, stop," I said, grabbing his fingers. "It is what it is. We can't change anything."

He held on tightly, then rubbed his eyes with his free hand.

"Mind you," I said, "if I ran into Brenda again, I might have to give her a quick slap."

He smiled slightly.

"Yeah, I'd like to see that." Then he frowned. "She felt really bad about what happened."

I released his hand, and leaned back in my chair.

"You spoke to her about it—what she did?"

I was amazed. Maybe even hurt. Brenda the Slut was the only memory I had of her. Yes, she'd certainly lit the fuse that had led to our explosive separation. I knew, deep down, that it would have happened anyway, but still. To hear that Sebastian had spoken with her, maybe even stayed in touch with her. Maybe even *slept* with her—I really wasn't ready to hear *that*.

"Well, yeah. She kept bugging Ches until I agreed to see her. By then it was kind of obvious why she'd done it."

"Obvious how?"

He sighed.

"She was pregnant—knocked up by that bastard Jack Sullivan. You remember that older guy who used to hang out at the beach? Yeah, well, when she found out she was pregnant, she freaked. Had this crazy idea in her head that if she could get back with me, she'd get me to sleep with her and pretend the baby was mine."

He shook his head in disbelief at the screwed up behavior of a scared 18 year-old girl.

"She thought if you were out of the way, we'd get back together. She had no idea what she'd done. Until after—and it was too late."

"And did you? Sleep with her?"

"For fuck's sake," he said, his anger evident. "I told you. I didn't even touch another woman for three years."

"Sorry."

"Yeah, well," he said, continuing with the grim little story, "she had to face her parents eventually. Jack wouldn't have anything to do with her, and she wouldn't say who the father was. Everyone assumed it was me anyway."

He rubbed his forehead tiredly. "But when Kimberley was born, she had all this dark brown hair and dark eyes, it was kind of obvious I wasn't the father."

"Kimberley?"

"She's a great kid. I see them sometimes when I'm on the west coast. Brenda married a car salesman a couple of years back. He's a pretty nice guy and good with Kimberley."

I nodded slowly, finding I couldn't dislike Brenda as much as I'd wanted to.

"Well, I'm glad it worked out for her—in the end." I paused. "You didn't tell me what happened to Donna and Johan. They were always kind to me."

"Shirley's stayed in touch with them. I saw them a few times after

... Johan retired a couple of years back, and they moved to Phoenix. I heard he was pretty sick—leukemia, I think."

"I'm sorry to hear that, they were a nice couple."

Oh, poor Johan. Such a decent man. Poor Donna. Maybe I should write ... no, they wouldn't want to hear from me.

He nodded but didn't reply.

"What about that funny little friend of yours—Fido? What was his real name ... um ... Alfred? Albert? Arnold! What happened to him?"

Sebastian didn't smile, which was never a good sign.

"He enlisted just before me. He joined the Rakkasans, 187th Infantry. He died eight years ago in Iraq—IED. Poor bastard never stood a chance. He didn't even make it to twenty."

"Oh no, I'm so sorry!"

And I remembered that sweet kid who used to try and flirt with me: dead. All those young men gone.

We finished our coffees in silence, each lost in the past.

Every time I thought we'd finished our stroll down memory lane, something else came along to hijack us, tugging us back to our turbulent history. It was like being on an emotional carnival ride—including the nausea, but seriously lacking the fun.

"Ready to head for Chamonix?" asked Sebastian.

I smiled at him, grateful that he'd interrupted my musings.

"Yes, ready as I'll ever be. Actually though, it's more comfortable riding on that motorcycle than I thought it would be. I just wish I'd worn something warmer."

"Put your hands in my pockets this time," he said. "That will help. And there's a shop in Chamonix where we can get you some good gloves."

"That's not necessary."

"I can buy you some fucking gloves, Caro!" he said, crossly.

"Fine!" I snapped, matching his irritated tone, "Although I have no idea what 'fucking gloves' are: made of latex?"

He laughed loudly. "God, I love you, Caro!"

He stopped when he'd realized what he'd said.

"Slip of the tongue," he mumbled.

I ignored his comment and waited until he mounted the motorcycle, before clambering on behind him.

Gratefully, I pushed my hands into the pockets of his jacket, winding my fingers into the soft leather.

∼

We crossed into France at the quaintly named village of Saint Gingolph. A border guard glanced at our passports, looked again when he realized we were American, sneered a few questions that Sebastian answered in fluent French—which seemed to annoy the man even more—then he waved us across.

The road on this side of the lake was more thickly wooded and less inhabited than the northern side. Small farmhouses dotted the hillside and winding roads threaded their way up into the Alps.

"This road leads to Italy," Sebastian yelled over his shoulder. "How about a quick trip over the border?"

"Two countries in one day is enough!" I shouted back, but the thought that I was just miles from my father's homeland tugged at my heart.

Chamonix soon appeared out of the low mist that had settled in the valley. To my left, I could see the awe-inspiring presence of Mont Blanc, thick snow capping the summit.

The town itself was empty—the winter skiers long gone, the summer tourists not yet arrived.

The ride through the Alps had been sensational, as promised, and Chamonix was lovely: a picture-perfect Alpine town, with an abundance of bijou shops selling everything from skiwear to expensive, designer jewelry.

Sebastian pulled up outside one of the former, and dragged me inside.

"We'll get you some ski gloves to wear," he said. "Best I can do for now."

The sales assistant was overly helpful. I couldn't decide if that was because she was delighted to have a customer so close to the end of the ski season, or because she got to stare at Sebastian's ass as he wandered around the shop.

As far as I was concerned, he had a very fine ass and, having been wrapped around it for the last couple of hours, I felt I was in a position to voice an expert opinion.

And then a very erotic image sprang unwelcome to my mind, as I recalled the numerous occasions when I had reason to know Sebastian's naked ass very well indeed.

I did my best to banish the memory, but I wasn't entirely successful. I wondered if all US Marines were in such good shape.

"How about these?" asked Sebastian, handing me a pair of black ski gloves.

"Ninety Euros! Are you kidding me? That's $115! For a pair of gloves!"

"Just try the damn things on, Caro," Sebastian growled.

"No. That's ridiculous. There must be something cheaper."

"If you don't try them on, I'll buy them anyway," he threatened.

"No! It's a waste of money."

He turned to the sales assistant and handed them over. "*D'accord. Je les prends.*"

"Wait! *Attendez!*"

I snatched them back from her and pulled them on over my hands. They fit perfectly.

Damn!

He grinned at me wickedly.

"You argue too much, Caro."

"I can't imagine why," I said, dryly.

We left the shop with my ridiculously expensive gloves tucked into my jacket pocket. Sebastian looked annoyingly pleased with himself.

"Should we find somewhere to have lunch?"

"What, you're actually asking me, Hunter? As in, seeking my opinion?"

He grinned at me. "Sure!"

"In that case, yes, but only if I treat you—non-negotiable."

"I love it when you tell me what to do, Caro," he leered at me. "Brings back memories."

And this time I couldn't help the blush that rose to my cheeks. I knew *exactly* what he was talking about. Other than Italian, the one thing I had taught Sebastian was how to give me an orgasm. And he had been a *very* good student.

He laughed out loud when he saw my blush. I couldn't think of a single comeback. Not one. Not a word. Not a single response, answer, reply, witticism, quip, jest or jibe. I was utterly mute.

He wrapped his arm around my shoulders and pulled me to him, kissing my hair lightly.

"Just teasing you, Caro."

I shuffled away, trying to look offended, but he knew better and just grinned.

"Do you want to try fondue?" he asked, still trying not to laugh.

"Fine," I muttered sulkily.

I regained some of my rumpled poise over lunch.

We both ordered the cheese *fondue* and were given a basket full of different rolls: *foccacia*, olive breads, breadsticks, and a *fondue* made up of *mozzarella*, *dolcelatte* and parmesan. It was the perfect winter warmer, especially on a chilly day in the spring.

"Mmm, this is good. Have you been here before?"

He nodded nonchalantly. "A couple of times."

"Ever bring your women here?"

He frowned, and looked irritated. "You make it sound like I had a fucking parade of them."

"Didn't you?"

He threw down his fondue fork angrily.

"What do you want me to say, Caro? I fucked everything I could get my hands on when I realized you weren't coming back. It was years before I trusted a woman enough to be able to make love to her, and even then..."

He stopped mid-sentence, scowling at me.

I'd done it again: forced him to say words that only brought pain to both of us.

"I'm sorry," I murmured. "I didn't mean..." I looked into his eyes. "It's none of my business, Sebastian. I apologize."

And it really wasn't. I was the one who had insisted that we couldn't change the past, and here I was, surgically opening old wounds, one by one.

"I'm sorry, too. I didn't mean to yell at you," he said, his voice aching with regret.

Then he took a deep breath and shook his head to clear away the anger and recriminations.

We sat silently for several minutes. I searched around for a more neutral topic of conversation.

"How long have you had the motorcycle?"

He leaned back in his chair.

"This one, about two years. But I've had one on and off since I was 19. Bought my first bike as a birthday present to myself. It's still in Ches's garage."

"Really? Well, there's another reason for his wife to think you're leading Ches astray. Or is he the responsible father-type now?"

Sebastian smiled.

"He's a great dad—really patient. He fucking loves those kids of his. But we still take the boards out and catch some waves when I'm there."

"Uh-huh, and how many meals have you made him late for, just catching 'one more wave'?"

He smiled knowingly.

"Too many! But he goes out when Mitch visits, too, so she can't blame me for that."

"I think I'd like her—a woman immune to the Hunter charm."

Sebastian laughed. "She's immune all right. But yeah, she'd like you. I'll introduce you when we're stateside."

"In case you'd forgotten, I live about 3,000 miles and ten states from San Diego."

"Yeah, well, in case *you'd* forgotten, they've invented airplanes."

"*Touché,* Sergeant Hunter."

He smirked at me, and raised his glass of water in a toast.

"What happened to that friend of Mitch's—Bill—the one who was at that wretched 'fun' day Donna dragged me to at the beach?"

"Why are you asking about him?"

Sebastian frowned at me and I rolled my eyes. Surely he wasn't *still* jealous because Bill had flirted with me once?

"Just wondering. He was in your surfing crowd, wasn't he?"

"Oh, right," he said, rather huffily. "He married again a few years back, I think. He was sent to Quantico. Mitch keeps up with him—Christmas cards—something like that."

Thank God Bill's story had a happy ending. I didn't think I could take any more bad news today.

"It felt good having you on the bike with me today, Caro," said Sebastian, thoughtfully, as if he was testing the water before adding something more.

"Hmm," I said, the sound filled with skepticism.

He laughed. "Well, I've had an idea about that..."

"Oh, another of your ideas? That sounds dangerous."

He grinned at me, a gleam of mischief in his eye.

"You know how we always talked about traveling through Italy? I just thought, while we're both here, why don't we?"

I frowned at him, not sure I understood what he was suggesting.

"Why don't we what?"

"See Italy. We could take the motorcycle and go see all those places we talked about: Milano, Verona, Capezzano Inferiore—see if your dad's relatives still live there."

Oh, he'd definitely found my weak spot.

"Don't you have work to do?" I replied, avoiding answering the question. "How come you've have all this time off?"

"I'm on leave," he said, quietly. "I'll be shipping back out to Afghan—in about three weeks."

"Oh," I said, feeling the blood drain from my face. "I didn't realize ... I thought you were stationed in Geneva."

He shrugged.

"I was, but they need interpreters, and they're getting antsy about using locals. Too many green-on-blue attacks." He brushed the thought away. "So, what do you think?"

I shook my head.

"I can't, you know I can't. My papers could come through any moment and I'll be on my way out there myself. Besides," I said, trying to lighten the moment, "three weeks with you—that's definitely a dangerous mission."

"Don't you trust me?" he asked, trying and failing to look wounded.

"No, not particularly."

He grinned, completely unabashed.

"Oh, don't say that. I'll be good. Scout's honor."

"You were never a boy scout."

"True," he said with a smirk. "What if I promise I'll behave myself: separate bedrooms and everything?"

"No way, Hunter. I've heard about your *reputation*, remember? Besides, I don't know how soon I'll get a flight to Leatherneck. I don't want to risk losing my slot."

"It won't happen for at least two weeks."

I narrowed my eyes at his tone.

"You sound very sure of that."

He just grinned at me.

And then realization dawned.

"What did you do, Hunter?"

His grin grew wider.

"Let's just say I know people in the right places."

I couldn't believe his arrogance.

"Are you telling me you've blocked my application?"

My voice started rising, and he had the grace to look almost contrite.

"It's not blocked, Caro, not entirely. I ... just threw a few well-aimed monkey wrenches in the works. It'll take at least a week to sort out—probably two."

Unbelievable!

Now I was really angry.

"This is my *work*, Sebastian," I said, the fury in my voice more than obvious. "This is how I get *paid*. How dare you interfere like this! You're unbelievable."

He scowled at me.

"You can't butt into my life like this!" I half yelled at him. "I'm not the insipid little woman I was ten years ago!"

"You were never that," he said, his expression burning.

Oh, how well I remembered that look.

"You'd better damn well get that monkey wrench out, Hunter! I mean it."

He sighed, looking disappointed.

"I can't, Caro, it's out of my hands now. But I promise it's temporary. I just ... after all this time ... I wanted us to be able to spend more than a few hours together." He stared at his hands. "I don't know when I'll see you again," he mumbled. "I've already waited ten years."

His admission was so astonishing and he looked so miserable, that my anger began to ebb. I was still annoyed, furious at his interference in fact, but I couldn't hold the same level of rage when he looked like that and, more importantly, once he'd explained his reason for doing it —that he still had feelings for me. But what the true nature of those feelings really was, I remained deeply unsure.

"Will you at least think about it?" he asked softly.

I nodded, still too angry to speak.

I let Sebastian have all the fondue, my appetite having vanished. He kept throwing me guilty glances, but it didn't stop him finishing both his plate and mine.

We spent the afternoon wandering through the town, stopping to look in shops and gazing up at the stormy face of Mont Blanc.

I was still irritated by his high-handed behavior, but there was nothing I could do about it, besides I was used to waiting, and I'd waited in a lot worse places.

"I wouldn't mind coming back here in the winter," said Sebastian, "try out the snowboarding."

"That's something else I've never done," I grimaced, trying to imagine hurtling down the steep, icy face of the lowering mountain on a piece of wood not much bigger than a skateboard.

"I'll teach you," said Sebastian, confidently.

"Oh, something you can teach me, Mr. Hunter?"

He raised an eyebrow and grinned at me.

I glanced at my watch. "I think we should be heading back now. I can't get a signal on my phone here. My editor might have been trying to contact me."

I threw him a challenging glance. Sebastian didn't look happy, but he didn't argue either.

We walked back to his motorcycle and I pulled on my very lovely, and very expensive new gloves.

Sebastian took the autoroute back to Geneva and we arrived in slightly under an hour. I didn't like to ask what speed we'd been traveling at—one that exceeded the limit, I suspected.

I climbed off the bike, and handed him back my helmet. He stowed it in one of the empty saddlebags and stared down at me.

"I really enjoyed today, Sebastian. Most of it, anyway. Thank you."

"You're welcome, Caro."

We stood gazing at each other. Without knowing why, I felt awkward, the tension rolling in waves between us.

"Okay, well, thanks again," I murmured, turning to go.

"Can I see you tomorrow, Caro?" he asked, his voice filled with intense longing. "Will you think about the Italy idea?"

I stared at him, certain the anguish was etched on my face.

His eyes darkened as he continued to stare at me.

"I want to kiss you, Caro. Very badly."

The breath caught in my throat as he took a step toward me. I knew I wanted that, too. *Very badly*.

I raised my hand to his cheek and he sighed softly as he leaned into it, closing his eyes. I ran my fingers down his neck, feeling the warmth of his skin.

He took another step toward me, and rested his hands on my waist. I pulled his head toward me and felt his lips on mine. So soft, so sensuous. I could feel his breath stroke my face, then his lips parted and his tongue swept into my mouth.

My God, the feelings that burned through me, scorching away every sorrow, every moment of regret. Instead, I remembered how his hands had learned every curve and hollow of my body, how our love had melded us into one, how his body had fit inside mine.

He pressed himself into me, his mouth hungrily devouring every breath.

"God, I want you, Caro. I want to make love to you," he whispered on my lips.

"Yes," I said. "I want that, too."

CHAPTER FOUR

SEBASTIAN HAD TO GO AND PARK HIS MOTORCYCLE IN THE HOTEL'S secure underground garage.

His absence gave me ample time to consider the consequences of what I was about to do. I still wasn't sure I trusted him, I had about a minute to decide whether or not to change my mind. But, in truth, there was no decision to make. My body ached to be touched, it had been a long time, too long perhaps, since I'd allowed a man this close to me. And the way I felt when Sebastian was near me, it was as if every nerve ending was sensitized simply by his presence. I hated it and I loved it and I hated it.

I waited for him in the lobby, sitting on the same sofa where he'd sat last night during our fractured heart-to-heart. The receptionist's curious gaze bounced off my back: I didn't have room in my mind to consider anyone else at this point, and I cared even less what she thought of me, if she thought anything at all.

And then he had returned and it was too late.

Watching him walk through the automatic doors into the lobby was extraordinarily arousing. I longed to feel his body intertwined with mine, to feel as I had felt once before. I could see the tension and expectation on his face, and the old insecurities began to worm their way to the surface. Ten years ago, I had been the experienced one and I had led the way, even though my 'experience' had been limited to my uncreative husband. Sebastian's experience, at the time, had been zero, but now? By his own admission, he had fucked every woman who'd let him. I had no doubt that his charm, superficial or otherwise, combined with his extraordinary good looks had gained him entry to a large number of bedrooms.

By contrast, the number of men I'd slept with since him could be numbered on one hand. I was afraid he would find me ... boring.

He crossed the lobby with long strides until he was standing in front of me, searching my face. He held out his hand, and I didn't hesitate. If it was a mistake, then it was one I made willingly.

A relieved smile flickered briefly across his face.

He pulled me to my feet and braided his fingers through mine, leading me toward the bank of gleaming elevators.

All were busy, crammed with tourists returning from day trips, politicians and businessmen retiring to their suites for the evening. Sebastian and I stood off to one side, wedged among a throng of men in suits. He wrapped his arms around my waist and pulled my back into his chest, bending down to place soft kisses in my hair.

Two men smiled knowingly, but Sebastian didn't so much as glance at them.

Several other people got off at the same floor, following us along the corridor, chatting noisily. Sebastian and I were silent.

I pulled the keycard out of my wallet with shaking fingers, and pushed the door open. I stepped inside, my heart racing, my nerves taut. I moved around the room, turning on the side lights, pulling the curtains and shifting my laptop from the neatly made bed. In other words, doing everything rather than look at him.

He hovered by the door for a moment, then walked in slowly and sat on the edge of the bed, his eyes following me around the room. He caught my hand as I fluttered past on another pointless circuit.

"Hey, it's okay. I'm nervous, too."

I stared at him in amazement.

"*You're* nervous ... why?"

"Because it's you," he said, simply.

He raised my hand to his lips and kissed it courteously, a sweet, old-fashioned gesture.

"Only if you want to, Caro."

"I do ... I just feel, I don't know, embarrassed. It's so stupid."

He lay back on the bed and gently pulled me down next to him. He began kissing my throat, his hands moving up from my waist.

I felt him everywhere, all over me, suffocating me, and I froze.

"No, Sebastian."

I pushed him away, and he stopped immediately.

I was half expecting him to get up and leave in disgust, but he surprised me again.

Suddenly, he rolled away from me to the other side of the bed.

"Let's just make out," he said, grinning at me.

"Make out? As in..."

"Lie on the bed, watch trashy TV in French or German—your choice—and make out."

He raised his eyebrows as he sat up, then he shrugged out of his jacket and dropped it on the floor, unbuckled and levered his feet out of his biker boots, before peeling off his socks.

He grabbed a couple of pillows, piled them against the headboard and launched himself back onto the bed.

"Where's the remote?"

I pointed to the cabinet on my side of the bed and watched as he stretched over me to retrieve it, exposing a delicious sliver of taut, naked stomach as his t-shirt rode up his body.

Oh, I really wanted some of that.

He surfed through a few channels before he found some badly-dubbed TV show, then grinned up at me, patting the space on the bed next to him.

I followed his lead, unlacing my boots and dropping them in the corner with my socks. I crawled up on the bed next to him, and he pulled me into his arms so I was resting against his chest. He kissed my forehead and settled back on his pillows with a sigh.

I snuggled into him, feeling surprisingly relaxed.

"This feels good," he said, happily. "Should we order room service?"

"I'm not hungry."

"Would you mind if I ordered myself a beer?"

Just one beer?

"No, I don't mind."

He pulled the hotel telephone toward him to order a beer and a sandwich, then settled back with his arm around me.

With typical Swiss efficiency, the beer arrived within five minutes, the 'sandwich'—an enormous French baguette—was stuffed with cold meats, lettuce and tomato.

Sebastian's eyes lit up.

"Food instead of sex?" I couldn't help saying, reminding him of a running joke we'd once had.

He grinned at me, and licked his lips.

"For now. I'm still kind of hoping the sex comes later."

"How's that going for you?"

"Not sure: she's playing hard to get. I was going to ply her with alcohol and have my wicked way with her, but I guess she's wise to my game."

"Women!" I said, rolling my eyes.

He laughed, and started to work on demolishing the sandwich.

When he'd finished and brushed the crumbs from his t-shirt, he lay back with the bottle of beer, and wrapped his free arm around me again. He sighed contentedly and stretched his long legs out in front of him, crossing his bare feet at the ankle.

"I could get used to this," he said, nuzzling my hair.

"What, badly dubbed reruns of 'Frasier' and TV dinners?"

"You know exactly what I mean, woman."

"Oh, 'woman', is it?" I said, thumping him on the chest.

"Yes, a beautiful, amazing, talented, gorgeous woman," he said, his voice serious.

The mood shifted immediately, from relaxed and playful, to heated tension.

He placed his beer on the bedside table, then pulled me gently into his chest. With his fingertips, his free hand caressed my ear, gently sweeping my hair aside. His eyes studied my face carefully as he leaned in to kiss me, the lids fluttering closed at the last moment, before his lips touched mine.

His mouth drifted across my face, sweet, gentle kisses, as light as butterfly wings, hovering over my eyelids, brushing over my chin, then returning to rest on my lips.

My hand crept across his stomach, and slowly up toward his chest, pausing for a moment just over his heart. Then I lifted my hand to cup his cheek, and he turned his head to kiss my palm.

He pulled me in more tightly, so I was half-lying across him, and he ran his hands up my spine while he kissed my neck. His kisses grew more urgent, and I felt him run his tongue over my throat. Then his teeth tugged on my lower lip, and his tongue dove into my mouth. I could taste beer and hot, delicious Sebastian.

I moaned into his mouth, and heard an answering growl from deep within his chest. I hooked my leg over his thigh, pulling our bodies closer together. Through his jeans I could feel that he was aroused, and the knowledge sent a jet of heat spiraling through my body.

His hands stroked my back through the thin cotton of my t-shirt as his kiss deepened. Then they dropped to the waistband of my jeans and he pulled the material free, running his strong fingers along my bare skin, toying briefly with the elastic of my bra, before dropping back down to cup my ass.

I shivered with desire, and his hands stilled.

"Are you sure, Caro?" he whispered.

I leaned away so I could gaze down into his beautiful eyes, softly massaging the small frown line between his eyebrows with my finger.

"I'm sure." I sat up and pulled off my t-shirt to add emphasis to my words.

His eyes were dark with desire and he swallowed quickly before sitting up and hauling his own t-shirt over his head. His silver dog tags chinked quietly as they settled back on his chest.

I reached over to touch him, needing to feel the warmth of his silky flesh, then stopped.

"You got a tattoo?"

He smiled slightly.

"Standard Marine issue."

I studied the delicate artwork and misty colors while Sebastian slowly stroked my back.

"The Marine insignia."

"Yep. The eagle represents the nation, well, protecting the nation —see the way its wings are spread out? The globe is our worldwide presence, and the anchor is because of our naval heritage."

The eagle was carrying a ribbon in its beak: I was just able to make out the tiny words.

"*Semper fidelis*—always faithful."

He nodded, his eyes serious.

I kissed his shoulder gently and lay back on the bed, pulling him toward me. Without speaking again, he pressed me down into the mattress, kissing me hard. His right hand roamed over my breast, gliding his fingers under my bra-cup and teasing the nipple until it was sensitized and rigid.

Then he slid his hand under my back, snapping open my bra, and pushed the shoulder straps over my arms, tossing the flimsy fabric onto the floor.

He moved his head to my breasts, his tongue dancing around the nipples, grazing his teeth over my aroused skin.

I moaned, arching my back, and he hooked one hand underneath me, half-lifting me off the bed. I responded by dragging my nails down his spine, making him cry out. He ground his hips into my pelvis and sucked the skin on my shoulder, biting so I could feel his teeth.

I ran my hands over his biceps and forearms, then slid my fingers inside the front of his jeans, feeling the large bulge pushing through his briefs. He groaned loudly, and I squeezed him through the material.

"Fuck, Caro!" he said, his voice hoarse with need.

Matching me move for move, he pushed his hands underneath my waistband, caressing my ass, pushing his fingers into the cleft between my buttocks. Then he pulled his hand out and toyed with the button on the front of my jeans, before twisting it open. He didn't bother with the zipper, but simply pushed his fingers under my panties, pulling gently on my pubic hair, massaging my mound in slow circles, before letting his index finger drift lower.

I knew I was wet, desperately aroused, and as soon as his fingers found me I cried out. He'd always known this part of my body so well, and he definitely hadn't lost his touch. In and out, in and out, torturing me, confined as I was by my jeans. My back arched, and I cried out again.

He sat up quickly and unzipped my jeans, hauling them roughly down my legs, before catching his fingers through the fragile fabric of my panties and tossing them to the floor.

I quivered as he splayed out his fingers and ran them from my chest, down across my stomach, down across my pubic bone and along my thighs. His hand rose upwards again, finding my sweet spot with his index finger, he began to press hard, back and forth.

I groaned, and pushed his hand away.

"No. You. I want you."

He smiled briefly, then unzipped his pants and stood to let them drop to the floor, kicking his feet free.

I knelt up on the edge of the bed, pushing my breasts into his chest, and running my hands over his ass. Then I peeled the briefs over his hips and his erection leapt free.

Wow! I'd honestly forgotten how well endowed he was. Truthfully, I'd not realized until after our ways had parted, that he was considerably above average.

I licked my lips and ran one hand over the length, gently cupping his balls in my other.

He breathed in deeply through his nose, his nostrils flaring slightly. I repeated the gesture and he swore lightly under his breath.

A bead of moisture glinted at the tip, and I swirled it around with my thumb. His body trembled.

"Are you on the pill?" he said, his voice rough.

I shook my head, a smile threatening to break out. "I don't usually have a need for it. Please tell me you have condoms, otherwise 'making out' is all we're going to be doing."

He smirked, and bent down to rifle through the pockets of his leather jacket.

"Just wondering," I said, casually, "but when did you buy them, or are they old stock?"

He grinned at me, and shook his head. "Nope, new packet. Check it out."

He tossed me the small box and I saw that it was true: the seal hadn't been broken.

"So, no need to practice putting one on then?"

I was teasing him—ten years ago, he'd admitted, somewhat shamefaced, that he'd practiced putting on a condom so he'd know what to do when the time came.

Sebastian laughed.

"Well, I haven't practiced recently, but I think I can remember what to do."

"You're avoiding the question," I said raising my eyebrows. "When did you buy these?"

"Second day of the hostile environment training."

"But you were still mad at me then!" I said, very surprised.

"Didn't stop me wanting you," he replied, grinning back at me.

"Hmm, well. Let me see if *I* can remember what to do," I said, raising one eyebrow.

His grin widened and he stood in front of me with his hands on his hips, his erection heading in my direction.

I tore open the box and pulled out a foil packet, running it down his length, and tapping him on his tip lightly.

"Whoa, careful!" he breathed out.

"Wimp! I thought you were a Marine not a mouse."

"Just be careful with my weapon," he shot back.

"Close your eyes and relax."

"Why, what are you going to do?" he asked warily.

"Don't you trust me?" I said, smiling innocently.

"Not with that look on your face," he said, but closed his eyes anyway.

I ripped open the foil and pinched the end between my thumb and forefinger, but before I rolled it on, I leaned forward and took him in my mouth.

"Fuck!" he hissed between his teeth, as I stroked my mouth up and down him.

He rested his hands on my shoulders and flexed automatically, sending him deeper into my throat. I pulled back slightly and bared my teeth, making him shudder.

I sucked hard, and he groaned.

"No, baby. I want to be inside you."

I gave another not-so-gentle tug, and released him.

He shook his head, his eyes amused but heated.

I smiled up at him and ran my hands over his ass, enjoying the defined dip where hip met muscle.

"Just put that fucking thing on," he said. "You're killing me here."

"Oh, don't be such a baby, Sebastian. We've waited ten years, you're not going to expire in the next 30 seconds."

"I wouldn't be too sure about that," he muttered.

I held the condom at the tip of his penis, and as slowly as was humanly possible, I rolled it down him, making every second, every millimeter count.

He brushed my hands away as soon as I was finished.

"My turn," he said, his voice allowing no argument.

I lay back on the bed, and raised my arms to pull him down to me.

"Oh, I don't think so," he said. "My turn, remember? Pull your knees up."

"Yes, sir!" I barked, and threw up a salute.

"Are you mocking the US Marine Corps, lady?" he snarled.

"Why? What are you going to do about it?"

The expression on his face changed subtly, and I had a feeling I was going to regret my challenging words.

I slid my feet up the bed as commanded, and watched with a mixture of anticipation and delicious foreboding as his head disappeared between my thighs.

His tongue flicked up and I was so aroused I nearly came on the spot, my body bowing to meet him.

For a second, he pulled back to glance up at me, grinned wickedly, and continued with his erotic assault that had me moaning at an embarrassing volume.

Then he hooked his shoulders under my knees and lifted my whole lower body off the bed, so my weight rested on my upper back.

And he was merciless.

My orgasm began to build quickly and even as the waves tore me apart, he didn't stop until every bone in my body had turned to liquid.

I couldn't help the nasty little thought that darted through my brain: practice makes perfect.

But he didn't give me time to think too deeply because he laid my hips back down on the bed, and positioned himself over me.

"I've waited a very long time for this," he said.

Then he slid into me, inch by slow inch, as my body adjusted to his invading presence.

"Fuck, you feel so good, Caro. I can feel you all around me. *So fucking tight!*"

And I could certainly feel every inch of him. My numb brain began to fill with memories, the times, the places, the many, many times he'd made love to me before. Many times, but somehow too few times.

I ran my nails down his back again, then pressed the tips of my fingers into his tight muscles.

He groaned, continuing to stroke slowly in and out.

Ten years ago, the boy he'd been had been unable to stop himself from racing to the finish line. Now I was benefiting from his experience.

He held his weight on his forearms, and gradually increased the speed. I felt the cool metal of his dog tags on my skin over my heart, which was beating furiously fast, as my body began to respond again and again.

Death by orgasm—what a way to go.

I moaned out his name, and he seemed to lose a fraction of his careful control because he started to move faster. Soon his hips were plunging fiercely, and I absorbed every delicious thrust as he ground into me.

His eyes were wide open, staring down at me, almost wild in their intensity, then his mouth was on mine, our tongues twisting and twining together.

I tilted my hips up to meet him and felt his body go rigid, he flexed deeply once more then stilled, his breath coming in rapid gasps.

I wrapped my legs around him, locking my ankles behind his waist and clenched inside, milking every last bit of him.

Then he let his arms give way, burying his face in my shoulder.

A slow minute passed, and gradually, our breathing began to return to normal, and I felt his lips pressing lightly into my neck.

He lowered his hand to where we were joined, making sure that the condom hadn't gone missing in action, and pulled out of me carefully.

He rolled onto his back, and peeled off the thin rubber, pulling a face as he tied a knot in the end of the condom before dropping it into the garbage can. Then he leaned up on one elbow to look at me, resting his free hand on my stomach.

"Are you okay?" he asked, tenderly planting a gentle kiss on the tip of my nose.

I wasn't sure how to answer that question.

I'd *promised* myself I'd never get involved with another man in the military, I'd been *determined* never again to be attracted to a younger man, I *knew* that revisiting the past was a bad, bad idea, and I sensed that Sebastian was a volatile mixture of intense emotions and unexamined anger at the past.

And yet, my reckless body sang every time he touched me.

"Yes, I think so," I replied, my voice carefully neutral.

I pushed his hand away and sat up, ignoring his confused expression.

"Where are you going?"

"Just to get some water," I said, without looking at him.

I felt his eyes on me as I walked into the bathroom, brutally aware that my forty-year old body couldn't match the exquisite perfection of his.

I pulled on the bathrobe and drank some water from the faucet. The bathroom mirror reflected my flushed face and tangled hair. I'd picked up my hairbrush to resolve one of the issues when I heard Sebastian, and turned to see him standing in the doorway behind me.

"Caro, what's the matter?"

"Nothing," I said, too brightly. "I'm fine."

His eyes met mine in the mirror and I could see that he didn't believe me, but he didn't challenge me either. Silently, he took the brush from my hands and slowly, carefully, brushed my hair until it hung in tidy waves down my back.

"You have beautiful hair, Caro. I'm glad you kept it long."

His tone was gentle, almost loving.

I shrugged.

"Every now and then I decide to cut it, especially after I've been somewhere I haven't been able to shower for a couple of weeks."

"That would be a crime," he said solemnly.

"You can talk!" I said, pointing my chin at the haze of golden hair that clung to his skull.

His lips twitched in a small smile.

"Believe me, babe, I'd grow it if I could. Maybe I should go to my CO and tell him my girlfriend wants me to..."

He stopped abruptly.

I sighed. "It's okay. I keep forgetting which decade I'm in, too. It's so strange."

He nodded in relief.

"Yeah, this is so weird, I feel the same. It's as if nothing's changed but everything's changed. It's like being in some crazy time machine. I keep expecting your husband to be banging down the door."

I winced.

"Fuck, sorry. I'm doing it again."

I smiled, painfully.

"Oh well, I imagine you've had some experience with husbands banging on the door."

"Don't, Caro."

I stared at him for a fraction of a second, then pushed past him, back into the bedroom.

I couldn't believe he'd mentioned my ex-husband. Didn't we already have enough painful memories between us? Apparently not.

I heard the faucet running, and he followed me, carrying a glass.

He handed it to me silently, and I took a small sip before placing it on the cabinet next to the bed.

"Thank you."

He sat back on the bed, covering his lower half with the sheet.

"Caro, I know this is fucking weird but it's good, too, isn't it? I mean, not everyone gets a second chance."

Is that what this was, a second chance? But a second chance at what? A second chance to rip ourselves apart again?

"Today was fun," I said, trying to think it through, "and tonight was … good, but the reality is I'm based in New York and spend between three and six months of the year away from home. You're a Marine and go wherever they send you. Presumably this next tour of Afghanistan will be six months or maybe longer? And then where, because let's face it, Sebastian, the chances of you getting posted to the Corps' Division of Public Affairs in New York is slim to none—especially with your record. So I'm not sure what sort of 'second chance' you have in mind."

Sebastian's body went rigid with sudden, suppressed rage, and then he leapt off the bed, glaring down at me, gloriously naked—and very angry.

"Christ, it's like listening to an old record, Caro! You *always* try to think of reasons why we can't be together!"

"What do you mean 'always'? I haven't seen you for ten years!"

"That's the whole fucking point, Caro! You used to say this shit to me when I was 17, and you're still doing it now. We wasted *ten years* and you're worried about a few thousand miles? Hell, we've got airplanes, we've got email, they've invented fucking cell phones. Jesus, if it comes down to it, I'll even write you a fucking letter!"

I bit back a rather hysterical giggle that began to bubble up.

"You write letters?"

His shoulders relaxed slightly, but his eyes were still tight with emotion.

"I'll write you on both sides of the fucking paper, Caro."

"How can I refuse such an astonishing offer?"

"Are you laughing at me?"

"Are you shouting at me?"

"Yes!"

"Then, 'yes' to you, too." I sighed. "Look, today, tonight—it's been fun. But like I said to you before, I'm really not looking to get tied down again. I work *a lot* and I love what I do. I'm still mad at you for screwing up my travel papers. I won't be paid until I've filed a story, and I won't be able to do *that* until I get to Leatherneck. All this time, I'm not earning—and I have a *very* expensive mortgage to finance."

He rested his hands on his hips, and looked me in the eye.

"I'm sorry about the money, Caro, and I'm sorry that I made you mad at me again, but I'm not sorry about what I did. I hoped I'd get a chance to spend some time with you, but I would have done it just to keep you safe."

I sighed. "This is getting us nowhere."

He sat down on the edge of the bed with his back to me, and rested his elbows on his knees.

I had the opportunity to study his finely muscled back, sculpted shoulders and glowing, gold skin—my golden boy.

"Caro, I have 17 days before I ship out. I'd like to spend them with you. That's all. If you don't want to see me after that ... well, I guess that's it."

CHAPTER FIVE

WHEN HE PUT IT LIKE THAT, WHAT DID I HAVE TO LOSE? I COULD see Italy with him or spend a pointless two weeks kicking around Geneva on my own. And, despite what I'd said to him about the sex having been 'fun', 'spectacular' and 'mind-blowing' would have been more appropriate adjectives. Plus, it was the most orgasms I'd had in one evening for a decade.

"I'm going to need a cushion to sit on if you expect me to ride on that motorcycle of yours all the way to Salerno."

His expression lifted at once.

"Really? You're sure?"

"Well, to paraphrase you, 'what the hell'." I paused. "But I reserve the right to fly back if you're being too much of an ass."

"Huh, well, you'd better give me a sliding scale of assaholic behavior, just so I know."

I raised an eyebrow. "That could be quite a long list."

"Try me."

"Okay," I said, sitting up straight, and diving straight to my mental list of his most assifying and irritating moments since we'd met up again. "First, no getting drunk and passing out in my bed; second, no more interference in my career *of any kind*—that's a deal breaker; third, no territorial displays of adolescent jealousy; fourth..."

But I didn't get to finish my list—he jumped on me, pinning me to the mattress, and kissed me hard.

I was breathless and aroused when he let me go, and I could also feel his renewed erection poking my hip through the bathrobe.

Of course—fast reloader. I'd forgotten.

"What was that all about?" I said, pushing him off me.

He shrugged.

"It sounded like a very long list, I thought I'd try to distract you."

"Diversionary tactics?"

"Yeah, we're schooled on that in the Marines," he smirked.

"I bet you are! And by the way," I said, pointing to his fully erect dick, "you can put that away—I'm exhausted. Somebody dragged me all over Switzerland and half of France today."

"Sure I can't persuade you?" he said, leaning down to bite my thigh.

"Quite sure, thank you. This forty-year-old woman needs her beauty sleep."

He scowled. "I wish you wouldn't do that, Caro."

"Do what?"

"Keep going on about your age. You're older than me—I get it. And guess what? I don't give a shit. I never did. I just wish you weren't so hung up about it. It's kind of annoying."

I was annoying *him? In what universe?* Oh, this one, probably.

I realized my mouth was still hanging open in a most unattractive way.

"Feel free to say what you really mean, Hunter."

He grinned at me. "Okay."

I shook my head, half-amused, half-irritated.

"So, we can go tomorrow? Start our road trip?" he said, his eyes glowing like a kid at Christmas.

"Well, I suppose so. But I don't know how we'll get my case on the back of your motorcycle."

"Don't worry about that. We'll just take what you need, and leave your case at my place till we get back." He paused, his expression turning challenging. "So, can I stay the night, or are you going to kick me out into the cold, dark world, all alone in a strange city, where foreign women might try and have their evil way with me?"

"That's a sob story, if ever I heard one, Sergeant Hunter, although I strongly suspect it's a highly edited one."

"Is that a yes?" he asked hopefully.

"It's a yes, providing sleep is what you had in mind."

"Mostly. Good enough?"

I shook my head. He really was incorrigible.

"Fine. You want to use the bathroom first?"

"No, go ahead."

As I brushed my teeth hard enough to remove several layers of enamel, I wondered how I'd got railroaded *again*. I really didn't seem to have the ability to say 'no' when it came to Sebastian. Had it always been like that between us? I thought back to some of the outrageous risks we'd taken ten years ago. Yes, I had to admit—it had always been like that.

When I'd finished, Sebastian took his turn in the bathroom, and I climbed wearily into bed. I'd forgotten what a workout it was, having sex with him. My thirty-year-old self had trouble keeping up, there seemed even less chance I'd be able to keep up now. I reminded myself that according to the consensus of opinion, a forty-year-old woman was in her sexual prime, while a man's was at the age of 19. Which meant Sebastian was already past his prime, although there was no evidence that anyone had told him that. Even so, it cheered me up slightly.

I enjoyed the floor show as he strolled out of the bathroom, unembarrassed by his nudity, wearing just his dog tags and a big smile. He was either very comfortable with me, or he was just used to wandering around naked—did they have open showers in the Marines? Hmm, maybe some research was in order—strictly on the grounds of professional integrity, of course.

Instead of walking around the bed, he deliberately sat on my side, then climbed over me.

"Sebastian, what are you doing?"

"Taking a shortcut," he said, as his body hovered over mine, and he dipped down to kiss me.

He tasted of mint.

I reached up and pulled him deeper into the kiss before pushing lightly on his chest.

"Sleep! Now!"

"Sure I can't change your mind?" he said, eyeing yet another erection, which was growing at an alarming rate.

"Oh, put it away! I'm tired."

He grinned at me and gave in, sliding under the duvet on the other side of the bed.

I stretched to turn off the bedside light and the room was plunged into darkness. I felt Sebastian's hand drift over my waist, and he kissed the back of my neck.

"Night, baby."

He fell asleep quickly, his arms wrapped around me, warming me and weighing me down. I listened to the sound of his quiet, even breaths, wondering if our differences would bring us together or push us apart.

~

It was barely light when Sebastian shook me awake from a confused and disturbing dream.

"Caro, are you okay?"

I rubbed my face as his worried eyes gazed at me.

"Oh, sorry, did I wake you up? I was dreaming."

"It sounded more like a nightmare."

"Sorry. Yes, I'm okay."

In truth, I'd been dreaming about Iraq again. It wasn't something that happened often, but it was always frightening when it did. The recurring images stemmed from the time I'd visited Victory Base near Baghdad's airport: the medical team had just heard that three 'Category Alpha' injuries were on their way. In my dream, it was the distinctive thrum of the medivac helicopters that filled me with fear.

Sebastian definitely didn't need to know what my nightmare had been about.

I shivered and sat up, the duvet slipping down to my waist. Sebastian's expression changed, and I realized his eyes were hungrily fixed on my breasts.

"Your eyes are going to fall out, Hunter," I muttered.

He grinned guiltily, acknowledging that he'd been caught staring.

"Just looking, boss," he said.

I didn't bother to reply. Instead, stretching stiffly, I shuffled off to the bathroom with the bathrobe pulled tightly around me.

I contemplated the bags under my eyes and frazzled hair, searching for any gray ones that I could ruthlessly root out. And then I realized the truth: this was as good as it gets. I was never going to be younger, or more toned, or less wrinkly. And maybe there would be a day, sooner rather than later, when Sebastian would want younger flesh under his expert hands. And if that happened, there was nothing I could do about it. But right now, he wanted me. It was *my* body that made his eyes pop out of his head, and *my* body that had so aroused him last night. He'd said again that he didn't care about the age difference, so what was my problem? Maybe I should just sit back and enjoy the ride, so to speak.

Perhaps I was having a breakthrough: *he didn't care*, so why should I?

I prodded my puffy eyes again. Nope, still luggage-laden. Then I remembered something: something Sebastian had said to me ten years ago, something we'd never done.

Hmm. That had interesting possibilities. I wondered if he'd let me ... one way to find out.

It would certainly take my mind off my inadequacies and, well, hopefully it would take Sebastian's mind off of everything.

Sebastian was lying back on his pillows with his hands behind his head.

"Hi," he said, his eyes glowing.

"Hi yourself."

"You seem better."

"Why, Sergeant Hunter, what masterful skills of observation you have."

He grinned at me. "Yeah, much better."

"Well, now you mention it, I am in a much better mood, although I'm rather hungry."

"Do you want to go down for breakfast or should I call room service?"

"Let me think about that for a minute."

Slowly, I untied the belt to my robe and pulled it out of the loops, winding it through my fingers.

I dropped the robe to the floor, and watched Sebastian's eyes as he followed its descent.

"I was thinking about eating you, Sarge, but as you're such a stubborn, annoying man, who makes me pissed with every other sentence he utters from between his beautiful, badly-behaved lips, I thought I should tie you up first. What do you say?"

Sebastian's mouth dropped open.

"I'd say, where is Carolina Venzi and what have you done with her?"

I smirked at him. "I'm just taking your advice, Sarge."

"I don't know what advice I gave you, but it must have been damn good."

"Let's find out. Put your hands on the headboard."

"Yes, ma'am."

He wrapped his hands through the metal framework, and I crawled up the bed and across his body. Kneeling over his chest, I threaded the belt through the headboard and tied both his wrists tightly.

"Have you done this before?" he breathed out, his gaze heated.

"Only in my dreams, Hunter. Now, be quiet, or I might have to gag you, too."

"Fuck!" he whispered.

"Maybe later."

I whipped the duvet from him in the same way that I ripped off wax strips from my legs. I wasn't surprised to see he was beautifully erect.

"Now that's a sight for sore eyes, Sebastian. Maybe I should just leave you here—the hotel maids might appreciate that. Or, better still, maybe I'll take a photograph of you on my phone. Don't worry, I won't post it on the internet, it'll just be my screensaver."

"Caro!" he said, a serious warning in his voice.

"Spoilsport," I said, pouting at him. "No sense of adventure."

He grinned back, but his expression was slightly wary. He flexed his arms, testing the knots. I was delighted to see he couldn't move them. I placed a gentle kiss on each of his biceps before sliding back down his body.

Oh, I was going to enjoy being the one giving the orders. Maybe I'd teach him how to be a good soldier and take them.

I knelt down on the bed, and ran my tongue from his balls to his tip, he groaned loudly. Nope, that wasn't going to work.

I clambered off the bed again.

"Where are you going?" he asked, rather nervously.

"Back in a minute," I called, as I wandered into the bathroom. I rooted through my toiletry bag trying to find a hair-tie.

"Caro!" he yelled. "What the fuck?"

"Are you getting impatient, Sebastian?"

He swore again and I heard him tug on the headboard, making it creak ominously.

I strolled back into the bedroom, pulling my hair into a ponytail. "Couldn't see what I was doing," I explained.

"There's going to be payback for this, Venzi," he said, his eyes dark and amused.

"Bring it on, Sarge."

I knelt back on the bed and ran my hands over his fabulous chest, enjoying the smooth tautness of his pecs, every ripple of his abs and washboard stomach. I took his dog tags in my mouth and sucked hard.

He closed his eyes, and breathed in deeply.

I smiled to myself. I was enjoying having him at my mercy—I suspected he was, too. Well, it was more than a suspicion, I had the evidence to prove it. Yes, about that evidence...

I kissed, nipped, bit, licked and sucked my way downwards. I must have found a ticklish spot, because his hips bucked uncontrollably and he swore again.

"Sebastian, your language!"

I ran my tongue down his full length, and gently held his balls in my teeth. His body was rigid, and I think he stopped breathing. I released him carefully, and heard the breath rush out of his lungs. I felt the urge to laugh, but thought better of it. I held his erection at right angles to his body, and leaned down. I planted a soft kiss on the tip, feeling his body quiver, and then I took him in my mouth, all of him, all the way up and all the way down. I used my tongue, teeth and lips to give him sensation in as many different ways as possible.

His skin was soft and silky to the touch, his erection hot, hard and delicious. I massaged his thighs and balls as I rode up and down him with my mouth.

He flexed his hips upwards, and moaned softly. That was my cue to increase the pressure and ramp up the speed.

I felt so turned on having him in my complete power. I'd never done anything like this before in my life, and I'd lied to Sebastian when I'd told him I'd dreamed about doing it. But there was something about his honesty and openness that made me feel strong and almost fearless. It was *me* giving him pleasure and making him writhe underneath me, not some nubile twenty-year old. Forty, and with fewer inhibitions: it wasn't a bad place to be.

With a feeling akin to triumph, I felt him come in my mouth as he cried out my name. I swallowed quickly, aware of the warm, salty fluid in the back of my throat. *Really don't want that going down the wrong way.*

I sat up, feeling a little stiffness in my neck and shoulders. Oh, well, it was worth it.

His eyes were still closed and his breathing was rapid. I watched him for a moment, then leaned over to the bedside table and drank some of the water that he'd left there last night.

I glanced at my phone to see the time, wondering if he'd regain the power of speech anytime soon.

I lay back on the bed and cuddled up on his chest, pulling the duvet over us.

"Jeez, Caro! That was ... that was ... wow!" He paused. "Are you going to untie me now?"

I shook my head sleepily. "Don't think so. I like having you as my beck-and-call boy."

He chuckled lightly, then rattled the headboard again. "Seriously, I want to hold you."

Grumbling quietly, I untied his arms and he flexed his hands. He worked the fingers a little, which made me wonder if I hadn't tied him a little too tightly. Oh well, live and learn.

"Where did you teach yourself to do that?" he asked teasingly, once I'd settled back on his chest.

"Night school," I said, with a yawn.

He laughed and kissed my shoulder. "Is it my turn now?"

"I thought you wanted to take me on a road trip."

"Yeah," he said, a salacious gleam in his eye. "But I could be quick…"

Hmm, fast, hard sex … with Sebastian.

No, my muscles were still feeling the sting of last night's activities.

"I'll take a rain check, Sarge."

His expression was rueful.

"Okay. In that case, I guess we should get going."

But his hands weren't obeying the words his mouth was speaking.

"What are you doing?" I asked suspiciously, my eyes still closed.

"Nothing," he said softly, as his fingers skated a little lower.

Then I gasped, and my eyes flew open. He was grinning at me, a devilish expression on his face.

"Sebastian!" I moaned.

"Shh, baby," he whispered, then covered my mouth with his.

It seemed it was my turn after all.

I showered quickly, shooing him out of the bathroom when he tried to join me. I knew if he did, our road trip would begin and end with this bedroom, which didn't sound so bad, but now, after all my arguments, I found I was looking forward to seeing Italy with Sebastian.

His shower was even briefer than mine, and he dressed quickly while I packed up my clothes, cell charger, laptop and notebooks. Carefully, I wedged my camera case in among my t-shirts to give it as much protection as possible.

The camera was a Nikon D2Xs and it meant a lot to me. It had been one of the first things I'd bought myself, once I started making some money from writing. There were other, better digital cameras out there on the market, but this one had accompanied me all over the world, and it had never let me down.

"Do you want to get breakfast here?" said Sebastian. "You didn't eat anything after lunch yesterday."

His thoughtfulness was endearing. Yes, I remembered that: those brief moments when someone had put my needs before their own. Sebastian had been the first person to do that.

"No, it'll take too long. You must know some little café we could stop at? Maybe on the lake?"

"Yeah, okay. But I need to swing by my place first and pick up a few things."

We headed down to the lobby, and while I settled my bill, pushing the receipt in my pocket, glad that my newspaper was paying for this expensive hotel, Sebastian went to retrieve his bike. I still wasn't sure how he was going to get my case onto his motorcycle, even for the short distance to his apartment.

I realized I had no idea where he lived. It was going to be fascinating seeing his private world.

I heard the bike's engine before I saw it, the throaty roar surprisingly familiar already.

God, he looked gorgeous in his leather jacket, and denim stretched tightly over his toned thighs. I could daydream for hours about those. And the black helmet made him look dangerous.

He lifted up the visor.

"Give me the case, Caro."

"Where are you going to put it?"

I handed it to him, feeling puzzled, but he just wedged it in front of him between the handlebars, and jerked his head at me to get on behind him.

Yes, sir!

I'd definitely have to tie him up again—he liked being in charge too much. Or maybe I should stop encouraging him by calling him 'Sarge'.

Certain that carrying luggage like this was highly illegal, we headed off into the city. I decided that if we were stopped, I'd try the innocent-and-clueless-tourist-abroad card.

Luckily, we made it to Sebastian's place without incident.

His apartment, if you could call it that, was in an older part of the city where the architecture looked more Italian than Swiss. The cobblestone street was narrow and very quiet.

Sebastian's apartment was in a tall, thin building, with peeling stucco and weathered shutters. It wasn't at all what I'd expected. I'd imagined some chic bachelor pad, all glass and chrome—somewhere to take his conquests.

I pulled off my helmet, and clambered inelegantly from the mean machine. Sebastian swung his long leg over easily, smirking at me.

"Nothing to laugh at, Hunter. Just because you're about a foot taller than me."

"Shrimp," was his generous comment.

I tried to swat his backside, but he dodged out of the way.

"You're feisty this morning. I think I like it."

He pulled an old-fashioned key out of his pants' pocket and grabbed my case with the other.

The door creaked open and I peered into a gloomy passageway.

"Sorry," said Sebastian, "no lights."

He led the way up three flights of dark, narrow staircase, and slid the key into another lock when we reached the top.

"This is it," he said, shortly.

As I stepped inside, a feeling of sadness welled up through me. The room was small and white, with a narrow single bed pushed against one wall. An ugly military-style blanket was neatly folded over the top, as if ready for inspection. A dozen, well-thumbed paperbacks lay on a plain, wooden bookshelf. The only color in the room was provided by his dress uniform, which had been arranged on a hanger inside a dry-cleaner's bag, and hung from a hook on the wall.

A wooden chair sat silently underneath the window, and a small chest of drawers stood sentry next to the door.

There was no carpet and no rugs, just bare, wooden boards; there were no pictures, nor photographs, just his iPod and laptop, which looked lost and oddly out of place in the Spartan room.

Sensing my shock, Sebastian pointed toward the window.

"It's got a great view," he said, defensively.

"Yes," I agreed, looking out over the tiled rooftops toward the lake, "very pretty."

He shrugged. "It's all I need."

I turned to flick through his books, needing a moment to blink back the tears that threatened. He wouldn't want my pity.

"Still the Conrad fan," I said, trying to control my voice, although my throat was tight with unshed tears.

"Sure," he said.

"You should get yourself an e-reader," I said, trying to find a normal tone of voice. "The whole of Conrad for two bucks."

"Yeah, I guess I should," he replied, his voice muffled as he reached under the bed for a small overnight bag, "if I knew there'd always be somewhere to charge it up when I'm in some shithole, Stone Age village."

He stood up and tossed his bag on the bed, then rifled through the chest of drawers, pulling out half-a-dozen white t-shirts, and some of his gray briefs and black socks.

"What happened to all the colors?" I blurted out.

He threw me a puzzled look.

"Sebastian, the most colorful thing in this room are your Dress Blues," I pointed out helplessly. "The first time I met you, you were wearing those ridiculously bright red board shorts."

He laughed lightly. "Oh yeah. I've still got those somewhere. In a box in Ches's garage, I think."

"It sounds like Ches has all your worldly possessions."

"Pretty much," he said, shrugging. "I didn't take a lot when I left my parents' place. But what the hell—it's easy to pack up and move on when you're not laden down."

My heart swelled with emotion. My poor, beautiful boy—his entire family was Ches's. He owned nothing, lived nowhere, and had no one.

Except, perhaps, me—if I let him. If he wanted me.

"Caro, how much of this stuff in your case do you need?" he asked, pulling me away from my forlorn thoughts.

"I definitely need my laptop and notebooks..."

"I mean clothes, Caro. I wouldn't dare suggest to a reporter that she goes anywhere without the tools of her trade."

"That's right, Sergeant. You'd just stop her going where she needed to go in the first place."

He pouted and I couldn't help smiling. He was so cute when he did that. I wondered how many other Marines used pouting as their primary weapon.

I picked out some t-shirts.

"See," I said, arranging a palette of pink, green, blue, yellow and orange t-shirts. These are called 'colors'. They're what you get when you're not wearing black, white or gray."

"My jeans are blue."

I rolled my eyes. "So they are, Sebastian. Way to go."

"I could maybe get into colors," he commented, holding up my favorite, lacy bra, which was a deep magenta.

"I don't think it would suit you."

He added it to the pile of clothes I was taking with me.

"No, but I'm really looking forward to taking it off you."

"That's assuming you get lucky, Hunter. You promised me separate rooms, remember?"

He looked like I'd just told him Christmas was cancelled.

"You're not going to hold me to that, are you, Caro?"

I smiled at him.

"I don't know—depends how irritating you are."

"What if I promise to be on my best behavior, ma'am?"

"Mmm, maybe. I was impressed how well you took orders earlier today."

His eyes darkened dangerously, and he licked his lips.

"Yes, and there'll be payback for that, Ms. Venzi."

I tried to step away but he caught me in his arms, running his nose down my neck and kissing my throat.

"And I'm looking forward to collecting. Maybe we should christen this bed."

"Christen it? I would have thought it had seen plenty of action."

He stilled and looked up at me.

"No, you're the first woman I've brought here. It's ... private."

I wrapped my arms around his neck and pulled his head down, kissing him softly on the lips.

"We'll christen it when we get back," I whispered.

I felt his smile on my skin.

"Something to look forward to."

I pulled away and continued with my packing.

"Okay, I'm done. By the way, where exactly are we going? It's a pretty long way to Salerno, so I presume we're going to stop somewhere *en route*."

"Yeah, it's just over 1100 kilometers, so..."

"Give me that in good, old-fashioned US miles, Sarge."

He chuckled. "Seven hundred miles. I thought we'd stop at Genoa tonight—that's just under 200 miles—take us about four hours."

Or less, the way he drove.

"How come you know all these distances off the top of your head?"

He hesitated, and I saw that he was stuffing a map of Italy into his jacket pocket.

"I've been planning to do this road trip for a while."

Oh. So not something special to do with me after all.

"You and I talked about it once, you remember? All the things we were going to do, all the places we were going to see? I just figured that as I was here, I'd go anyway. And ... I remembered that you said your dad came from that village near Salerno. I thought I might find ... I don't know what I thought. I just wanted to see it."

I shook my head. Every time, *every time*, he surprised the hell out of me.

"Then let's get going," I said, smiling up at him.

As I made my way down the gloomy stairs, I heard the lock click as he closed the door. I still felt sad that this was the only place he had to call home. But when I tried to imagine him in my tiny bungalow at Long Beach, somehow the picture didn't fit. I shook the thought away, concentrating instead on the here and now.

"We could go straight to Genoa, using the Mont Blanc tunnel," he said, pulling me from my maudlin thoughts again, "but I really like the idea of going up through the high pass. There'll still be quite a lot of snow around—you up for that?"

Hmm, snowy roads, two wheels: I didn't like the math. On the other hand, long tunnel and large trucks.

"I vote for the route over the Alps," I said, sounding a lot braver than I felt.

Sebastian dropped our bag to the ground and picked me up, swinging me around. I laughed delightedly, happy that he was happy. When he finally put me down, he kissed me sweetly.

"God, you're amazing, woman!"

"Wait, I should write that down," I replied, making a grab for my notebook.

"No way! You might use that against me in court. Do I have the right to an attorney?"

"Get on the damn bike, Sebastian, before I change my mind."

He grinned and stowed our overnight bag in one of the saddlebags. I was impressed how light we could both travel, something we had in common after all.

We had a quick breakfast of sweet rolls and coffee in a café overlooking the lake, then headed up into the mountains. I was very glad I had my expensive ski gloves to wear, because we hadn't gone far before I started seeing heaps of snow at the sides of the road. Some were as high as six or seven feet. I assumed they'd been piled up as snowplows cleared the road. A couple of miles later we really began to climb, the blacktop disappeared and we were riding on compressed snow. Sebastian dropped the speed as the hairpin bends began to live up to their name.

The bike wobbled dangerously, and Sebastian pulled to the side of the road. He twisted around and lifted up his visor.

"Baby, you're going to tip us over if you do that, and I don't know about you but it looks like a helluva long way down to me."

"What ... what did I do?" I asked, nervously looking down the sheer drop.

"You're trying to sit upright on the bike: don't. You have to lean into it or the balance goes for shit. Don't try and do anything, just sit real tight and hang onto me."

"Okay, good safety tip, Sergeant. Glad you mentioned it."

His eyes crinkled in a smile, and he snapped the visor down again.

We took off slowly, zigzagging our way up the mountain. The views became more spectacular the higher we climbed, but commensurately more terrifying. My arms were wrapped around Sebastian's waist with a death-grip that was probably crushing his ribs. I was thankful he couldn't see my face because half the time my eyes were closed. So much for being fearless, so much for enjoying the view.

Twenty minutes later we reached the highest point of the pass, and Sebastian stopped again. He pulled off his helmet and grinned at me.

"It's really something, isn't it?"

Awkwardly, I clambered off the bike, tugging at my helmet and shaking my hair loose. Then I turned to look at the view.

"Wow," I breathed.

Geneva was spread out below us, the lake mirror-like in the chilly sunshine. Disappearing into the valley, I saw the Z-bends that we'd just driven up. Even here, from the safety of the summit, they looked hair-raising, and I still had to make it down the other side. But it was beautiful, too—the air was crystal clear and the sky too blue to be real. I felt grateful to be here, enjoying this moment with this man. Second chances didn't come any better.

"Thank you for this, Sebastian. Thank you for bringing me."

I leaned against him and he wrapped his arm around my shoulder, kissing me softly. I twisted in his arms so I was facing him, and gave his kiss the attention it deserved, expressing my gratitude wordlessly, pouring all my happiness into that one moment.

When I pulled away from him, my face felt flushed, along with other parts of my body. Sebastian's expression told me that outdoor sex at the top of a mountain pass in the snow was suddenly on his 'to do' list.

I stroked his cheek.

"Save it, Sergeant. We've got a long way to go yet."

He smiled reluctantly and waited while I snapped some photographs, then helped me climb back on the mean machine. We started the descent down through the Alps and toward a new country.

A short while later, Sebastian pointed to a road sign: *Italia*. I felt a thrill of excitement ripple through me. At last I was in the country where my dear papa had been born. The idea was fanciful, but in an odd way it felt like coming home.

The border guard gave our passports the briefest of examinations before waving us through with a cheerful smile. I really was in Wonderland.

We traveled onwards, and I felt almost sleepy on the back of Sebastian's motorcycle. I wondered if it was possible to fall asleep in this position.

I was beginning to feel the need to stretch my legs when we passed a sign that announced, 'Genova 20km'—and I saw the sea. It was calm and of the deepest ultramarine, fringed by delicate, white villas. Italy's Mediterranean coast.

Sebastian took us along the shore road, and it became apparent that Genoa's seafaring tradition was not just historical. We passed dock after dock lined with every kind of yacht, boat and ship I could imagine, from sleek motor-cruisers to enormous, ugly cargo vessels.

Modern Genoa seemed to be thriving, with housing creeping higher and higher up the sides of the mountain that loomed behind us.

Sebastian aimed for the towering beacon of the Torre della Lanterna as we headed into Genoa's bustling center. Skimming past the Piazza de Ferrari, we passed palatial buildings built at the time of the Renaissance, and up on the hill I could see a medieval castle. I drank in the history as we roared past.

I thought Sebastian would stop soon, but he cruised on and soon Genoa had fallen behind us. Was he going to try and reach Salerno tonight after all?

I was relieved when he finally pulled over, but when he didn't cut the engine, my hope that we'd finished for the day evaporated.

"Just checking the directions, baby," he shouted over the noise of the engine, and waved the map at me. "Not far now."

I gave him a quick thumbs up, and we took off again, climbing back up the mountain that seemed to have grown directly out of the sea.

He stopped once more to check the map, then turned off the main road, and we bumped up a steep, gravel track. A sign next to a small, whitewashed villa welcomed us to 'Casa Giovina'.

He stopped and let the engine idle.

"This is it. It only has one guest room, but it's out of season ... want to try it?"

Sebastian's expression was wary. Perhaps he thought his simple tastes didn't compare with the upscale hotel where I'd stayed in Geneva. We still had a lot to learn about each other—and I didn't mind at all.

"It looks charming. Let's go and see, but if the owners have a pretty daughter, we're out of here."

He rolled his eyes, and chose to take my words as a joke, which they were. I think. Sort of.

An elderly woman in the severe, black clothing of a widow opened the door.

"*Posso aiutarvi?*"

"I hope you can help us," I replied, in Italian. "We were wondering if you had a room for the night?"

I could see her eyeing Sebastian's 6'2" of solid muscle and evaluating how much trouble he was going to be. I could have saved her wondering and just answered 'a lot'.

"Are you married?"

As I stuttered out a surprised answer, a man in his fifties came stomping down the corridor.

"Mama! You can't ask people questions like that! I apologize—my mother is very old-fashioned. Are you French?"

"No, American."

"But you speak *Italiano*! Americans never speak our language."

Sebastian decided it was time to demonstrate his own linguistic abilities, if a little less fluent than mine.

"We mean no disrespect to your mother—this beautiful woman is my fiancée," he said pointing to me, "but if your mother would feel more comfortable, I will happily sleep in a separate room."

Oh really? Two lies in one sentence, Sebastian: see you creeping into my room after dark.

"No, no, that won't be necessary," said the owner, as his mother rolled her eyes to heaven and crossed herself twice. "Besides, we have only one room."

A fact which Sebastian already knew.

"Please, come in. Let me show you the room."

The room was airy and simply furnished. A pine wardrobe stood in one corner, and a matching chair was the only piece of furniture besides the large, old-fashioned bed. A mosquito net hung in a pool of lace above it, making it look like a rustic boudoir. But the views out toward the coast were spectacular.

I smiled happily at Sebastian, and he nodded his agreement.

"The bathroom is across the hall, *signore*, it is to share."

He shrugged helplessly, as if to apologize for the smallness of his establishment, but I didn't care. I imagined making love to Sebastian in that bed looking out over the Mediterranean.

"Breakfast is at 8AM, *signore e signorina*. There is a *ristorante* just two kilometers up the road. It is very good—run by my brother."

"That sounds great," said Sebastian.

"Ah, *signor*, one more thing: if you would mind not riding your motorcycle after dark. My mother doesn't sleep well, you understand, and she has the room next to yours."

"That won't be a problem," I muttered, once he'd gone. "I'm not getting on that thing again tonight if you pay me."

"Feeling a little tender, Ms. Venzi," said Sebastian, grabbing me and rubbing my ass soothingly.

"Not really. It's more the feeling that I'm still in motion."

"I know something that will cure that," he said, wickedly.

"Would that have anything to do with taking off our clothes and making mad, passionate love on that bed?" I said, frowning at him.

"It might have," he said, eyeing me warily.

"Oh, all right then. I'll try anything once."

His double-take was almost comical. "Is that a yes?"

"Yes, that's a yes. But you'll have to hurry, Sarge—the *ristorante* probably closes before midnight."

He glanced at his wristwatch, completely confused. "It's only five o'clock?"

"Like I said—you'll have to hurry."

Understanding brought a smile to his beautiful lips.

"Well, in that case, woman, you're wearing too many clothes."

Finally, he was on the same page as me.

"By the way," I said, before he got too caught up in the moment and knowing from experience that he could only concentrate on one thing at a time when sex was on the menu, "your *fiancée?*"

He grinned. "Seemed like a good idea at the time."

"Hmm, well, I like *my* idea better—the one where we commit as many sins as possible in the shortest amount of time."

And, to make my point, I unzipped his jacket and ran my hand down his chest, before tracing a finger around the waistband of his jeans.

I was interrupted in my further exploration by a knock at the door.

Looking irritated, Sebastian pulled it open.

"*Ah, mi scusi, signore e signorina.* I have just telephoned my brother: he is closing at 7.30PM tonight. If you wish to eat there, it would be best if you leave now."

"Thanks," said Sebastian shortly, and the little man darted away, not knowing how close he'd just gotten to a *very* pissed off Marine.

I couldn't help laughing at his expression. "Rain check, Sarge?"

He sighed, "Looks like."

"Never mind. Come on, let's get you fed and then I can have my wicked way with you."

"How wicked?"

"Not that wicked, so stop drooling. Just moderately naughty—it's been a long day."

CHAPTER SIX

HAND IN HAND, WE CLIMBED UP THE STEEP LANE TO THE *ristorante*. I couldn't imagine how a place that was so out of the way could attract much business, but when we poked our heads through the door, I saw that my assumption was very wrong.

It was thronged with families, and children of all ages were sitting at the long, trestle tables like little adults.

The happy noise tailed off when they saw us, and an unsubtle whispering began. I heard the word '*Americani*' several times before a man in a white shirt and black pants, whom I assumed was the owner, came hurrying over.

We agreed that yes, we were the Americans and yes, it was an astonishing thing that we both spoke Italian and yes, we'd have whatever was on offer. No, we weren't fussy, and yes, we were happy to have the locally made *dolcetto* red wine.

We were seated at the corner end of one of the trestles, wedged in next to a family of seven. At first, our neighbors seemed a little shy, but then Sebastian shrugged out of his jacket and pushed up the sleeves of his t-shirt. A little girl in the party, a dark haired ragamuffin aged about five, noticed his tattoo and asked her mother about the 'picture'.

Her mother tried to hush her, but Sebastian smiled and explained to her that it was because he was a sailor and a soldier, and the 'picture' reminded him of his work.

"Is that because you forgot?" asked the child, clearly puzzled.

The whole room burst into laughter. I joined in, but seeing how at ease he was with the little girl made me sad for things that might have been.

It was clear the child was completely smitten with him, because she asked her mother if he was an angel, then reached up to stroke his short-cropped hair.

The meal finished with a small bowl each of *gelato di miele* honey ice cream, a local specialty. Sebastian ate most of mine, as I'd already eaten enough. He really was a bottomless pit when it came to food.

By the end of the evening we were practically family, and all on first-name terms. It had been a wonderful evening, full of laughter and quiet enjoyment, Sebastian chatting to his new, little friend. But I also couldn't help noticing that Sebastian had drunk almost a whole bottle of wine by himself, although it didn't seem to have had much effect. On the other hand, I was feeling a little lightheaded after two glasses.

"Having fun, baby?"

"Do you realize this is our first dinner-date?"

He frowned. "What about back in San Diego—that Sicilian place?"

"That doesn't count—you wouldn't let me finish our meal because you wanted to drag me back to the hotel."

"Oh yeah, I definitely remember that!"

"Besides, your *friend*, Brenda, was spying on us. I'm half expecting to see her now, tossing her hair over her shoulder and thrusting her boobs in your face like she used to."

His expression was amused. "She thrust her boobs in my face?"

"Don't pretend like you didn't notice. Anyway, if any boobs are to be thrust in your face, they'll be mine. Right, Hunter?"

He laughed. "Anything you say, boss. Looking forward to it."

"But then I was thinking," I went on, "if this is our first date, I probably shouldn't sleep with you. I don't want you thinking I'm easy."

Sebastian gazed at me appraisingly, then pulled out his phone and started scrolling through the numbers.

"Who are you calling?"

"Well, my date just told me she wouldn't sleep with me, so I thought I'd see if I had Brenda's number on speed dial."

Ouch. He was much better at this game than I was.

"Fine, fine. I'll sleep with you. But if my reputation is in ruins, it's all your fault."

Sebastian grinned at me, then stood up to pay the bill.

I realized we hadn't discussed how we were going to split up the costs for this vacation. Maybe if he paid for one night and I paid for the next—that would be fair.

We left the *ristorante* with the good wishes and prayers of our new friends, the little girl blowing kisses to her 'Angelo'.

But the angel proved he had a devilish streak because the moment we left the *ristorante*, he pushed me up against the wall and kissed me hard, holding my waist with one hand, and running his other hand up between my thighs.

He pressed his body up into me and I could feel his arousal by my hip. I was seriously considering taking him there and then, when the ristorante started emptying, and we were very nearly caught *in flagrante delicto*.

The women looked envious, and the men called out several coarse suggestions. I was very glad the darkness hid my embarrassment.

"Should we try and make it back to our room this time?"

"Good idea," muttered Sebastian. "I don't think I could take a third interruption in one evening."

The moon lit our path as we strolled back down the hill. The air was mild, much warmer than chilly Geneva, but, of course, we were at sea level on this side of the Alps. I marveled again that in just a few days, we would be in the town where my father had been born. I don't know why that filled me with expectation, but I was looking forward to walking where he'd walked, looking at the views that he'd seen, maybe even talking to people he'd known. Italy was changing, but there were still places where the old folks lived and died in the villages where they'd been born.

When we got back to Casa Giovina, the villa was in near darkness. One, small lamp glowed in the hallway, and we crept up the stairs as if we were naughty teenagers.

I grabbed my toiletry bag before Sebastian could distract me and dashed into the bathroom, scrubbing the wine stains from my teeth, and then massaged a little moisturizer into my face with hope, rather than expectation, that it would erase any wrinkles.

When I returned to our room, Sebastian was already barefoot and shirtless. I dropped my toiletry bag from nerveless fingers, and he laughed at me.

"Seems like *your* eyeballs are the ones in danger of falling out, Ms. Venzi."

"That is true, so hurry up and get your ass back in my bed."

"Yes, boss!"

I stripped off my clothes, tossing them onto the chair, and threw myself into bed. Instead of it being the fairytale boudoir with the lacy net curtains that I'd imagined, the bed creaked alarmingly with every movement. I was horribly aware that the owner's mother was in the room next to ours *and didn't sleep well*. I stifled a giggle: it was not our night.

Sebastian returned, looking all hot and predatory. I was getting aroused just looking at him. But the thought of our noisy bed was making it hard not to laugh.

"What?" said Sebastian, annoyed that his entrance hadn't had quite the effect he'd anticipated.

"Nothing," I said, snorting back a giggle.

"What's so funny?"

I shook my head, holding a hand over my mouth.

Huffily, he pulled down his pants and kicked them off, then slid his briefs down his slim hips. For practically the first time, there was no hint of an erection. My laughter obviously had a dampening effect.

He threw the sheets back on his side of the bed, looking sulky, then sat down and started to slide over to me.

The bed creaked loudly and his eyebrows shot up. I laughed out loud.

"Sorry! I think we got the you're-not-married-so-you-damn-well-won't-be-getting-any bed. It's got a built-in anti-screwing alarm."

Sebastian smirked at me. "You think a noisy bed is going to stop me?"

"The old lady is right next door! She 'doesn't sleep well'—remember?"

"I can't help that. Besides, it'll bring back happy memories for her."

"Huh, you think you're that good?"

Uh-oh, wrong question.

He gave me a dark smile, and then his head disappeared under the sheets. I really wasn't laughing now. I tried to stifle a groan as a powerful sensation, beginning at my toes, raced up through my entire body. I pulled a pillow over my face and moaned into the soft mound of feathers.

"Oh, God!"

"Yes, baby?" said Sebastian, his amused voice muffled by the sheets.

I heard him crawling back up the bed, the mattress articulating every movement, and he tugged the pillow from my face and grinned down. His long, skillful fingers continued to dip in and out of me, bringing me to the edge of orgasm. When he fastened his teeth over my left nipple, I fell, spiraling down and choking out his name.

"Still embarrassed by the bed?" he said, smiling at me wickedly.

The question was unfair. I wasn't capable of speaking, let alone forming a rational answer.

The mattress creaked again as he slid off it to dig a condom out of his toiletry bag.

"You want to do this, baby?" he said, holding out the condom toward me.

He waited for all of two seconds before he gave up trying to get an answer. As if from a long way away, I heard the foil being ripped and the distinctive sound of a condom being tugged up an impressive erection.

"Roll over, baby, I want you from behind."

When I didn't move, Sebastian sucked my right nipple until he was guaranteed a reaction.

"Give me a minute," I grumbled.

But this Marine had waited long enough. He picked me up bodily and tossed me face down on the bed, before hauling me onto my knees so my ass was pointing to the ceiling.

He stroked my cheeks and then I felt his hot tongue between the cleft of my buttocks.

Oh, that was new.

I wiggled, not sure I was liking that. Hmm, okay, maybe.

But then he pulled away and I felt him position himself before sinking into me.

"Fuck, Caro!"

He groaned loudly. Maybe it was the alcohol, or maybe it was because he'd finally gotten around to fucking me from his favorite position, but he seemed to have less control than usual. He started pounding into me and I could feel him unraveling rapidly. The bed creaked in sympathy, the antique springs urging him on.

Oh! Not another orgasm! I forced my face into the pillow and moaned into it. We were racing toward the finish, and I was afraid the bed was going to collapse before I did.

But then Sebastian shuddered into me and stilled, and I gasped out some wordless sounds.

"Oh fuck!" he hissed, pulling out of me roughly.

My body gave way, and I lay splayed on the bed, thoroughly fucked.

And then, through the thin wall that separated us from the owner's mother, I heard the sound of someone clapping, and her reedy voice called out, "*Bravo! Bravo!*"

"What the fuck?" said Sebastian, still breathless.

I started to laugh. "I think ... I think we just got a round of applause!"

"You're fucking kidding me!"

I shook my head weakly. "That's what it sounded like. I guess she was impressed by your performance."

I heard the bed creak again as Sebastian sat up and called out loudly, "*Grazie, signora!*"

"*Prego!*" she replied.

He lay back on the bed, his hands behind his head. When I rolled onto my side to look at him, he seemed very pleased with himself.

"Something making you smile, Hunter?"

"Yeah! I never got a round of applause before."

"Maybe she was applauding me."

"Nah, she thinks I'm a stud, I can tell."

He peeled off the used condom as if to emphasize his words.

"Well, it's a good thing you don't have performance anxiety, that can put a man off his stride, so they say."

He smirked at me, then his smile faded and he looked serious.

"Do you ever think about the first time we were together? You know, when..."

"Sebastian," I said, softly. "You don't have to remind me—it's not something I'm likely to forget."

"Sorry. It's just ... I thought about it a lot at the time and, seeing you again this past week, well, it's brought it all back."

"For me, too."

He smiled and leaned over to run a long finger down my cheek, before lying back again.

"Do you know how amazing you were that night? You took care of me after my dad had beaten the shit out of me." He closed his eyes. "I thought my heart was going to fucking stop when you undressed me and you took your clothes off. And then you touched me and my cock just exploded. I thought you'd laugh at me or something. It was so fucking humiliating." He paused, remembering that awful and wonderful and dreadful night. "But you didn't. You made me feel like a man. I remember every word that you said. You told me it was going to be okay, and I didn't know how it could be, but somehow you made the world go away, like it was just you and me."

I was silent, remembering how crushed he'd been that night, how broken, and how the act of making love had somehow healed him. I wondered, now, if it had been the same for me. It was certainly the moment when my life took a completely different road from the one I'd been on.

His admission touched me deeply. I'd forgotten how painfully honest he could be. Even though he'd been so young when I'd known him before, or maybe *because* he'd been so young, he'd never held back with me. I couldn't help thinking that in some ways I'd had the best of him then, before life had made him bitter. Although his early life had been far from perfect, he'd been the sweetest, kindest person, the gentlest, most thoughtful and selfless lover—and a good friend.

"That's how you make me feel, Caro, like the world just goes away and it's just you and me. I ... I didn't think I'd ever feel like that again. All those other women, I know it bothers you, but it was just sex. It wasn't ... this."

"So, there was never anyone special, where it was more than just sex?"

He looked thoughtful.

"There was one girl, Stacey, that I sort of dated for a while. She was ... okay, but I wasn't interested in anything long-term."

"What happened?"

He shrugged and looked away.

"I heard her telling her girlfriend that she'd 'tamed' me."

I winced inwardly.

"Oh, I can guess how much you enjoyed hearing that. What did you do?"

He twitched his shoulder in an irritated gesture.

"I slept with her best friend."

I took a sharp intake of breath. "I see."

He didn't look guilty or upset, and I felt a brief frisson of sadness for Stacey and the way he'd treated her, especially when I knew he was capable of such gentleness.

"You asked me why Ches's wife didn't approve of me, and that's the reason," he went on. "Stacey was a friend of hers. And before you ask, no, I didn't sleep with Amy—it was another girl. I would never do that to Ches."

I took a deep breath.

"Well, I'm not surprised Amy doesn't like you after you did that to her friend ... and it's not very reassuring to hear that you've shown your dick to half the female population of California—and Paris, or so I've heard—but that's your business. But surely you see that you made things difficult for Ches."

"How's that?" he said, rather testily.

"You put him in the middle, making him choose between his best friend and his wife."

"What?" he said, angrily. "How was I making him 'choose'?"

"Well, I bet you anything Amy would have said she didn't want you in the house if you were going to treat her friends like that, and Ches would have had to find some way of defending what was, frankly, indefensible behavior."

I paused, wondering if Ches would have explained about Sebastian's history—our history—as a reason for his friend's actions. I hated the thought that Sebastian had used 'all those women' because he'd imagined that I'd left him without a backward glance. It was such an ugly distortion of the truth.

"You get on your fucking high horse damn quickly, Caro," he snapped.

I was taken aback at his angry tone. "I'm just saying..."

"What? What the fuck are you 'just saying'?" he said, his voice growing louder with each syllable. "You were a fucking journalist, Caro! You could have found me any time if you'd wanted to. It would have been so easy for you. So easy! I didn't even know your fucking last name. I was so desperate to find you that I even tried to see that prick of a husband of yours, but he slammed the door in my face and called my CO. I was on fucking punishment duties for weeks after that. But you didn't give a shit, did you? It's just lies. You just tell me what you think I want to hear. How can I ever trust you?"

"Sebastian, I..."

"I really want to hear this, Caro. I really want to hear how hard you tried to find me," he jeered. "You knew my fucking father was forcing me to enlist *because of you*, but you didn't even bother to make a few fucking phone calls. *Three years* I waited for you, Caro. *Three fucking years*, while you were off building your career and having a great life traveling all over the world. So yeah, I fucked some women who deserved it, because I'd already been fucked over once and I wasn't going to let it happen again."

I felt sick. All that hatred and anger pouring out of him.

"It wasn't like that, Sebastian. Just listen to me for a moment! Let me explain, because I..."

"Go tell it to the Marines," he sneered, "because I'm not listening."

I needed to get some space and t he bathroom seemed like it could be a place of refuge until he'd calmed down. His anger was scaring me and I didn't want to say anything that I'd regret later, although it was clear he wasn't having the same reservations.

I sat on the edge of the bed and reached for my t-shirt.

"Where are you going?" he shouted. "Running away again? Yeah, well, it's what you do best, isn't it? Run away. Fuck that! I'll save you the trouble."

He leapt out of bed, pulled on his jeans, thrust his bare feet into his boots and scooped up his t-shirt and jacket.

And then he walked out.

A moment later I heard the throaty roar of his motorcycle.

I pulled the sheet around me tightly, wondering what the hell had just happened. It was hard to believe that the man who'd made such sweet love to me could talk to me like that. Or rather, yell at me like that.

So much anger at me.

It seemed clear now that the gentle side he'd shown had simply been a mask that hid his true feelings.

But he'd gone and I had no idea if he was coming back. Well, *fuck him!* He wasn't the only one who'd suffered, he wasn't the only one who'd had to struggle. Oh sure, my life had been so easy: I'd cleaned other people's toilets for nearly three years before my writing earned me enough to give it up. *How dare* he speak to me like that!

I jumped out of bed and whirled around the room shoving everything into his small overnight bag. I knew his phone and passport were in his jacket, so he hadn't left anything that he needed. *Not even me*, said the sad, little voice in my head.

I thought through my options: I could book a cab to take me into Genoa, and from there, take a flight to Geneva. Then it was back to Plan A: wait for my permits to come through for Leatherneck—assuming Sebastian didn't try to screw that up again, although the odds didn't look good, given his current rage—do my job and get on with my life. And then I'd write off this episode to experience. Or something.

But it hurt. It really hurt. Just as I'd begun to trust him and let him back into my life...

And then I wondered if he'd be back after he cooled off. I really didn't want to face very-angry-and-scary Sebastian again tonight. But if I wedged the chair under the door, I wouldn't be the least surprised if he'd just decide to kick it in. Not that we'd be welcome staying at Casa Giovina after tonight's stunt anyway, but I didn't want to add a broken door to our troubles.

In the end, I pulled on my t-shirt and panties and tried to get some sleep. After thrashing around for several hours and replaying the whole horrible scene over and over, I finally lapsed into unconsciousness about an hour before dawn.

~

My alarm pulled me awake at 7AM and I immediately looked over to the other side of the bed: it was cold and empty—like me.

Fierce disappointment mixed with relief washed over me. At least I didn't have to face his recriminations again. Wake-up arguments definitely didn't do it for me.

I headed for the shower, but the tepid water did little to relieve my heavy mind. I didn't feel much like breakfast, but the least I could do was apologize to the hosts for our behavior. His behavior.

I wandered out to the patio and saw that the little table had been laid for two. I felt hot tears prick my eyes and I angrily scrubbed them away.

When I heard footsteps behind me, I turned hopefully. But it wasn't Sebastian and it wasn't the owner, instead the little grandmother was walking stiffly toward me, carrying a pot of coffee.

"Sit, young woman," she said. "And don't worry: it will all seem better once you have eaten. He'll be back."

I swallowed and tried to smile. She patted my shoulder sympathetically and left me alone.

The coffee was very good: rich and strong and just the shot in the arm that I needed. I drank almost the whole pot, then managed to eat a small plate of *fette biscottate* with salted butter. And I did feel better. And angry. *Really fucking angry.* How dare he talk me into this road trip, then drop me in the middle of nowhere the minute it suited him!

Or maybe this was his plan all along: maximum humiliation. *Screw him!*

I marched back to my room, scooped up the overnight bag and went to find the owner.

"Ah, *signorina*," he said, worriedly.

"Please accept my apologies for last night's disturbances," I said, with polite formality. "How much do I owe you for the room?"

He twisted his fingers unhappily. I could tell he felt bad about charging me, but I was determined to pay my debts. I pulled out my wallet expectantly.

He sighed. "Forty Euros, *signorina*."

"Thank you, *signore*. You have a very pleasant establishment."

"*Grazie, signorina.*" He bit his lip and tried to smile.

"Can I get a cab to pick me up and take me to the airport?"

"Ah, regretfully, *signorina*, taxis do not like driving up my narrow road, but if you walk two kilometers toward Quinto Al Mare, you will find a taxi office."

I thanked him, hefted the bag over my shoulder, and strode out into the beautiful spring morning.

I'd reached the main road when I heard Sebastian's bike roaring up behind me.

My stomach lurched, twisting with anxiety. When I heard him cut the engine, I put my head down and walked as quickly as I could.

"Caro, wait!"

He jogged up behind me and grabbed the handles of the bag, forcing me to stop.

"Caro, I'm sorry. Okay? Are you going to talk to me?"

"I think you've said enough—for both of us."

"Fuck, Caro! It was the alcohol talking, that's all."

"It was more than that and you know it, Sebastian."

"Can't you take a fucking apology?"

"I don't know—can you make one?"

We stood staring at each other, both hurt, both angry.

He ran his hand over his hair and scowled. "Can we just go somewhere and talk? Or are you going to walk back to Geneva?"

I folded my arms and glared at him. "Yes, frankly. I was going to get a cab to drive me to the airport. I'm sure I'd have no trouble getting a flight."

"Don't leave like this, Caro," he said, in a slightly less aggressive tone. "Let's just talk. If we can't ... fix this, I'll take you to the airport myself."

Damn him!

I nodded coldly and let him carry the bag. Silently he passed me my helmet, and stowed our solitary piece of luggage in the saddlebag.

He climbed on the bike and held out his hand to help me, but I preferred to scramble on by myself. And, instead of fastening my hands around his waist, I held onto the small grab-bar at the rear of my seat. It was uncomfortable and I didn't feel very safe, but it was preferable to touching him.

He swung the bike around in a slow U-turn and headed southeast, away from the airport, following the coast road. After a few miles, he pulled into a parking lot next to a beach café in the small town of Bogliasco.

"Do you want a coffee?" he asked stiffly.

"An espresso and a glass of water, please."

He placed the orders with a bemused waiter, who clearly hadn't been expecting any customers so early. In fact, I suspected that we'd interrupted his morning gossip with his cronies, a group of grizzled old men who eyed us curiously, but relaxed when they heard Sebastian speaking in Italian. The waiter ambled away with reasonably good grace.

I stared across at Sebastian's beautiful sullen face, wondering why we were even bothering. I realized his eyes looked rather red. Obviously he'd chosen to dive straight into a bottle of whiskey last night, or *grappa*, perhaps. He stared out at the water, refusing to look at me or to speak. Not a great start to 'talking'.

Our coffees arrived along with a basket of rolls, and I wondered who was going to break the silence first.

He pushed the basket toward me.

"No, thank you. I've already eaten."

"Did you check out of that place?"

"Yes."

"Did you pack up my stuff?"

I blinked at him. "Of course!"

"Okay, thanks. What do I owe you for the room?"

"Nothing. Forget it."

"Just tell me what I owe you, Caro."

"Seeing as you didn't stay in it, I don't see why you should pay."

"Is this how you're going to be?"

"How would you like me to be, Sebastian? Because, honestly, I just don't know."

He grabbed a roll and started tearing it into pieces.

"Look, maybe we should just cut our losses," I said. "I'll get a cab to the airport and you can ... do whatever you want, Sebastian."

For a moment I thought he was going to agree, but then he looked down at the crumbs on his plate.

"I don't want you to go," he muttered.

I waited for more, an explanation for his behavior, perhaps. But he was silent.

And then realization hit me with the force of a Sherman tank, why he was struggling to find the words: he'd never done this before. Ever. He hadn't had a girlfriend in any real sense of the word since he was 17, and that relationship had ended abruptly without any desire for reconciliation on his part. From there, he'd plunged into a turbulent affair with me, which hadn't exactly honed his relationship skills either.

By his own admission, he'd fucked Stacey's best friend as his version of solving their problems. He had no clue how to cope with the complex emotions of an adult relationship. Last night, his first reaction had been to run and hide in a bottle. No wonder he was finding this so difficult. As far as relationships went, he was on virgin territory.

I considered the fact that he actually wanted to talk to me was a step forward.

I'd been married for 11 years, and although that had ended in dismal failure, at least I had some vague idea of how relationships worked, or should work. And I'd dated two guys since Sebastian. Sort of. Sure, those hadn't panned out either, but for quite mundane reasons. Bob had moved to Cincinnati with his job, and Eric had traded up to a younger, wealthier model. I didn't count the one night stand with Allessandro, a reporter I'd met in Mexico. We were still in touch, occasionally.

"Sebastian, you're going to have to tell me why on earth you'd want me to stay," I said, gently. "Last night you said some pretty unpleasant things, and I'm not going to accept your explanation about drinking too much. It's pretty clear that you've been hanging on to a lot of anger —toward me. And I don't know what I can do about that."

He slouched down in his chair, looking for all the world like a sulky teenager. He seemed to be waging some sort of internal battle, but eventually he straightened up and looked me in the eye.

"Caro, did you really try and find me when I turned 21?"

And here we were again.

"I'll tell you exactly what I told you before: I wrote to Shirley, and I wrote to Donna. But no, I didn't try and find you directly, because I simply wanted to know that you were okay. When both letters were returned unopened, I took it as an omen that it wasn't to be. I didn't feel I had the right to interrupt your life and risk doing further damage. I felt a great deal of guilt at the devastation I left behind me: I didn't want to remind you of all that, or make you feel any obligation toward me. It never occurred to me that you ... that you'd be waiting for me."

He leaned forward, his eyes intense and angry. "But I *said* I'd wait for you. I promised I'd wait. Hell, Caro, it was the last thing I got to say to you. And you ... you said..." he bit his lip, hesitating.

I'd promised to love him forever.

An ugly wave of guilt rushed through me, and finally I could see how it had looked from his point of view: I hadn't tried hard enough— I'd let him down.

"Oh, Sebastian ... I'm so very sorry."

What could I say that would wash away so many years of hurt?

His voice dropped to a whisper. "Did you mean it, Caro? Did you mean it when you said you loved me?"

"Yes, *tesoro*, I did. I loved you very much. But you're not the person I knew ten years ago. The Sebastian I knew was sweet and gentle and loving, but you ... you can be like that, but your anger scares me. The hatred I saw in your face and heard in your words—that was hard for me. I can see that you think I let you down badly ten years ago, or seven years ago ... and I can't tell you how sorry I am for that, but I can't fix it either—I can't change the past."

He turned away, staring out at the sea.

"I'm confused about what you want from me, Sebastian. One minute you say we've been given a second chance and that we should try again, and the next minute you're blaming me for every bad decision you've taken in the last ten years. If you hate me that much, if you resent me that much, why am I here?"

"I don't hate you, Caro," he murmured.

"Sebastian, you called me a liar, you said you could never trust me."

He winced, but I was determined to see this out.

"You asked me to come with you on this trip, and then the first time something goes wrong, you fling the past in my face. If you really believe I did what I did because I didn't care, then I don't see how we're going to get past that."

I hoped he'd offer something, some insight as to what he was thinking, but his lips remained pressed together.

"Listen, I wouldn't be who I am now if I hadn't met you—that's the truth. I'd probably still be locked in a loveless marriage. But that's only half the story."

Finally he looked at me.

"It was really tough for me in New York. I had almost no money, no contacts, nowhere to live, no job. Do you want to know how I survived? I cleaned people's houses, I scrubbed their toilets. For three years. Until eventually I earned enough from my writing."

"I didn't know," he said, softly.

"No, because you didn't give me the chance to answer you last night."

I wondered if he could see how cruelly he'd behaved, but his next question took a different turn.

"You said you dated a couple of times."

"Excuse me?"

"The first night we talked. I asked you if you were seeing anyone, and you said you'd dated a couple of times."

"Yes, so?"

"When?"

"What, you want dates?"

"Yes."

I sighed. "I met Bob on my 35th birthday when I was having drinks with friends. We dated for three months and then he was transferred to an office in Cincinnati. Eric was a couple of years later: we dated for about six weeks before he dumped me for a younger woman."

"That's it?"

Oh, what the hell.

"I had a one night stand with a reporter when I was on assignment in Mexico. That's it. Now you know my entire sexual history. Although I very much doubt you could be as succinct about yours."

For a moment, he looked angry, then he gave a wry smile. "I deserve that."

I closed my eyes and leaned back.

"Are you okay?" he said, quietly.

I shook my head slowly. "Not really."

He sighed. "I am sorry, Caro. I just get fucked up in the head sometimes."

"You can't deal with it by lashing out at me. And *I* can't deal with it if you keep blaming me for something I can't change."

He put his head in his hands. "Don't give up on me, Caro."

"Last night I thought *you'd* given up on *me*."

A pained expression crossed his face.

"Can we start again, Caro? I promise I'll try not to fuck up again."

I took a deep breath.

"Sebastian, it's not a case of 'starting again', it's about working things through when we have a problem. Funny enough, it was you who taught me that, ten years ago: you made me face up to things. You can't promise me you won't fuck up, because you will. And I can't promise you that I won't fuck up, because I will. We can deal, and we can move on. Or, we can say it's been an interesting few days, and go our separate ways."

He reached over and tentatively took my hand.

"I want to go on. With you."

I wasn't even sure why I was agreeing to this. My head was screaming for me to get out now, but my heart had gone in another direction entirely.

I nodded my agreement. "Okay, then. Let's try."

"And I promise not to sleep with your best friend, especially if it's that scary British woman I saw you with in Geneva."

I could see he was trying to lighten the mood, but I wasn't quite ready to joke about it.

"Sorry," he said, quietly. "Another foot-in-mouth moment."

I tried to smile, but I probably just grimaced at him.

I pulled my hand free, and sat back to sip my lukewarm espresso.

He picked up some of the pieces of his eviscerated roll and chewed solemnly.

"Did they say anything about last night? The people at the villa?"

"Not really. They were mostly embarrassed. I think we've managed to ruin it for any other Americans who might want to stay there. But the old lady told me that you'd be back."

Sebastian looked surprised. "Really?"

"Yes, and I'm pretty certain it was me not you she was applauding last night. She probably thought I should get a medal for putting up with you."

"Yeah," said Sebastian, smiling softly, "a Purple Heart."

"Wounded in action?"

His smile slipped away. "I'm really sorry about what I said."

"We're moving on, remember? But, for the record, apology accepted."

He shifted uncomfortably in his chair and ate some of his roll, more for a distraction than anything else, I guessed.

"I got drunk and fell asleep on the beach," he muttered. "In case you were wondering."

His voice was so quiet, I could hardly hear him.

"Well, thank you for telling me."

"I panicked when I woke up and I thought you might have gone. And then I saw you walking along the road. At first I was relieved but then ... I just thought you'd walked out on me. That's why I was..."

"...such an ass?"

His smile was rueful.

"Yeah, that about sums it up."

"Well, like I said, thank you for telling me. Now, what's the big plan for today?"

He smiled his first, genuine, relieved smile of the day.

"I thought we could go to Pisa—take a look at that big, old leaning tower. It's about two hours away."

"Sure, that sounds fun."

I'd always found it hard to fake enthusiasm—something my ex-husband had pointed out on numerous occasions. But I was trying. For Sebastian's sake. For our sake.

He finished his breakfast, threw some Euros on the table and stood up to go. He held his hand out to me and, a little awkwardly, I took it.

His hand was warm and dry, the skin across the top, soft, while the palms were slightly rough, as if he'd done some manual labor recently. I hadn't noticed that before. I wondered why I did now.

When we got to the bike, he fiddled with the zipper on his jacket.

"I really want to kiss you," he said, gazing at me, a mixture of anxiety and need etched on his face.

I hesitated, and it was just long enough to see his expression change to hurt.

"Okay," I said, quietly.

He rested his hands lightly on my waist and I raised my face to his. He touched his lips to mine and I felt the familiar tug of desire. I pulled back quickly.

"Caro..."

"Just hold me, Sebastian. Just hold me."

I laid both my hands on his chest and leaned my cheek against his shoulder. He wrapped his arms around me, hugging me tightly.

"I'm sorry," he whispered. "I'm so sorry," and I felt him kiss my hair several times.

Eventually, he let me go and I gave him a brief smile.

"We'll get there," I said, quietly.

Whether I was reassuring Sebastian or myself, I didn't know.

CHAPTER SEVEN

IF I HADN'T KNOWN THAT PISA WAS A UNIVERSITY TOWN BEFORE, I knew it as soon as we drove along the main thoroughfare. The streets were packed with twenty-somethings, all casual-chic in that way foreign students do so effortlessly. By comparison, I felt scruffy, dusty and well-traveled. Being dog-tired didn't help either. I was looking forward to finding accommodation where I could have a long, hot shower and sleep in a quiet, comfortable bed—alone.

It was clear that we'd arrived during some sort of festival, because music blared from every café and *ristorante*, competing with the street entertainers and musicians who seemed to be performing on every street corner.

Sebastian carefully steered his bike into the corner of an overwhelmed municipal parking lot, surrounded by battered Fiats and old Renaults. I was a little nervous about leaving my laptop, but at least I had all my notes stored on a flash drive in my wallet, if worst came to worst.

"Are you taking your camera?" Sebastian asked me.

"Might as well. Who knows, maybe I'll be able to sell a travelogue of motorcycling through Italy."

Sebastian raised his eyebrows. "It's got to beat reporting from shitty military camps in fucked up countries."

I shrugged, not feeling in the mood to explain my obsession. Sebastian caught the hint and wisely let the subject drop.

The famous leaning tower was only one of a number of architectural marvels. The central plaza, the Piazza del Duomo, was also home to the beautiful Romanesque cathedral and the 900 year old *Battistero* or Baptistry.

It was a strange feeling, wandering among such antiquity while surrounded by irreverent youth, one of whom kept trying to hold my hand. I was glad that I had my camera as a chaperone. I didn't feel ready for the level of intimacy Sebastian clearly felt was needed. It was hard to explain to myself: I'd said I'd try, but I felt on edge being near him, as if I was waiting for him to explode again. Our earlier, relaxed mood was going to take some effort to achieve. Instead, I felt tense and ill at ease.

After an hour of wandering, I could tell he was beginning to get bored just ogling old buildings, although he did his best to hide it, which I appreciated. I recognized that he preferred action to introspection, but right now I needed to let my mind rest on the centuries of mysteries I saw all around me. I found it soothing and I couldn't help wondering if my father had ever visited Pisa. There was no particular reason why he should have, but still, he might. I liked to imagine that he wandered around here as a young man before deciding to try his luck in the New World. After all, in the sixties, he'd have heard the siren call of Janis Joplin, Bob Dylan and Woodstock. By comparison, Italy would have seemed dull and dreary, dragged down by postwar depression.

"A penny for your thoughts," Sebastian asked quietly, interrupting my musings.

"I was just thinking about Papa—wondering if he ever came here."

Sebastian's eyes lit up and he smiled.

"I really loved your dad, Caro. I was kinda jealous of you when I was a kid—I wanted so badly to have a dad like him, not the sack of shit I was saddled with."

He scowled at the memory.

"Do you ... keep up with your parents at all?"

He shook his head.

"Last time I saw the old bastard was at my graduation from boot camp."

"Oh," I said, surprised, "that was ... nice of him."

"Are you fucking kidding me? He only did it because he knew it would piss me off to have to salute him."

"Oh, right. What about Estelle?"

He shrugged. "She's still in San Diego. Ches sees her around now and again. He banned her from the country club—drinking."

He raised his eyebrows as he looked at me. I didn't say anything, but I hoped he was aware of the parallels in their behavior. Of course, being in the military didn't make for many teetotalers.

"They divorced a few years back. Dad shacked up with some stripper. I don't really know. What about your mom? Do you see her?"

I shook my head. "No, we're not in touch. I know she's living in a retirement home in Florida, but that's all."

"Why aren't you in touch? She couldn't have been as bad as my mom."

"Don't be too sure about that."

He hesitated, but I could tell he was curious. "What did she do?"

"She didn't do anything, Sebastian. That's the point. When I … when I left David, she told me I'd 'made my bed so now I could lie in it'. She didn't want anything to do with me. Wouldn't lend me a red cent to help out when I went to New York. She wouldn't even send me any photographs of Papa. I only have a couple of old pictures of him."

Sebastian tried to pull me in for a hug, but I resisted him without even being aware of it. He shoved his hands in his pockets.

"Do you see anything of him … David?"

"No. We had to correspond over the divorce papers, but that's all. I believe he stayed in the Navy. You said you tried to see him … when was that?"

Sebastian frowned and stared off into the distance.

"About four months after you'd left. It was killing me not knowing how you were, or where you were, or how to get in touch with you. Dad had already trashed my computer and deleted all my email accounts before I went to live with Mitch and Shirley. I didn't even think the bastard knew how to do that stuff. Took my cell off me and smashed that, too. Anyway, I was getting pretty desperate, so I went to your old house—but it was a waste of time. The asshole yelled at me that I'd ruined his marriage, I told him he didn't deserve you and was a bastard for the way he'd treated you. He threatened to call the police. That was it."

I sighed.

"You don't feel sorry for him do you, Caro?" Sebastian said angrily.

"A little. He just married the wrong woman, but he wasn't a bad man."

I could tell from Sebastian's expression that he disagreed strongly.

"But you didn't ruin my marriage. David and I managed to do that all by ourselves. You … freed me."

His angry expression dissolved, and his eyes gazed at me with wonder.

"Please let me hold you, Caro. It's driving me crazy that you won't let me touch you."

He reached out, but I stepped away from him.

"Just ... just give me some time, Sebastian. I don't deal with rejection well."

"Is that how you see it? That I rejected you."

I stared at him. "Of course. There's no other way to see it."

He ran his hands over his hair in frustration.

"Fuck, Caro! Last night was about my shit, not about you. Don't you see that?"

"No, I don't. Not really. But I don't want to go over that again. I'm trying to put it behind us ... I just need time."

He sighed and his shoulders sagged slightly. "Okay."

There was an awkward silence, but I'd learned that there were two ways to guarantee Sebastian's good humor—and sex was off the menu.

"Do you want to go find somewhere to eat?"

He gave a small smile.

"Yeah, I was hoping you'd say that. Do you feel like Italian?"

"Oh, very funny. You should be on 'Saturday Night Live'."

We wandered through the crowded streets, trying to enjoy the party atmosphere. I began to relax—a little.

"What about that place over there because...?"

Suddenly, I was shoved from behind and I lost my balance. Sebastian caught my elbow but my camera strap had been tugged off my shoulder.

"My camera!"

I pointed at the fleeing figure but Sebastian was already off the blocks and running. The would-be thief made it a hundred yards down the road before Sebastian tackled him, knocking him to the ground.

By the time I arrived, the man had blood pouring down his face from where Sebastian had punched him—more than once, by the look of him.

"Sebastian, no!" I gasped, as I ran up behind him.

At the sound of my voice, he uncurled his fist and stood up, handing my camera back to me. An angry crowd had started to gather, and without knowing what had happened, their sympathies were with the bleeding man.

"We'd better get out of here," Sebastian muttered.

"What about the police?" I gasped, my eyes mesmerized by the blood fountaining from the man's nose.

"Fuck them!" he snorted, and grabbed my hand, towing me through the ring of people who were watching the show with grim fascination. There were a few angry voices aimed at our backs, but no one tried to stop us.

Sebastian darted down a side-alley, pulling me after him and a moment later, we emerged into a wide piazza. I began to breathe normally again, but I was feeling shaky. I knew it was a combination of an adrenaline rush on top of an empty stomach.

"Are you okay, Caro?"

"I'm fine," I lied, weakly.

He didn't look convinced.

"Come on," said Sebastian. "You should eat something."

I nodded, and didn't argue when he led us into a small café that looked like a fifties diner, with high stools ranged along a Formica bar.

"Thank you for saving my camera," I said, quietly.

Sebastian looked surprised, then pleased. "I was waiting for you to chew me out for hitting that guy."

"Well, I'm glad you stopped punching him when you did, obviously, but I'm very fond of my camera. I worked hard to afford to buy it. Thanks, Sarge."

"You never cease to amaze me, Caro," he said, shaking his head.

I didn't know what he meant, but right there and then, I didn't really care either. I reached over and took his hand. "How are your knuckles?"

He chuckled quietly. "Much better now," he said, running his thumb over the back of my hand.

The waitress sauntered over to take our order and I could see her taking a keen interest in Sebastian. He saw the direction of my gaze and smirked at me.

"Not my type," he whispered.

"I'm glad to hear it. She's not mine, either."

For just a moment, Sebastian was caught off balance, then he smiled wickedly at me.

"Not interested in threesomes?"

"I don't know," I replied, casually. "Do you have friends in the Marines who are as cute as you?"

He frowned. "No. I don't."

I laughed. I'd finally won a round of verbal teasing. Things were looking up.

Over dinner, we began to talk naturally with each other again. Sebastian told me more about his life in the Marines and the work that he did—although I sensed there were things he couldn't tell me, as well.

He asked me about my assignments, and more about Liz and Marc, when and how I'd met them. And I told him about my little bungalow in Long Beach, and about Jenna, Alice and Nicole, and how they'd been among the first people I'd met when I'd arrived in New York.

I was relieved to see that he stuck to just the one bottle of beer, which also helped me to relax. I was putting off the moment when I'd have to tell him how much he scared me when he'd been drinking. But not now.

I stifled a yawn.

"Are you tired, Caro?"

"Yes, definitely ready to head for bed, Sebastian. To sleep."

He smiled, but didn't comment.

"Okay, let's see what we can find. There were a couple of streets I saw online that are mostly *pensiones*. Should we try one of those?"

I liked the idea of staying in one of those small hotels. They were usually family run and, although modest, friendly and fun, too.

"Sounds good."

Sebastian paid for the meal, waving away my suggestions that we take turns to pay, or split the bill. I was too tired to argue, but added it to my mental list of 'things to talk about'. It was quite a long list.

There was, however, a tricky subject that I wanted to bring up, and I didn't know how he was going to react.

"Sebastian, don't get mad at me, and don't read too much into this..."

His expression was already worried as I plowed on.

"...but I'd really like to have separate rooms tonight. Just..."

My voice trailed off as a kaleidoscope of emotions flitted across his face. The predominant emotion seemed to be hurt, but there was anger and frustration mixed in there, too.

My body tensed, a primal fight or flight reaction, but he nodded his head slowly.

"Whatever you need, Caro."

I let out a long, relieved sigh.

"Thank you."

But our relaxed banter had, predictably, vanished, and we walked in silence.

"This is the street," he muttered, pointing toward a long line of narrow townhouses.

The first two *pensiones* were full, and the third could only offer a single room. It wasn't looking too good.

"We could try going more upscale," said Sebastian, obviously irritated, although whether that was with me or the accommodation, I couldn't tell.

"Well, we have to walk along this street to get back to the main hotel area, so we may as well try a few more on the way," I suggested.

"Yeah, okay."

At the fifth *pensione*, we struck gold. Sort of.

"I'm sorry, *signora*," said the owner, a stout lady aged about sixty. "I have one room with two single beds, but that's all. It's the Festival, you see," she said, gesturing helplessly. "You're lucky—I had a cancellation."

I could see out of the corner of my eye that Sebastian was willing me to take it. I turned to look at him.

"Pajama party," he mouthed.

I couldn't help smiling. "*Si*, we'll take the room. *Grazie*."

The *pensione* was narrow and old-fashioned, but clean and welcoming, too. Our hostess went by the name of Signora Battelli, and when Sebastian informed her that my surname was 'Venzi', she went off into paroxysms of joy that 'Mr. and Mrs. Venzi have come home', meaning we'd returned from America to the mother country. She had delightfully misunderstood him.

Our room looked like it was last refurbished in the 1970s, decorated with an astonishing clash of vivid patterns, and garish pictures of saints. But I was so tired I didn't care. There was a small sink in the room, and the shower was down the hall, shared, she assured us, by just one other couple.

She bustled off, calling over her shoulder that breakfast was at 8AM.

Sebastian threw himself down on the bed and it groaned slightly.

"Not as noisy as last night," he said, smiling up at me.

"I don't think that's even possible," I agreed.

He unpacked our overnight bag and tossed my toiletry bag onto the second, narrow bed.

"Thanks for packing up my stuff," he said, looking over at me. "I thought I'd probably seen the last of these shirts."

"What a tragedy," I said, cattily. "You might have had to do something shocking, like buy t-shirts in different colors."

He smirked at me, but didn't reply.

The bedroom window had old-fashioned slatted shutters instead of curtains. Sebastian leaned over to open the window, and the sounds of revelry drifted up on the night air.

"Listen to that," he said, dreamily. "Sounds like being in Italy."

I stood and listened for a moment, a smile on my face. "Yes, it sounds, I don't know ... happy."

He turned and looked at me. "Are you happy, Caro?"

I nodded slowly. "Getting there."

"Good," he said, quietly.

I collected my toiletry bag and headed for the shower. As I glanced over my shoulder, he was still staring out of the window.

When I returned, he was leaning out as far as he could, soaking up the mild, night air. He looked relaxed and had a serene expression on his face. I didn't often see him like that: it reminded me of how he'd been when I'd known him in San Diego.

"Back in a minute, baby," he said, smiling at me.

While he was gone, I pulled on a baggy t-shirt that I used for sleeping in, and pulled out my laptop to catch up with emails.

My editor was fuming, still unable to expedite my travel documents. With a frisson of guilt, I realized that I hadn't even told him I was on the move. I tapped out a hasty email of explanation, and offered him a light travel article as a bonus.

Jenna and Alice had sent long and chatty emails about a new gallery they'd been to see in Manhattan, mentioning how the cheap wine had been undrinkable. I wrote to tell them I was traveling through Italy with an old friend, and that I'd finally seen the Leaning Tower of Pisa for myself. It made me feel comfortable to be connected and have news from home.

True to his word, Sebastian returned quickly from the shower. He seemed relieved when he walked back through the door. Perhaps he thought I'd run away while he was gone.

"You doing your writing?" he said, nodding at the laptop.

"No, just catching up with my girlfriends."

"Did you tell them about me?"

"I told them I was traveling through Italy with an old friend."

He looked disappointed, but didn't question me further.

"So, what do you want to do tomorrow?" he said. "Look at more old buildings?"

I was amused by his tone—he was obviously trying to please me, but the look on his face screamed *no more old buildings or I'll want to stab my eyeballs with a fork!*

"Whatever. This is all a bonus anyway. Where would you like to go?"

"There're a couple of surf spots I'd like to check out, if you don't mind," he said, looking hopeful.

"I don't mind, Sebastian. I could use some beach time—sleeping in the sun sounds perfect about now."

"Okay, cool!" he said, clearly relieved. "The surf isn't great in the Med, but there are a few breaks that look like they might be rideable."

He peeled off his t-shirt while he was talking, and I couldn't help my eyes drifting over his chest. *Damn, he was in good shape.*

I dropped my eyes back to my laptop before he caught me staring.

I heard, rather than saw, the rustle of fabric as he tugged off his jeans. I couldn't help glancing up, and noticed that he'd kept his briefs on. That was thoughtful. I knew I wanted him in my bed again, but not yet. This time last night, he'd been yelling at me, calling me an untrustworthy liar. Memories like that took some swallowing.

He jumped into his bed and lay back with his arms behind his head, smiling across at me.

"Are you going to tuck me in?"

I laughed. "I think you're old enough and ugly enough to do that yourself."

"Ugly?"

"Hideous. I can hardly bear to look at you."

"You could close your eyes."

"I could, Sebastian, but I might get the urge to peek."

He thought about it for a moment. "Well, can I get a goodnight kiss?"

"Sure. I'll ask Signora Battelli if she's available."

He pulled a face. "I've never kissed a woman with a mustache."

"First time for everything, Sebastian."

"Please, Caro," he said, pouting cutely at me. "I'll be good. Promise."

"Hmm, I've heard your promises before."

He looked so sad and sort of lost, I couldn't resist him anymore.

"Okay, one kiss. But that's all!"

He grinned at me, delighted to have his own way.

I stowed my laptop back in its case, and sat on his bed. He wrapped his arms around me and pulled me down gently.

I snuggled next to him and lay my head on his chest while he stroked my back.

"We're okay, aren't we, Caro?"

I could hear the anxiety in his voice.

"Getting there."

I wriggled free of his arms and planted a quick kiss on his lips. He held me briefly, then let me go, an expression of regret on his face.

"Night, Sarge."

I turned off my bedside light and heard him murmur.

"Night, boss."

The helicopter was so loud I had to hold my hands over my ears. The whirling blades kicked up plumes of yellow dust that coated my nose and throat so I could taste it. A man in desert fatigues was yelling at me, but I couldn't hear the words. And then his face disappeared in a bloody mist.

"Caro, wake up!"

Sebastian was shaking me hard. I sat up, wide-eyed and trembling.

"Fuck, Caro," he said, more quietly. "Another nightmare?"

I nodded silently.

"Come here, baby."

He wrapped his arms around me and pulled me tightly into his chest.

I gulped in air, my lungs burned as if I'd been holding my breath for a long time, and I could almost taste the acrid dust in my mouth.

Damn, that had been a bad one.

"What was it about, baby?"

I shook my head. "Just a nightmare."

"You can tell me anything, Caro," he said, rocking me slowly.

No. Not anything. Not that.

But he didn't press me, and I was happy just to have him hold me.

After a few minutes, my heart rate had returned to normal.

"Scoot over," he whispered. "I'll just stay till you go back to sleep."

"Thank you."

He slid down next to me and I felt his warm body press into mine. There was no anger, no ugly accusations, no tension, just his gentle hands around me.

Finally, the nightmare drifted away, and I slept.

∾

When I woke up the next morning feeling happier and refreshed, bright sunshine was filtering through the shutters, and Sebastian's body was still twined around me in the narrow bed. His breath was hot on the back of my neck and his heavy arm pinned me down.

I tried to wriggle out from underneath him, but he mumbled something unintelligible and pulled me in more tightly.

It felt good waking up in his arms. Hell, it felt better than good, it felt right. We still had some issues to resolve—pretty important ones —but I began to feel hopeful that we were getting there. Like I'd said.

I stroked his long fingers that were resting across my stomach, and I felt him move, stretching out in the bed like a big, old sleepy cat.

I shifted around so I could look at him.

A slow, sexy smile appeared on his face as he rubbed the sleep out of his eyes.

"Wow, I have this beautiful woman in my bed. I really like this dream."

"Actually, Sebastian, you're in *my* bed."

"Oh, yeah. You must be one of those fast women I heard about at boot camp."

"Hmm, well, I think that lecture was supposed to warn you off them."

"Oh, I guess I didn't hear it right. I suppose that explains why I didn't get into Officer Candidate School."

"Did you try?"

He shook his head slowly. "Nah, not really. Not my thing. I took some college classes for a while, but then ... I was already fucking around. Guess I pissed off the wrong people."

"You'd make a good officer, Sebastian. Maybe you should think about it."

He shrugged. "I'm a Master Sergeant—three ranks up from Sergeant." He correctly interpreted my expression. "Yeah, you know that stuff. Sorry. I did get asked to join the Navy SEALs, though."

"Really? That's great! I mean, that's a real honor, isn't it? You'd like that—all that super-macho stuff."

He smiled, and ran a finger down my arm. "I turned them down."

I gaped at him. *Nobody* turned down the chance to join the Navy's elite team. "Why?"

He looked at me as if the answer was obvious.

"Caro, there's no way I'd join the same service that my father is in. Fuck that! Can you imagine if we ended up at the same Base? I'd end up killing the bastard."

"Shh," I said, resting my finger on his lips, as his voice started to get louder. "We're in Italy, it's a beautiful day, and we're going to go and find some waves for you to surf."

He took a deep breath and smiled. "Okay," he said, happily.

Then his hand drifted down to my thigh and he circled, slowly, his fingers tugging at the material of my panties.

"You know what would make this day even better?" he said, suggestively.

"Oh no, Sebastian. I'm not falling for that. I'm going to take a shower, and you'd better have some damn clothes on by the time I get back."

I rolled out of bed before he could stop me, and stomped around the room picking out clean clothes to wear.

"Are you sure?" he said, smiling lasciviously, as his hand disappeared under the sheets. I could tell he was stroking himself, and the thought of what I could do with the result was very arousing.

I shook myself out of my reverie. No, I'd promised myself that we had to get through at least another 24 hours without having another major meltdown before I'd give in. It was just being smart. If I let him in any further without some sort of proof that I could trust him with my heart, I was a damn fool, and deserved everything that happened to me.

I headed for the shower, cursing myself for not having taken a photograph of him lying there in my bed, all hot and wicked. I'd need something to entertain myself with during the dark, lonely nights when I was an old woman, and boring anyone who'd listen about that summer vacation where I'd had more sex than Madonna. Well, maybe —I was still thinking about it.

The shower was cool enough to put out the flames of passion that Sebastian had been stoking in me.

Twenty-four hours I chanted to myself.

When I was back at our room, he'd gotten as far as pulling on a pair of jeans, but that was all.

"You shouldn't wander around like that," I admonished. "You'll give Signora Battelli a coronary."

He winked at me but took no notice whatsoever, as he sauntered out of the room.

While he was gone, I searched through his jacket pockets until I found his map. I scoped out the beaches that might have enough swell for surf, then Googled them on my laptop. There were two possibilities within an hour's drive. We'd already gone past one of the best surf spots at Levanto. The next best spot was outside Rome, but that was a five hour drive. I decided we could save that for another day.

"Whatcha find?" said Sebastian, as he wandered in from his shower, still only wearing his jeans.

He knew damn well what that was doing to me!

"We seem to be in between surf spots here, but about 30 miles away, there's a place that looks like it might be okay. There's a big campsite there and it says they rent out boards, so it seems like a good bet. Want to try it?"

"I'll try anything with you, baby."

"Sebastian, focus."

I pointed at the map.

"Sure, baby," he said, smiling. "I just need to fill up the gas tank, but otherwise we're good to go."

He wrapped his hands over my shoulders and kissed my hair.

"Come on then, Hunter," I said, throwing him one of his ubiquitous white t-shirts. Let's go see what Signora Battelli has for breakfast."

Breakfast: the word was deeply inadequate for what Signora Battelli had laid out. It was more like a banquet of breakfast foods: fresh oranges and wild berries, *panini*, sweet rolls, *fette biscottate*, muesli, three different homemade yogurts, *caciotta* and *pecorino baccellone* cheese, and a chef's delight of *salumeria*—cold meat—including the local specialty of wild boar.

Sebastian's eyes glowed, and he completed at least three circuits of the buffet table before he was satisfied, or possibly too embarrassed to go around a fourth time. Maybe not: I didn't think Sebastian did 'embarrassed'.

At the next table sat a couple of American students who were wide-eyed at the spread in front of them. One of the girls was asking Signora Battelli's opinion on different types of fresh pasta.

"But how much should I give guests at a meal?" she said. "How will I know how much to buy back home?"

"Young woman," said Signora Battelli, swelling with knowledge. "You buy a half pound of fresh pasta per person ... except for my son: he eats one pound of pasta!"

I was rather hoping the son would appear so I could see if he lived up to expectations, but we were to be denied that pleasure. Signora Battelli explained that her son had taken a job in Rome.

It was the same story everywhere: young people leaving their small towns and villages to seek their fortunes in the big city. But wasn't that always the case?

As soon as they realized that we were Americans, too, the girls were determined not to leave us alone. Well, I'm sure I could have disappeared in a puff of purple smoke and they wouldn't have noticed—their eyes were welded to Sebastian instead. I couldn't blame them, and I was sort of curious to see how he behaved with them.

One of them reminded me of his ex-girlfriend, Brenda. Maybe it was her propensity to toss long, shiny hair over her shoulder, and gaze at him from beneath her long lashes.

She was flirting with him right in front of me like I didn't even exist!

Sebastian answered their questions pleasantly. It was obvious they were angling for a ride with us, and it was almost comical how far their faces fell when he told them we were traveling by motorcycle.

"I've never ridden a motor-sickle," said the one called Lydia.

And today won't be the day either, lady.

"Well, I'm sure you'll enjoy it when you get the chance," said Sebastian, evenly. He stood up to go, and held out his hand to me. "Come on, baby," he said.

I placed my hand in his and he pulled it to his lips, kissing the inside of my wrist. A warm feeling traveled up from my feet, and settled somewhere in the area of my groin.

He was delicious and dangerous and my resolve to wait another 24 hours crumbled away.

The girls looked like they were in agony, and I couldn't resist smiling at them as Sebastian and I walked away hand in hand.

"What?" Sebastian asked, catching my eye.

"Sometimes you can be very sweet."

I heard his breath catch in his throat, he looked so raw and vulnerable as he stared down at me.

"*Tesoro*, what did I say?"

He looked into my eyes, then let his forehead rest on mine.

"I love you, Caro," he said.

CHAPTER EIGHT

STANDING OUTSIDE SIGNORA BATTELLI'S BREAKFAST ROOM, MY world changed.

"I love you, Caro, so much."

I couldn't believe he was saying these words to me.

"I haven't changed how I feel. I still love you—I've always loved you. It's only ever been you."

I thought my heart would stop beating.

Ten years ago he'd said these words to me, told me that he loved me. I'd believed they were the words of a lonely, infatuated boy: real, but not lasting. Now the same man was standing before me, saying that he'd loved me all this time—and that it was real. He didn't care that I was older than him, he didn't care that I was ridden with insecurities, and he'd forgiven me for doubting him.

Was I brave enough to accept his love? Could I accept that he wasn't perfect, that he had his own problems to deal with, that he drank too much, and his hot head led him into trouble more often than not? Could I accept that he did a dangerous job in a dangerous world, and that we would be apart for months on end?

He'd asked me once if I was brave enough to take a chance on love. I finally knew the answer.

"I love you, too, Sebastian. More than you'll ever know."

He gasped, staring at me with wonder. And then he kissed me.

Not the boiling, surging kisses that heated my blood and shredded my resolve, but a kiss so sweet and gentle, so honest and simple, that my heart cracked open and filled with love.

He pulled me to his chest and we stood in silence, our arms wrapped around each other.

I was vaguely aware of the continuing quiet tide of humanity flowing around us, but for that moment, we were the only people in the whole world.

"You mean everything to me, Caro." Sebastian spoke softly into my hair.

"You're so brave, *tesoro*," I said, quietly. "You've never been afraid to love."

I felt his smile. "That's because I learned from you."

I shook my head.

"It's true," he said, gently.

I sighed and pulled my arms a little tighter around him.

He laughed softly and stroked my cheek.

We continued to stand there, basking in a love that came from within, warming us and filling us.

Eventually, Sebastian rubbed my arm and stood up straight.

"I guess we'd better get going before Signora Battelli decides to start vacuuming around us."

"Okay," I said, smiling up at him.

At that moment, I'd have followed him to the four corners of the Earth and the very gates of Hell.

We walked back to our room in blissful silence, and every now and then I felt Sebastian's fingers squeeze mine.

"I can't stop smiling," I said, stupidly. "I think I've pulled a muscle in my mouth."

"I know what you mean," said Sebastian, grinning back. "Although I have some ideas about how you could do that for real later."

I slapped his arm.

"You don't change, do you, Hunter!"

He threw himself back on his bed and grinned up at me.

"Do you want me to change?"

"Oh, you could do with a little polish here and there, but otherwise, no, you'll do."

"I'd like you to polish me right now," he said, smiling wickedly.

"Well, I'd love to oblige, but Signora Battelli is going to be knocking on our door in about two minutes."

He pouted. "We could make it quick."

"Oh no, I want to take my time."

"How much time?" he asked, his gaze heated.

"Hours, possibly days ... whole months even," I said, staring back at him.

He groaned and closed his eyes. "Months?"

"Years," I said, softly. "A lifetime."

He sat up, his gaze serious. "Do you mean it, Caro, a lifetime?"

"Yes."

He closed his eyes, breathing in deeply. Then his head sank to his chest. Slowly, he opened his eyes and looked up at me. His smile was glorious.

"Okay," he said, his face glowing with happiness.

Yes, I did mean it. There was no doubt. And I could tell from Sebastian's reaction that he was overwhelmed with happiness. I felt the same way. Overwhelmed, over-brimming, over-full, flooded with joy.

We packed up our small bag, moving easily around the room, touching each other as we passed, as if there was a physical necessity to express our happiness somehow.

Sebastian paid a relieved Mrs. Battelli. We'd taken so long, she was obviously wondering if we were planning on moving in permanently.

Sebastian thanked her beautifully for her delicious breakfast, telling her that he'd never enjoyed a *pensione* more. Then he kissed her hand, and the stout widow blushed.

"You are so smooth, Hunter!" I scolded him as we headed out to get the bike.

"I was just telling her the truth," he said. "I think we should come back here, and book the same room every year—then spend the night fucking."

"You're such a romantic."

"Yeah, I know, baby."

Sebastian's motorcycle had survived the night. I pulled on the now familiar black helmet and settled myself onto the seat, enjoying the comforting smell of old leather, with my thighs pressed into Sebastian. I'd almost go so far as to say I felt comfortable—although a car with a roof and doors also had a lot to be said for it. Hmm, hot, steamy car-sex with Sebastian. On the other hand, now beds had been invented...

We headed out of town and southeast along the coastal road, burning out of Pisa and racing into the sun.

I wrapped my arms around Sebastian's waist and thought what a difference a day can make. Yesterday, I'd been unhappy and abandoned. Today ... well, it was the start of the rest of my life.

～

The campsite I'd found was just an hour from Pisa, outside the village of Polveroni. The Mediterranean stretched before us and the sun heated the sea gently. Better still, from Sebastian's perspective, long breakers rolled in, providing perfectly rideable waves of between three and four feet.

His eyes lit up at the surf barreling up the beach, and just when I thought the day couldn't get any better, we saw a shop with boards to rent.

"Game on!" he said to himself.

We parked the mean machine and Sebastian practically sprinted inside, talking animatedly with the owner. He returned a few minutes later with a battered longboard, a huge beach towel, and a pair of garish board shorts.

"Hey, Sarge! You're in danger of doing color!" I teased him.

He smirked at me. "Yeah, well, it was all they had. Either that or I'd have to do it in the nude. What do you think, Caro, naked surfing?"

"It could catch on, or you could get arrested. But I'm telling you, Sebastian, if you do get arrested and I don't get laid tonight, I'm going to be mighty pissed at you."

He laughed delightedly.

"Now you're talking. By the way, the guy in the shop said that he rents out rooms. He said it's pretty basic—just a big, old bed and a small bathroom. But I thought it would be kind of cool to be able to hear the sea tonight. Is that okay?"

"Very okay."

He grinned at me, but his smile slipped away as he gazed in horror at the sensible, navy-blue one-piece that I was holding in my hands. It was the swimsuit that I usually wore to the public pool.

"Wait," said Sebastian, "*that's* what you're going to wear?"

"Yes, why?"

I stared at him, utterly baffled.

"Stay here."

He strode off back toward the beach shop. He returned a few minutes later with a tiny bit of string and a few triangles of material and handed it to me.

"Here. Wear this."

I held out the skimpy bikini. It left absolutely nothing to the imagination. It was barely big enough to cover my nipples, let alone anything else.

"I can't wear that, Sebastian, there's nothing to it! I'm forty, not twenty!"

"You'll look amazing, Caro. I want every guy on the beach to know how hot my woman is."

"I may as well go topless!"

His eyes heated, and a licentious expression appeared on his face. "Yeah, baby."

I shook my head at him. "You're crazy."

"Crazy in love," he said, scooping me into a kiss that made my bones rattle.

"Fine, I'll wear it," I said, breathlessly.

He gave me a dark look that said I damn well would.

Sebastian held up the beach towel to cover my modesty while I changed into the tiny bikini. Although 'modesty' and 'tiny bikini' in the same sentence didn't really seem to be a good fit. Like the bikini. Whichever way I tugged it, more flesh than seemed acceptable was exposed.

"I can't wait to take that off you," he whispered in my ear.

"Sex or surfing, Sebastian?"

"Sex," he said, at once.

I laughed, even as my body overheated.

"Well, you'll have to take a rain check—we haven't reserved that room for the night yet. And I've warned you what will happen if you get arrested."

He smirked at me.

"You owe me a lot of rain checks, Caro. I'm going to enjoy cashing them in."

He didn't bother using the towel when he changed into his board shorts—he just dropped his pants and briefs right out there in the open.

"Sebastian!" I muttered, glancing around to see if anyone was watching.

He'd already pulled on the garish board shorts by the time my eyes flickered back to him. He laughed at my surprised expression.

"Years of practice changing out of my wetsuit in windswept parking lots along Sunset Cliffs, Caro," he said. "I'll show you how quick I can get out of my clothes now if you like?"

"Go. Surf."

"Here—look after these for me."

He pulled off his dog tags and placed them around my neck, where the small metal tags nestled between my breasts. He stood back for a moment.

"Those look hot on you, Caro. Really fucking hot."

He scooped me up in a ridiculous Hollywood kiss, dipping me so low, my hair was touching the sand, then he put me back on my feet. I was still off balance as he ran down to the water.

I loved to watch him surf, it brought back many good memories of our time in San Diego. There had been too few from that turbulent summer, but being on the beach with Sebastian, watching him in the waves, those had been happy times. He was so graceful out there, charging down the glassy, green surfaces, diving through the foam.

I'd taken my camera with me, so I zoomed in and snapped some photographs of Sebastian surfing. I had a pretty decent lens, and I got some really good close-ups of him in action.

Hmm, photographs of Sebastian in action, now there was a thought to warm a cold winter night.

I lay back on our beach towel, relaxed and filled with a quiet happiness. Once again my life had swung across the pendulum from bitterness and despair to an overwhelming sense of love and being loved. And this time I would allow myself to believe in it.

The warmth of the sun was pleasant, adding to my sense of peaceful well-being. It wasn't really hot, maybe a balmy 68°F or 69°F. Enough to be relaxing: not enough to worry about getting burned.

Suddenly I realized someone was standing over me.

"*Buon giorno!*"

An attractive man about my own age was smiling down at me.

"*Ciao?*" I replied.

I sat up, wondering what he wanted.

"It's a beautiful day, isn't it?" he said, in Italian.

"Yes," I agreed, rather puzzled.

"It looks like you're enjoying the sun."

Oh crap! He was hitting on me. Was he hitting on me?

"Um, yes. It's very pleasant."

"Are you here on vacation?"

"Yes, we are," I replied with the faintest emphasis on the plural.

"Ah," he said, looking around him for my absent companion.

"My boyfriend is surfing," I explained, with a small smile.

"Then he will be having some good rides," replied my new friend, who then winked at me and ambled away.

I could see Sebastian jogging up the beach to join me.

"What did he want?" he asked, looking none too pleased.

"Don't blame me, Sergeant," I said, raising one eyebrow, "You're the one who bought this itsy bitsy teeny weeny bikini for me. Anyway, I told him my boyfriend was surfing, so you don't need to worry."

Sebastian scowled.

Oh boy, talk about double standards.

"Did you have fun?" I asked, trying not to laugh at him.

"Yeah," he agreed, looking in the direction where my 'friend' had vanished, "not bad. Had some good rides."

"I know, I was watching." I pointed to the camera, "I got some great shots, too."

"Really?" he sounded delighted, and turned his full attention to me. "I've never seen any pictures of me surfing."

My heart gave a quick, unhappy flop. My poor boy had never had parents who cared that he was good at something.

He sat down on the towel next to me, his skin glistening with drops of seawater. Trying not to get distracted, I showed him the shots I'd caught, and he raised his eyebrows.

"Wow! You're a really good photographer, Caro."

"I have excellent subject material," I said, then snapped a close-up of his exquisite face and chest.

"What's that for?" he asked, blinking in surprise.

"Just so I know you're real," I told him. "I think you're a figment of my overwrought imagination, and you might disappear when I wake up. But now," I said, waving the camera at him, "I have proof."

He grinned and shook his head, as if I was a little crazy. Which I was. Like he'd said: crazy in love.

He pushed me down onto the beach towel with his damp body, and kissed me in a way that told me how he felt. I stroked my hand over his wet hair and smiled up at him.

"You're so cute when you're wet."

"So are you," he said, with a leer.

We ate lunch on the beach, panini from the shop and some fresh fruit sold by a bored teenage boy, who was slouched under a sunshade.

Sebastian continued to flirt with me, tease me, and toy with my bikini straps, which I found ridiculously adorable. It was all I could do to stop myself from leaping on him there and then. But we were both enjoying just touching each other, playing and spending time together, without having to worry about what anyone else thought, said or did.

In the afternoon, he fell asleep in the sun and I lay watching him for nearly an hour, almost unable to believe my luck—he was really mine, and that I was his.

We spent the rest of the day on the beach. Sebastian even persuaded me to go for a surf with him, although I thought the water was really too cold to be pleasurable.

"Come on, Caro, I've wanted to try this for a long time. Let's take the board out and catch a wave together. I'll do the paddling and I can stare at your gorgeous ass while I'm doing it."

Which was an offer I couldn't refuse.

I lay on the board first, and Sebastian jumped on behind me. He couldn't resist giving my ass a quick bite.

We paddled out to just behind where the waves were breaking, then as the water started to rise, Sebastian turned the board around and we began to speed down the front of the wave.

"Get ready to pop up!" he yelled, above the crashing surf. "Go!"

I scrambled to my feet and felt the board wobble slightly, then Sebastian was behind me, one hand steadying my hip as we raced down the face of the wave.

It was the most extraordinary feeling, riding that wave together. In some ways it was a metaphor for the life we were starting out on. Who knew when we'd fall off? But by trusting each other and moving as one, the ride would be longer.

Eventually, Sebastian conceded that I really was cold, and we belly-boarded back into the beach.

"Your nipples are hard," he said, pointing out the obvious.

"Well, what a shocker," I said. "I've never seen them like that before."

"Is that right? I'll see what I can do about it later."

"Promises, promises," I sighed.

His eyes widened and his nostrils flared with the challenge.

"Bed, woman. Now."

"Don't you want to find somewhere to have dinner first?"

He shook his head. The Master Sergeant wanted sex, not food. I really, really wasn't going to argue.

We paid for the room behind the beach shop, but were interrupted en route to our sexcapades by the owner, who was desperate to talk to Sebastian about surf spots in California. I left them mulling over whether San Diego or Monterey had the better breaks, even though I could feel Sebastian's eyes following me across the beach.

I collected our overnight bag from the bike and carried it into the small room.

It was like being in a log cabin: wooden walls, wooden floors, wooden furniture. But Sebastian was right—the bed was huge. I tested it out gingerly. Nope, no creaking springs to distract us tonight.

While I was waiting for him, I checked my emails. I was surprised to see that there was one from Nicole.

> To: Lee Venzi
>   From: Nicole Olsen
>   Re: WTF
>   Venzi! WTF are you doing in Italy? How come I had to hear about it secondhand from Jenna? Don't you think it's time you had mindless sex with an Italian stallion? Call me for tips. Have fun. Nx

That was so like Nicole. If only she knew. I decided I'd send her a photo of Sebastian to cheer up her gray, New York morning.

I picked the one of him sitting back on the beach towel, his beautiful face and divine chest in full view. I wasn't going to send her the one where his board shorts showed the ammo he was packing: Nicole would probably implode.

> To: Nicole Olsen
>   From: Lee Venzi
>   Re: Re: WTF
>   Thinking about your advice. Traveling through Italy with an old friend. Thought you'd like this eye-candy to brighten your day. Lx

I was still smiling to myself about Nicole's message and my reply, when Sebastian strolled in.

"What's so funny?"

"Oh, I just had an email from my friend Nicole in NYC. She wants me to have mindless sex with an Italian stallion."

Sebastian didn't look amused. "Why is she saying stuff like that to you?"

"Oh, don't be such a prude, Sebastian! It's just a joke. She's always nagging me to find a man."

"What about me?" he asked, sounding ridiculously hurt.

I rolled my eyes. "I haven't told anyone about you. I like having you to myself. But I will, if you want me to."

"I want to know your friends, Caro. Although I'll fucking tell *Nicole* that she can keep her comments about 'Italian stallions' to herself."

Uh-oh, the Master Sergeant was riled.

Now *that* was going to be an interesting meeting—Sebastian and Nicole were both fiery. I wasn't going to place bets on who'd win that encounter.

Suddenly my phone started ringing. I stared at it in amazement, as if it had suddenly grown wings. Why on earth was Nicole calling me?

"Nicole, hi! Wow, it's great to hear from you. How are you?

"Don't give me that, Venzi. Where did you get that smokin' hot picture? Have you turned into one of those women who ogles younger men?"

"Like you, you mean?"

Nicole snorted. *"Exactly! Since when did you start taking photos of hot guys? And who's this 'old friend' that you're suddenly traveling around Italy with?"*

"Nicole, I sent you a picture of him. His name is Sebastian."

Sebastian glanced over at me, a smile on his face.

"Come on, Lee. Why won't you tell me who you're traveling around with?"

"No, seriously, Nicole. That's a photo of my friend."

"The Stud Muffin is your 'old friend'?" she yelled down the phone. *"You're bullshitting me, Lee!"*

I laughed. "I promise you, Nicole."

"Have you been holding out on me? Where did you meet him?"

Her words poured out in a torrent.

"I'll tell you some other time," I said, shaking my head, as Sebastian gazed at me quizzically.

"No! Tell me now!" she shrieked.

"I can't. Later."

"Why not now?"

"Because he's standing right here, Nicole."

Sebastian raised his eyebrows.

"Bullshit! I don't believe you."

"It's true."

"Put him on the phone."

"What?"

"I think you've been without sex too long, Venzi. You're hallucinating."

I handed the phone to Sebastian. "She wants to talk to you."

He took the phone, looking amused. "Hi, Nicole. This is Sebastian."

I saw him listening intently, a slight frown on his face. I wondered what on earth Nicole could be saying to him.

"You don't want me to use her?" he said, glancing toward me. "Well, Nicole, I was planning on taking her to bed and using her in ways that aren't even mentioned in the Kama Sutra, but now you've told me, I think I should go take a cold shower instead."

I snatched the phone back, glaring at him. Sebastian just smirked at me.

"Sorry about that, Nic!"

There was a long silence at the other end.

"Nic?"

"Fuck me!" she said, huskily. "Don't be sorry, Lee. That is the hottest thing I've heard in years. He sounds like a sex machine! Look, I think you should write a sex manual with this guy, but you'll have to take photographs ... lots of photographs."

I laughed. "I'll get back to you on that, Nic."

At which point, restive and impatient, Sebastian started untying the straps of my bikini. I tried to shoo his hands away, but it was awkward, what with trying to hold onto my phone and continue the conversation. I gasped as he tossed my bikini top onto the floor and massaged my nipples with his fingers.

"Oh my God, Lee! Are you guys doing it right now? Can you put it on speaker on?"

"I'll have to call you back, Nic," I said, breathlessly.

I cut the call while she was still yelling, and launched myself at Sebastian.

My phone clattered to the floor, and one part of my brain was already assessing what damage that might have caused, but the greater part of my brain, by far, already had Sebastian stripped and ready for action. My fumbling fingers had to play catch up but luckily my tackle had knocked him backward onto the bed.

I straddled him and pinned his wrists back with my hands, my mouth crushing his, my breasts forcing themselves into his chest.

He could easily have overpowered me, being about fifty times stronger than I was, but he seemed content to let me have my wicked way with him. I had some serious catching up to do, and he had rain checks that needed cashing.

Our tongues were gliding together, our teeth clashing, and I could feel Sebastian getting aroused beneath me.

He sat up suddenly, cradling his arms around my waist, as mine flew up in surprise. He kissed my neck, running his hot tongue over my throat.

"You taste like the sea," he murmured, "and your skin smells like sunshine."

He ran his fingers up my back, and let them tangle in my hair, pulling my face down to his.

"I want to be inside you, Caro."

I smiled against his lips, and then rolled off him, scooting down to the bottom of the bed.

"Raise that glorious ass," I said, tugging on the hem of his board shorts.

He grinned at me and lifted his hips from the bed. I pulled off the shorts, threw them behind me, then sat back to enjoy the view.

His legs were long and tan and muscled like a runner, his thighs and hips pale, and his rich, pubic hair was light brown. My eyes wandered up his body, taking in his erection that hovered above his tight, toned stomach, where his skin turned to gold again. He propped himself up on his elbows and smiled at me, his head on one side, as if he was asking what I found so fascinating.

"You're beautiful, Sebastian. I love to look at you. I love to see you like this, when it's just the two of us. Why does it feel so right?"

He shook his head slowly.

"Maybe it was just meant to be. I mean, shit, could we have had any more challenges thrown at us?"

I could think of one big challenge that we still had to face, but I refused to let that spoil the here and now.

"We've certainly had our share," I sighed.

He sat up and held my cheek with his hand.

"Don't be sad, Caro. We've got our second chance ... or maybe we're on our third ... I kinda lost count already."

"That is very true." I laughed, lightly. "Now you seem to have a very desirable hard-on there, so should we have some fun with that?"

"I'm all yours."

I grinned and jumped off the bed. "Are the condoms in your toiletry bag?"

"Yeah, baby."

I rooted through the overnight bag until I found what I was looking for.

"Sebastian, there's only one condom left in here," I said, shaking the now empty box at him.

"Shit! You're kidding! Fuck, how did I ... ah, crap. Give me that fucker—I'm going to make the most of it."

"Oh no, Hunter," I smiled, waving the foil packet at him, "this one is all mine."

His eyes heated instantly and his cock twitched.

"Feeling a little needy, baby?" I said, continuing to tease him, as I walked around the bed.

"Fuck, Caro!"

He lunged for me but I danced away.

"Dear me, someone is impatient."

"Yeah, very!" he said, sounding both amused and slightly annoyed.

I stood at the end of the bed.

"Would you like me to take these off?" I asked, tugging gently on the delicate laces of my bikini bottoms.

He nodded silently.

"Or maybe you'd like to take them off me?"

He swallowed and nodded again.

I climbed up from the foot of the bed and crawled all the way up him, the foil packet held in my teeth. I hovered above him and he reached down to untie first one, then the second ribbon, and the small strip of material fluttered to the floor.

I took the condom packet out of my mouth while his right hand drifted up my thighs and his index finger slid inside, slowly massaging me. My eyes were locked on his: watching him, watching me, watching him.

Then he pushed another finger inside me, moving faster, and my breath began to come in short gasps.

"Come on, baby," he said, his voice tight.

My body responded and I tried to push his hand away, not being able to take any more.

"No, baby," he said softly, "you can take more."

"I can't! I can't!" I begged him, but he wouldn't stop, and the most intense, demanding, draining orgasm arched my spine and made my body shudder, the tremors coursing through me like the aftershocks of an earthquake.

Because my legs were apart, still kneeling across him, it seemed to go on and on and on.

I collapsed onto his chest, and I felt his fingers stroke my back, tracing my spine through my skin.

Gently, he rolled me onto my back, and kissed me across my neck and chest, sucking and tugging on my nipples with his teeth. My over-sensitized body responded quickly. It was as if the lightest touch sent a charge of electricity racing through me.

He pushed up my knees and before my brain had caught up, I felt him plunge inside me.

"Sebastian, no! Don't!"

"Come on, baby, you feel so good."

He rolled his hips, and sensation flooded through me.

"No!"

I pushed hard on his chest and, reluctantly, he pulled out, his sea-green eyes accusing.

"What are you doing, Sebastian?" I gasped, staring at him in shock.

"I just want to make love to you, Caro."

"I know ... but, you're not wearing a condom."

I opened my hand, begging him to look at the foil packet that I was holding, still unopened.

"We don't need that, Caro."

Did I hear him right?

"What? Are you crazy, Sebastian? I could get pregnant!"

He stared down at me.

"Would that be so bad?"

"You *want* me to get pregnant?" I stammered.

He sighed and closed his eyes, rolling onto his side.

"I want to have a life with you, Caro, for the rest of my life. Look—kids—whatever. If it happens, then great, if it doesn't, that's fine, too. Just as long as we're together. This time, forever."

I flung my arm over my eyes, shutting out the vision of his beautiful face, trying to regain some order among the craziness.

He pulled my arm away from my eyes, forcing me to look at him.

"Caro?"

"Sebastian..." I stuttered, not sure where to start. "We were apart for ten years. I saw you again a week ago, we had sex, a couple of dates, more sex, we fought, we broke up ... and now you're saying you want to have children with me?"

He smiled and raised his eyebrows. "Yeah."

"Do you know how crazy that sounds?"

"That's our story, Caro. Crazy in love."

I didn't know whether to kiss him, hit him, or have him committed.

"I ... I don't know what to say."

He shrugged. "You don't have to say anything, Caro. You don't have to *do* anything. Like I said: if it happens or not ... whatever ... we'll deal."

"And what ... you'll give up being a Marine to look after the kids?"

His mouth dropped open, then he grinned at me. "Kids? As in, plural? Sure, why not?"

"You ... you'd do that?"

By now I was gaping at him.

"Caro, I'll do whatever it takes to be with you. I've been in the Marines for nearly ten years now and I've had tours in Iraq and Afghan, been stationed in Germany, Paris and Geneva. I didn't care because I didn't have anywhere to go home to. But with you, we'll have a home, and I won't want to be away from you."

I struggled to sit up, still feeling tremulous from my very recent orgasm. Or it might have been the complete head-spin Sebastian had just thrown at me.

"I ... I..."

He smirked at me. "I thought you were supposed to be the one who was good with words, Caro."

"Usually," I choked out.

He stroked my stomach suggestively, letting his hand drift lower.

"So, what do you think? Should we just keep going?"

"I ... no ... look, just give me some time to think about this. We've got this lonely, little condom, so let's use it and talk again later. Okay?"

He sighed and looked resigned, but I could tell he was disappointed. Then he glanced down at his dick, which had lost some of its delicious hardness.

"Feeling a little flat here, baby. You wanna pump me up?"

His mood swings left me reeling, but I couldn't help smiling at the hopeful expression on his face.

"Yes, I think I can do something about that. Lie back."

He grinned up at me. "What are you going to do?"

"Absolutely nothing."

"What?" he said, frowning.

"I'm not going to touch you, Sebastian, and you're not going to touch me. Yet. I'm going to show you how good I am with words."

"I have no idea what you're talking about baby, but it's making me feel horny."

I smiled. "That's the point, Sebastian. I'm going to make you so hard, I'm going to get you so wound up, I'm going to turn you on so much, that all I'll have to do is touch you with one finger to make you come."

"Fuck!" he breathed, his eyes wide.

I lay down next to him so we were close, but not touching.

"Close your eyes," I breathed.

He gave me one, long, hot, lingering look, and then did as I asked.

"I want you to see it all in your mind, Sebastian. Imagine

everything I'm saying: see it, hear it, taste it, feel it, breathe it in. Understand?"

He swallowed and nodded.

"You're lying on the bed and it's very quiet. It's night time, but there's a full moon, and the shadows on the floor are almost blue. You hear the door open, but your eyes stay closed. You hear my footsteps across the wooden floor, you know it's me because you recognize the soft sound of my footfalls. I'm standing right next to you, looking down at your naked body. You can hear the rustle of my clothes as I slowly start to take them off. You can hear the zipper of my dress. I must be wearing silk, because the material whispers as it falls from my body. Then you feel the mattress moving under you and my weight presses down on your body. My naked breasts are brushing against your skin, it's cool and my nipples are hard when you take them in your mouth."

He groaned softly and I saw that his cock was almost completely erect again.

"I move up your body, hovering over you. I moan slightly and you know it's because I'm touching myself, turning myself on for you. My fingers are inside me, circling slowly, and when I pull them out, I place them on your lips and you suck them hard. You can taste me and you can smell the muskiness of my scent. You long to touch me, but then I take your fingers in my mouth, sucking them one by one. You imagine what my mouth would feel like around your cock: my lips, my teeth, my tongue swirling around. You can imagine what it would feel like when you move into my mouth and your tip touches the back of my throat."

I could see that his cock really was hard and ready for action.

Not yet, Sebastian.

"My hair brushes the skin on your chest as I arch away from you, and your skin is so sensitized you can feel every strand, every wave, every individual hair. I take your hand and move your fingers against my clitoris. I'm wet, very wet, and you know it won't be long before your hot, hard cock is stroking inside me. I run my fingers around you, gripping you, squeezing you, and you know that I want you—every inch of you—inside me. You're at the entrance of my sex, and you sink into me: slowly at first, then getting faster and harder, going deeper and deeper. Your control is unraveling because you can feel that hot, soft, sweet flesh all around you. My body starts to buck under yours and you know that I'm close. You can feel ripples of pleasure pulsing through me and you're wondering how long you can hold on before you come. You're trying so hard to hold it back but then I clench around you, squeezing you, milking everything you have. And I'm begging you to give it to me again. I'm begging you to take me from behind, so you pull out, even though you're aching to come, your balls hot and heavy, and then you're looking at my ass, knowing that I want you so badly, waiting just for you."

By now Sebastian's breathing was becoming rapid and his hands were hovering over his body as if he was desperate to touch me or to touch himself. My own words were making me moist and needful, but I carried on.

"You plunge into me and it feels so deep this way, it's never felt this good before. You're so hard, your cock is aching for release but you want to enjoy every moment of it, so you hold back, hold back, hold back. But it's hard, so hard, because I'm coming again and you desperately want to come with me, but you want me to have every second, every ounce of pleasure, so you hold back, hold back. And then I'm coming hard, like you've never felt before, and it's so hot and wet and sweet—you spill into me, on and on and on."

And with those words, I grasped his cock, hard, and Sebastian came in my hand immediately. I stroked him a few more times, watching the creamy fluid spill onto his stomach, his chest muscles heaving with the effort of breathing, his eyes screwed shut.

I kissed him softly on the lips and lay back next to him, snuggling into his shoulder.

Eventually he opened his eyes and looked down at himself in amazement.

"Fuck, Caro!" he croaked. "How ... how..."

"So, you're the one who's speechless now?" I said, smugly.

I watched him for a while, as he tried to pull all his shattered pieces together. I reached over to my toiletry bag and grabbed a Kleenex to clean him up.

He watched me with vacant eyes as I stood up to throw the tissue away, then I sat back on the bed and smiled wickedly at him.

"Enjoy my bedtime story?"

"Fuck, yes! I still can't believe you did that to me, Caro," he said.

"Well, Sebastian, now you have something to think about when we're apart, or when you're doing a tour. Now you can imagine me talking to you."

"Are you fucking kidding me? With twenty other horny Marines sharing the same grot?" He groaned. "Oh, God! I won't be able to get rid of that image now."

I laughed, "That's kind of the point, Sebastian."

He shook his head, slowly.

"Fuck, Caro! You are so fucking amazing. Did I ever tell you that?"

"You may have mentioned it once or twice, but feel free to repeat yourself."

He still looked baffled: it was so cute.

I slapped his chest. "Come on, let's go shower. I'm hungry. For food."

I jumped off the bed and headed for the shower. I'd already shampooed and conditioned my hair, soaped myself clean and dried off with a towel, before the Marine managed to stagger into the bathroom.

I thought these guys were supposed to be in good shape?

Nicole would be so disappointed.

CHAPTER NINE

THE SHOWER REVIVED SEBASTIAN ENOUGH THAT I FELT ALMOST SAFE letting him take us on the bike.

"You okay?" I said. "You seem a little discombobulated."

"Fuck, yes, and I don't even know what that means," he said, nodding his head. "Fuck, Caro, I can't get over that. I mean, you barely touched me. It was just ... hot."

I smiled. "Ah, the power of words."

"There's going to be payback," he promised, with a devilish smile.

"Sebastian, if I wasn't so damn hungry, I'd be dragging you back to the bedroom now and tying you down until you made a dishonest woman of me."

He stared at me with admiration and not a little surprise.

"Jeez, you've gotten so ... bossy. I like it."

I laughed delightedly. "Oh, Sarge, I think you've been taking orders from the wrong people—but I'm going to help you with that."

"Can't wait," he said, shaking his head in disbelief.

Then he pulled me into a hug and buried his face in my neck, tickling my skin with his warm breath.

"I have missed you so much."

"I've missed you, too, *tesoro*."

We stood there quietly, his arms around me, each of us unwilling to break the spell.

Eventually, he rubbed my back and kissed my hair lightly. "Let's go eat."

Just three miles down the road was the pretty Marina di Cecina.

Our friend at the beach shop had recommended that we eat at one of the restaurants on the waterfront. It probably belonged to an uncle or cousin, but it looked nice and had sensational views over the Mediterranean.

"What the hell is that?" said Sebastian, pointing at the menu. "*Cipolline agrodolci alla Cinque Terre.* Is that onions?"

"Yes, sweet and sour onions: it's a local delicacy. You want to try them?"

"Normally I'd say yes, but I'm really craving ... steak," he said, apologetically.

I rolled my eyes. "You're so American! You want fries with that?"

"Yeah, now you mention it. Anyway, I have to keep my strength up. This woman I've met is milking me dry. She can't keep her hands off me."

"What a slut."

He smirked at me. "Well, she hasn't been that slutty, but I'd really like to see her in slutty stockings and garter straps—no panties."

"Hmm, well I'm sure we can arrange it at some point, but I have to admit, Sebastian, I don't actually own anything like that."

He looked surprised. "Not at all? I thought all women..."

He stopped mid sentence, looking embarrassed, and wishing he could bite back the words.

"Maybe all your previous women, Sebastian," I replied, rather cuttingly, "but no, not me, I don't."

Wisely, he buried his eyes in the menu.

"Sebastian, apart from you, I last had a date nearly three years ago. And there's not a lot of need for slinky underwear on assignment to military bases—well, not for me, anyway. Maybe you know differently?" and I raised my eyebrows at him.

"Why don't you date, Caro?" he asked, looking up, his voice puzzled. "I mean, you're fucking gorgeous, anyone can see that, and you're clever and funny. Any man would have to be blind not to want you."

And I realized he meant it. Would I ever get used to hearing him say things like that to me? I hoped not.

"I've just ... not been that interested. No one's really caught my eye."

He shook his head in amazement.

"Oh, wait, Major Parsons asked me out: Mike. He was pretty cute," I said, casually glancing at Sebastian.

"That fucking bastard!" he snarled, sounding really angry.

"Sebastian, I said no. And actually, he was really sweet about it. He wasn't pushy or anything."

I was regretting making Sebastian jealous, but damn, it made me feel wanted. And I really wasn't used to that.

I decided to change the subject before his temper spoiled our meal.

"What were you thinking, that first day, when we saw each other at the press training? You looked really mad."

His gaze became distant, remembering the day, only one week ago.

"Just so fucking shocked. I saw the name 'Lee Venzi' on the training list. I recognized it because I'd read some of your articles..."

"Really?"

"Yeah, sure. I check out all the journos who go on these gigs. I want to know what kind of shit ... sorry, what kind of writing they do. I thought yours was good."

I shot him a look.

"No, really. I'm not just saying that. I kind of assumed you were ex-forces because of the way you understood the military. And we were all expecting you'd be a guy. Obviously somebody screwed up on the background checks. But as far as your online presence, you're definitely a man."

I smiled serenely at him. "That's the general idea. I've had quite a few assignments given to me because people assume I'm a man, jobs they wouldn't give to a woman."

Sebastian frowned at me. "Yeah, but there could be a good reason for it, too. I mean, some of the places you go are dangerous and..."

I caught his hand and placed my fingers over his lips.

"Shh, *tesoro*. They're a lot less dangerous than where you go, and we're not having this conversation."

He scowled and started to argue.

"No, I mean it. This is my work. Please drop it."

He didn't look happy about it, but he didn't argue further either, instead he gave me a look that said the discussion wasn't over, merely postponed.

"You were going to tell me what you thought when you first saw me," I reminded him.

"Shock. At first I thought you'd done it deliberately somehow. And then I saw the look on your face, like you didn't know what to say to me either, and I realized it was just as weird for you as it was for me."

"And then?"

"I just kept thinking how mad I was at you, blaming you for all the shit. I kept trying to hold on to all that anger, but you just looked so ...

you looked just the same. And I kept thinking, maybe I got it wrong. And then I remembered that you hadn't come looking for me and ... it was so fucking confusing, Caro."

He stared out at the water washing over the beach.

"And then you tried to talk to me and I just freaked. I couldn't ... not in front of all those people, not with all the things I wanted to ... I found a bar and just started drinking ... getting up the courage to go see you. I really screwed that up, didn't I?"

"Completely," I said, nodding my head.

He looked apologetic and stared at his hands.

"It doesn't matter now, Sebastian," I said, quietly.

He shook off the memory, but I could tell it still bothered him.

"What did you think, when you saw me?" he said.

"You mean after the oh-my-God moment? I thought you looked bitter: your eyes looked so cold and hard. Gorgeous, of course, but you looked like you'd really changed. I was ... intimidated. And then Liz told me you'd got this reputation ... as something of a ladykiller..."

Sebastian scowled.

"Well, you did ask."

"Yeah, well ... what else did you think?"

"She said you were brilliant, too, if that makes you feel any better."

"Not much."

I sighed. "I just thought I'd try and talk to you by yourself, but you kept avoiding me. So, I assumed you didn't want anything to do with me. I was ... hurt, but I guess I accepted it. Can we talk about something else? This is making me feel blue."

"Sure, baby," he said, smiling softly. "How about we plan the rest of the trip?"

I smiled back. "Yes, please."

He reached over to his jacket, which was hanging from the back of his chair, and pulled out the map.

"Well, it's up to you, Caro. We could keep going down the coast road to Salerno, look up your dad's old village. Or take it slower, go see some of Tuscany. Siena is supposed to be amazing and there's this old hilltop town, Montepulciano that looks really cool. Or go right down to the bottom—check out Sicily."

"What do you want to do, Sebastian? I don't mind having another day on the beach if you want to do some more surfing—it's your vacation, too."

"Nah, that's okay—it's going to be flat tomorrow—I already checked."

I rolled my eyes. "Of course. Silly me."

"It's about 200 miles to your dad's village. We could be there this time tomorrow. If you want."

I thought about it for a moment. I was probably investing too much in what would inevitably be a big disappointment.

"No, let's take it easy. I'd like to see some more of Tuscany. I've heard of Montepulciano: they have good wine. And honey."

He smiled at me, amused. "How come you know all this food stuff?"

I stared back as if, for once, *he* was missing the blindingly obvious. "I'm Italian, Sebastian."

He laughed out loud, and swept my hand off the table to kiss my fingers.

The waiter arrived with our order, interrupting our moment, although he smiled apologetically.

The food, including Sebastian's enormous *Bistecca Alla Fiorentina* steak with fries, was good, and we were quiet for several minutes as we ate.

I toyed with my question for some time.

"What is it?" said Sebastian, at last, laying down his knife and fork.

"What do you mean?"

"You have that look on your face—like you want to ask me something. You can ask me anything, Caro."

I was amazed—people didn't usually read me that well. But then again, Sebastian knew me better than anyone. How strange.

"Well, there was something ... did you mean what you said about quitting the Marines?"

"Sure. I mean, I re-upped two years ago, so I'd have to do another two before I punch out..."

Disappointment flooded through me. *Two more years.*

"And Afghanistan soon."

He looked at me thoughtfully.

"They're short of interpreters, especially non-locals, and military intelligence..."

He stopped abruptly, realizing he'd said too much.

"Sebastian, whatever you tell me, that's between us. I would *never* use it in my work."

"I know that, baby, but there are some things I can't tell you ... and some things that it's better you don't know."

I wasn't happy that there were secrets between us, but I understood.

"They're not going to be pleased that you're dating a journalist."

He glanced away, briefly, then smiled at me. "Nope. Don't think so, although they couldn't stop me..."

"So ... I guess it would be better to keep this between us, just for now?"

He nodded, then leaned back in his chair.

"Would *you* give it up, Caro? Working in war zones, traveling all over the world?"

I'd been waiting for him to ask me that question, but I still didn't know how I was going to answer it. The truth was I didn't want to give it up. I'd worked hard to achieve the position I'd reached—and I enjoyed it. Yes, my work took me into dangerous areas, but it was rare that I was on the frontline, not like Sebastian. Oh, yes, my hypocrisy knew no bounds.

So, what was the compromise? He gave up everything and I gave up nothing? But if I did give up my work, how long would it be before I felt resentful and tied down. *And* he wanted us to have kids. Whatever he said about 'seeing what happened', I knew that was high on his list of priorities.

"I wouldn't want to give it up completely, Sebastian, that's the truth. But I could agree to a maximum amount of time I spent away in a year, maybe."

He nodded slowly and sighed. "Okay, I guess."

He stood up and stretched, gazing around the restaurant.

"Where are you going?"

"Restroom. I'm hoping they have machines that sell rubbers."

I smiled. "We still have one left."

"Yeah, but that's not nearly enough for what I have in mind ... unless you want to do what we talked about earlier?"

I could hear the hope in his voice, but I shook my head.

"That's another discussion for another time, Sebastian." He pouted, and I couldn't help smiling. "When you've finished this next tour, we'll talk about it then, I promise."

He returned a few minutes later, scowling.

"Fucking useless!" he fumed. "They didn't have any in the restrooms and I checked with the waiter—all the nearby supermarkets and pharmacies are closed on Sunday evenings."

"Oh, dear," I said, smiling. "Well, never mind. We'll just have to get creative."

"Yeah, okay," he said sulkily.

I raised my eyebrows at him. "I hope you're not getting bored with me already!"

He rolled his eyes. "You're like a freakin' drug to me, Caro. I can't get enough of you. And I really like wake-up sex."

I couldn't help laughing out loud. "We'll figure something out. Don't sweat it, Hunter."

Sebastian was still in a bad mood when we left the restaurant. Okay, it wasn't the ideal situation for two apparently sex-starved adults who were behaving like rampant teenagers, but I thought we'd already proved that we could be creative—and I had one or two things in mind. Besides, I'd brought the rest of the bottle of wine from the restaurant, so we could always have a quiet evening with a glass of vino and watch the stars appear.

Sebastian, however, was a lot less relaxed, accelerating hard out of the parking lot in a shower of gravel, tires squealing.

I gripped him tightly around his waist, hoping that he'd slow down, but instead he went faster, taking the turns on the coast road at such a speed that our knees were ridiculously close to the ground. I closed my eyes and hung on, until he slowed abruptly. I soon saw the reason. Two Italian police officers were waving their table tennis-shaped batons at us.

Crap.

We'd been caught speeding.

Sebastian pulled over to the side of the road and swung one, long leg over as he climbed off. Watching as he removed his helmet, I decided to follow him. He was so hotheaded, I could imagine him mouthing off at them and spending a night in a cozy, Italian jail.

"French?" asked the first policeman, looking at the license plates on Sebastian's motorcycle.

The officer looked like Groucho Marx, which was rather distracting. The second one was younger and stared at us through his Aviator shades, even though it was dusk.

"No, American," replied Sebastian.

The policemen looked surprised.

"Is this motorcycle yours, *signor*?"

"Yes."

"You have papers for it?"

"Yes, in my wallet."

Sebastian started to reach into his jacket, and the younger officer immediately went for his gun.

I gasped and Sebastian swore. The next second, they were forcing him to kneel on the ground and put his hands behind his head. I could see the older man reaching for handcuffs.

"No, please!" I called out. "He was just trying to show you his papers."

"*Signora*, he was driving at 120km an hour, the speed limit here is 90km an hour."

"Please, let him show you. I'll get his wallet!"

I moved slowly so they could see exactly what I was doing. I reached into Sebastian's inside jacket pocket and carefully lifted out his wallet.

"What am I looking for?" I whispered, urgently.

"The *Certificat d'immatriculation*—the papers in gray. Caro, I..."

"Just don't speak, Sebastian," I hissed at him. "Let me handle this."

Silently, I handed over the document, although it was clear neither of the officers could read French.

"Are you authorized to ride this motorcycle, *signora?*" said the older, gentler officer.

"No, but..."

"Then we'll arrange to have it removed," he said, kindly.

"Please don't arrest him!" I begged. "He's only on leave for two more weeks, then he's going back to Afghanistan."

The two men looked at each other. I was hoping that the military/police solidarity that existed back home also held true in Europe. I pulled Sebastian's ID card out of his wallet, the one that identified him as a US Marine, and showed it to them.

"We only have two weeks," I repeated, not needing to fake my desperation.

"My son-in-law is serving out there," said the older officer, shaking his head. "Very well, we will let you go, but this one time only. Obey the speed limits."

They let Sebastian stand, and handed back his papers.

"Thank you so much," I said, feeling slightly tearful at our reprieve.

"Make him obey the speed limits, *signora*," said the older officer, wagging his finger at me.

"I will. Thank you!"

"I will pray for you both," he said, simply.

We watched as they wandered back to their car, chatting amiably to each other.

"You were great, Caro," said Sebastian, grinning.

I slapped him hard on the arm. "No more speeding!"

"I don't know ... I have my own Caro-shaped 'get out of jail free' card."

"Yes, well, do that again, and you might be finding out what Italian jails are like."

"You wouldn't let that happen to me, baby."

"Don't bet on it, Sarge! I have enough gray hairs without you giving me anymore."

He pulled me in for a hug.

"Nope, can't see any," he said, kissing my hair.

I pushed him away, crossly.

"Another two weeks with you and I'll have to color my grays," I said, grumpily.

He laughed.

"It's not funny!"

"God, you're beautiful, Caro!"

I climbed back on the bike, irritated to see that Sebastian was still grinning, but at least he drove to the campsite at a more moderate pace.

When we arrived back, Sebastian parked the bike while I stomped off to our room, feeling very irritated with him. If he was this reckless in Italy ... no, I really didn't need to start thinking like that.

I hunted around for a corkscrew to dig out the damn cork that the waiter had managed to ram back in. I was just contemplating smashing off the neck and sieving the wine through a clean sock to remove any broken glass, believing that desperate times called for desperate measures, when Sebastian sauntered into the room.

"I can't open the fucking wine!" I snarled at him.

He looked taken aback.

Yeah, well, he wasn't the only one who knew how to swear.

"What's the matter, Caro?"

"I just told you!" I yelled, "I can't open the wine!"

Quietly, he took the bottle from my hand, produced a Swiss Army knife from his pants pocket, and proceeded to dig the cork out using a small blade.

"I think some of the cork fell in," he said, placing the bottle on the table.

"Thank you," I muttered, rather sullenly.

"Caro..."

"What, Sebastian? You could have been arrested back there? That was so stupid and reckless!"

He stared at me in amazement. "Nothing happened..."

"It could have!" I shouted at him. "And if you take chances like that out in…"

But I couldn't finish the sentence. Angry and frustrated, I was furious when I felt tears spring to my eyes. I scrubbed them away with my fists, while Sebastian watched me in silence.

"Hey, come here," he said, softly. "It's okay."

He pulled my stiff body into an embrace, but I stood rigidly, fighting back tears, willing anger not fear to win out.

"Caro, tonight was just dumb, I admit that, okay. I'm just enjoying being … free, here and now, with you. Don't cry."

"I'm not crying!" I yelled. "I'm mad at you!"

"Yeah, got the message, baby."

Eventually, I pushed him away, grabbing the wine bottle as I walked past the table, and took a good slug. Then I threw myself on the bed, piled the pillows behind me and tipped another large quantity of wine into my mouth, rubbing the back of my hand across my face to catch the drips.

"Are you going to share that?" he asked, at last.

"No. You drink too much."

"You're just going to sit there and finish the whole bottle by yourself?"

"Yes."

"You don't like drinking."

"I do tonight."

"It'll make you sick."

"I'm being reckless. You do it all the time."

"Caro," he said tiredly, rubbing his forehead, "come on, that's enough."

He pulled the bottle out of my hands and put it on his side of the bed.

"Give me my goddamn wine, Sebastian."

"No," he said, evenly, sitting next to me.

I tried to reach over him to get it, but he blocked me.

I wanted to scream with frustration, even though I knew I was behaving childishly.

"Fine."

I slammed out of the room and walked down to the beach without a coat. It was cooler now that it was night. Oh well, I'd wanted to see the stars.

I sat down on the sand and moodily wrapped my arms around my knees. A light breeze was blowing off the sea, and moonlight glimmered on the water. The surf had almost completely dropped away. Sebastian was right:,it would be as flat as glass tomorrow.

I buried my boots into the still-warm sand and listened to the tide lapping against the shoreline, as regular as breathing.

I was irritated with myself for my tantrum, but I was more than annoyed with Sebastian for nearly getting himself arrested—and for not appearing to think anything of it. But at the heart of it was my fear that his recklessness would lead him to doing something really stupid when he was *out there*. I didn't even want to think about where he was going—where we were going.

It wasn't long before I heard his quiet footsteps in the sand. I pulled my arms around my knees more tightly as Sebastian sat down next to me, gently placing his old, leather jacket around my shoulders.

"Want some wine?" he asked. "It tastes great straight from the bottle."

I leaned against his shoulder, and he wrapped his arm around me.

"Sebastian, promise me you won't be reckless. I couldn't stand it if anything happened to you now."

"Caro, I'm never reckless when I'm working. Well, maybe some of the off-duty stuff, but not when I'm working, I promise. I'd never have gotten promoted if I was a complete fuck-up. Don't worry about me. Besides, I have a reason to come home now, okay?"

"I will worry."

"And I'll worry about you, too. You still have a chance to go home where I know you'll be safe, Caro. Please?"

I sat up stiffly.

"Don't even think about screwing up my papers again, Hunter!"

"Whoa! Slow down!"

He held out his hands defensively.

"I promised I wouldn't, Caro, even though I really fucking want to." He paused. "So, have you finished stomping all over me with your boots?"

I sighed. "For now, unless you ask me to, nicely."

He laughed gently. "I'll bear that in mind. Can I kiss you, or am I risking serious injury?"

I pushed him back onto the sand and made myself comfortable lying across his chest.

Under the moonlight his skin was pale and silvery, every hint of tan bleached away. I traced his profile with my finger, and then tilted his face toward me, kissing him lightly on the lips.

"This brings back memories," I said, feeling soothed.

He smiled up at me. "Yeah! Sex on the beach was one of those things that everyone at school used to brag about, and then I got to do it with you. That first time, that was one of the best nights of my life."

"The first time we ever spent a whole night together."

"You want to relive good times, Caro?"

"Can't."

"Why not?"

"I left our one and only condom in the room."

He sighed and closed his eyes.

"Besides," I continued, "I kind of have a thing for beds these days. Call me old-fashioned."

"Yeah, I guess," he said, wistfully. "I really liked having sex in your car though. That was hot."

"Oh my God, yes! Although I'd have to say that sex in that closet at the country club was pretty amazing, too. No, wait, the hotel in Little Italy. That room looked like a wild animal had rampaged through it by the time you'd finished!"

"Wild animal, huh?" he said, looking pleased with himself. "Yeah, well, I think I can improve on that now, baby."

"Oh, you do, do you? Because I have to tell you, Sebastian, you never ran out of condoms when you were 17."

"Ouch! Low blow, Ms. Venzi."

I laughed. "True, though."

"Yeah, well, I'll fix that tomorrow and then you won't be having *any* sleep, woman."

"Heard it all before, Sergeant, but it ain't happened yet."

I lay back down on his chest, and drew pictures on his t-shirt with my finger.

"So, who was your first woman, after me, I mean?"

I felt his arms tense.

"Why do you want to know that?"

"Just curious."

He sighed. "I don't really want to go there, Caro. It was ... a bad time for me."

"Okay, I'm sorry. You don't have to answer."

We lay there in silence for some minutes.

"Will you tell Ches that we're ... back together?"

"Of course I will, Caro. Ches is my brother," he said simply.

"He'll be surprised."

"Fuck, yes!"

"Do you think he'll be okay about it? I mean, I'm sure my name would have been dirt with him."

"Ches isn't like that. He was pretty shocked by everything that went down that day at your place, but he knew that what we had was real. He'll be pleased."

"When are you going to tell him?"

"I hadn't really thought about it. When are you going to tell your friends about me?"

"Are you kidding?" I laughed. "After your little stunt with Nicole it'll be hot news in NYC by now. Your photograph will be on screensavers everywhere."

"Yeah?"

"Oh, don't be all coy with me, Hunter. You know you're cute."

He grinned up at me. "Just as long as you think so."

"I think you're devilishly handsome, with the emphasis on 'devil'."

"Yeah, well as it happens, Ms. Venzi, I think you've got some devil inside you, too."

"Oh, I'd really like to have some devil inside me right now, Sebastian."

He sat up, pulling me with him.

"Let's go," he said.

It wasn't a request.

I stood up and brushed some of the sand from my pants, while Sebastian retrieved the bottle of wine that he'd stashed in the dunes.

We strolled back to our room, and every now and then, Sebastian would pull my hand to his lips and kiss my fingers gently.

But once we were in the room it was a different story. It was as if someone had flicked a switch in his body: gone was sweet, gentle Sebastian, in his place was a man on a mission who knew what he wanted, and he wanted it now.

No sooner had we closed the door than he pushed me up against it and started kissing me hard, one hand molding my breasts, the other pushing down inside my jeans.

"Where's that fucking condom?" he muttered.

"Bedside table," I gasped.

He strode over and snatched up the condom, and had already ripped the foil off before I'd taken three steps.

"Sebastian, the bed?"

"No, here."

He unzipped his pants and expertly rolled the condom over his erection with one hand. Then he yanked down my zipper and lifted me up by my hips.

"Wrap your legs around me," he said, the tension evident in his voice.

"How?" I gasped, pointing at my jeans, still trapped around my knees.

He swore and yanked them further down, but found they were caught by my boots. Instead of waiting the 30 seconds it would take for me to kick them off, he stepped over the denim and ignored the trailing material.

He rammed into me and I cried out. His face was buried in my neck, his breath coming in loud gasps as his body worked faster and faster. I held onto his shoulders while he pounded me into the door. It was so raw and urgent, so completely unexpected, I thought I could see stars.

And then his phone rang.

"Oh, fuck!"

"What? Don't stop, Sebastian!"

He carried me over to the bed, still joined together, and pulled his phone out of his jacket pocket.

"Sebastian," I whimpered.

"Just a minute, baby, I have to take this call. It's my CO's ringtone."

What?!

"Hunter, sir."

Then there was a long pause and I shifted uncomfortably, still clinging on, and Sebastian frowned at me.

Fuck you, Hunter! You're answering the phone during rampant sex, and you're frowning at me?

He raised one eyebrow, smirked, then started moving again in a way that should not be permitted while carrying on a phone conversation.

Thrust.

"Yes, sir."

Thrust.

"No, Italy, sir."

Thrust, thrust, thrust.

I gasped and bit back a moan.

Thrust, thrust, hip roll, thrust.

"Um ... I've just been out for a run."

Thrust, thrust.

"Yes, sir."

Hip roll, thrust, thrust.

"Yes, sir."

Pound, pound, pound, thrust, thrust, thrust.

"I'll be there."

Then he threw the phone in the corner, dropped me onto the bed, angling his hips in a way that made me gasp, and I threw my head back. He fastened his mouth over my nipple so I could feel his teeth through my bra and t-shirt.

I came loudly and he followed with two quick moves.

"Sebastian?" I gasped, astonished by what he'd just done.

He pulled out and looked down at me, grinning wickedly. "Did you get what you wanted, baby?"

"Excuse me?"

"You said you wanted some devil inside you. I aim to please."

I slapped his arm and tried to wriggle away from him, but his body was still pinning me down.

"Sebastian, you just fucked me while you were talking to your CO!"

"What, you think men can't multitask?"

I stared up at him in astonishment.

"I can't believe you did that!"

He laughed. "Felt good! Don't tell me you didn't enjoy that because either it was you moaning, baby, or my CO had a stomachache."

"I ... you ... that ... unbelievable!"

He lay down next to me, pulling me onto his chest.

"I haven't even taken my boots off," I muttered, to no one in particular.

"Me either," he said, with a grin.

He sat up and peeled off the condom, tossing it in the garbage can. Then I heard the sound of him zipping up his pants.

I was still trying to decide whether I was mad at him, or too well fucked to care that he'd taken a phone call during sex with me.

He wandered off into the bathroom, and I heard the shower running while I was still prone on the bed.

He strolled back in, looking completely relaxed and at ease. I felt him pick up my left foot and he started to undo the laces. He tossed the boot over his shoulder where it landed with a thump, then peeled off my sock, and sucked my toes one by one.

"Sebastian," I whimpered, "you're supposed to do foreplay *before* sex."

He grinned but didn't reply, simply copying his movements with my right foot. Then he reached up to tug off my jeans and panties. It didn't take much effort as they were already hanging off me. I was now naked from the waist down.

"Very nice," he said, planting a soft kiss on my belly button.

He pulled me up and hauled my t-shirt over my head, then reached around to unhook my bra.

"Mmm," he said, tasting both my nipples, his eyes glinting with mischief.

I slapped him away.

"Don't start what you can't finish, Sebastian."

"Who says I can't finish? You were the one who said we should be creative. I'm just following orders, ma'am."

He unbuckled his heavy biker boots and kicked them into the corner, tugged off his socks and dropped his jeans and briefs to the floor in one quick movement.

Then he tugged his t-shirt from the back of his neck and pulled it over his head, scooped me up and carried me into the bathroom with military efficiency.

The shower was deliciously hot: so was Sebastian.

He lathered up the soap, and carefully washed every inch of my skin, stopping only to kiss me softly.

"You want some more, Caro," he asked, smiling down at me, and suggestively massaging between my thighs.

"I'd love to say yes, but really I just want to go and sleep. Rough sex during phone calls always does that to me."

"Always?"

"Always."

"Hmm," he said, frowning.

"By the way, why was your CO calling? What did he want at this time of night?"

Sebastian sighed and looked away.

"He wanted to know where I was."

"I gathered that. Because?"

"I'm sorry, Caro, I'm going to have to be back in Geneva in four days. And then back to Afghanistan."

"Four days?"

Oh no.

"I'm so sorry, baby."

"Well, we'll just have to make the most of the four days then."

"I'll make it up to you, I promise, Caro."

"Sebastian, don't worry. Every day with you is a bonus. And we've got the rest of our lives to see Italy."

"Promise?"

"I promise."

I pulled him into my arms and we stood together in the tiny shower, letting the hot water flow over us, trying to reassure each other that it would be okay.

Eventually the water began to cool and I turned off the faucet.

"Come here, let me dry you, *tesoro*."

Sebastian stood with his arms outstretched, as if waiting for an embrace that didn't come. Instead, I used the large, fluffy towel to dry his back and shoulders, chest, stomach, arms and legs, slowly, carefully, methodically, soaking up each droplet of moisture.

"There you are—all done."

He handed me a fresh towel to wrap around myself, then carefully rubbed my hair with a small hand towel.

"You shouldn't sleep with damp hair," he scolded me.

His words made me smile.

"Sebastian, I've done a lot of foolish things—reckless, you might say—since I met you: sleeping with damp hair doesn't figure particularly high on that list."

He scowled.

He looked so cute when he did that.

I kissed him on the tip of his nose.

"Race you to the bedroom!"

I ran from the bathroom before he could move a muscle, and launched myself onto the bed.

"You're so slow, Hunter," I laughed at him. "You're really out of shape. Maybe you should go for a run, like you told your CO."

"Tomorrow, Caro, I'm getting a fucking sack-load of condoms, and I'm going to make you regret every word you've just said."

I smirked at him. "Like I said, Sebastian, promises, promises. I keep hearing about these fuckathons, but nothing ever happens."

His eyes flared with the challenge, and I knew for sure that I'd live to regret my taunts. I was looking forward to it.

I yawned loudly, and he looked amused.

He lay down beside me, his body warm and still slightly damp from the shower, pulling the sheets over us. I snuggled into him, and he wrapped his arms around me so I was curled up on his chest, our legs entwined.

"God, Caro. You make it all worthwhile," he said, kissing my hair. "Thank God for you."

"I love you, *tesoro*," I whispered.

CHAPTER TEN

Waking up in the morning, the first thing I saw was Sebastian's beautiful blue-green eyes gazing down at me.

"Hey," he said, smiling.

"*Ciao, bello!* How long have you been awake?"

"Not long. Just enough time to remind me that I'm a lucky bastard."

I smiled and stretched, feeling his warm body against mine.

"I could get used to this, Sebastian, waking up next to you."

As soon as I said the words, I felt a breath of sadness. Our time was limited.

I forced a smile, certain that the last thing Sebastian needed to see before he shipped out was a miserable, moping face.

"So, what's the new plan, Sarge? Do you want to see some more of Tuscany, or should we go further north?"

He looked bemused. "What about Salerno?"

"It's too much driving, Sebastian. We don't have a lot of time and you..."

"Hell, no! I want to see where your dad came from as much as you do. Fuck the driving, Caro! We're going to Salerno. If you get your beautiful ass out of bed, we can be there in maybe five hours."

I felt the pull of Salerno and the warm south. I'd tried to be selfless but Sebastian had once again weakened my resolve, as in so many things.

"Anyway," he continued, "we're out of condoms, and much as I'm enjoying being creative, I really just want to fuck you into next week."

"Such sweet words, Sebastian. How did you get to be such a smooth talker?"

He grinned at me. "I don't know, baby, but it works every time."

"Every time, huh? But you know, I have to say, last night wasn't particularly creative—we weren't even naked."

He laughed happily.

"Not creative? Hell, Caro, I managed to keep a conversation going with Cardozo, I thought that was pretty fucking creative."

"Is that the name of your CO?"

"Yeah, he's an okay guy."

"He must have his hands full dealing with you." I paused. "What's his wife like?"

Sebastian grinned wickedly. "Blonde, attractive ... about forty. Why, are you jealous?"

"Of course," I said, evenly.

He kissed me softly on my lips, his eyes gentle with love. "You've got nothing to worry about, baby."

Love, lust, passion—all swirled through me, his touch blinding me with desire. I kissed him back, pushing my tongue between his parted lips as our bodies began to move together. At my hip, I felt his cock twitch. I wanted him badly. It was, as he'd said: total addiction.

"Caro," he groaned, quietly, as I ran my hands over his thighs.

"Shh, *tesoro.*"

Ten minutes later, we were both lying on our backs, panting. There was a lot to be said for a quick burst of hand-to-mouth creativity before breakfast.

I was filled with a warm, satisfied glow, as Sebastian lazily stroked my thigh.

"You ready to get up, baby?"

I sighed, happily. "Mmm, if I have to. But to tell you the truth, I'd be quite happy staying here all day, if someone brought us food. And condoms."

Sebastian kissed me quickly on my chest, then kicked the sheets back, the cooler air making me flinch.

"Hey!" I complained.

"Up," he said, as he stood over me.

Then he leaned down and fastened his teeth over my nipple, tugging gently.

"You cheat," I grumbled, staggering the short distance from the bed to the shower.

He swatted my ass, which I felt was unnecessary: he'd already made his point.

The water wasn't hot, which didn't encourage us to linger, and I stood in the bedroom, shivering slightly as I dressed.

"It doesn't take you long to get ready, does it, Caro. You never even bother to put on makeup."

Sebastian was sitting on the bed, smiling at me as he buckled up his boots.

I was slightly taken aback by his remark. Did that mean that he wanted me to wear makeup—that he thought I should?

"I do sometimes," I replied, trying not to sound defensive, "if I'm going out somewhere dressy. But not usually, no. Why?"

He shrugged. "Nothing. Just saying. It drives me crazy when women spend hours getting ready to go out."

I felt relieved—and annoyed at myself for feeling relieved. I was a modern woman who didn't need a man's approval on how I dressed. Except, maybe ... yes, damn it! I wanted Sebastian's approval on how I dressed. I craved the way he looked at me, like he'd never seen anything so precious. Maybe I ought to make a little more effort. Just for the next few days: give him the best memories I could, before we were parted.

I vowed to buy some lipstick and mascara in the next pharmacy or supermarket we found.

"You remember that time we went clothes shopping in San Diego?" he asked, pulling me out of my self-flagellating thoughts. "You had to buy a new dress?"

"Oh, sure, I remember that! The sales assistant was flirting with you?"

He looked surprised. "She was?"

I rolled my eyes. "Don't you remember, she was asking you if you were a pilot from Miramar?"

Sebastian shook his head, amused and puzzled at the same time.

"Well, I'm not surprised," I said, smiling to myself, "in those days you never used to notice other women flirting with you: you were such an innocent. Not like now."

"Hell, you shouldn't complain, Caro! You were the one I lost my innocence to—a hot, older woman."

I slapped his arm. "You know what I mean."

His look of amusement faded and he caught my hand, pulling me down, until I was sitting across his knee.

"Caro, you're all I want. You don't have to worry about other women. Yeah, so I fucked around a lot, but you know what? It was just a game—I was using them, they were using me. It gets pretty old after a while." He paused to tuck my hair behind my ear and kiss my throat. "But I might have to hunt down those old boyfriends of yours and beat them to a pulp."

I laughed. "Double standards, Sebastian?"

"Nope, just two sets of rules ... but I was thinking about the cute, black dress you bought. You looked so fucking hot in that."

"I've still got it somewhere, although I haven't worn it in years."

"We should do that, Caro, go out somewhere upscale."

I sighed. "I used to fantasize about seeing you in a tux."

"Really?"

"Sebastian, I spent far too many hours fantasizing about you in a variety of, um, situations. And just recently, it's become my new hobby."

He laughed, delightedly. "I've never worn a tux."

"Never? Not even at your high school prom?"

"I didn't go. I hadn't met you again, and I'd split up with Brenda. Ches didn't have a date either—he swiped some of Mitch's beer, I scored some weed—and we got trashed on the beach instead. It was a pretty good night—I think. I don't remember that much about it. We didn't need any women," he said, looking at me with a sly expression. "But that was before I met you again."

"Hmm, very virtuous of you. But didn't you wear a tux for Ches and Amy's wedding?"

"Nah, Amy kind of got off on the whole military thing, even though she didn't want Ches enlisting, so she asked me and Mitch to come in our Dress Blues. I don't know, I think she thought it would look cool in the wedding pictures."

He rolled his eyes.

"She turned into a complete nightmare-bitch-from-hell over the whole wedding thing. Ches was freaking out, thinking he was about to marry some crazy person. She even tried to ban him from having a bachelor party," he said, indignantly.

"Gee, I wonder why ... maybe she didn't trust *you*," I said, sarcasm dripping from my voice.

He grinned at me, wickedly.

"Yeah, well, she was probably right about that..."

"I don't want to know, Sebastian!"

He kissed me again. "So what do you think?"

"About what?"

"Going somewhere upscale? I'd love to see you like that again."

"Well, okay. Let's do that when you get back from this tour. Then we can really celebrate."

"Let's do it *now*," he said, decisively. "There must be some place in Salerno you can get women's stuff."

"Stuff?!"

"Yeah, silky dress, stockings, high heels ... stuff. And then I could undress you—slowly."

His eyes heated at the thought, and my heart skipped a beat.

"Okay, I'll do it if you do."

He laughed. "Sure, if I can find somewhere that will rent me a tux, why not? It'll make a change from being in uniform."

Then he kissed me quickly, scooped me off his lap and set me back on the floor.

"We'd better get going. Got me a date planned with a really hot woman."

∼

Instead of traveling along the pretty coast road, Sebastian headed inland for the Autostrada del Sole, the highway that ran from Milan to Naples. It was terrifyingly busy, with huge trucks roaring too close to us, but the route was designed to get us to Salerno in the least amount of time. I clung on and gritted my teeth.

We stopped briefly just outside of Rome, at a café on the highway where they produced fresh pasta to restaurant standards, then carried on south, past Naples and on to our final destination.

Sebastian finally pulled up at the curb when we ran out of road. Behind us, the small town of Salerno clung to the cliffs, the buildings square and white with terracotta roofs, and glistening below them, the Mediterranean was azure in the afternoon sunshine.

He pulled off his helmet and stretched out his back before climbing off. I felt as if the bike was still in motion and my ass had been molded into the shape of the saddle.

Sebastian grinned at me, then helped me take off my helmet. It was as if I'd been underwater and I could finally hear properly again.

"You all right, baby?"

"I'm fine," I lied. "How are you?"

"Yeah, good. Look, I think it might be easier to find a *pensione* or hotel in Salerno than in your dad's village. We're only a couple of miles away so we could easily shoot on over there in the morning. What do you think?"

"Anything that doesn't involve getting back on your bike sounds good, Sebastian," I grimaced. "My ass is numb already."

He pulled me into a hug, and rubbed his hands over the portion in question.

"Better, baby?"

"Mmm, much."

He kissed me lightly. "Come on then, let's walk for a while. We'll find a room—and a pharmacy."

"Good to see you've got your priorities in order, Sebastian."

"Trained by the Marines, baby, what can I say?"

We strolled through the sunlit streets, listening to the rumble of local traffic, which seemed to consist of crazy drivers in beaten up cars, and teenagers on scooters buzzing around. Everywhere, people chatted, gossiped, talked, yelled and waved their hands in the air, animated conversations surrounding us. It reminded me of Papa when he got excited, and I could imagine him as a child running down the hill from the village, and climbing back in the evening, dusty, tired and happy.

Sebastian slung his arm around my shoulders with casual possession, and I let my fingers creep around his waist.

It was too warm to wear the leather biker jackets for long, so we found a small pavement café and gratefully sat, relaxing in the sun.

"I could really use a beer," said Sebastian.

I wasn't sure if he was just commenting or asking my permission. Either way, I had something else in mind.

"This is the home of *limoncello*, Sebastian, the real thing—made with Sorrento lemons. I think we should try some."

"Yeah!" he said, enthusiastically. "You used to make those amazing ones when I was a kid." He frowned, and I knew what he was thinking —he didn't like to be reminded of our age difference either.

I shrugged. "Sure, but these are alcoholic." I glanced at him sideways and smiled. "We could order them with a pitcher of water, too."

"Sounds good," he said, raising an eyebrow.

The young waiter slouched over, seemingly unconcerned as to whether or not he would serve us. But when I spoke to him in Italian, he seemed to cheer up slightly, his demeanor a fraction less surly.

"And would you know of anywhere we could rent a room for a couple of nights—nothing too expensive?" I asked, with a smile.

"My uncle might," he acknowledged, surprising me with a friendly grin. "I'll go and ask him."

When I glanced over at Sebastian, he was scowling at me.

"You didn't have to flirt with him, Caro," he spat out.

I stared at him, utterly astonished.

"Excuse me? Flirt with him? I was being friendly, that's all."

"Well, it didn't look like that from here," he said, obviously angry.

I shook my head in amazement. "Rule number three, Sebastian, of my conditions for coming on this road trip with you: no displays of adolescent jealousy. Remember?"

He leaned back in his chair and folded his arms.

Oh, great—sulky Sebastian. I should have added that to my list.

Our waiter returned with the *limoncellos*, water, and an older man with jet black hair and dark olive skin.

"My nephew tells me you're looking for a room. For how long?"

"Just a couple of nights. Somewhere in town—nothing too upscale —although somewhere with a bath would be great. We've been on our motorcycle all day."

"I have just the thing," he said, happily. "My mother-in-law's sister's neighbor rents rooms. Her villa overlooks the sea—very pretty rooms. Only €50 a night. I could call her for you, if you like?"

"Thanks," said Sebastian, deciding to take charge. "We'll take a look."

The waiter's uncle—Aberto—soon returned, smiling.

"You're in luck, *signore e signora*. She has a room available. I've written the address down for you."

"Thank you," I said, "that's very kind of you."

He nodded and turned to leave.

"Aberto, can I ask you something else? My father was from Capezzano Inferiore. He left many years ago, but I was wondering, do you know anyone with the surname of 'Venzi'?"

I held my breath as he scratched his head.

"No, I'm sorry, *signora*, I don't know that name. I could look in the phone book for you?"

"Thank you. That would be so helpful."

Sebastian held my hand while we waited for Aberto to return.

"Ah, I'm sorry, *signora*," he said, "there's no one with that surname in the town—some in the province, but none within 70km."

I breathed out slowly, feeling everything deflate inside me. How ridiculous. I'd allowed my hopes to get blown out of proportion.

"Thank you for looking, Aberto."

He nodded, and walked away.

"Sorry, baby," murmured Sebastian. "I know you had gotten your hopes up."

"I was just being stupid. I just wanted ... I just hoped I'd find some family."

He kissed my hand gently.

"Hey, I get that. I know what it's like."

"I never even asked you, Sebastian, but do you have grandparents? You never mentioned any."

He shrugged. "No, not really. Mom's parents died when I was a kid, Dad never spoke to his. Big surprise. I don't even know where they live."

"And you've never wanted to find out?"

"I thought about it once. Anyway, I'm not sure I'd want to find anyone who was related to that bastard. Besides, they never showed any interest in me ... it made me wonder if the bastard was really my dad. I dunno..." he shrugged. "Ches and his kids, Mitch and Shirley—they're my family."

"And Amy," I said, teasing him gently.

He groaned. "Yeah, and she's thrilled about that."

"Well, she'll be much happier when we show her the new, improved Sebastian Hunter. I could tell her that I've tamed you."

He gave me a knowing look. "You're treading on dangerous ground there, Venzi."

I sat back and smiled at him. "You're so masterful when you talk like that, Sebastian."

He leaned forward and stared at me. "Yeah, well, if we can find a fucking pharmacy, you'll find out just how 'masterful' I can be."

"Looking forward to it."

We sipped our *limoncellos* as we watched the world go by: yachts and fishing boats in the harbor, scooters, bikes and cars, people of all ages, strolling, chatting, enjoying the afternoon sunshine.

"You know what we should do, Caro?" said Sebastian, stretching his arms above his head. "We should drive up to Amalfi. The coast road has some gnarly mean bends—see what the bike can really do. There should be some great views, too."

I swallowed hastily. I could just imagine Sebastian tearing up the mountainside and carving his way around another terrifying set of hairpin turns.

"That sounds fun," I said, trying to restrain the quaver in my voice.

I didn't fool him at all, and Sebastian laughed out loud. "That's my girl!"

After we'd paid Aberto, we wandered through the town, on the lookout for Via Roma, which turned out to be a wide avenue running alongside the harbor.

To Sebastian's delight, we also found a pharmacy, where he purchased two boxes of 12 condoms, much to my embarrassment and the amusement of the elderly woman serving him. I think she may have given me a sympathetic glance, too.

I felt a little lightheaded when I did the math: 24 condoms, three nights.

But I also found cheap mascara and a dark cherry lipstick.

"Looking forward to tasting that lipstick on you later," whispered Sebastian.

"Looking forward to tasting you later," I whispered back, which earned me a very hot look.

Signora Carello's villa was a small but pretty, whitewashed building overlooking the sea, as promised.

I'd expected another well-built motherly type, but the Signora was a bone-thin racehorse of a woman, perhaps 70 years of age, with swept-up black hair and immaculate taste in clothes.

"Ah, the young travelers Aberto mentioned. Welcome to my home. Please, come in. Let me show you the room."

She led us up a flight of shallow steps that looked like they could have been carved out of marble, or some other polished, creamy stone —and opened the door into a beautiful, dreamlike room.

A large, white bed dominated, with fronds of net curtains hanging down, and a wardrobe that was Oriental style, made from a wicker material. The balcony doors were open, and the curtains drifted on the breeze, brushing across a small mosaic table with two matching chairs.

"Oh, this is just lovely!"

"Thank you, *signora*," she said, obviously pleased by my reaction.

"Actually, it's *signorina*," I said, not wishing to mislead this charming woman.

"I'm working on that," said Sebastian, challengingly, and I saw Signora Carello try to hide a smile.

"The *bagno* is on the right," she said, gesturing elegantly toward a white door.

The bathroom was plain and white, but, joy of joys, it had a gigantic enamel tub in the center of the room, as well as a small shower in the corner.

I clapped my hands together and grinned at Sebastian.

"We have a motorcycle," he said, smiling at my obvious happiness. "Do you have somewhere I could park it overnight?"

"Oh, I used to enjoy riding on a motorcycle in my day!" she said. "Oh, yes, young man ... I was quite fast in my youth."

And Sebastian blushed. He actually blushed. I hadn't seen him do that in ten years. I was almost jealous of Signora Carello.

She smiled pleasantly at him and when she looked at me, she winked. I grinned back. Oh, I liked this woman.

"I'll go and get the bike," he muttered.

"Sebastian, would you mind if I stay here and take a bath?"

"No, that's fine, Caro," he said, suddenly brightening up. "I'll see you later."

Hmm, what was on that tricky Hunter mind now?

I shrugged and left him to walk back down the stairs, chatting animatedly to the *signora*.

I was delighted to see that two enormous, fluffy, white towels had been laid out for our use. I started running the water immediately and peeled off my sticky clothes, enjoying the cool stone of the bathroom floor beneath my bare feet.

I ran the water as hot as I could stand it, then climbed in, luxuriating in the sensation. I wished Sebastian was there to share the moment—and to scrub my back—but it was rather wonderful to stretch out, too.

I lathered my hair, using shampoo that smelled like lemons, from the small pot that the *signora* left out for us, and then wallowed for a good half an hour. By which time, the water had cooled, but Sebastian still hadn't returned. I let the water drain away and wrapped myself in the huge towel and boldly sat out on the balcony, enjoying the late afternoon sun.

I heard the mean machine before I saw it. I watched Sebastian drive along the street and stop at the villa's entrance, before cutting the engine and pushing it around to the yard at the back. I wondered what on earth he'd been doing, he'd been gone ages.

I heard him running up the stairs and I called out to him.

"You missed a great bath. I've been sitting here enjoying the view— naked, except for a towel."

He walked up behind me and kissed my damp hair.

"I was beginning to think you'd gotten lost."

"Had some business to take care of, baby."

I twisted around to look at him. He was grinning like a Cheshire cat.

"Come on, Hunter, spill. What business?"

Sebastian grinned and bit his lip, but I knew he was dying to tell me. It took about three seconds before he caved.

"Signora Carello told me somewhere I can rent a tux, so it's game on for tomorrow night. We're going upscale, baby."

"Really?" I said, excitedly. "Where?"

He grinned down at me. "Can't tell you. Not even if you torture me."

"Are you sure about that? Because I think it can be arranged, Sebastian."

"I was hoping you'd say that."

He picked me up out of the chair and carried me into the bedroom. I fastened my arms around his neck and kissed him hungrily.

"Ugh, you're all sweaty!" I complained.

"Yeah? Any objections if I get you all sweaty, too?"

"None whatsoever."

And those were almost the last words we spoke for the next two hours, although I may have moaned his name several times. We got through three condoms and had seven orgasms between us.

I was a wreck, and I had no one but myself to blame. All my teasing and taunts had quite an effect on the Master Sergeant. It was time to pay or play: I did both.

"Oh my God, I can't move!" I gasped.

"Fuck!" said Sebastian, who was somewhat less loquacious than usual.

I lay there panting for several more minutes. I felt the bed move, but I was too exhausted to open my eyes.

"I know you're looking at me, Sebastian," I grumbled, "but whatever you have in mind you can just forget it. I admit it all: you're an animal in bed, and I will never, ever question your virility again."

He laughed softly.

"You can question it as often as you like, baby, because that just means I have to prove it to you."

He dragged the sheet over us, and pulled me into his arms, where I flopped unattractively.

"Do you want to go find something to eat?" he said.

"Go? As in, leave the room? No, no. Bad, bad idea. Call takeout."

"I don't think they deliver to naked people in hotel rooms, Caro."

I groaned.

"Come on, baby, time to get up."

"I can't," I whined.

He left me lying in bed while he showered, I was nearly asleep by the time he returned. I heard him moving around the room, dressing and pulling on a pair of sneakers instead of his biker boots.

He sat on the bed next to me, and I realized he was holding my pink t-shirt in his hands.

"Not your color, Sebastian," I mumbled.

"No, baby. I want you to wear it."

"Why?"

"You look cute in pink."

Oh!

"And I got you something while I was out."

I sat up, ignoring several aching muscles.

"You got me something?"

I could hear the excitement in his voice, and he handed me a shopping bag from a woman's clothing store.

"You bought me clothes?"

"Just look in the goddam bag, Caro!"

I reached in and my hands fastened around a small piece of folded cloth: black with a design of tiny, pink flowers embroidered along one edge. It was a skirt, a miniskirt, a *very short* miniskirt.

I was astounded. Was this how he saw me? Barely-there bikinis and micro-miniskirts? These were the clothes a twenty-year old would wear, they weren't right for me. Maybe it was just wishful thinking on his part.

"Don't you like it?" he asked, sounding hurt.

"Sebastian, I ... it's very pretty, but..."

"But what?"

"It's not really me. I'm more a jeans and t-shirt sort of person these days. Besides, I don't have any shoes—I've only got my walking boots."

He smiled, and pulled another bag out from under the bed.

Inside was a pair of soft, black leather ballerina flats. And in my size.

"Do you like them?" he asked anxiously.

I slipped them on my bare feet and held them out for him to look at.

"So, you'll wear the skirt?" he said hopefully.

It seemed a small thing to do to make him happy.

"Yes, *tesoro*, I'll wear the skirt."

I carried my new outfit into the bathroom and stared at myself in the mirror. I was horribly afraid I'd look like mutton dressed as lamb. Did all women with younger men feel like that? Like they had to dress to match the age of their boyfriend?

The skirt was so short, I could hardly bring myself to look at it, and I certainly wouldn't be able to bend over in it with any degree of modesty.

I brushed my hair out and applied some of my newly purchased mascara and lipstick. I felt awkward and uncomfortable, a fraud, like I was trying to be something I wasn't.

But Sebastian's appraisal was very different from mine.

"Wow! I mean ... wow! You look awesome, Caro. Really fucking sexy!"

He ran his hand up my bare thigh and cupped my behind.

"Mmm, this skirt is great: it's making me horny."

"Thank you for my gifts," I said. "But right now, I need food more than I need your body, Sebastian."

He smiled, kissed my neck, then walked over to the door to hold it open for me.

"After you, baby."

The evening air was still warm, although I suspected it would feel chilly later. I'd brought a sweater with me to wear, although there wasn't much I could do to keep my legs warm, and I was wishing I hadn't gone along with Sebastian's whim. It didn't help matters that two men walking in the opposite direction whistled at me and called out endearments—rather crude ones.

Sebastian scowled and started to turn, as if he was going to go after them.

"Oh no, eyes front, Hunter. You bought this skirt, and now you're suffering the consequences: suck it up."

He frowned, but let me lead him out of the danger zone.

When we found a pizzeria that we liked the look of I couldn't help noticing that Sebastian made sure I was seated so that my legs were hidden by the tablecloth. Talk about double standards, it was almost comical. And time for a new topic of conversation.

"What do you want to do tomorrow, Sebastian? Apart from spring your surprise on me?"

He grinned, his good humor instantly restored.

"I thought we could walk up to Capezzano Inferiore, take a look around. Even if there aren't any Venzis there, it would be kinda cool to see where your dad grew up, wouldn't it?"

He was so sweet. A complete pain in the ass, but really sweet.

Our pizzas arrived, pepperoni for Sebastian, *quattro formaggi* for me, and he also ordered a light beer. Then he surprised me.

"Tell me about your place in Long Beach, Caro."

I didn't know why it surprised me: maybe because it didn't seem to be part of 'us', maybe I'd been unconsciously avoiding it.

"Oh! Sure, okay. Well, it's small, a bungalow in an area called the West End. It was built about ninety years ago, and it was pretty beaten up when I bought it. I restored the porch at the front so I can sit out and watch the ocean, and in the winter the windows are covered in salt from the wind coming off the Atlantic. I have some really great neighbors, and they look after the place while I'm away. My friends like to come out from Manhattan on the weekends. You spoke to Nicole, she works in merchant banking; and then there's Jenna, who's a bitch-on-wheels attorney, but actually she's really lovely; and Alice, she's a Professor of literature at NYU. I met her when I was going to school there…"

I stopped suddenly.

"What's wrong, Sebastian?"

He'd stopped eating, and was staring at me with dark, angry eyes.

"How am I going to fit in with your life there, Caro? All your friends have these amazing careers … and I'll just be a jobless grunt with a high school diploma."

"Sebastian, no!"

"You know what they'll think: Muscles Are Required Intelligence Not Essential."

"Hey! No one will think that, and you know what? I don't give a shit anyway. Sebastian, haven't we had to listen to enough crap in the past to care less what anyone else thinks now? Isn't that what you've been telling me?"

He shifted in his seat, but didn't answer.

"Sebastian, do you love me?"

He looked up instantly.

"You know I do, Caro. *Sempre*."

"Then whatever happens, we'll deal. I vaguely remember someone saying that to me. Oh, wait, that was you a couple of days ago. Sebastian, the only thing my friends will care about is that I'm happy."

I took his hand in mine.

"What about your plans to be a personal fitness trainer? And, jeez, Sebastian, we'll be in New York, you could do something amazing with your language skills. Don't go and get all shy on me now, Hunter!"

He took a deep breath, forcing himself to relax.

"Yeah, okay. Sorry. I just kinda freaked for a moment there."

"I know and I understand. It's weird for me, too, and we haven't been doing this for very long. I guess you could say we're out of practice with the whole dating thing. I feel very un-me sitting here in this shockingly short miniskirt, but I tried it, for you."

"Shockingly short?" he said, his grin returning.

I took his hand under the table and let him run his fingers up my thigh.

"Yeah," he agreed, "shockingly short."

"Okay, Columbus, you've discovered enough for one evening," I said, slapping his hand away as it began to travel even higher.

He pouted at me, and I laughed out loud.

"Come, *tesoro*, take me home."

When we returned to our beautiful room, and our beautiful, large bed, Sebastian made sweet, slow love to me. Maybe it was the romantic setting, or the way we were gradually getting to know each other again and defeat our fears one by one, but the way he touched me seemed to have a new depth and intensity. I was dreading the moment, just a few days away, when we'd have to say goodbye. Again.

We woke with yet another day of bright sunshine spilling in through the open windows.

"*Ciao, bella*," he said, copying the words I'd said to him the day before.

"*Ciao*," I said, smiling back at him.

I stretched, and several muscles grumbled at me. I'd thought I was in pretty good shape, but I'd been worked over by a US Marine, for several hours. There was definitely something to be said for a having the services of a personal trainer.

Sebastian's morning wood poked me in the side and his hand drifted over my hip.

Uh-oh, round two. Or three. Were we up to four? What the hell—seconds out.

Signora Carello served us breakfast on a small, private terrace to one side of her villa. She had a tiny garden filled with bougainvillea that was just coming into its full glory.

We invited her to have her coffee with us, and she happily accepted our invitation.

"So, you are hoping to find family in Capezzano Inferiore?"

"Well, that would be the icing on the cake, but really, I just want to see the village where my father came from. If I find family, well…"

She smiled sympathetically and patted my hand.

"Perhaps you will find family in a different way," she said, glancing at Sebastian, who grinned back at her.

There were several ways I could interpret her remark, I chose to ignore all of them. Although, it wasn't easy with Sebastian sitting opposite, smirking at me.

We wandered through Salerno, stopping to admire the neat yachts lined up in the harbor.

"I should take you sailing some time," said Sebastian, staring out at the deep, blue waters of the Mediterranean. "If we had more time, I'd rent us a boat and teach you how to sail."

"I already know," I said, smiling at him. "Although I haven't been out on a sailboat for years."

"Really?" he said, intrigued. "I didn't know you could sail."

"Ah, you don't know all my talents yet, Hunter."

He smiled. "I'm looking forward to finding out. But when did you learn?"

Damn, I should have kept my mouth shut—we were definitely sailing into dangerous waters.

"David taught me," I said.

Sebastian's face clouded over at once. "The asshole?"

It was his favorite name for my ex-husband.

"The very one."

His good humor evaporated and I sighed. I could have predicted that response—I *should* have predicted that response.

"It was a long time ago, Sebastian. And we agreed we couldn't change the past, so stop looking so mad, or I'll have to kiss you indecently in public."

His expression changed to one of surprise, then darkened perceptibly to lust.

"Nope, still pissed off, Caro. You'll have to kiss me. I don't know if it'll work, but you could try."

His eyes were challenging.

"Are you sure, Sebastian?" I said, in my most sultry voice. "Because I don't want to get you all hot and bothered."

"I'll risk it," he said, arrogantly.

I turned to face him, standing so close that our bodies almost touched. And then in full public view, I ran my hand over his ass, up beneath his t-shirt, and dragged my nails down his back. With my other hand I pulled his head down toward me and kissed him hard. And I might have also rubbed him over his zipper, causing him to take a sharp intake of breath.

"Fuck, Caro," he whispered. "Let's go back to our room right now."

I laughed. "No, Sebastian. That was just my distraction technique, which, by the way, I didn't learn in the Marines."

He groaned and had to adjust his pants.

"Should we go to Capezzano Inferiore now?" I asked innocently.

He gave me a look that said payback would be a bitch.

It was a steep walk to my father's village, but the view more than made up for it. Salerno glittered jewel-like below, the Mediterranean a polished glass of an implausible cerulean blue. In the crystal-sharp air, we could see a landmass on the horizon that I guessed must be Anacapri.

The village itself was quiet and dusty: a few cars passed us, all heading downhill. There was a fountain in the center that coughed and spurted arthritically, and a skinny dog idly scratched itself. All the life seemed to have been bled out of it, draining down the hill to the more confident town of Salerno. For the first time, I truly understood why my father might have wanted to leave, why America, with all its garish, New World charms, advertised by a thousand color movies, had been such a draw. And, perhaps, why my blonde, blue-eyed mother had seemed like a dream worth chasing.

It was making me sad, and it felt like a mistake to have come here.

"We don't have to stay, Caro," said Sebastian, squeezing my fingers.

I sighed. "It's okay. I don't know what I was expecting: Papa always said it was a one-horse town where the horse had died. I guess he was right."

"Look, that guy over there is just opening up his café—let's go get a drink, okay?"

The café owner was surprised but delighted to have some business. I imagined he didn't get many customers.

Sebastian ordered a beer and I opted for an espresso. Maybe a shot of caffeine would help to lift my mood.

The beer was served in a frosted glass, and my espresso arrived in a miniature coffee pot with raw cane sugar and a glass of water.

"Excuse me, sir," said Sebastian, politely. "But my girlfriend's father came from this village. We were wondering if you might have known him: his surname was Venzi."

The man scratched his head. "That name seems familiar, but I'm not sure. Let me ask my wife—she's lived here her whole life."

My heart began to beat more rapidly, and I sat up anxiously in my seat.

"Don't get your hopes up, Caro," Sebastian said, gently.

"No, I'm not," I lied, unable to beat back the sudden expectation that had flared.

A moment later, the owner's wife appeared.

"*Buon giorno*. You are asking after the Venzi family? How can I help you?"

"I was just wondering ... my father, Marco Venzi, he was born here. Did you know him?"

"Goodness! Marco Venzi! That's a name I haven't heard in a very long time. He was the boy who left to live in America. Your father, you say? Yes, I knew him."

She knew him. She really knew him. I felt tears welling up in my eyes.

"It's so exciting to meet someone who remembers Papa," I choked out, gazing at the woman's warm and sympathetic face.

"Yes, we were at school together: he was a few years older than me, and always in trouble. He had the devil in him, that one."

"His daughter is just the same," said Sebastian, with a quiet smile.

The woman laughed. "And how is dear Marco? Did he make his fortune in America like he said? He was crazy for your American movies. Said he was going to be a big star, like Valentino."

"Mr. Venzi died some years ago," answered Sebastian, knowing I was finding it hard to speak.

"Ah, I see," she said. "Forgive me, young woman, my condolences. Your father was always so full of spirit. Too big for this little town."

"Do you know if he had any relatives here?" said Sebastian.

"Well, there was his mother, but she died a long time ago. Marco had a sister who was much older than him, I remember. But she married and moved away, to Naples, I think. I'm sorry, I don't remember the name of the man she married, so that's all I can tell you."

She nodded, and moved back inside the shadowy café.

Sebastian held my hand, stroking his thumb over the back of my knuckles.

"We could try and find her," he said, gently. "She might have had kids—you could have cousins you don't know about."

"Yes, I might. I probably do."

I closed my eyes, remembering the happiness my father found in everything to do with America: the music, the movies, the TV shows, the cars—especially the cars. A large, pale blue Cadillac had been his pride and joy. The damn thing drove like a bus. I used to get seasick just from sitting in the back seat.

But that was in the past, it was all in the past, and I was planning a future.

"It doesn't matter, Sebastian," I said, slowly. "Signora Carello was right: even if there are cousins, they're not my family—not really. I have my friends and I have you. You're my family now."

He bowed his head and held my hand to his lips. Then he stood up, taking me by surprise.

And in that dusty little square, in that nondescript, one-horse town where the fountain coughed and spluttered and the cars passed by without a second glance, he sank to one knee.

"Carolina Maria Venzi: I love you, and I want to spend my life with you. Will you marry me?"

CHAPTER ELEVEN

I STARED DOWN IN AMAZEMENT AS SEBASTIAN KNELT BEFORE ME, HIS beautiful face torn with anxiety.

I could think of a thousand reasons why marrying him was sheer lunacy, and only one reason why it wasn't.

I took a deep breath, willing all my doubts and fears away.

"I love you, too, Sebastian. And the answer is yes."

He let out a shout of delight and leapt to his feet, pulling me into his arms, and holding me tightly as if he'd never let me go. I laid my head on his chest, listening to the pounding of his heart through his thin t-shirt.

"I'll do everything to make you happy, I promise, Caro," he whispered. "Everything, baby. You are my life."

"And you are mine, *tesoro*. We'll find a way—we always do."

He sat back down on the hard, wooden seat and pulled me onto his lap, nuzzling my neck.

"Oh, fuck!" he said, angrily.

"What? What's the matter?" I asked nervously.

Had he changed his mind already?

"I forgot to give you the fucking ring," he snarled. "Fuck it! I wanted this to be so smooth. Jeez, I said it enough times in my head."

"You did? You practiced this?"

I loved that he'd practiced.

He smiled, slightly abashed. "Yeah, once or twice. Maybe a few times more … maybe a lot of times more… Ah, fuck it, Caro. See if the damn thing fits."

I couldn't help laughing out loud from sheer happiness—plus, he was so damn funny.

"You're in danger of sweeping me off my feet again, Sebastian. How can I resist such sweet words: I'll treasure your proposal forever, 'See if the damn thing fits'."

He grinned at me, then pulled a small ring box out of his back pocket, opened it, and laid it on the table.

Nestled in the dark blue satin was a small but breathtaking blue-white diamond solitaire, simply mounted on a gold band.

I gasped, as the diamond blazed in the sun, scattering tiny rainbows across the table.

"Sebastian, it's beautiful! Where on earth did you get it ... and *when?*"

"Try it on."

He lifted the ring out of the box and slid it onto the third finger of my left hand.

"Perfect."

"Yes, it is. Thank you, *tesoro*."

I twisted around and kissed him softly, leaning down to enjoy the feel of his lips on mine.

Sebastian looked as if he'd just climbed Mount Everest or defeated the Mongol hordes single-handedly.

"So, *fiancé*," I said, "what should we do now?"

My new name took him by surprise.

"Wow, *fiancé*, huh? I didn't think it could sound so cool."

"I disagree, Sebastian. I think it sounds *hot*. Maybe we can agree to disagree, or just accept that it's an all-temperature sort of title."

He laughed loudly, the sound filled with a ridiculous and infectious joy that I couldn't help sharing.

"Well, *fiancée*, I thought we could check out those gnarly bends on the Amalfi coast. What do you think?"

"I think you're crazy, probably certifiable, and I'm horribly afraid it's contagious."

He grinned at me and stood up, tucking my hand under his arm, as we floated back down to Salerno.

The sun was blazing in the sky, the air warm, and the feeling that filled me, indescribable. I felt both calm and fizzing with joy, happy and anxious, loved and terrifyingly in love. I was falling off a cliff, one I'd thrown myself from willingly, hoping I'd fly. Crazy in love.

When we reached the villa, Signora Carello was standing in her garden, watering the bougainvillea.

"Did you have any luck finding your family, my dear?" she asked kindly.

"Yes, I did," I said, gazing stupidly at Sebastian.

Sigora Carello gasped as she saw my ring flashing in the sunshine.

"Oh, felicitations, *congratulazioni per il vostro fidanzamento*, my children! I'm so happy for you."

And she kissed us each three times, while Sebastian grinned away as if nothing could ever dim his happiness.

"And now for your surprise?" she said, patting Sebastian on his arm.

He winked and nodded.

I actually felt jealous that I wasn't in on the secret, but I couldn't help smiling anyway.

"Some lunch before you go? I was going to fix myself *insalata tricolore*—you're welcome to join me."

We sat in the *signora*'s pretty garden, enjoying the tranquility that came from within.

"So, when will you marry?" she asked, with keen interest.

We answered simultaneously.

"I don't know," I said.

"As soon as possible," said Sebastian.

The *signora* laughed.

"Oh, you two have some talking to do, I can see that. Never mind, my dears, you'll work it out. Have you decided where you'll live?"

"Caro has a place near New York," said Sebastian, "but I could be stationed anywhere."

"You're in the army?"

"No, ma'am, US Marines."

Signora Carello nodded slowly, a frown of concern crinkling her eyes.

"He has to do two more years," I said, staring at my plate, and trying to keep the tremor out of my voice. "And he's being sent out to Afghanistan. On Thursday."

"Ah," she said, and shook her head sadly.

"Hey, it'll be fine," said Sebastian, emphasizing the final word. "Besides, I might see you out there."

Signora Carello looked confused.

"Caro is a reporter—a foreign correspondent," said Sebastian. "But I wish she..."

He stopped mid-sentence.

"Well," said the *signora*, forcefully, "you young people don't choose the easy path, but it is your own path. I wish you both well. Please come back and have your honeymoon here."

"Honeymoon!" said Sebastian, looking as if he'd just won the lottery. "Hell, I'd forgotten about that! Yeah, we should definitely have a honeymoon, Caro. With room service—so we don't have to get out of bed."

I felt hugely embarrassed he'd said that in front of the *signora*, but she just laughed and he winked at her.

When Signora Carello took the plates back into the villa, I elbowed Sebastian in the ribs.

"Don't say things like that in front of her—she'll be embarrassed!"

Sebastian laughed. "You're the only one who's embarrassed, Caro, which is pretty fucking funny. Signora Carello used to be 'fast', remember? Anyway, I didn't say anything that wasn't true."

And then I recalled that the *signora* had already cleaned our room that morning, I cringed, thinking about the large number of condoms that we'd deposited in the garbage can. Oh, God, how embarrassing was that? Sebastian's inappropriate comment paled to nothing when faced with more tangible evidence of how we'd spent our time.

We collected our leather jackets from the tidy room, and Sebastian changed into his heavy boots before we headed off for the 'surprise'. He looked so sexy bending over to fasten the buckles. What was it about jeans, boots and leather jackets? I wondered what it would be like riding through upstate New York on Sebastian's mean machine. Now *that* would be fun.

I was puzzled when the *signora* cornered us by the front door and kissed us again, whispering something to Sebastian, and patting his arm.

I had the distinct impression that they'd planned something together: no doubt the Hunter charm and the Italian love of intrigue had been cooking up something.

The Amalfi coastline was like a huge James Bond set. Dizzying, narrow roads arced up the mountain, with the cliffs falling away into the sea, many hundreds of feet below.

I clung onto Sebastian, as he took the turns with terrifying speed. I could tell he was enjoying himself, but I had my eyes closed and grit my teeth so hard, I was afraid I would grind them into chalk dust or make them come flying out of my mouth like so many peanuts.

At the top of the path, above the small town of Pontone, Sebastian pulled off the road next to a lemon grove, and cut the engine.

"It's a great view, baby. You want to get your camera out?"

I opened my eyes and pulled off my helmet. He was right—it was stunning. And, with my blood pressure returning to normal, I felt able to capture the astonishing landscape in the lens. I snapped a few of Sebastian, too, looking all bad-boy next to his motorcycle.

I climbed a little higher to get some more views of the sea, when I slithered back down the mountainside, I was surprised to see that Sebastian was digging around for something in one of the bike's saddlebags.

"Don't you want to ride on a little further?" I asked, puzzled.

"Nope, we're staying here. Picnic," he grinned at me, holding a miniature bottle of champagne in one hand, and two crystal flutes in the other. "Borrowed from Signora Carello," he said, answering my unspoken question.

"I think the *signora* has a soft spot for you, Sebastian."

"Must be my animal magnetism, baby."

I rolled my eyes at him.

"Hey, don't knock it—it works on you."

"That is true, Sarge."

He led us to a patch of dry, springy grass and opened the champagne, where the cork flew off like a rocket, making us both duck.

"Huh, guess it got shook up on the road."

Yeah, and it wasn't the only thing that got shook up, I thought, uncharitably.

He poured the champagne, half-filling the glasses with froth and bubbles.

"Here's to us, Caro," he said, softly and seriously. "Today, tomorrow, forever. Promise?"

"Yes, *tesoro*. Forever, I promise."

We sat, high above the Mediterranean, as if at the top of the world, sipping our champagne and speaking quietly, promises and words of love. Then we lay in each other's arms, feeling the warm sun on our faces.

"I love my surprise, Sebastian," I said, contentedly.

He chuckled quietly. "This is only part of it, Caro. There's more."

"More?"

"Much more."

"Such as?"

"You'll see."

Feeling a little lightheaded from both the ride and the champagne, I mounted the motorcycle once more, and we headed back down toward the sea. This time, I screwed up my courage and managed to open one eye as Sebastian raced down the hill, taking the curves with what, to me, seemed like reckless speed.

We arrived in the village Conca dei Marini without incident and, to my surprise, Sebastian pulled up in the forecourt of Il Saraceno, a hotel so grand, I was sure it must be frequented by the great and good, the wealthy and the beautiful. Sebastian fit right in—especially on that last one. I looked dusty and travel-stained, as if I'd just crossed the Sahara on the back of a smelly camel.

Il Saraceno clung to the cliffs, a series of fortress-like arches that mimicked the ancient Moorish architecture of Spanish Grenada. The views down to the sea were in danger of bringing on an attack of vertigo.

"Here?" I asked uncertainly, aware that my hair resembled a squashed bird's nest.

"Here," he said, with a smile.

I was surprised when he unpacked the bike's saddlebags, and handed the keys of his machine to a man at the reception desk. I couldn't imagine him letting anyone else park it, I supposed the valet would simply wheel it around to the parking area.

The receptionist smiled, and handed an envelope to Sebastian, along with a room key.

"We're staying here? But we left all our things at Signora Carello's?"

"Actually, we haven't. I asked the *signora* to pack us up while we were out this morning. She was cool about it. Besides this is kind of her idea. Well, she helped me pick out somewhere special."

"But a place like this must cost a small fortune, Sebastian!"

"I can afford it, baby. This is my first night as an engaged man—and I want to enjoy it. Hey, don't worry. The only thing I've spent my pay on in the last ten years is booze and bikes. I'm good for it."

Which wasn't the point, but he was in such high spirits, I didn't have the heart to argue with him.

But the surprise didn't end there. At the door to our room, Sebastian swept me up into his arms and insisted on carrying me over the threshold, his wonderfully romantic gesture leaving me breathless.

The bed was huge, almost seven feet wide. I'd never seen anything like it—but I quickly formed plans for how we could use it. I barely noticed the opulence of the rest of the room, the chandelier and long curtains trailing across our own private balcony. The bathroom alone was an essay in magnificence: an enormous whirlpool bathtub, plus a vast hydro-massage shower. Both were fashioned from marble, and could probably have accommodated an entire soccer team. I couldn't wait to try them out with my very own United States Marine.

Sebastian pulled open the wardrobe doors and didn't seem at all surprised to see two suit carriers hanging up inside.

"This one is for you, baby."

Staring at him in amazement, a smile creeping over my face, I unzipped the carrier that he handed me, to reveal a stunning, floor-length evening gown, in midnight blue.

"Sebastian, it's beautiful! What have you done?"

He grinned at me. "And I have a tux—like you wanted. Except mine is just rented. You get to keep the dress."

I laid my beautiful gown on the bed, and wrapped my arms around his neck.

"How did you get to be so perfect, Sebastian, because I could have sworn you were a giant pain in the ass."

He laughed. "Next time I piss you off, I'm going to remind you that you said that, baby. Which will probably be in about five minutes."

"Probably," I agreed, with a smile.

"Come on, let's shower, and then I want to see you in that dress."

"Why, Sergeant! You want to put me *into* clothes?"

"You have another idea?" he murmured into my neck.

"Oh, yes, most definitely, and it involves getting you naked on that bed, having my wicked, wicked way with you *before* we take a shower."

His smile grew even bigger.

"So, let me get this straight, Caro, that's *two* lots of wicked?"

"The thing is, Sebastian," I said, stroking his cheek and watching his expression of amusement turn to lust, "if you're going to make an honest woman of me, I want to get in as much sinning as possible first."

I pushed him back on the bed, just in case he wasn't on the same page as me, and ripped his t-shirt over his head, loving that moment when his eyes heated with desire. I knelt across him, then ran my tongue from his waist to his throat, making a delicious diversion where I tugged his nipples with my teeth.

Yes, two could play at that game.

I gripped his wrists with my hands and held them over his head, trapping him. Then I leaned down to kiss him, tracing his soft lips with my tongue and letting his warm breath wash over me.

"Mmm, you taste so good, Sebastian, I won't want anything else to eat tonight."

He laughed lightly, and gently pulled his hands free, before running them down my back.

"Yeah? Well, I'm starving, so unless you want me to eat downstairs alone, baby, you'll have to put up with a three-course meal. And I guarantee you'll need your energy later."

I pouted at him. "Sure you don't want the starter now?"

He didn't answer with words, but moved his hands around to my waistband, tugging my t-shirt free, and pulling it over my head. It landed somewhere on the floor, while he unfastened my bra one-handed.

There had been a time when bras had presented him with something of a challenge—not any more.

"Mmm, I like this position," he said, sitting up and nuzzling my nipples, then sucking hard. I moaned and arched my back, pushing my breasts into his willing hands.

He fished a condom out of his jeans pocket and handed it to me.

"Take your pants off, baby."

"I will if you will," I replied, teasingly. "Race you!"

I bounced off him and quickly unlaced my boots, dropping my jeans and panties to the floor in record time.

"Ah, hell," muttered Sebastian as he struggled to unbuckle his boots.

"You're a slouch, Hunter," I jeered at him. "Just look at what you're missing."

I gave a quick twirl, which didn't help his concentration.

"Fuck!" he hissed, hopping around the bed, one boot on, one boot off.

"Maybe you should have been a fireman instead of a Marine, then you'd be used to undressing quickly."

There was a loud thud as his second boot landed on the floor, a moment later his pants and briefs hit the deck, too.

Damn, he looked so fine standing there, all tall and erect, all hot and devilish. I definitely wanted some of that.

"Lie on the bed," I ordered.

"Yes, ma'am."

I decided to have a quick taste, feeling his hips arch upwards so he filled my mouth. Okay, maybe not so quick: he tasted salty, his skin silky and delicious.

I held the condom in my hand as I continued to enjoy feeling his arousal between my lips, in my mouth, under my writhing tongue. I ran my fingernails up and down his chest as I continued to stroke him with my mouth. I was beginning to resent the intrusion of our little rubber friends, and wondered what would be the best time to start taking the birth control pills: perhaps a month before he got home on his next leave? That would be a good surprise for him. A welcome home present for both of us.

"Baby, I'm going to come if you keep doing that," he growled, his voice strained.

Oh, I'd completely lost track of what I was doing. Hmm, better not admit to that.

I released him and sat back, watching the rapid rise and fall of his chest as he tried to pull himself together. Before he got the chance, I rolled the condom down, and positioned myself over him, sinking down slowly. Very slowly.

He moaned softly and I leaned down to kiss him. At the same time, he flexed his hips upwards, filling and massaging me at just the right place, causing sensation to spill through me.

"Fuck, Caro! I can't control myself with you!"

He started pumping his hips, bouncing me up as I slammed down to meet him.

He came quickly and used his fingers to make sure that I followed him.

I slumped down on his chest.

"Sorry, baby," he said, breathlessly.

"You have nothing to be sorry about," I gasped, impressed I'd managed to string a whole sentence together.

He smiled and stroked my back. "Ready for the main course?"

"You've got to be kidding me, Hunter? I'm still..." and my body clenched around him.

"Oh, wow," he said, his eyes wide, "I really felt that."

"Good," I said, rather grumpily. "So did I."

He laughed, and lifted me off him as he sat up.

"I'm going to go shower."

With bleary eyes, I watched him saunter into the palatial bathroom, snapping off the condom as he went.

I glanced down at my hand and caught sight of the unfamiliar ring on my finger. I still wasn't certain how that had happened. But it felt good. It felt right. Although explaining it to my friends would be interesting. I shook my head: hell, explaining to myself would be pretty damn interesting, too.

I heard the bathroom door open again, and Sebastian strolled out drying himself. Or rather, the way he looked, the way he looked at me

—that was explanation enough for our impetuous engagement, certainly as far as I was concerned.

"What?" he asked, smiling.

"Just wondering how the hell I ended up engaged to such a hot Marine. It's been quite a week, Sarge."

He frowned. "You're not having second thoughts, are you, Caro?"

I shook my head. "No, Sebastian, I'm not. But you have to admit, it's all been pretty fast."

"It's been ten years, Caro," he said, seriously. "I've waited long enough."

His response floored me: he had a way of just cutting through all my bullshit.

"I love you so much, *tesoro*," I said.

His eyes softened. "Love you, too, Caro. Now get your ass in that shower, before I throw you in there."

"Fine, fine," I grumbled. "I'm going."

He waited until he was sure I really was moving.

"I'll meet you in the restaurant, Caro."

"You're not going to wait for me here?"

"Nope. I want to see you coming down that staircase, and have all the other bastards wanting you, but knowing I'll be the one taking you to bed later." He saw the expression on my face. "Humor me: it's a guy thing."

I shook my head. Honestly!

When I climbed out of the shower, the room was empty, except for my beautiful dress which Sebastian had laid across the bed. I didn't want to think how he'd gotten so good at choosing women's clothing.

I hunted through the drawers until I found a hair dryer. Luckily, I had some hairpins in my bag, and, after a couple of false starts, I managed to sweep my hair up into a reasonably elegant chignon.

I realized then that Sebastian had laid another set of bags on the bed. What the hell had he done now? Inside the first was the most exquisite set of silvery-gray silk bra and panties, all chic and obviously designer—they must have cost a fortune. I'd never owned anything so glamorous in my life. In the second bag was a pair of high-heeled satin pumps in the same midnight blue as the dress. In my size. Of course. I dreaded to think how big a hole this had put in Sebastian's savings. Things were going to be a lot tighter when we were married.

Married.

I hadn't had time to think about what that meant. I'd been married for 11 years from the age of 19, and they had been difficult and unhappy years. I'd promised myself I'd never marry again, and I'd had absolutely no intention of getting involved with a man in the armed forces. Nope, never, no way. And yet here I was: promising myself to Sebastian forever. It helped that he wasn't planning on staying in the Marines, because there was no way I'd want to live on a military base ever again, despite my fascination with reporting from, and writing about them.

There were so many things Sebastian and I had to work out. We'd both been single for so long that blending our lives together wasn't going to be easy.

I'd promised Sebastian we'd find a way. He deserved to be loved for everything he was. And for whatever crazy reason he had, he loved me, too.

I shimmied into the tiny silver panties, enjoying the whisper of the sheer material over my damp skin. The bra hugged my breasts and felt incredibly sensual. It made me feel sexy—and Sebastian had chosen them. And I realized that's how he saw me, as someone desirable, someone he desired. Well, tonight I was going to do my best to live up to that.

I applied some mascara, cursing when I managed to deposit a gluey lump on my cheek. I had better luck with the lipstick. By some miracle, I'd managed to buy one that went on creamily and didn't bleed. For the second night running, a stranger's face stared back at me in the mirror.

But the dress ... oh, the dress was something else. It was a floor-length, flowing gown, cut low at the back, and plunging dangerously at the front, and with a thigh-high slit that only revealed itself when I walked. And yet it was so cleverly constructed, that I felt safe. Well, I wasn't afraid that anything would be revealed by mistake. I was fairly sure I wouldn't be safe from Sebastian later. I was looking forward to that. I hoped he didn't tear anything when he took it off me, because that would be a crying shame.

Before I left the room, I put the packet of condoms on the table next to my side of the bed—they'd need to be where we could find them in a hurry.

Now, if I could just get down the main staircase without breaking my neck in those perilously high heels...

I took a deep breath and left the safety of our room.

At the top of the stairs, I glanced down. My breath stuttered in my throat. I thought I'd slipped through a crack in time because in front of me, my fun-loving surfer boy, my rough, tough, sexy Marine, had transformed into a nineteenth century gentleman.

He was dressed in black: the pants legs edged in a narrow, satin stripe, an elegant, fitted tuxedo-jacket rested on his broad shoulders, over a fine cotton piqué shirt. A black bowtie accentuated his beauty still further.

And the woman he was talking to, looked like she was stripping him with her eyes, before dragging him to her room.

I eyed up the competition. She was perhaps two or three years younger than me, expensively dressed in a vivid purple halter top about the size of a handkerchief, with long, sexy harem pants. There was no doubt she had the figure to carry off such an outrageous outfit, although if I was inclined to be critical, I'd say that her boobs had the volume, shape and rubbery bounce of beach balls, her teeth were whitened to a degree that could cause snow blindness, and she had fake talons that could remove an eyeball at a hundred paces. But only if I was being critical.

And she was flirting with my fiancé.

I was about to be seriously pissed off when she laid a predatory hand on his arm, in an apparently friendly gesture.

I saw Sebastian turn slightly, so she was forced to drop her hand. I felt like cheering. He wasn't interested in her.

Then he glanced up at the stairs and his eyes widened as he saw me, before his face broke out in a huge grin.

The Orangeade woman turned to see what he was staring at, and if looks could kill, I'd have shriveled on the spot. But I didn't shrivel. I gave her a small, oh-so-magnanimous smile, before I carefully made my way down the stairs.

Sebastian strode across to meet me and took my hand, lifting it to his lips.

"You look beautiful, Caro."

"Thank you, kind sir."

He held out his arm. "May I escort you in to dinner, ma'am?"

"Why, yes you may."

Sebastian glowed with happiness, although the glint in his eyes was still wicked. I'm sure, that evening, that I reflected his joy, felt it wash over me, I basked in it and bathed in it. At that moment, at that time, there was nowhere in the world I'd rather be.

The dining room was exquisite, a small piece of perfection, with the Mediterranean at its feet. The chairs were swathed in linen that matched the tablecloths, and the starched napkins had been folded into shapes like a bishop's miter.

Sebastian led me to a table in a small alcove, where the arched windows looked down onto the sunset over the sea. A waiter rushed forward to pull out my chair, but Sebastian waved him away, carefully seating me himself, before brushing his lips over my bare shoulder in a soft, lingering kiss.

"I can't wait to get you out of that dress," he whispered in my ear, as he ran a long, cool finger from my earlobe down to the base of my neck.

Then he sat across the table from me and smiled smugly.

"Every man in this room wants you, Caro. I'm so fucking proud, I can't stop smiling."

"Hmm, well I think you may be a little biased, I thought I was going to need a crowbar to pry that woman off you. Is it just me, or had she overdone the fake tan, because I haven't seen that shade of orange outside of a drag review."

He raised his eyebrows. "My girl's got grit: I like it."

"I felt like swinging her around by her hair extensions. Maybe some of your Marine training is rubbing off on me."

"That comes after the main course," he said, confidently.

"Thank you for today, Sebastian," I said, serious for once. "It's been perfect. Thank you."

He smiled at me across the table.

"It's been a long time coming, Caro, but it was worth the wait."

I could see in his eyes that he meant what he said.

"Where did you get this beautiful ring?" I murmured, admiring the way it glinted on my finger. "Because I didn't see any shops in Salerno that..."

"I didn't buy it in Salerno," he said, interrupting me.

My mouth popped open in surprise. "Then where?"

"Geneva," he said, grinning at me, completely unabashed. "You know I was supposed to be at that fucking dull hostile environment briefing—which they'd given me as part of my 'rehabilitation' after Paris..." he raised an eyebrow, "but after I saw you ... I couldn't face going back. I was wandering around trying to get my head straight, and I saw it in a jeweler's shop."

I was dumbfounded.

"But ... you still hated me then!"

He shook his head vehemently. "I never hated you, Caro, although I tried, I really fucking tried. But I just couldn't do it."

He sighed and rubbed his hands over his hair.

"That ring has been burning a hole in my pocket ever since. I was just waiting for the right time to give it to you."

I blinked back tears: tonight was not a night for crying, although I was certain that would happen in the lonely days to come.

"You've always been so sure," I whispered, "I don't understand why."

"I told you, Caro," he said, softly. "It's only ever been you."

I stretched out my hand, admiring the ring as it sparkled under the light of the chandelier. "Thank you for giving it to me."

He caught my fingers and kissed the ring. "Thank you for wearing it."

The wine waiter arrived with an expensive-looking bottle and opened it with an understated flourish.

Sebastian held his glass and watched the bubbles effervesce. Then he looked up, staring into my eyes.

"Thank God for you, Caro," he said, his voice low and aching with sincerity.

"And you, Sebastian, *semper fidelis*."

As the hours passed, the tension that had been so briefly and beautifully absent from our relationship began to creep back. Once again, our summer was slipping away, and we could count it in minutes and seconds.

Tomorrow, the dream would be over—but, for now, tonight was still ours. I had to remember that.

We dined on *antipasti di frutti di mare*, a *primo* of ravioli with pumpkin and almonds with sage, and as *secondo*, a melt-in-your-mouth *ragú di pecora*, as the sun set, sinking into the sea beneath us. It was a perfect and poignant end to a magical few days.

We walked back up the grand staircase, hand in hand, and my gentleman escorted me to our room. I was waiting for him to revert to my sensuous and very physical lover, but there was one more surprise to come.

He led me out onto the balcony, where two glasses of Galliano liqueur blazed in the light of a single candle. And next to that, in a crystal vase, was a perfect pink rose.

In silence, he handed me the drink and took the second for himself. His gaze was heated, and his eyes never left mine.

The golden liquid burned as it trickled down my throat, but the burn was not as fierce as the way my *fiancé* looked at me.

He finished his drink and placed the glass back on the table, then took mine. With a look that made my body tingle and dried my throat, he held out his hand and led me toward the bed.

In silence, he cupped my face with his hands and kissed me until I was breathless and dizzy.

Then he turned me around, and rested his hands on my waist, gently unzipping my dress, stroking my bare flesh as the material shivered to the floor. I stepped away from it, and regarded him intently as his gaze flowed up and down my body.

My turn.

I moved toward him, and slid his jacket over his shoulders, tossing it onto the chair. I loosened one end of his bowtie and undid the top button of his shirt while he gazed down into my eyes.

He kissed my neck, his warm lips sending ripples of desire through me, then he dipped down, scooping me into his arms, and carried me to the bed.

I lay, looking up at him as he undid his cufflinks, then slowly he unfastened each button on his shirt, never taking his eyes from mine.

He shrugged the shirt off and my gentleman became a soldier again, his dog tags glinting in the candlelight, his tattoo a dark bruise on his golden skin.

He bent down to untie his shoes and peel off his socks, then he stood up, watching me silently, with wonder on his face.

I sat up and hooked my finger into the waistband of his pants, and pulled him toward me. I held his eyes as I slid the button free and lowered the zipper.

He pushed the material over his hips and threw the black pants onto the chair with his jacket.

As he stood in front of me, I could see the defined muscles of his stomach, diaphragm and chest moving with each breath.

I let my fingers drift over his bare skin and felt a shiver run through him, his breath caught in his throat, and his eyes fluttered closed.

I pushed his briefs down his long legs and he stepped free.

The way he looked at me took my breath away. Desire, need, love and lust: the emotions chased each other across his beautiful face, the candlelight throwing shadows that emphasized the perfect symmetry of his cheekbones.

I sat up, wrapping my arms around his waist, and placed soft kisses across his chest and stomach, before dipping down to plant a gentle kiss on the tip of his erection. He breathed in deeply and closed his eyes.

I kissed him again, then reached over to find a condom, tore the packet open and slowly rolled it down his length. He sat next to me on the bed and carefully pulled out my hairpins, one by one, until my hair fell down my back and shoulders. Then he tangled his long fingers in my hair, and tipped my head back to kiss my throat.

His hands traveled across my body, and I felt him unhook my bra, sliding the straps over my shoulders, before leaning down to kiss my breasts. I stroked his short, soft hair as he continued to run his tongue over and around my nipples, teasing them into rigid points.

I lay back on the bed, my arms stretched above my head, and he hovered over me, his erection probing softly at the entrance to my sex, before he kissed his way down my chest and belly, running his tongue along the edge of my silk panties and rubbing his chin over my mound.

He hooked his fingers under the delicate material and threw the panties somewhere behind him.

He kissed me softly and sweetly, then nuzzled his way back up my body.

I lifted my knees, ready for him, running my hands over his strong forearms and biceps, tracing his tattoo with one finger.

His dog tags jingled softly as they fell onto my chest, and Sebastian's body loomed over me, his eyes locked on mine.

He pushed inside me slowly and I groaned loudly, feeling his body filling me. I lifted my hips, taking that extra length, and I heard his breath exhale sharply.

He gazed into my eyes, his hands stroking my face, as his hips moved and flexed rhythmically. My body trembled in response and he lowered his face to kiss me deeply, his tongue twining with mine.

He pulled back slightly, nuzzling my throat, and rolling his hips so every part of me felt him inside. I clenched around him and I heard a responding growl deep in his throat.

A quiet moan escaped me and his body recognized the sound, moving one degree faster. I lifted my hips again and I heard the breath hiss through his teeth. I cried out, on the edge of all sensation, then he buried his head in my neck and started thrusting rapidly until he reached his climax, and his body went rigid.

For a moment, his full, crushing weight pinned me to the bed, then, with a soft sigh, he pulled out of me and rolled onto his back, one hand resting across my stomach.

No words had been spoken, there was nothing that needed to be said.

For the rest of that night, we slept, woke briefly, made love and slept again, until dawn turned the sky gold and purple, with flames of orange reflected in the sea. We had spoken quietly, describing our love, and expressing our need for each other with our bodies.

We slept late, and Sebastian insisted on ordering a decadent breakfast of a dozen fresh fruits, a range of olive breads and light pastries, freshly squeezed orange juice with Sorrento lemons, and a large pot of coffee.

We sat on the balcony in our bathrobes to enjoy the feast, but our carefree happiness had slipped away with the night. Today, we had to return to Geneva. And this time tomorrow, Sebastian would be headed out to one of the most dangerous countries on earth. I would follow when I could.

I sighed, staring out at the sea, and Sebastian held my hand, lifting it to his lips at intervals.

"As much as I hate to say it, *tesoro*, but I think we should get going. We've got a hell of a long drive ahead of us, or rather you have, and you didn't have much sleep last night."

He smiled at the memory. "Yeah, but it was worth it. Anyway, don't worry, Caro, we're not taking the bike, we're flying back from Naples. Our flight is at 4PM, we've plenty of time."

"Flying? But what about your bike?"

"Sold it, baby. I can't take it with me, and they won't send me back to Geneva after this tour."

I was astonished. "When did you organize all this?"

"When we were in Salerno, I didn't think you'd mind."

"I don't, it's your bike, but I wish you'd told me—it would have been one less thing to worry about."

He smiled at me. "Sorry, baby. I guess I'm just used to doing stuff on my own."

I frowned. "Yes. Me, too. I suppose we'll just have to practice the whole sharing and communicating thing. I promise that I'll write to you every day, *tesoro*."

"Really?" he said, looking both pleased and surprised. "That would be cool. I never get mail. Well, Shirley always sends me a birthday card, but that's about it. Ches is shit at staying in touch. So am I."

"Well, I will expect an effort from you, Sebastian. Will you be able to email me?"

He pulled a face. "Maybe, I'm not sure. For a few days, but then ... I'll be out of range. Caro, don't worry if you don't hear from me regularly." He paused, watching my expression. "The places they send me, I can be away from the main Base for days, sometimes weeks, in shithole little villages, trying to persuade the locals to work with us. Nonmilitary comms is limited. Your letters will catch up with me— eventually, but emails—probably not that often."

"I understand," I said, a chill creeping across my heart. "But in an emergency, what's the procedure for contacting you?"

I could see he was toying with an answer.

"I'll give you a number you can call but only in a real, fucking emergency, Caro. I'm not supposed to give it out."

"Okay," I said softly, then steeled my nerve to ask my next question. "If … if anything happens that I need to know about, how will anyone know to contact me?"

He leaned back in his chair and closed his eyes. "Same as you, Caro. We have to do a call-list—the Emergency Contact Form—of who to notify. I've been wondering how, I mean, I can't put you down as 'Lee Venzi' or even 'Caro Venzi' because they'll recognize the name, they'll start in asking questions, and you could be in deep shit."

"What about Carolina Hunter?" I suggested, looking across at him. "They'll just assume I'm a cousin or something, in fact, why don't you do that? Put me down as a relative."

I could tell by the look on his face that he'd been hoping I'd make that suggestion.

He smiled. "Yeah, that would work."

I hated having to talk about these things, but it was important, very important.

"Hey, baby, nothing's going to happen to me. I can take care of myself. I'm more worried about you. Reporters get … hurt all the time."

"I know, Sebastian, but I'll be embedded with a Marine unit from Leatherneck, safest place to be. I heard US Marines are tough, and I know for a fact they're hot. In fact the word 'embedded' has me thinking all sorts of interesting things."

I could tell he didn't know whether to smile or scowl.

"You stay away from those bootnecks, Caro. They're a bunch of horny bastards."

"I've noticed! But really, don't worry about *that*. I've learned to say 'no' in even more languages than you."

He took my hand, fiddling with my ring.

"Well, at least they'll know you're taken when they see this."

I didn't answer. He'd be hurt if he knew I wasn't planning on wearing it. I couldn't tell him that it would draw too much attention. I could either cover it up with a band-aid, or wear it around my neck on a chain—my own, unique dog tag.

"How long do you think you'll be in Afghan?" he asked, still running his finger over the diamond.

"Assuming my papers arrive," I said, giving him a look which he wisely ignored, "maybe a month, six weeks. Certainly no more. I'll have a couple of days in Kabul, maybe in Kandahar, too—meeting some of your top brass. Then I'm hoping I'll be able to hitch a ride out to Leatherneck. I'll just have to see how it goes. Maybe I'll see you out there?"

He frowned. "I want you home, safe, Caro."

"Likewise, Sebastian."

We stared at each other, aware we'd reached an impasse.

He shook his head and changed the subject.

"Do you want to take a swim?" he asked suddenly. "I'll be God knows how many miles from the nearest pool out there, and hundreds of fucking miles from the ocean."

"Sure," I said, relieved at the new topic. "And I get to see you in those ridiculously loud board shorts again."

"And you'll wear the bikini?"

"Only if you promise not to punch anyone who looks at me."

"Can't promise that, baby," he said, with a smirk.

～

The time passed too quickly, and it seemed just moments later that we were sitting in the back of a taxi taking us to the airport at Naples, a short drive away.

It felt strange to be traveling in a car again and, much as Sebastian's driving had scared the living daylights out of me, I missed the mean machine—it had been so sexy feeling his hard body through the leather jacket, my thighs clamped around him. I wondered if he'd get his other bike shipped over from Ches's garage. I hoped so. I wanted him to feel that his home was in Long Beach, not a bunch of boxes in San Diego.

I decided to broach the subject.

"Sebastian, when do you think you'll tell Ches about us?"

He turned to look at me, a slight frown on his face.

"I don't know. Why?"

"Well, I just thought I could have all your belongings sent over from the west coast, but it's going to make it tricky to organize if Ches doesn't know about me."

He blinked at me in surprise.

"And there are some beautiful places in upstate New York that we could ride out to on your other bike ... if you want."

A happy smile spread over his face. "You'd do that?"

I was confused by his question. "Of course. Why wouldn't I? You'll need your things when you come home."

I couldn't understand Sebastian's surprise, he was shaking his head and smiling at me.

"Okay. I'll email him tonight," he said with a grin. "He'll be pretty fucking surprised."

I laughed darkly. "Yes, that probably about sums it up—to say the least."

He pulled my face toward his, and kissed me hungrily, ignoring the fact that our driver had a grandstand view in the mirror.

The airport was a small, modern, glass and steel structure with a single runway.

We were separated by security, and I watched anxiously from a distance as Sebastian was questioned and patted down. It wasn't until he was able to persuade them to look at his US Marine ID card, that they finally let him go.

He smiled as he walked over to me. "Guess I have a criminal face or something."

"I could have told you that," I laughed. "I'm just glad they didn't have one of the female security guards or you'd never have gotten away."

He rolled his eyes.

The flight was short, less than two hours and we were back in Geneva, carless, bikeless and sunless.

The city was much cooler than the southern Mediterranean, but I felt colder inside, too. Our time together could now be counted in hours.

We took a taxi to Sebastian's attic-like room, and I hovered by the door as he threw back the shutters, letting the thin, gray, northern light of dusk into the room.

He saw the stricken expression on my face.

"We can check into a hotel, Caro."

"No, this is fine. It's not the room..."

"Don't say it, Caro," he said, softly. "Please, baby. I can't bear it when you look at me like that."

"Sorry," I whispered. I made an effort to pull myself together, for his sake. "So, single bed, huh? That's going to be cozy. We'll have to improvise."

He smiled at me gratefully.

"I just gotta pack up my shit, baby, then we'll go find somewhere to eat, okay?"

"Sure, go ahead. I'll write up my notes and check my messages."

Predictably, I had long emails from both Jenna and Alice begging me to tell them if it was true that: a) I'd met a man, b) I'd actually had sex with him, and c) could it possibly be the hottie in the photograph. Nicole's email was much shorter and so explicit in her demand for information, that I angled my laptop screen away from Sebastian, in case he happened to glance over.

There was also an email from my editor saying that my credentials were on their way and I had a flight booked to Kabul 12 hours after Sebastian. I decided not to tell him, knowing it would give him something else to worry about—or possibly try to delay again, no matter what he said to the contrary. Although I did wonder if he'd perhaps put a word in for me after all, to expedite my papers.

It didn't take Sebastian long to pack, he owned so little. He wouldn't need his civvy clothes or the majority of his books, which were boxed up to be sent back to the U.S., everything else went in his duffel bag.

"You can stay here if you like," he offered, rather apologetically. "It's paid up till the end of the month. The owner is Madame Dubois. Just leave the key with her when you go: she's cool."

"Thank you, I'll do that."

He smiled, glad to be able to do something for me.

"Any interesting emails?"

"All my girlfriends are drooling over your photograph," I said, skating over the news that my editor had been in touch. "They can't quite believe you're real. Neither can I sometimes."

He smirked and pulled me into a hug. "I could prove it to you now if you like," he said, pushing himself lightly into my body.

I didn't answer, but ran my hands across the front of his jeans and squeezed, not very gently. His eyebrows shot up, making me laugh.

"Sex instead of food, Caro?"

"Yes," I said, kissing his neck, "I don't know what's come over me— you must be a bad influence."

He responded with enthusiasm, and I'd gotten as far as stripping off his t-shirt when his damn phone rang. I recognized the ringtone—it was one I wasn't likely to forget—Sebastian's CO. I'd have to have words with that man.

I raised my hands in defeat, and Sebastian scowled as he answered.

"Hunter. Yes, sir. Back in Geneva."

He listened intently for almost two minutes without speaking. I was squirming with curiosity, desperate to know what his CO was telling him, certain it was to do with where he was being sent.

He ended the call with a curt, "Yes, sir," then he looked at me. "Pick up 05:00."

I wrapped my arms around his neck and clung to him.

We stood together, unmoving, needing that closeness for as long as we could.

Eventually, Sebastian kissed my hair.

"Let's go get some food," he said, quietly.

I nodded without speaking.

We stepped out into the evening, and I shivered in the chilly air. Sebastian held my hand and we walked slowly, the mountains behind us silent sentinels of our unspoken misery.

He led me to a small, intimate bistro, where the owner nodded at him familiarly, seemingly surprised to see him with company.

"I come here most days," he said, shrugging slightly.

I'd noticed that his room didn't have anywhere to cook. In fact, he didn't have so much as a kettle. My love lived simply.

I tried to lighten the mood, wanting him to remember our last night together for something other than the crushing pain I felt.

"Hmm, seems to me you need some cooking lessons, Sebastian. When you come home—to Long Beach—we'll have to have some fun with food."

His eyes glinted with mischief.

"Yeah, that would be great! Remember that chocolate sauce you bought that time? That was amazing—and I don't even like chocolate that much. Although it tasted damn fine on you."

"Don't use language like that with me, Sebastian. Chocolate is not something I joke about."

He grinned. "Okay, I get it. How do you feel about peanut butter?"

I wrinkled my nose. "I'll buy some for you: crunchy or smooth?"

"Crunchy," he replied, making the word sound incredibly dirty.

I smiled, happy to see him planning for our future, wishing it could be sooner, wishing things were different.

We didn't linger in the bistro. Even though it wasn't busy, we didn't want to spend our precious hours with anyone else.

Sebastian's room was barely warmer than outside when we climbed that narrow staircase for the last time, and I shivered.

"Cold, baby?"

"A little. Can we turn the heat on?"

He smiled at me. "No heating."

I stared at him in amazement. "None? Not even a space heater?"

He shook his head, amused. "Don't worry, Caro—I'll warm you up."

Oh well, who needed space heaters when hot Sebastian Hunter was an option?

I brushed my teeth in the chilly bathroom, and leapt into the narrow bed, still wearing my t-shirt and panties.

Sebastian was far hardier, strolling into the bedroom naked.

I feasted my eyes, trying to fix the image in my mind, and had to restrain myself from whipping out my camera for a more permanent memento. I reminded myself that I had many photographs to treasure from the last few days: pictures and memories, good memories.

He slipped in next to me, wrapping his body around mine.

"You know, Sebastian, while I really enjoyed the floor show, you'll have to wear more clothes at home."

He frowned. "Why?"

"Because," I smiled, "I live in a bungalow—and I have elderly neighbors. We have elderly neighbors, and I don't want you giving them a heart attack."

"Okay, boss," he smirked.

On the other hand, it would be a shame to miss out on that every night. Hell, I could buy thicker drapes.

He pulled me against his body and kissed me slowly, deeply and seriously. And then we made love, again and again, unwilling to waste a single second where our bodies were not intimately connected.

Sebastian moved inside me slowly, filling me inch by inch, rolling his hips, so I could feel him in every part of my core. Then he rolled onto his back, pulling me with him. He laid his hands flat on my belly as I arched up over him.

I placed my hands over his.

"Can you feel yourself inside me?"

"Yes," he said, with a smile, "I can."

We both remembered that I'd said those words to him the very first time we'd made love, when his eyes had been as wide with innocence, as they were now, with experience.

Too soon the night was over.

It was still dark when the alarm summoned him. Sebastian had left it as late as possible, needing every last minute with me, just as I needed him. I insisted on getting up and showering with him, sliding my hands over his body for one last time.

Then I watched him dress, and my lover became the soldier, pulling on his desert khaki utility uniform. It was the first time I'd seen him in the clothing he'd wear in combat. I wanted to scream and cry and cling to him and beg him not to go. I did none of those things. I pulled him to me, kissed him again and again, told him how much I loved him, again and again.

"*Tesoro*, go with my love, but take this with you. It's just silly, but I've always carried it with me when I leave home—but now I have your ring to wear."

I handed him a tiny pebble of polished quartz.

"I found it the first time I went to Long Beach."

He closed his eyes and kissed my hair.

"I've never had something to come back to before, Caro. Don't worry about me—just take care of yourself."

He kissed the little pebble and slipped it into his pocket.

"I love you, *tesoro*. Stay safe for me."

A car horn sounded in the street below us.

"Time to go, baby. Love you."

I watched from the window as he tossed his duffel bag into the car that waited for him. For a second he stared up at me, smiled, and then he was gone.

CHAPTER TWELVE

I WATCHED AS HIS CAR DISAPPEARED INTO THE DAWN, AND THE emptiness I felt inside spilled out around me. I lay in Sebastian's bed, drinking in the scent of sheets that still smelled of him, stretching my hands into the cold void where he had slept, and cried myself into an exhausted stupor.

He had gone: when and where we would meet again was out of our hands. I hoped desperately, of course, that I would see him in Afghanistan, but beyond that, a long six months apart seemed more likely. I tried to tell myself that we'd weathered ten years. What was another few months?

With the sun rising higher in the cool, gray sky, I forced my eyes to open and stare around the empty room. My throat hurt from crying, and the skin on my face felt stiff from salty tears. Tough. Get on with it. Do your job and do it well.

Despite my mental ass-kicking, Sebastian's small shaving mirror offered a view of red, puffy eyes, lined with dark rings. I was glad he couldn't see how ghastly I looked. I wondered where he was now. Probably on his way to some military airfield in Germany, before being cooped up in an uncomfortable C5 troop transporter airplane with perhaps as many as 200 other soldiers, for six or seven hours.

Sebastian's possessions were piled into two boxes, ready for shipping stateside. I opened one, and placed inside the beautiful evening dress and matching shoes, silvery-gray underwear, and miniskirt that he'd bought for me. The leather ballerina flats I left out to take with me.

I laid out the rest of my clothes and equipment on the bed, checking and re-packing it for departure. I had kept hidden my own set of body armor from Sebastian. We'd both colluded in the illusion that our work was nothing to worry about, nothing to fear—a walk in the park. Hiding evidence of the lie had made it easier.

I'd acquired the body armor after my first visit to Sudan, when I discovered that the standard issue didn't fit someone who wasn't a six foot three, two-hundred pound soldier. After two weeks of wearing ill-fitting equipment day and night, I had backache that felt terminal, abs that would have thrilled a bodybuilder, and no boobs to speak of. My custom fit equipment was slightly smaller, but only a little less heavy. It was blue, to distinguish me from the military, although that was a double-edged sword: I wouldn't be shot as a soldier or a spy, but sometimes journalists and nonmilitary personnel were targeted as the more valuable kill. Even insurgents knew the value of PR.

The rest of my things were, perhaps, a little eccentric, but based on experience of several previous assignments to hostile environments. When working within US military zones, I always included Copenhagen Black tobacco as a gift for the soldiers who'd be assigned to babysit me. I'd learned that many of the men, especially those from the south, appreciated that little piece of home. I also carried garlic tablets, as one of the best means of avoiding insect and mosquito bites, and several packs of gum to counter the remedy. I had a pair of flip-flops, which were useful for crunching across floors where cockroaches had the run of the place in the night, a large sarong that could double as a towel, lightweight sheet, sleeping bag or mosquito net, and a knee-length man's shirt that I wore in Muslim countries, to provide some modesty over skimpy t-shirts. I'd tried wearing a burka but found I couldn't run in one, and somehow, it seemed more disrespectful to the local customs than simply showing that I understood their culture by covering up. I always carried a black headscarf: useful across the spectrum, from Catholic churches in Portugal, to bazaars in Baghdad.

Dry shampoo was a luxury as far as my male colleagues were concerned, but for me, it made the difference between feeling revoltingly and disgustingly dirty when there was no chance to shower for several days, and just a little less grubby. And thank heaven for whoever had invented baby-wipes. One other essential nonessential was a humble bottle of *tamari* soy sauce. People laughed at me when I produced my small bottle, but by the time they'd had MREs ration packs, three times a day for two weeks, the flavor my soy sauce could add, made me the most popular person around. Mango chutney was also a favorite.

I also carried lavender oil, earplugs, an eye-mask, and a thin, inflatable mattress given to me by a US Army captain whom I kissed when I realized how comfortable it was. Which wasn't something I'd be telling Sebastian about. His jealous streak was only ever a heartbeat away, and I had to remember that. I didn't like to see that side of him, but damn, it made me feel wanted.

I tried to keep my mind on the job—thinking about him would have me in tears again.

I checked my first aid supplies: dehydration tablets were important, but one of the most useful things for a woman, was a Mooncup, for those awkward times when sanitary napkins and tampons were impossible to find. I usually carried condoms with me, too. I'd never needed to use them, but I'd given them out to colleagues on a fairly regular basis. I'd been planning to buy some in Geneva while I was waiting for my permits to come through, but I'd met Sebastian first. Funny the way things worked out.

I also kept photocopies of my passport and Press ID badge, and would print out a dozen copies of my new credentials when I arrived at the airport. I kept JPEGs of important documents, which I emailed to a secret account that only I could access.

There was one more important job to do.

I booted up my laptop and emailed all the photographs of Sebastian to the same private account, then deleted everything from my camera, memory stick, laptop and phone. I couldn't risk anyone seeing them and identifying him as a US Marine. I was sorely tempted to keep one photo to look at, but it wasn't worth the risk, for either of us.

The tears began again as, one-by-one, those photographs that recorded our all too few days of happiness were wiped from my camera's memory. I knew Sebastian didn't have a photograph of me either. All he had was my stupid little pebble. Suddenly that seemed terribly important and I was glad I'd given it to him.

I stared at my beautiful engagement ring, then pulled it off my finger, placing it on a thin, gold chain around my neck, where I could imagine it was near to my heart.

I followed Sebastian's instructions for having his belongings shipped home, and then returned his door-key to a confused, elderly woman who answered the bell at his landlady's apartment.

I smiled and explained that *Monsieur* Hunter had left. She kept asking me if he'd gone back to America and, in the end, it seemed the easiest explanation to give her. I don't know who she thought I was, but she shook my hand and kissed me on both cheeks.

My taxi dropped me at the airport ninety minutes before my flight. From Geneva, I'd fly to Frankfurt and then pick up a charter to Kabul with a Turkish airline. There were a few commercial flights to Afghanistan, and I expected that I'd either be seated with NATO servicemen and women, or private contractors, engineers, doctors and builders, who were trying to help put the poor, broken country together again, plus a few Afghans, bravely returning home.

By the time we touched down to land in Afghanistan, I'd been traveling for nearly 18 hours. I'd slept a little on the plane overnight, but I was exhausted, although keyed up and excited as well.

My first sight of Kabul showed a sprawling, thriving city, squatting at the bottom of the Koh Daman Mountains of the Hindu Kush. Many of the ugly, boxy homes that had begun to creep up into the foothills were made from the same dusty yellow as the soil itself.

It was a city of contrasts where ancient palaces stood next to a few modest skyscrapers, small mud houses snuggled next to gaudy compounds, narrow alleys led out to wide, modern roads thronged with vehicles of every brand, age, and stage of decay, and modern opulence walked side by side with biblical poverty.

Men with Rolex watches had their Mercedes washed by children who had no shoes. International aid had flooded the desperately poor country with money, but the distribution left much to be desired, and it was whispered that billions of aid dollars had flowed out of the country into private numbered accounts in Swiss banks.

The streets were full of people going about their business: women in blue headscarves, men in a mixture of traditional robes and western clothing. Cars coughed fumes into the hot, dry air, and motorcycles with carpets for seats roared around, ignored by the donkeys pulling carts, and herds of goats that seemed to roam freely. The ever-present sound of people talking, arguing and selling their wares poured from rows of dimly-lit doorways.

But everywhere were signs of war: bomb-blasted buildings, walls with bullet holes, and ugly, burned out patches where cars had been used as weapons, exploding to shower hot fragments of metal over anyone who had been too close.

The bulletproof car that collected me from the heavily guarded airport now dropped me in a secure parking compound at the Mustafa Hotel. I was escorted inside by a burly Marine sergeant who answered to the name of Benson. I didn't know if that was his first name or last, but his comfortable bulk made me feel safer.

The hotel was a favorite with correspondents, as was the owner, a regular Mr. Fix-it. And, even better, I'd heard from Liz before I'd left Geneva: she was still in Kabul, waiting on a ride out to Camp Bastion to report on how British troops were training the Afghan National Army, with a view to a complete handover by 2014. There were few who didn't think 'the sooner the better', but it was hard to see how the country would ever be ready to rule itself. Perhaps democracy didn't suit a land where decisions were traditionally made at a tribal level. But I was there to report, not have an opinion or look for solutions —thank God.

Liz had sent me a message saying that she'd happily share her twin-bed room at the Mustafa Hotel, which was perfect. There was safety in numbers, especially for women traveling alone. She'd also ensured that the room was not on the ground floor (too unsafe, for obvious reasons), and no higher than the third floor, as the fire escapes in Kabul were notorious for their shoddy construction.

I checked in, and was then escorted to my room by a cheerful boy in dirty white robes whose only English seemed to consist of 'Hello', 'yes' and 'jolly good'. I suspected Liz had taught him the latter phrase.

The room was eye-wateringly colorful, decorated in a discordant array of oranges, yellows and reds. But it was comfortable and reasonably clean. Better still, it had its own bathroom. A luxury I'd be doing without once I was at Leatherneck.

I was grateful to drop the heavy bags and read the note that Liz had left. She informed me that we'd been invited to a dinner party being held by the UN for local military, Press, and important Afghan government officials. It was taking place at the Intercontinental Hotel —and I had 40 minutes to get my 'arse' over there.

So much for having a rest.

The shower sputtered intermittently, but it was nearly hot, and washed away most of the yellow dust that seemed to coat every part of me.

Formal functions in some Muslim countries could be a cultural minefield. Since this dinner was including women, it wasn't going to be truly orthodox, so I wasn't too worried about what to wear. I had my tried and trusted black cocktail dress, and planned to match it with the black ballerina flats that Sebastian bought for me. My ring was on the necklace hidden beneath my dress, but I could feel it, and that was important.

The dress had long sleeves, a high neckline, and a knee-length skirt. It passed in more conservative circles, and Liz had thoughtfully informed me that there would be a number of Muslim guests tonight. And although they were likely to be of the more liberal persuasion as women would be present, I didn't want to risk giving offense. I had my plain, black headscarf in my purse to cover all eventualities.

It was lucky I was dark haired and dark eyed, because once I'd donned my headscarf, I attracted little interest. If I'd been blonde haired and blue eyed, it would have been a very different story. As soon as my sweet Sergeant Benson escorted me to the Intercontinental, I went to the restroom to take off my headscarf and brush out my hair.

My attention was caught by a stunning woman in a jade-green, designer gown, with plunging neckline and exposed back. She would have been perfect for a glitzy LA premiere, but here she was jaw-dropping—and not in a good way.

I suspected she was with the UN—certainly no journalist would be so ridiculously overexposed and underprepared, and I was surprised that no one had warned her to dress more appropriately. In the spirit of sisterhood, I decided to give her a heads-up.

"Excuse me, hi. My name is Lee Venzi, I'm with the Press. Forgive me, your dress is really beautiful, but it might give you some problems here tonight: for Muslims, green is Mohammed's favorite color—they might find your choice, as a Western woman, disrespectful. And a more ... conservative style usually goes down better."

"Oh, I never bother with formalities like that," she sneered, rolling her eyes up and down my simple, black dress with obvious contempt.

I was left speechless by her arrogant attitude. I seriously considered jamming her head under the faucet to see if her heavy mascara really was waterproof.

She left me standing, and turned to her friend who was applying an indecent amount of lipstick, although at least her dress was more respectful and less revealing.

"You're dressed to impress, Natalie," said the second woman, in a heavy, German accent. She gave her friend's designer gown the same visual appraisal as my own, but with less honesty. "I wonder if I can guess who you have your eye on—seeing as you mentioned you'd bumped into him again."

The woman named Natalie smiled coolly.

"What can I say, Hanna? He's a five-star fuck: stamina and expertise, with fabulous packaging. Paris was memorable. I'm planning on having another night to remember. Who'd have thought Kabul could be so entertaining."

I followed the two women out of the restroom, shaking my head.

"What a bitch!" I muttered to myself.

"You don't know how right you are," said a familiar voice.

I whirled around, beyond thrilled.

He looked dashing and so handsome in his Dress Blues, my heart leapt with joy, reveling in the fact that he was here, that I was here—that we were together so much sooner than either of us could have hoped.

"Sebastian! What are you doing here? I thought they were sending you to Kandahar?"

"Change of plan," he said, his eyes dancing with happiness. "I've had a two-day stopover and I'd heard the Press would be here tonight, so I wangled an invite. I wasn't sure when you were arriving." He grinned at me wickedly. "But now that you're here, I'm planning on seducing you behind the potted palms."

"Or somewhere a little more private, I hope," I breathed out.

His eyes flared with excitement. "Yes, ma'am."

"By the way, do you know her?" I asked, jerking my head in the general direction of the rude woman.

He smirked. "Her name is Natalie Arnaud. French. She's a PA for some guy at the UN; she likes people to think she's important."

"And you know her because...?"

He didn't answer, looking away.

"One of your Parisian conquests."

'He's a five-star fuck.' Oh no.

"It was just a warm body, Caro," he said, correctly reading the expression on my face.

"I understand that," *sort of*, "but she's going to get herself into trouble. She's only dressing like that to impress you, Sebastian, so you'd better speak to her."

I felt proud of myself for taking the moral high ground. Sebastian scowled at me, clearly unhappy with the mission I'd just given him.

"Suck it up, Hunter," I smirked at him. "You could say that you created this situation, so you have to deal with it. And then find somewhere private for us."

He shook his head in irritation at my insistence he deal with the woman, but smiled and threw me a cocky salute.

"Yes, boss."

Then his smile faded and his eyes darkened in a way that made me long to run my hands over his strong body, and push my tongue between his soft, sensual lips.

I knew he was on the same page, because he glanced around, took my hand and tugged me down the corridor. We were clearly in the staff area of the hotel, because we passed several cramped rooms full of desks and crammed with filing cabinets.

But when Sebastian found an empty office that was larger than a closet, he pushed me inside, slammed me against the door, and kissed me roughly, the buttons of his uniform pressing painfully into my breasts.

His hand was under my dress, dragging the skirt up to my waist, his fingers circling the edge of my panties, and then he ran one long finger under the material and inside me, making me cry out.

"Fuck, you're wet," he hissed.

I moaned in reply.

"I am so fucking hard right now," he growled into my ear. "Here and now: yes or no, Caro?"

"Yes!"

He unzipped his fly quickly, rolling a condom over his erection, while I shimmied out of my panties.

"Bend over the desk," he ordered, as he gripped my hips.

"Sebastian, the door!"

"Fuck," he snarled, spinning around and wedging a chair against the handle.

I leaned over the desk, completely aroused by the unexpected and illicit nature of the moment.

He hauled my dress up over my ass, forced my feet apart with his, and plunged inside me. I heard his breath hiss out through his teeth. He pulled out slowly, then pushed back in, making me feel every inch of him.

He angled his body and rolled his hips, making me clutch hold of the edge of the desk. My insides quivered in response, and I could hear his soft grunts as he continued to thrust deeply.

I pushed my hips backward to meet him and he groaned loudly, picking up the pace and pounding into me frantically, almost desperate in his desire and need.

I couldn't take any more—I thought my legs were going to buckle when I came—but he didn't stop, pounding on and on and on, in a way that would leave bruises across my hip bones from the wooden desk.

I felt his body shudder and empty into me, and his chest rested on my back for a brief moment before he pulled out. I sank to my knees, and collapsed onto the floor. He lay down next to me, his breath hot on my neck. I twisted around to gaze into his eyes, softly brushing the tips of my fingers over his face.

I didn't need to ask why he'd fucked me like that, with such desperation: it was an adrenaline rush—the heightened sense of awareness that came from being in a war zone and close to death. It was an intense need to prove that you were still alive, to reaffirm life.

"Fuck, that wasn't enough, Caro. I want you again."

"We can't, Sebastian," I panted. "As it is, we'll be missed if we don't hurry."

He frowned unhappily and tugged my limp hand to his lips, sucking my fingers, one by one.

"I need you, Caro. Let me come to your room tonight, please, baby."

"You can't, I'm sharing with Liz."

"Get rid of her!" he whispered, persuasively into my ear.

Suddenly someone rattled the door handle, and I could hear men's voices outside.

"Fuck it," he hissed, tucking himself in quickly.

"My panties," I said, feeling panicky.

Sebastian grinned at me, and searched around until he found them hanging disconsolately from a handle on the desk drawer like the flag of a defeated army.

"I think these are yours, ma'am."

"Thank you," I said, hurriedly pulling them on and straightening my skirt.

The door handle rattled again, and I held my breath, but the voices receded into the distance, arguing with each other.

Sebastian helped me up, and listened intently at the door. He hesitated, glancing back at me, then opened it cautiously.

"You're good to go," he said, quietly, his eyes searching the corridor in both directions.

I raised an eyebrow. "You're not so bad yourself, Sarge."

He grinned wickedly. "Later?"

But then we heard more voices coming toward us, I smiled once, and hurried away.

He let me go first, and I made my way into the reception area, where people who'd been invited to the dinner were circulating.

I was concentrating on calming my breathing when I heard someone say my name.

"Hello, Caroline."

I recognized that voice. And only one person called me 'Caroline'.

A cold shiver ran down my spine, and I turned slowly.

My ex-husband stood in front of me, a stiff smile on his face. He looked handsome, in a silver fox sort of way.

"Hello, David," I said warily, as feelings of dislike and distrust swept over me.

"I heard you were here tonight: the famous war correspondent 'Lee Venzi', as you're known now."

I listened out for the sarcasm in his words, but I wasn't certain I could hear any. How odd.

"I see you've been promoted, Captain Wilson," I replied, keeping my voice neutral. "Congratulations, David."

He looked pleased and surprised. "Thank you."

Meeting one's ex-husband was never going to be a Kodak moment, but this was perhaps more than usually awkward, bearing in mind my cheeks were still flushed from screwing Sebastian in an office about 40 yards away.

But David's next comment took me by complete surprise.

"I've enjoyed reading your articles, Caroline. They show great insight."

He gestured around him to indicate all things military. Compliments from David were rare. Very rare.

"Thank you very much," I said, as my eyebrows rose up to my hairline. "I'm ... flattered."

I thought David was going to say something else, but what he saw over my shoulder made him lose his composure, and a familiar expression of haughty disdain transformed his features.

"I see you're still with him," he said, coldly.

I knew immediately who he was talking about, of course.

"I must say I'm surprised, Caroline."

I felt the heat of Sebastian's furious glare as he came storming over.

Military protocol demanded that he salute a superior officer, even one from another service, and David was Navy, not the Marine Corps. Instead, Sebastian shoved his hands in his pockets with deliberate insolence.

David frowned, but just when I was sure he would insist on his dues, he simply ignored Sebastian and looked back at me.

"Good to see you, Caroline. You look lovely tonight. I hope you enjoy the evening."

And he strolled away, greeting a few people as he moved through the room.

"What the fuck were you doing talking to that asshole?" snarled Sebastian.

"What are *you* doing making it so damned obvious that you care?" I shot back angrily.

"Why aren't you wearing your ring?" he asked, sounding hurt.

I guess he'd been too busy fucking me over a desk to notice before.

"I am wearing it—just not where anyone can see it. But right now I am so furious with you: all you've done is make it absolutely necessary for me to go to my ex-husband and beg him not to tell anyone about us. Have you any idea how that makes me feel, Sebastian? Do you? Because he's the last person I'd want to ask a favor from."

"I'll handle him," said Sebastian, arrogantly. "I'll..."

"You'll do nothing," I hissed. "Absolutely nothing, do you hear me? Now leave me alone. You've already attracted enough attention tonight."

I walked away, leaving him standing, his expression wounded, angry and defiant.

I forced myself to smile politely as I moved through the crowd, but inside I was fuming: Sebastian wasn't particularly risking his own career, but he was damn well risking mine—again. Who the hell did he think he was?

I made myself concentrate. I was here to meet the unit commander that I'd be embedded with, a Captain Ryan Grant. In all likelihood he'd resent having a journalist assigned to him. As far as he'd be concerned, having some hack looking over his shoulder when he was trying to do his job was nothing more than an irritating, additional worry. I just hoped he'd behave with polite tolerance rather than make my position more difficult. At least I knew that someone senior to him had made the decision to give me access, which meant I shouldn't have a problem with open hostility. I hoped.

I'd been informed that I'd be seated next to him at dinner. I could wait until then for introductions.

First, thanks to Sebastian's ridiculous territorial display, I had to go and grovel to David. I hated the fact that he'd handed David the power to ruin my career with a few, quiet words in the right ear.

My former husband was standing talking to an Army Major when I walked up.

"Hello, again," I said, blandly.

He blinked, looking surprised, then politely introduced me. I was taken aback when he used my professional name: that was decent of him.

We chatted casually for a few minutes, before the Major was claimed by a colleague and moved away.

"David," I said, taking a deep breath, "I won't insult your intelligence. I'm here to ask you not to reveal what you know about me and Master Sergeant Hunter."

He raised his eyebrows.

"It was certainly a surprise, Caroline, but no, of course I wouldn't dream of saying anything that could hurt your career."

I was shocked he was being so magnanimous. I'd expected that he'd take the chance to belittle me. He'd been an expert at it while we were married.

"Thank you, David. That's very good of you."

"I would suggest, however," he said, calmly, "that you advise him to act with more circumspection."

"Yes. I've already mentioned it," I said, a little bitterly.

He gave a thin smile.

"He seems just as hotheaded as ever."

Yes, you could say that.

"You were taking a great risk, continuing your relationship," he couldn't help adding. "But despite what you may think of me, Caroline, I have never wished you ill."

I met his eyes, but saw only sincere concern.

"Thank you for that," I said, with more warmth than I thought I'd ever feel for him. "I will try to minimize any more … risk."

He cocked his head to one side and looked at me quizzically.

"I meant it was a risk to continue seeing each other when he was … well, younger."

I stared at him, finally realizing what he was alluding to.

"David, that's not it. I haven't seen Sebastian for ten years. We met again by accident, eleven days ago in Geneva."

He looked dumbstruck. "But I thought … the way he behaved just now … well, I see I was mistaken."

At which point an announcement was made in English, French and Pashto to call us in to dinner.

"I do wish you well, Caroline," he said, briskly. "And I meant what I said: you look lovely tonight."

He smiled briefly, and then offered his arm to escort me in to dinner.

I accepted, baffled by his pleasantness and consideration.

He helped me into my seat, then with a half-smile, disappeared toward his place at another table.

CHAPTER THIRTEEN

I SAT AT ONE OF THE LONG BANQUETING TABLES IN A STATE OF MILD shock. I had never known David to be so considerate, especially when it was anything concerning me. During our 11 years of marriage, he'd been a domineering bully and ... no, 'domineering bully' said it all. Since the divorce, I'd had nothing to do with him, I certainly hadn't known he'd be in Afghanistan. Maybe he was working at the hospital at Bagram Air Base north of Kabul.

My attention was diverted when I noticed that the woman in green had swooped into the room and was eyeing the place cards. I had a strong suspicion that if I kept watching her, I'd see her swapping them around. Well, that was Sebastian's lookout, I doubted he'd have too many problems with her—I was pretty certain he'd had plenty of practice dealing with overly friendly women. I tried to brush the thought away—I had other, more important issues to concentrate on tonight.

"Excuse me, ma'am, I think you might be in the wrong seat."

I looked up to see a man in the Dress Blues of a US Marine Corps captain gazing down at me. He was perhaps a few years younger than me with a strong face, and clear, gray eyes.

"Captain Grant?"

"That's right, ma'am," he said, looking puzzled. "And you are?"

"Lee Venzi. I'll be embedded with you for the next month. It's good to meet you."

He looked bemused. "*You're* Lee Venzi?"

"Let me guess," I said, with a polite smile, "you were expecting a man. I get that a lot."

He gaped, looked thoroughly pissed off, then settled for a cool disinterest.

"It's a pleasure to meet you, ma'am."

We shook hands as he eyed me cautiously.

Don't worry: I won't bite—you're not my type.

"Please don't be concerned, Captain Grant. This is not my first time being embedded with US troops, and I don't expect any level of comfort beyond that of the average private. I will try to impact on your command as little as possible. I would suggest we meet soon to discuss protocols for the next month. I'm not here to do a hatchet job, Captain."

"Then you'll let me read what you write before it's filed?"

"That's one of the protocols we can discuss, but no, my editor is the only person who sees my work prior to publication."

It was important to explain up front how I worked. I didn't particularly want to do that over the dinner table, but as he'd asked, I'd give him the courtesy of a clear and concise answer.

A reluctant smile crept across his face.

"Something to discuss, ma'am."

"Certainly there will be many things to discuss, Captain," I said, politely. "I have agreed to the rules of being embedded with your unit, but beyond that, my authorial independence will not be something we discuss."

He raised his eyebrows but wisely didn't pursue the point.

From the corner of my eye, I saw Sebastian enter the room and move toward a group of Afghan men dressed in the traditional *salwar kameez*, worn with the oval *qaraqul* hats. He exchanged some pleasantries, then went to search for his place card. He looked puzzled because it wasn't in the general area that he'd expected. When he saw the Green Bitch, comprehension washed over him and he looked pissed.

I couldn't help feeling a mean little frisson of self-righteousness.

Your problem, Hunter.

He seated himself politely next to the French woman, who looked like she wanted to perform a lap dance before the antipasti.

At first, he seemed to shrug off her advances, but then I saw her lay a discreet hand on his thigh, and my blood boiled.

"Lee! Are you stalking me, woman?"

Liz's dulcet tones turned heads and I couldn't help smiling, more than a little grateful for her timely interruption of my silent fuming.

She was wearing an ankle-length dress in navy blue, so voluminous, that she looked like a ship in full sail.

"Hi, Liz. Thanks for the room-share. Let me introduce you to Captain Ryan Grant; Captain, Elizabeth Ashton—she's a correspondent for *The Times* of London."

They shook hands, each weighing up the other.

"Have you seen that miserable bastard Hunter is here?" Liz said to me, as soon as the brief pleasantries were over. "Up to his old tricks with the French floozie."

I winced, and saw Captain Grant frown.

"Yes, there are a few familiar faces, Liz. Stroud and Van Marten are here."

"Really? I must go and chew on their earflaps for a minute, Lee. I'll see you later. Captain," and she hurried off.

"A colleague of yours, ma'am?"

"Yes, and a friend."

I could see that Captain Grant was beginning to be grateful that it was me and not Liz who was going to be embedded with him. But then his eyes flickered back to Sebastian, who was staring coldly at his dinner companion. When she laid a proprietary hand on his arm and leaned across to touch one of his medals, Captain Grant's eyes narrowed.

"Excuse me, ma'am," he muttered.

He stood up abruptly and walked toward them. Sebastian rose to his feet and saluted sharply. It was clear the Captain was asking about the seating arrangements, and Sebastian was trying to point out he'd just followed the place card's instructions.

I watched as Captain Grant took him to one side and seemed to be giving him a dressing down. Sebastian stood to attention, and I could see that he was gazing about three inches above the Captain's left shoulder.

After that, Sebastian left the room, leaving the disappointed woman by herself, and Captain Grant returned to my side.

"Is there a problem, Captain?" I asked, casually.

"No, ma'am, just my interpreter, he'd been seated at the wrong table."

"*Your* interpreter," I said, feeling a shiver travel down my spine.

"Yes, newly assigned to my command."

Oh crap.

"I gather you know him, ma'am?" he said, looking at me astutely.

"We've met," I said, maintaining a casual smile. "Master Sergeant Hunter was the languages expert when I had my hostile environment briefing in Geneva. He lectured on useful phrases in Pashto, Dari and Arabic if I remember correctly."

Captain Grant nodded, accepting my words at face value, and we talked about the forthcoming deployment to Leatherneck and beyond.

I didn't see Sebastian again during the meal, and the Green Bitch had an empty space next to her for the entire time. I also noted that someone must have spoken to her, because she now wore a black pashmina that covered up her cleavage and shoulders for the rest of the evening.

It was fascinating to see who had been invited to the dinner and who had not. There were a number of UN officials that I recognized, as well as British, German, and American officers. Among the Afghan men—and there were no women—I sensed there was something more going on than a simple meet and greet. I kept track of the comings and goings, who was talking to whom. There was definitely excitement in the air.

The evening ended without any more tangible developments occurring. Captain Grant nodded politely and said he'd send a driver to my hotel at 5AM the following morning. We'd be loading up and heading out to Camp Leatherneck, 350 miles away along the notorious Kabul–Kandahar Highway.

Two decades of war and neglect had left the road connecting Afghanistan's two main cities in disrepair. The US had funded the rebuilding of three-quarters of the road, with Japan chipping in another chunk of money. It was currently in slightly better repair, but it had become a favorite target of the Taliban—and not a journey to be undertaken lightly, even by the mighty US armed forces. Certainly not by a woman-journalist from Long Beach.

I waited in the lobby for Liz, and when she finally emerged, she was fizzing with excitement. She eyed our driver, the same bulky Sergeant Benson who'd dropped me off at the start of the evening, before allowing him to escort us to our car. She grabbed my elbow and began whispering at top speed.

"I picked up some very interesting snippets, Lee. Something is definitely in the air."

"Yes, I thought so, too. Azimi was talking to Chalabi, and you don't often see Sunnis and Shiites being that friendly."

Liz raised her eyebrows. "Interesting! Well, I'd say, looking at the bigwigs there tonight, it's a US op. Could be going down from Leatherneck, Lee. Keep your ear to the ground for me, will you?"

"You think I'd hand you a scoop?" I asked, teasing her.

"No, of course not, but I'm sure you won't leave your old mucker out in the cold, either."

"I'll take it under advisement."

"Huh, bloody colonials," she snorted.

I laughed. To Liz, half the population of the world were 'colonials'.

We drove quickly through the busy streets, people hurrying home before the night-time curfew.

Back at the hotel, Liz tried to persuade me to have a drink with her in the bar. She'd heard that someone had gotten hold of alcohol from the local market. Apparently the blanket ban wasn't taken too seriously by some of the locals despite the Sharia law, although punishment for those who bought, sold or consumed the evil brew could be a fine, imprisonment, or even 60 lashes with a whip.

"Come down with me, Lee, it should be a laugh. After I get out of this god-awful frock," she said, tugging on the hem of her blue tent.

"No, thanks, Liz. I'm going to take a hot bath. Since it'll be my last for a month, I want to enjoy soaking in an actual tub."

Liz had just changed out of her dress and into her usual Berghaus hiking pants and long-sleeved shirt, when there was a soft tap at the door.

We were immediately on the alert: it was a golden rule never to let anyone know which room you were staying in. If you needed to meet a contact, you met them in the lobby. Journalists were deemed to be easy targets—and our bodyguard was long gone.

"Who knows you're here?" Liz hissed at me.

"My embed liaison and my editor. You?"

"Same. Stay away from the door and get ready to phone for help."

I picked up my cell, checking that I had Sergeant Benson on speed dial. I nodded at her, my finger poised over the button, and she called out aggressively,

"Yes?"

"Ma'am, I'm looking for Lee Venzi?"

I recognized Sebastian's voice at once, relief, lust and irritation each took their turn as I moved toward the door.

"What are you doing?" Liz whispered, grabbing my arm.

"It's okay, I know who it is."

She relaxed a fraction, but still hung onto my arm.

"Is this a romantic assignation, Lee?" she said, with surprise and some annoyance.

"Kind of," I muttered, "although I didn't know he'd come here tonight. It wasn't planned. I'm sorry, Liz."

"This really isn't like you," she said, frowning.

"I know," I said, apologetically.

I pulled open the door, and Sebastian quickly stepped into the room.

Liz's face was a picture.

"Sebastian, you've met my friend Liz Ashton."

"Yes," he said, stiffly.

"Sergeant Hunter," replied Liz, glaring at him with obvious dislike.

I rubbed my forehead.

"I'm sorry about this, Liz, but can you give us some time alone?"

She snorted and shook her head, muttering something that sounded like, "bloody fool".

I presumed she meant me, although her words fit Sebastian just as well. I had a few choice words of my own to say to Master Sergeant Hunter.

"Two hours, Lee," she said, glancing at her watch with zero subtlety. "I'll be downstairs in the bar if you need me."

She threw a final, accusing look at Sebastian and left.

I was still deciding what to say to him as I shut and locked the door, but before I could speak, he tugged me into his arms and kissed me.

His tongue was in my mouth and his hands pressing into my flesh, chasing all thoughts but one from my overheated brain.

When he finally let go, I was breathless and aroused—which was probably his plan—but I wasn't letting his outrageous behavior go unchallenged either.

"What the hell are you doing, Sebastian?"

He shrugged and grinned at me. "I thought I'd kiss you before you yelled at me. Guess it didn't work."

"You think this is a joke?" I asked, my voice rising with frustrated disbelief. "First David, now Liz. Why don't you just skywrite it?"

"What did the asshole say to you?"

I sighed. "He's not going to tell anyone—he was really nice about it."

Sebastian scowled.

"Liz won't say anything to anyone either—I'll just have to listen to her chewing me out later. But I'd have much rather she didn't know just now—she's my *work* colleague. You've got to stop taking these risks, Sebastian. For my sake, if you won't do it for yourself."

He grimaced. "I'm sorry, Caro. I just go a little crazy around you."

Not good enough.

"Well, you have to get it under control. Now please, please tell me your assignment to Ryan Grant is temporary."

He stared at me. "Fuck! I was wondering why they'd seated you next to him. Are you embedded with him? Shit!"

"Exactly my thoughts. He can't know, or it'll really screw things up for both of us—well, mainly for me. Sebastian, you're going to have to act like you did in Geneva, as if you still dislike me—or at the very least, ignore me. Can you do that?"

"Fuck, Caro," he sighed. "Yes, I can do it. But I'll hate every fucking minute."

"At least if we're in the same Camp, I'll know what you're doing and that you're safe."

He gave me a small smile.

"Same goes for you. Yeah, there is that. And we might get a chance to hook up?"

I shook my head, even as the image took shape.

"No, too dangerous. You can't risk it and I *definitely* can't risk it. Grant isn't an idiot."

"No, he seems on the ball."

"On the plus side, Grant already thinks you dislike me."

Sebastian frowned. "Because...?"

"Liz—she mentioned that we'd met in Geneva, and at that stage, she still thought you were an ass. Well, that hasn't changed, but just a different sort of ass now."

He gave me a crooked smile.

"An ass?"

"Big time."

He leaned against the door and crossed his arms, his head cocked to one side, a damn sexy smile on his face.

"What happened with your friend Natalie?" I asked, not prepared to let him off the hook just yet.

His smile vanished. "She's no fucking friend. She wouldn't take no for an answer, and then Grant kicked me out because of her."

"What did he say to you?"

Sebastian shifted uncomfortably.

"Oh, well, never mind—I can guess. She didn't look pleased either

—I think she was planning to have you for dessert. Was it you who told her to cover up?"

"Yeah, not that it made any difference."

"She must have listened to someone. At least you tried. And you are *very* trying, Master Sergeant Hunter. Part of me wants to slap some sense into you…"

"And the other part?" he murmured, wetting his lips with his tongue.

"Well," I said, running a finger down the red braid that edged his uniform jacket, "I was wondering what we could do for the next…" I checked my wristwatch, "…115 minutes?"

I thought Sebastian would leap on me but he closed his eyes, as if he was in pain.

"What's the matter, *tesoro?*"

"I really fucking hate this, Caro. We're always running in different directions, we're always running out of time. I just want to wake up with you in my arms every day."

Oh, he could say the most romantic things at the time when I most needed to hear them.

"I know, Sebastian, and I feel the same. But it won't be like that forever—we will be together. We just have to be patient." I stroked his cheek, "And for now, we have 113 minutes left."

His eyes snapped open.

"Fuck!"

Suddenly we were all fumbling, hurried hands, panting into each other's mouths, as Sebastian tried to tear off his uniform and undress me at the same time. I was naked and ready long before him, so I lent a helping hand, which didn't seem to help much.

"Damn it, Caro," he groaned, as I pressed myself against him, feeling the thick material against my heated skin.

He backed me toward my bed, his erection rigid against my thigh. I fell backward and then burst into laughter.

"What?"

"The whole pants around the ankles thing—it's not a great look."

He grinned ruefully as he toed off his shiny shoes.

"Guess I'd better lose the socks, too."

"Definitely."

When every item of clothing had been stripped off, he stood next to the bed and gazed down at me. I didn't feel like laughing now.

"You like what you see, Caro?" he asked, with a low, rough voice.

I nodded, my mouth suddenly dry.

"After tonight, well, we don't know when ... so I want you to remember me like this ... when you look at me—see me like this, wanting you."

And he stroked himself, his eyes half closing as he breathed in deeply.

"And when I look at you, this is what I'll be thinking about: close your eyes."

Reluctantly, I let my eyelids flutter down.

The mattress moved beneath me, and I felt Sebastian's warm hands on my ankles. Slowly, he moved my legs apart, then he kissed his way up to my thigh, and my breath caught in my throat.

He didn't stop, and I didn't want him to stop. I wanted him loving me forever.

Sometime later, we lay in each other's arms, peaceful and blissfully sated.

Suddenly, an enormous explosion erupted outside, rattling the windows of the hotel. Sebastian grabbed me and pulled me onto the floor by the side of the bed, away from the window. He waited for ten seconds, then cautiously rose to his feet, standing to one side of the window to peer out.

"Probably a car bomb—about half a mile away."

I was still shivering on the floor.

"It's okay, Caro. We're okay."

I'm sure we were both thinking the same thing: we were okay, but somewhere out there in the night, people had lost their lives, even now lying on the ground, bleeding into the dust. I wondered if Liz would be off to the site, to report on what had happened. Sometimes it felt important to be on the frontline, telling people back home what was happening in this far away war, but sometimes if felt like we were no better than war pornographers, capturing the misery of other people on film or in photographs, asking them at their most desperate moment to give us a sound bite to file and send home. Job done.

It was a fine line to tread, and not one we always got right. But I still thought that what we did was ultimately worthwhile—I had to.

I stood up hesitantly, naked and feeling exposed.

Usually when I was on assignment in a dangerous location, I wore clothes day and night. You never knew when you might have to evacuate your hotel room in a hurry, when the time it took to put on pants and a t-shirt was going to be the difference between life and death.

But with Sebastian, I broke all the rules.

"Caro, are you okay, baby?"

"Yes, I guess so. Just knowing that out there ... you'll be facing that soon."

He strode over to me.

"Christ, I know that, Caro, and it kills me to know that you'll be out there, too. Please, baby, please, go home while you still can. I'm fucking begging you, Caro!"

He held me tight against his chest, and I could feel his heart hammering as he buried his head in my hair.

"Please, baby. I need to know you're safe. If anything happened to you now..."

My arms crept around his neck, and I pulled his face down to kiss him softly.

"I have a job to do, Sebastian, you know that. So do you, and I will worry about you every day. I pray to God that you'll come home to me. Please, *tesoro*, promise you'll look after yourself—no unnecessary risks?"

He sighed. "I promise, Caro."

"Then come back to bed with me," I said, tugging his hand.

Time was slipping away too fast.

He lay on his back and I snuggled into his arms, one hand on his waist, and my head resting just above his heart, listening to its firm, even rhythm.

I didn't want our last night together to be filled with such sadness.

My fingers drifted over his muscular chest, across his ribs and down to his flat stomach. I pushed the sheet down, exposing his hair and the tip of something even more desirable and arousing.

"Sebastian, if that's what I have to imagine every time you look at me, I'm not going to get any work done."

He smiled and kissed my hand.

"Let's go back to Signora Carello's place for our honeymoon, Caro. We could fuck for days without getting out of bed."

I could tell that he was trying to lighten the mood, too, I was happy to play along with the fantasy.

"What, you think she could just push food under the door so you can keep your strength up, because I have to say, Sebastian, you were getting a little out of breath just now. I really thought the US Marines had higher standards of fitness: I might have to write about that in my next article. Of course, the research is incomplete—I've only documented one Marine's fitness levels in detail..."

"And it's going to stay that way," he said, firmly.

I laughed. "Feeling threatened? Me alone with all those horny Marines, I'm quoting, of course."

"Not funny," he grumbled.

"Okay, I won't tease you. Yes, we could go back to Signora Carello's, but there are lots of other places I'd like to see in Italy. Florence, the open air opera in Rome—I'd love to do that. But you know, I really like the idea of taking your old motorcycle and seeing upstate New York. What do *you* want to do?"

"Other than have a lot of sex?"

"My God! That's exactly the same answer you gave me ten years ago when you were a horny teenager!"

"So? I'm consistent. I thought women liked that in men?"

He had a point.

Lazily, he ran one hand between my breasts, toying with the chain that held my engagement ring.

"You have the most fantastic breasts, Caro. I can't stand those fake ones, they just feel so..."

He realized what he'd said, or nearly said, and stopped abruptly.

"Hmm, I was thinking, Sarge, maybe you should be one of those men who are strong and silent. You know, nice to look at, not so good at the talking."

He playfully bit my shoulder and twisted around, pushing me into the mattress.

"Is that right?"

"Yes. Hearing you talk about your *conquests* when I'm in a state of post-coital bliss isn't going to earn you round two."

"Huh, so I can't *earn* round two—does that mean I can pay for it instead?"

I slapped his ass, hard. "You couldn't afford me."

"You sure about that, baby? What's your price?"

"What have you got to offer, Sebastian?"

He used his hips to pin me down, his chest hovering over mine. "An orgasm?"

"That's just *quid pro quo*."

"Fuck, I love it when you talk dirty. What about two orgasms?"

"Two? Beginning to sound interesting, but do you think you're up to the job?"

One thing about Sebastian: he was always up for a challenge. Up and up.

Over an hour later, we were collapsed on the bathroom floor, flushed and breathless.

"I'd forgotten you had a thing for bathrooms," I gasped.

He kissed the back of my neck. "I like the mirrors."

"You know, that's a little kinky, Sebastian."

"You think? I'd like to get kinky with you, Caro," he said, tugging on my earlobe with his teeth and running his fingers over my hipbone.

The thought was intriguing.

"What did you have in mind?"

I felt him shrug. "You could tie me up again: that was hot."

"Hmm, well, I could talk to one of the MPs at Leatherneck— maybe I'll see if I can borrow a pair of handcuffs, Sebastian."

He didn't answer, so I nudged him in the ribs.

"Yeah, if you like, Caro."

"If *I* like? What do *you* like?"

He hesitated. "There's some stuff we could try."

"Such as?"

There was a soft tap at the door and I heard Liz's voice.

"Oh, hell. You'd better get dressed, Sebastian, unless a three-way with Liz was one of your fantasies?"

He shuddered. "Fuck, Caro! I'm going to have that image in my head now."

I grinned at him. "Better get your pants on then, Sarge."

I pulled on a baggy t-shirt and some pajama bottoms, checked Sebastian was halfway decent, and opened the door.

"Lee, I ... oh, is he still here?"

"He's just leaving, Liz."

Sebastian was sitting on my bed, tying his shoelaces when Liz marched into the room.

"There's a curfew on, Hunter," she said, crossing her arms across her substantial chest.

"Thanks," he said, shortly.

"You must have heard the car bomb: three dead, multiple injured. Bastards packed the bomb with nails."

"So evil," I murmured.

Liz nodded silently, and Sebastian pressed his lips together without speaking.

He stood up, pulled on his jacket and fastened the buckle on his white web belt.

He ignored Liz's chilly gaze and pulled me into a tight hug, leaning his forehead against mine.

"Remember what I said, Sebastian."

"I'll try, baby. And you remember what *I* said, what I'm thinking about when I look at you."

He rested his lips gently on mine.

"Never take my ring off, Caro," he whispered.

"*Ti amo tanto*, Sebastian."

He smiled softly. "*Sempre e per sempre*."

He glanced briefly at Liz, and then quietly left.

Liz closed the door behind him, and looked at me sternly.

"Bloody hell, Lee. You've fallen for him, haven't you? The priapic bastard has lured you into his lair to be one of his foreign territories. How can you be so damn stupid?"

Her words stung, but, to be fair, I could see exactly how it looked from her point of view.

I had two choices: I could say nothing, and leave her with the view that I'd been naïve and duped by a man who was a Casanova in a US Marine uniform, a total player, or I could tell her the truth.

"It's not like that, Liz," I said, rubbing my eyes tiredly.

"Don't give me that bullshit, Lee, you're lucky I'm the only one who knows what's going on. Otherwise, you'd be on the first plane home, and Hunter ... well, I don't know what they'd do to him. Not that he'd care, but it would be your career down the drain. Is that what you want?"

"No, of course not," I snapped.

"Then would you please tell me what the hell is going on, because I've never known you to behave like this—and it's not like you haven't had offers. Why him, Lee? Of all people—he's shagged half the female staff at the UN. Is that what you wanted—just a young stud? What if he tells someone? Bragging about his Kabul conquest?"

She was really building up a head of steam. I had to head her off.

"We're going to get married, Liz, as soon as his tour is over."

Silence.

I waited.

More silence.

"Have you lost your mind, Lee!" she bellowed suddenly, making me jump. "Is this some kind of hormonal surge or midlife crisis? You've let him shag you a few times and you're imagining he'll marry you? You barely know him!"

"I know him better than anyone, Liz. I've known him since he was eight years old."

She gaped at me.

"I think you'd better tell me the whole bloody story, Lee, because otherwise I'll have to assume that one of us is barking mad, and right now my money is on you."

I sighed. I'd never told anyone the full story before—not even my closest friends: guilt, sadness, and a wish to move on with my life had kept me silent.

"Fine. Make yourself comfortable, Liz." I took a deep breath, trying to marshal my thoughts.

"I met my husband, David, when I was 17, and we married a month after my 19th birthday. He was in the Navy, so we moved around. We had six months in San Diego after we'd been married about a year-and-a-half. Sebastian was the son of David's CO. He was a sweet, lonely child—his parents were just monstrous—and we became friends. That's all, I swear it. He used to come by after school and we'd talk about books and listen to opera. Then David was posted to Lejeune and that was that. But nine years later, we were back in San Diego again. Sebastian … found me. He was nearly 18 and God, Liz, he was gorgeous even then. At first, I just thought of him as the kid I used to know, but it soon became obvious that he … had other feelings for me."

Liz was watching me intently, a deep frown of concentration on her face.

"And … one thing led to another. I'd been unhappy in my marriage for a long time. And Sebastian was just so loving. He was sweet and funny—fun to be with. And he encouraged me with my writing: if it hadn't been for him, I don't think I'd ever have become a journalist. Well, his parents found out … and because he wasn't quite 18, it was a felony in California. His parents said they wouldn't prosecute me if I left quietly and didn't come back. The statute of limitations was three years: they threatened me, saying that if we tried to stay in touch, they'd have me arrested. Even if I didn't do jail time, I'd have had a criminal record. So I stayed away."

I paused, trying to scrub away the desolate feelings that thinking about those events always wrought in me.

"But Sebastian waited for me. When he was 21 we tried to find each other, but it never happened. I won't go into the details, but he realized eventually that I wasn't coming for him … and that's when all the drinking and womanizing started. I hadn't seen him for 10 years when we met in Geneva again. He still loves me, Liz. He says he's always loved me—and I love him: desperately. We're engaged and we're going to be married. But no one can know while I'm still out here. No one."

She looked at me steadily and shook her head slowly, a worried expression etched on her face, her eyes kind and concerned.

"Bloody hell! That's quite a story." She shook her head. "You and the beautiful Sergeant Hunter. I hope you know what you're doing, Lee, I really do."

She stood up and paced to the window, then turned to look at me.

"I'll say one thing: if Shakespeare had known you, he wouldn't have had to steal all his plot lines, because that's one hell of a yarn. I hope you're right about him, because the man you're describing is not the one I've seen in action. Take tonight, for example, that French tart was all over him."

"I know," I said, with a small smile. "One of his Parisian conquests. I asked him to tell her to dress more appropriately. It was his fault she was dressed like that. Of course, that was after Sebastian and I had sex in one of the hotel's offices. Over a desk."

She stared at me, then laughed out loud.

"You are extraordinary, Lee, you really are! I thought I knew you. I mean, I knew you were tough on the quiet, but you must have balls of iron—or tits like Exocet missiles. Fine, if that's what you want. Far be it for me to tell you you're making a giant, Hoover dam-size mistake."

She paused.

"Is he as good as they say?"

My jaw dropped and I gaped at her, far, far beyond embarrassed that she'd asked me that question.

"I'll take that as a 'yes'," she said with a wry smile.

I winked, but didn't reply.

CHAPTER FOURTEEN

What would have been a six- or seven-hour journey back home, turned into 15 hours of baking sun, choking dust and gut-churning fear.

The fear was sporadic, triggered every time I saw turbaned men with AK-47 rifles. I was traveling in a heavily armored car that looked more like a tank than anything else, and I was told it had been designed to withstand roadside bombs, but every time I saw the Afghan forces at checkpoints, a chill went through me. Green-on-blue attacks were escalating to the point where each International Security Assistance Force unit had appointed at least one soldier as a 'guardian angel' to act as a lookout—to keep an eye on our Afghan allies.

It had been both unnerving and arousing to see Sebastian armed with his M16 for the first time. He looked so damn hard and kick-ass. I wanted to go and run my teeth down his exposed neck, and then expose a lot more of his body. What the hell was happening to me? I couldn't stop thinking about sex.

I blamed Sebastian.

The convoy I traveled in was well-armed, but I would be relieved to get off this exposed stretch of road, pockmarked with bomb craters, and with blackened carcasses of burnt-out cars strewn at the side.

It was comforting to know that somewhere in the back of the line of trucks and armored vehicles, Liz was traveling with British forces on their way to Bastion. We'd agreed to try and meet up but, as ever, nothing was guaranteed.

Our destination, 50 miles west of Kandahar, housed 28,000

British troops, several thousand Afghan National Army soldiers at Camp Shorabak, and 20,000 US Marines. Altogether, the three sections must have covered nearly 4,000 acres. Leatherneck, by itself, was bigger than many small towns, supported by four gyms, a vast dining area that could serve 4,000 people at a time, three chapels and, best of all as far as many of the troops were concerned, calling centers where they could phone and email their families back home.

The housing arrangements were restrictive, so the two- or three-thousand female soldiers and contractors were kept segregated, not that there was much privacy for anyone, should a romance develop. A fact which didn't go unnoticed by me. In any case, most of the female staff didn't go outside the wire, unless they were needed on a special assignment to speak to Afghan women.

When we finally crawled into Leatherneck, I was allocated a bunk in a tiny room shared by Private First Class Mary Sullivan from Beckville, Texas, a small town, some 150 miles east of Dallas—or so she told me. She was 24 and duly impressed that I worked as a journalist. She was one of a team of 15 women who worked in the motor pool, repairing damaged vehicles—and she was truly envious when she learned that I'd be traveling into the countryside and beyond the wire fence.

She chattered away about her hometown as I unpacked, shrugging off the sadistic body armor, then she showed me the way to the female shower area. A hot shower: what bliss.

It was less blissful when she insisted on continuing to chat while I washed myself. Despite being surrounded by people 24/7, I got the impression she was lonely. And she called me 'ma'am', which made me feel old.

"Do you have a boyfriend, ma'am? I couldn't help noticing you were wearing a ring on that chain around your neck."

"Yes, I do. You?"

"Nah, and it's not so easy to hook up with people here. I only enlisted because I thought I'd meet loads of cute guys, and get a free college education. So, what does your boyfriend do? Is he a reporter, too?"

"No, he's not. I have friends who are reporters—one of them is over at Bastion right now."

"Uh-huh. Where's your boyfriend at?"

She really was tenacious: maybe they taught that in the Marines. Either that or the forces attracted tenacious people.

"I don't really like to talk about him, Mary. It just makes me sad that we're not together."

By this time I was drying myself off, and I could see her eyes widen with interest at my words.

"Oh, my God! You must really love him!"

So not going there.

"You know, I'm surprised, Mary, a nice girl like you—haven't you seen anyone that you think is cute?"

She twisted her dog tags around her fingers, as she thought about my question.

"Yeah, there's this one guy..."

"And?"

"Nothing."

"Why? If you like him, go talk to him. I don't know—offer to change his oil."

She giggled.

"You think I should?"

I shrugged. "It's up to you, but all I can tell you for sure is that life is short. And wouldn't you rather know once and for all if he liked you or not? If he does, great, if he doesn't, it's his loss and you can stop worrying about him."

After that piece of advice, which I was so much better at giving than taking, PFC Sullivan escorted me to the briefing room where I was due to meet Grant and the rest of his officers.

But the first person I saw was Sebastian, looking hot, dusty and pissed. Clearly he hadn't had the luxury of time for a shower and a friendly chat about his love life.

His eyes lit up as he saw me and he started to smile. When he remembered we were trying to be discreet, he dropped his eyes back to the map he was studying.

Luckily, Captain Grant had been focused on the map spread out beneath his hands, so he hadn't noticed Sebastian's slip.

I caught the tail end of Grant's monologue.

"If a guy sticks his head around the corner he could very easily have a gun. If you can't see his hands, he could have something, a hand grenade, say. Pulling a trigger is easy—we need to bring him in. It's not about that one person, it's about the team. I'll need you to go in first and..."

He became aware of my presence and ground to a halt, looking irritated.

"I can come back," I offered, calmly.

"No, that's fine, Ms. Venzi. We're done here."

He nodded to Sebastian, who saluted and left the Nissan hut-type room, throwing me a quick smile as he passed.

"We'll be moving out in the morning, Ms. Venzi," continued Captain Grant. "It's going to get a lot less comfortable—and a lot more dangerous. We'll be heading out to a remote location further north in Helmand. We'll have BGAN satcomms, but I can't guarantee you'll always be able to get your stories out."

"I understand, Captain."

He sighed, and I suspected he'd been hoping I'd change my mind.

We ate our long-delayed evening meal with Lieutenant Crawley, the executive officer, four second lieutenants, and Sebastian. How very cozy.

Sebastian spent most of the meal staring at his food, or gazing into the distance. I could tell that he was irritating the hell out of Grant, who was burdened with the lion's share of trying to make polite conversation with me, although Crawley made a good stab of asking me about my work. My poor *fiancé* was trying hard to ignore me: he wasn't very good at it, and it just made me love him a little bit more.

I was well chaperoned, and I knew that there was absolutely zero chance of 'hooking up' as Sebastian had eloquently put it and, to tell the truth, I was so tired, I was almost on my knees.

The men stood up as I left our table in the dining area, Sebastian looking at me longingly.

"Sleep well, gentlemen," I said quietly.

As they sat down again, at least six of them relieved by my absence, I saw Sebastian glance over and smile again. I ran my finger along the chain around my neck and smiled back. It was enough.

Back at my bunk, PFC Sullivan was waiting for me, practically dancing on the spot with unrestrained energy. I felt every single one of my forty years as I eyed her exuberance wearily.

"I did it! I totally did it! I asked him out and he said 'yes'!"

We swapped a high five, and she then proceeded to tell me all about Frank, a mechanic in the motor pool. Halfway through her description of his 'fine ass', I fell asleep. I had my own memories of a fine ass to dream about.

∽

"Hey, Lee! Wake up!"

"Huh, what?"

Mary was shaking me awake, her little face puckered up with concern.

"Captain Grant is after your ass!"

My ass?

"What? Why?" I stared at my watch. I stared at it again, utterly horrified, and willing the hands to rewind at least an hour.

"I'm sorry," whimpered Mary, "I thought you were awake, you *said* you were awake an hour ago. He's really kinda mad at you."

"Oh, crap!"

She giggled. "At least he can't give you cleaning duty."

"Want to bet?" I muttered, hastily pulling on my boots.

Mary helped me carry my gear out to the waiting vehicle, and a very sullen and irritated Captain Grant was waiting for me impatiently.

"I'm so sorry," I mumbled, "I overslept. It won't happen again."

He couldn't even bring himself to reply. I didn't blame him. He was responsible for 160 men, and one stupid woman reporter, who was fucking things up on day two of a one month embed. I'd be pissed, as well.

I pulled my body armor over my aching body, swept my hair into a rough ponytail, and slapped on my helmet.

Grant scowled, and did the one thing he could to show his displeasure: he seated me next to Sebastian. I climbed in creakily, annoyed at myself for being so unprofessional, but as soon as I saw Sebastian grinning in my direction, I realized that the gods were on my side for once, and I couldn't help smiling to myself.

"Good morning, Ms. Venzi," he purred. "I trust you slept well?"

"Too well, thank you, Sergeant Hunter," I politely replied, and saw him smirk at my response.

He looked fresh and delicious. I probably looked like old ham next to him, but I didn't care. Which was something of a revelation —it didn't matter what I wore, or how much sleep I'd had or not had, he always looked at me as if his world began and ended with me. How could I not be affected by that? By the certainty of his love?

As we headed north into the dusty, barren landscape, bumping along a broken road, heading up into the foothills, the heat was already building and I was starting to sweat. We'd all be soaked and stinking by the time we stopped for the night—and I already knew that there wouldn't be any showers.

I squinted into the harsh light, staring at the stark surroundings. Our road followed the side of a riverbed, and for a hundred yards in each direction, a strip of green vegetation broke up the bleakness of the lunar landscape.

Scattered in the scrubby fields, we saw several fortified farms with high walls, built from a mixture of mud and straw so they blended into the very dirt they were made from. Some were gathered into loose hamlets for company and protection, but most seemed to be abandoned. The only signs of life were a few skinny goats. If the owners were around, they were hiding from us.

I was still staring out of the window, when I felt Sebastian's hand drifting up to rest casually on my thigh. I shifted my daypack slightly, so that his hand was hidden, and slowly lowered mine, allowing our fingers to entwine on my leg.

In the middle of that blighted country, bumping along a dirt road in 90-degree heat, I felt a moment of peace.

～

Our destination was the town of Now Zad, grim was too kind a word. It might have been prosperous once, with evidence of a market area, but now it looked like it had been blasted by the desert.

Broken shops hung open to the elements, shutters drooping loosely. Only one person seemed to exist in this ghost town—an elderly man selling a few potatoes and eggs from a rug outside an empty building. He waved as we went past and called out something to us. Maybe that was a hopeful sign.

I glanced at Sebastian.

"What did he say?"

I saw Grant's head incline toward us, also waiting for the answer.

"Nothing I'd like to repeat, ma'am," he said, running his thumb over the back of my hand.

I nudged my knee against his and held back a grin. Playing footsie with Sebastian and having Grant sitting in front of me, gave me an almost irrepressible urge to laugh. Among other things.

My light heartedness disappeared when I saw the place that was to be our home for the next month.

Our compound had been a police station at some point in its life, but used many times over by ISAF soldiers from both British and US forces. It was basic, to say the least. There was no fresh water, no electricity, and the men were to sleep in the old cells, up to a dozen per room. I was given a space the size of a closet: I could just about stretch out there—it certainly wouldn't have done for anyone taller than me. I felt lucky to have a room to myself and that level of privacy. No one else did—not even Captain Grant.

I kept out of the Captain's way while he was organizing the camp. Instead, I tapped out notes on my laptop and blew up my oh-so-comfortable mattress.

PFC Sullivan had given me enough material for my first article, and the dreary town of Now Zad would supply plenty more. Being stationed here was a very different prospect from the relative comfort and safety of Leatherneck. I couldn't believe that our flimsy-looking mud walls would do much to protect us from an attack where rocket propelled grenades were used.

After a long while of being ignored, I started to feel hungry—particularly since I'd missed breakfast, and lunch had been a strange, flatbread sandwich on the road. No one had come near me, and I suspected I'd been conveniently forgotten. But now I saw men lining up near the area which I presumed had been designated as the kitchen. I joined the end of the line and looked hopeful.

The Marines all seemed so young. Most were in their early twenties, several were only nineteen. I remembered that Sebastian had been even younger than that when he'd first been sent to Iraq, and Fido hadn't made it to twenty.

They were all sweetly shy around me, calling me 'ma'am', of course, and insisting I go to the front of the line. We were having MREs (meal ready-to-eat) ration packs. I was told the food was chicken and noodles; the noodles I recognized, the anemic-looking meat I was less sure about.

I squatted down with the group nearest to me, and brought out my trusty bottle of soy sauce. It wasn't long before it was doing the rounds —even among the boys who'd never heard of soy sauce, let alone the *tamari* variety.

I asked each of them where they came from and what had made them enlist. For some, the Marine Corps was a chance to have a real family for the first time in their lives, for others it was a means to an end: learning a trade, or a college education, several said they wanted to serve their country, motivated by the events of 9/11. And for a few, I guessed, it was the difference between a slippery slope into a life of crime, and a chance to contribute something useful and make something of their lives.

I saw Sebastian once. He was standing at the compound's entrance, next to one of the sangar observation posts, talking to a group of locals. He looked tired, and I wondered if he'd had a chance to eat.

"I don't know how he talks that Greek shit," said Larry, a friendly kid from Pittsburgh, who was nodding at Sebastian.

"It's not Greek, fool!" snorted Ben, a native of Kansas City. "It's Arabic, isn't that right, ma'am?"

"Whatever, man: it's all Greek to me," said Larry, with a wide grin.

"It'll either be Dari or Pashto," I said, gently amused when Ben looked crushed by my correction. "I'm sure he'll teach you a few words if you're interested."

He shrugged, noncommittal. I understood: Sebastian was an unknown quantity—one of them, yet not one of them.

Gradually, the men became more relaxed in my presence, and the laughter and joking attracted more people to our corner of the compound. Laughter that petered out the moment Captain Grant wandered over to see what was going on.

I think he was mildly surprised to find I wasn't being a pain in the ass for a change, because he was almost civil to me, my early indiscretion forgotten, or at least forgiven.

Eventually, I decided to call it a day, and despite being implored to stay and shoot the breeze, I headed to my closet.

The bathrooms were basic, and I was dreading becoming familiar with them. But at least I wouldn't have the incredibly gross job of burning the waste every day. I wondered if it would be reserved for a punishment duty.

I brushed my teeth and rinsed with a mouthful of tepid water from my canteen, swiped some of the dust off my face with baby-wipes, kicked off my boots and laid my body armor where I could reach it in a hurry. I knew I was probably a little ripe from a day of constant sweating, but I was too tired to care, and it wasn't as if I could slip on my yoga pants after soaking in a hot tub.

Instead, I listened to the sounds of the camp around me: men going to their sleeping quarters, others going on watch. I realized what was missing—there was no birdsong. Nothing, not a single sound of any animal at all. The thought disturbed me, waking me more thoroughly than the alarm I had slept through this morning.

And then I heard a soft footfall outside my door.

"Caro?" he whispered.

I pushed open the door, and saw Sebastian crouching in the dim light. He wound himself through the narrow opening and wrapped his arms around me, holding me tightly.

"It's like a dream having you here," he murmured. "I keep thinking I'm going to wake up and find I've imagined you."

I clutched him tightly. "My dreams aren't usually this good."

"Mine are," he whispered, softly. "Or they used to be. When you first left, I dreamed about you all the time."

"What was I doing?" I said, stroking his cheek.

He leaned into my hand, breathing deeply. "Mostly, we were just by the ocean, walking on the beach."

"Mostly?"

He grinned. "Sometimes we did other stuff."

"Stuff? I'm not sure I know what you mean by 'stuff'," and I rubbed the front of his pants suggestively, hoping he'd feel the need to elucidate.

"Caro!" he groaned. "Fuck, I just came to make sure you were okay in here. I have to get back to the comms room."

"Right away? You can't take a few minutes?"

He kissed me hungrily. "I really can't, baby. Grant's waiting for me."

"You're such a tease," I said, slapping his ass. "You come in here, raising my expectations..."

"That's not the only thing that was raised," he said, dryly.

I smirked at him. "Well, I'd have been happy to meet those expectations, but apparently you have to go be a soldier."

"Actually, I have to go be an interpreter ... I could try and come back later, Caro."

"Sebastian, seriously—do what you need to do. You know where I am, and I trust you to know whether or not it's safe to take that risk. It worries me that I'm a distraction here for you. The most important thing is that you focus on your job. We have the rest of our lives after that."

He kissed me again, then rested his forehead against mine.

"I'm a lucky bastard—thank God for you, Caro."

"I'll see you at breakfast, Sarge," I said, running my hand over his hair.

"One other thing," he said, looking at me seriously, "there's been some radio chatter and the Taliban definitely know we're here. I don't think they'll do anything tonight—they're not in position, from what I can work out, but if you hear someone yell 'incoming', get your body armor on, keep your head down, and stay in here away from the windows. Whatever happens, Caro, stay in here. Everyone out there knows what they're doing: we don't need your help. You know what I'm saying, baby?"

I hugged him tightly. "I promise. I don't want you thinking about me when you have more important things to concentrate on."

He smiled briefly. "There isn't anything more important than you."

Then he kissed me gently, pressing his soft lips against mine. A moment later, and he was gone.

I settled back on my mattress, enjoying the relative coolness of the night air. I hoped Sebastian would be able to come back later, but I wasn't counting on it. Just knowing he was nearby was soothing.

The alarm on my wristwatch awoke me shortly before dawn. I sat up abruptly, my heart hammering in my chest. I could see a dark shadow curled up in the corner of my room. It moved and stretched.

"Sebastian!" I whispered. "What are you doing?"

"Hey, baby," he mumbled, sleepily.

"How long have you been there? Why didn't you wake me up?"

"Couple of hours, I think. I didn't want to wake you—you looked so peaceful."

I crawled up the mattress and wrapped my arms around his neck. I could feel the stubble on his cheek.

"You didn't even take your boots off," I said, burying my face in his neck.

He chuckled quietly. "Didn't seem much of a point." He kissed my hair and climbed to his feet. "Gotta go, baby."

"Already?" I said, disappointed.

He smiled. "Yeah, need to get a wash and shave before dawn patrol."

"You're lucky," I said, with a wry smile. "I'm relying on baby-wipes while I'm here. You'll get to know me in a whole new way, Sebastian."

He laughed quietly. "Looking forward to it, baby. See you later."

I quickly completed my morning ablutions (two baby-wipes over my face and under my arms, and a tiny squeeze of toothpaste to brush my teeth). I was touched, more than touched, that Sebastian had slept at the foot of my mattress, making sure I was okay, when he would have been better off crashing on his own bedroll for a few meager hours. Somehow that told me far more about the way he felt than if he'd woken me up for a rousing bout of illicit sex. I wouldn't have minded that either, and I'd been disappointed that he'd had to go so quickly. I knew he was trying damn hard to keep our relationship a secret. God love him for trying.

Which reminded me, he'd gone outside to wash and shave. I grabbed my camera and headed out.

The sun was just beginning to appear behind the mountains, weaving pink and purple clouds around the summits, when, like a gift from heaven, I saw a row of Marines, naked above the waist, who were washing outside in the cool air. Nicole would have gone crazy: all that taut, toned male flesh on display. It was a damn fine sight, but I was on the lookout for one sexy, muscular back that I'd gotten to know very well in the last two weeks.

I hid behind my camera, and snapped images of compound life. Yeah, right. Finally, I had a photograph of Sebastian that I could keep legitimately while I was working.

Then one of the older Marines spotted me.

"You gonna blow up a nice big print of me, lady?"

And then the catcalls started. Marines of all shapes and sizes started flexing their biceps and even rubbing their nipples in my general direction.

I couldn't help laughing, more at the furious scowl on Sebastian's face than anything else.

"Gentlemen," I said, "it's too early in the day for all that. I haven't even had my breakfast MRE yet."

The good-natured teasing continued as I made my way across the compound to the line for chow. Hmm, more noodles and meat in dinky little plastic packs. No wonder this food was also known as 'Meals Rejected by the Enemy' or even 'Man Ready to Eat'. I was really hoping we'd have a helicopter drop of some fresh fruit and A-rations at some point over the next three-and-a-half weeks. Otherwise, my bottle of soy sauce wasn't going to last long.

Captain Grant stuck his head out, searching for the source of gratuitous good humor. When he saw me, he looked surprised and nodded politely. I nodded back, but couldn't help grinning at him.

He smiled cautiously, then bobbed back inside.

Ten minutes later, I joined the officers and gunnery sergeants for the morning's briefing. Sebastian was there, too, freshly-shaven and looking grumpy.

"This morning we'll have four patrols moving out. Crawley, I want you and your team with me heading northeast along the river bed wadi. Romero, northwest by the edge of town. Jankowski, your men take the old market area with Holden flanking you at 100 yards.

"Hunter, you're in charge of the terps—brief them before we go. The population here are Sunnis. Are any of your men Shiite?"

"Two, sir," said Sebastian. "I've told them to stay behind today."

"Does that leave us short?" said Grant, frowning.

"No, sir, but one of the teams will have to use Angaar: his English is so-so."

"Then send one of the others with him."

"They don't get along, sir. Could cause problems."

"Then damn well make sure it doesn't, Hunter!" snapped the Captain.

Sebastian didn't argue the point further, but I could tell he was slightly pissed.

As the meeting broke up, I ventured to put my hand in the air. Part of me hoped I'd be with Sebastian's patrol, part of me hoped I wasn't, because I knew I'd be a distraction for him.

"Which team would you like me with, Captain Grant?"

He looked up, clearly irritated.

Well, fuck him! He wasn't the only one doing a job here.

"Perhaps 'like' was too strong a word, Captain," I suggested, coolly.

I saw Sebastian's lips quirk up in a small smile, before he quickly stifled it. He wasn't the only one—I saw two of the other officers grin openly.

"You'd better come with me, Ms. Venzi," the Captain muttered, somewhat unwillingly. "And you, Hunter."

"I feel like Fox Mulder," I murmured loud enough for Grant to hear, but not loud enough that he'd feel the need to reply. "The Marines' 'most unwanted'."

The Captain's forehead creased in a frown, but I thought I detected a hint of humor in his eyes, too.

The dawn patrols left the compound on foot. Today's mission was to scout the area and get a hands-on idea of the terrain. The two patrols checking the old marketplace probably had the most dangerous job—although there weren't really any safe ones. But those old bazaar buildings provided places where IEDs could be planted, or gunmen could hide.

By comparison, my stroll up the river wadi would be easy. Or perhaps 'easier' was a better way of describing it, because the heat was already building uncomfortably, and nothing would be easy today.

I'd been positioned in the middle of the patrol for safety. Sebastian was up front with the Captain when we saw our first locals.

Four small boys, aged about eight or nine, were sitting in a patch of dirt when they saw us. They stood up in a hurry, looking scared, but Sebastian called out to them, and they stared at him in surprise. He said something else and I saw the biggest boy, who seemed to be acting as the leader, shake his head. Then the boy pointed up into the foothills.

I snapped a quick picture while no one was looking.

"He says there are Taliban up in the hills, sir," Sebastian said to

Grant, quietly. "They moved into position during the night. He doesn't think they'll come out in daytime. Not sure I'd take that as an ironclad guarantee, but it could mean they'll hit us at dusk, or first thing in the morning."

I saw him glance at me.

"Anything else?" said the Captain.

Sebastian sighed. "He said his father has promised to get him a rifle like mine when he's ten."

I couldn't help wondering how long this war would go on, when children were being used to carry it forward.

Then one of the boys spotted me and gaped, openly pointing me out to his friends. They rattled off a question and Sebastian grinned.

"They want to know if Ms. Venzi is your wife, sir, or if you just brought her to do the cooking."

I'll get you for that, Hunter!

Some of the troops laughed, but Grant looked slightly flustered.

"Tell them she does the cooking," he said.

Sebastian gave them the answer and the boys nodded wisely. Then he handed each of them a hard candy, and we moved on, watching as they waved goodbye.

From a distance, I snapped another photo of them waving, then hurried to catch up with Grant.

"Would you like to explain that to me, Captain Grant," I asked mildly, while secretly giving him the evil eye.

"I don't want word getting out that we have a journalist with us," he said, shortly.

He had a point, and, despite the heat, I felt a shiver go down my spine. As I fell back to my place in the middle of the patrol, I glanced over to see Sebastian looking at me, a serious and worried expression on his face.

We moved slowly next to the dried riverbed when one of the Marines on point yelled out, "Incoming!"

I looked up to see a bright flash in the sky and heard an intensely loud roaring overhead. I half-dived, half-fell into the wadi, following the Marines who'd hit the deck the second their colleague had shouted.

The rocket propelled grenade shook the ground as it exploded, and the percussion from the hot air deafened me. Even though I was terrified, I could tell that the noise wasn't dangerously near to us.

"RPG, sir!" shouted the gunnery sergeant. "Bastards missed by 300 yards. Up in the foothills, sir. They'll have us in range any second."

He was right: we were in their sights and pinned down. The wadi gave us good protection but we couldn't move either.

Sebastian crouched down next to me.

"You okay?"

"I'm fine, don't worry about me. I won't move. Promise."

He gave an anxious look, then made his way back to Captain Grant.

Two men moved forward with a small mortar and fired off a couple of rounds. The rush of sound was distinctly comforting.

"Hewitt," shouted the Captain, "call in air support. I want the shit bombed out of those fuckers. Give them the coordinates—now!"

I managed to turn around in the confined area and took photographs of the Marine on the radio calling air-support, and of the two Marines firing the occasional mortar round.

Two more RPGs came in, each landing a little closer, although not close enough to concern the men around me. I thought I was having an out-of-body experience: everyone seemed so calm, including me, although another, quieter, rational part, was scared witless.

Luckily, I had something else to focus on. Despite the heat and despite the fact I'd sweated enough to leave salt marks on my clothes, I was dying to pee. Maybe it was just fear after all, but I didn't know how much longer I could hang on.

Another fifteen minutes passed and the pressure on my bladder was becoming intolerable. I was seriously considering just peeing my pants right there. It was so hot, my clothes would dry quickly, the sting of humiliation would, however, last considerably longer.

I felt better when I noticed several of the Marines discreetly peeing into the wadi. God, it was so much easier for men. I should have worn a long skirt like the local women, then I could have just squatted down in the dirt and no one would have been any the wiser.

At that moment, I heard the sound of a jet streaking past overhead.

"Harrier," muttered the bored-looking Marine who was kneeling down next to me.

There was an explosion so loud, it sounded as if a whole mountain had been blown up. A second explosion followed shortly afterward. I pressed my face into the dirt at the bottom of the wadi and tried to remember to breathe. I counted to a hundred before I dared to look up again. A thick cloud of dust and smoke hung over the foothills, lazily drifting down into the yellow valley.

I sat up to take a quick photo. I even remembered to take off the lens cap, which I thought was pretty damned impressive under the circumstances—and I still wanted to pee.

Then I noticed that several of the men were grinning at me.

"Was that your first time under fire, ma'am?"

"First time it was that damn close," I said, with a thin smile. "I almost peed my pants."

They laughed easily. "Well, you looked pretty cool, ma'am. We should make you an honorary Marine."

"I'm sure Captain Grant would be delighted with that suggestion," I muttered, and winked at them conspiratorially.

I looked across to see Sebastian smiling at me. I pressed my hand over my heart, and smiled back.

After waiting to see if there would be any further RPG attacks, we slowly made our way back along the dried up riverbed.

By now, my bathroom needs had intensified and I practically sprinted the last hundred yards to what passed for restrooms in the compound. 'Sprinted' might have been an exaggeration: I was wearing nearly 22 pounds of body armor, 'staggered' was probably more accurate.

But the relief could not be exaggerated. I floated out, oblivious to the catcalls and helpfully unhelpful comments from the Marines who were watching me with wide grins on their faces.

All I needed now was a hot shower, a good book, and a hot man. I'd come very near to an up-close-and-personal encounter with the Taliban: some life-affirming sex would be very welcome. I couldn't see Sebastian among the sea of desert utility uniforms, but I hoped he'd find me later.

I dragged my sorry carcass to my room, dumped the body armor gratefully, then took my laptop and solar charger outside, and sat in the shade, writing my notes.

I could see a small flurry of activity going on at one side, with Marines hoisting up bits of rope and old jerry cans. My body was too weary to wonder what they were doing, and my brain was too stunned to care. But then I noticed that Sebastian seemed to be organizing the work party. After another ten minutes, he strolled over casually and squatted down next to me.

"How you doing, baby?" he said, in a low voice.

"Pretty damn good, Sarge," I replied, "considering I nearly got my ass shot off today."

He chuckled quietly. "You are so fucking amazing, Caro."

"You're not so bad yourself, Sebastian."

We both noticed the speculative gazes we were garnering at the same time. He stood up abruptly. "We've fixed you up a makeshift shower."

"Excuse me?" I said, certain that I'd misheard.

"The guys wanted to do something for you—they think you're a ballsy woman. So they've made you a shower. You've got about two-and-a-half minutes of lukewarm water. How's that sound?"

"What? How?"

I gaped at him and he smiled back.

"I just left some cartons of water out in the sun during the day. They got pretty warm: all we had to do was hoist them up and make a shower head. You're good to go. Except you won't be able to take off your clothes, but it's better than nothing, I guess."

"God, I love you!" I murmured. "But I think I love them, too!"

He snorted, but thankfully looked amused as I waved at the shower-building team.

"I'll be right back!"

I hurried to my room and grabbed a small sachet of shampoo. I hadn't thought I'd need it, but I was so happy that I'd included it after all.

The shower felt wonderful: washing the salt and dust out of my hair felt even better. I even managed to make a stab at washing my clothes while I was wearing them, before the water ran out. Then I sat out in the afternoon sunshine and let my clothes dry on my body, while I chatted to some of the guys, listening to their stories.

Captain Grant came out to check on me and I even managed to get a smile from him. I hoped the truce would hold—provided I managed not to oversleep again, of course.

Another box of MREs, four hard candies, and a really bad coffee later, I crawled into bed. If Sebastian came into my room in the night, he'd have to poke me awake with a sharp stick. My shoulders ached from wearing the heavy body armor all day. I couldn't imagine how the guys must feel: their armor was even heavier, plus they had to carry their packs, ammunition and an eight pound rifle.

Their entire equipment and packs probably weighed more than I did.

And with that thought, I was asleep.

CHAPTER FIFTEEN

IT WAS DARK WHEN I WOKE UP, I REALIZED I WASN'T ALONE.

"Hey, baby," he whispered. "I didn't mean to wake you—I just wanted to see you."

He was sitting at the bottom of my mattress again. I peered into the dark, his outline faint against the darker shadow of the wall.

I rubbed my gritty eyes and reached out for him. "You're too far away," I grumbled, holding up my arms toward him.

He uncoiled himself from the floor, and tried to stretch out next to me, but his boots hit the door.

"Fuck," he muttered, "they've given you a damn hutch to sleep in."

"At least it's private, Sebastian," I said, running my finger across his stubbly chin.

He smiled. "Yeah, that's something."

He leaned over me, taking his weight on his arms, and kissed me, softly. I think he just had a simple goodnight kiss in mind, I certainly didn't.

I wrapped my arms around his neck and locked our faces together. Needing more, I pushed my tongue between his lips, and explored his mouth hungrily. He tasted of salt and mint gum. Desire bloomed inside me and I ran my hands down his back, resting them on his fine ass, feeling the rough material beneath my fingers, and squeezed hard.

"Are you sure, Caro?" he breathed.

"Yes," I whispered back. "Here and now."

He groaned softly, and I felt the weight of his body press down onto my chest.

"But you're going to have to get naked," I added.

He sighed and pushed back from me.

"It's going to take some explaining if the Taliban attack and I run out of your room with my ass hanging out," he replied.

It was a fair point, and he was only trying to protect my honor and act professionally, just as I'd asked. And yet ... I weighed up the pros and cons, realized he was right, and decided to strip him anyway.

We'd come under enemy fire today, and faced it together. I realized how lucky I was: surviving had made me damned horny, and I craved a bout of rough, life-affirming sex with my gorgeous *fiancé*. I felt, quite literally, that life was too short not to grasp something so good with both hands.

This man, lying in my arms, had told me over and over again that he loved me—that he'd always loved me. And, despite everything that fate had thrown in our path—time, distance, and age difference—we were in love. The why and how didn't seem to matter anymore: finally, finally I'd accepted that this was real and that it wasn't going to go away—that Sebastian wasn't going to go away. I'd accepted that he was beautiful and sexy and younger than me, and that women with far better bodies and far fewer years would want him, too. And I'd accepted that he wasn't perfect, and had a string of conquests on at least three continents, and I'd accepted that life was going to continue to throw new hurdles in our path—and I didn't damn well care.

It wasn't perfect. So what? Life isn't perfect—life is what happens while you're waiting for your moment in the sun and if you miss it, waiting instead for the perfect illusion that Hollywood sells, then more fool you. I'd spent half my life waiting for the right moment. I was done with waiting.

"Time to get naked, Sarge," I ordered.

"Make me," he shot back.

Oh, willingly.

"Okay, what can I trade you to take your shirt off?"

His eyebrows shot up.

"Trade?"

"Yes. I want you to take your shirt off, but it seems like I'll have to give you something in return. If I agree to your terms, you lose the shirt. If I don't agree, you get to keep it on."

"For real?"

"Yes, Sebastian," I said, pleased with my invention, but also intrigued to see what he'd come up with.

"A shirt for a shirt, Caro."

Okay, so he was starting out easy. But I was wearing fewer clothes than he was.

I undid my shirt and watched his eyes widen as he took a deep breath, his gaze drawn to my breasts. His jacket and t-shirt hit the floor and we were both naked from the waist up.

"So far so good. I want you to take off your boots and socks."

He thought for a moment.

"Okay, but I want you to touch your breasts, Caro, touch yourself until your nipples are hard."

I ran my hands lightly over myself, toying with my nipples while I stared into his eyes.

"Fuck!" he said, wetting his lips with his tongue.

"Boots," I said, my voice sharp with need.

It took a minute for him to unlace his boots and tug his feet out of them, then peel off his socks. His coordination wasn't helped by the fact that I continued to massage my breasts, turning myself on with my hands and his dark gaze.

"I want you to take off your pants, Sebastian."

"And you have to lose those pajama bottoms, Caro,"

I slipped them off quickly, adding them to the pile of clothes in the corner.

Sebastian matched me, unzipping his pants and tossing them away. My eyes were drawn to the very noticeable bulge in his briefs. But I needed to get them off him first—and I didn't have any clothes left to trade.

"I want you naked, Sebastian," I whispered.

"I want you to touch yourself between your legs, Caro. I want to see you come."

I pulled a face.

"What?" he said, looking confused.

"Sebastian, I can do that any night of the week. Frankly I was hoping you'd do it for me."

He grinned. "Yeah, but it'll be a real fucking turn on for me."

"All right then, but you, too."

"Me, too, what?"

"Lose the briefs, get handy, and make yourself come."

He hesitated for a moment. "Ah, what the hell."

He lay on his back and lifted his butt, so he could slide his briefs over his hips. His erection leapt free immediately.

Then he pulled himself into a sitting position, leaning against the wall facing me, and started stroking himself. I knelt up, spreading my knees wide and began to rub my clitoris slowly.

I felt utterly aroused watching him touch himself so intimately, staring into his eyes as his breath began to come faster, as I listened to myself moan softly. He wrapped his right hand firmly around himself, and started gripping harder, and I copied him, matching him stroke for stroke, my back arching as my insides began to tremble and my body begged for release.

"Oh, fuck this," he snarled. He launched himself forward, forcing me onto my back, and slammed into me, pumping hard.

I smacked his shoulder and pushed him off. "Condom!"

"Fuck! Fuck! Fuck!"

He pulled out of me hurriedly, grabbed his pants and dragged them toward him, fumbling in the pocket for a foil packet. He swore again as he dropped it and had to search for another.

"I'm sheathed up," he hissed, at last.

"From behind: make it rough."

I heard his breath catch, but he didn't need to be asked twice. I rolled onto my hands and knees and felt him grip my hips. He rammed into me so hard, I had to stifle my cry with one hand. I collapsed onto my forearms as he let himself go, hammering into my body, using me for sex, just like I'd told him to. It was rough and raw and just what I wanted—what I needed.

I pushed my ass back against him, and felt his balls slap against my skin as he plunged into me again and again.

He leaned over and reached down to palm my left breast, squeezing the nipple hard enough to make me cry out. Then he let go and moved his hand lower, his fingers circling me and reaching far enough back, so that I knew he was touching his shaft at the same time, feeling himself move in and out of me.

I brought my hand up to meet his, and we twined our fingers together, quite literally feeling our connection.

My body gave way as I came, and Sebastian hooked his arm around my waist to hold me up, until his own climax had him collapsing onto my thin mattress.

I was gasping for breath, on the verge of passing out, and Sebastian was breathing hard. I could feel the sweat on my chest and back.

Sebastian pulled out of me, a movement that made me wince. I'd asked for rough sex and I'd got it. Oh, boy had I got it.

I felt his breath on my neck and his hand rested on my hip.

"Are you okay?" he breathed, softly.

"Yes," I gasped. "Apart from the fact tomorrow I'll be walking like I just rode a camel across the Gobi desert. You?"

"Yeah, I think I ripped my foreskin—what's left of it," he muttered.

"Really?" I turned around to face him. "Are you okay?"

He smiled and stroked my cheek. "Kidding, Caro. That was fucking awesome. You were like some wild woman."

"You were pretty wild yourself. But you're right—I don't know what got into me—other than you, of course. Do you want to go again?"

"Christ, Caro! Are you trying to kill me?"

"Hmm, death by orgasm. What do you think? A handful by morning?"

"If you want, Caro, but you know what I'd really like to do now?"

"Thrill me."

He pulled me into his arms and looked at me seriously. "I want to make love to you, Caro. I freakin' loved that, but it was just sex. Can we take it slow, baby? Take our time? I want to touch every part of your body."

He kissed me gently and ran his hands across my shoulders and down to my waist, expressing with his hands what he'd told me in so many words.

His movements were tender and loving and gentle. There were so many different sides to this complex man. It was an education learning all his facets, and learning how trust was growing between us.

At last he fell asleep, his body curled around mine, his head resting on my chest.

As the night drifted past, and morning was just a breath away, I was reluctant to wake him. He'd missed a lot of sleep to take care of me the last two nights, and he needed to be alert. I waited until the very last possible second to wake him.

"Time to get up, Sebastian," I said reluctantly, running my hands over the silky skin of his back.

He blinked and tried to stretch, but ended up kicking the door again.

"Very stealthy, Sarge," I remarked, watching him sit up and search for his briefs.

He grinned back at me. "Yeah, trained in stealth, camouflage and concealment, baby."

"You were certainly concealed in me last night—several times, I seem to remember."

"Did ya lose count, baby?" he smirked.

I didn't bother to answer that one, instead, I had another question. "By the way, how come you're managing to get in here without anyone noticing you're not where you're supposed to be?"

He frowned. "It's not that hard—I'm kind of separate from everyone. I'm on attachment so none of them know me. I'm in charge of the other interpreters, but they're all Afghan, so I'm not part of that either. It was different when I was still with my unit, but this way no one knows when or where I'm on duty. Except Grant, and he has more to worry about than where I sleep. Works out pretty well, huh, Caro?"

I realized that his job must be lonely on occasions, and spending time with me meant he wasn't bonding with other members of the unit.

The military machine worked at its best when everyone knew their job and did it: lives depended on that. But when it came down to it, I couldn't help thinking that men fought for their friends, for the guys in their unit, rather than for their country. That came into it, sure, but in this kind of guerrilla warfare, your life usually depended on the other guy you broke bread with. They were your family.

I looked up and saw that Sebastian was gazing at me, his head on one side, as if he was trying to read what was going on in my mind.

I smiled at him, hiding my concern.

"Time to move your ass, Sebastian. I'll see you later?"

He kissed me quickly, and then darted out through the door. Half a minute later I saw him strolling casually across the compound, greeting some of the other men who were either waking up or coming off watch.

I yawned and stretched, and took a moment to freshen myself up with some more baby-wipes, before heading out to join the line for chow.

The day's new gossip was that fresh rations would be dropped in by helicopter in the next couple of days. Other than the butt-clenching fear of being under fire, it was as exciting as things got.

I realized that if there was going to be a food drop, then there might well be mail, too. I decided I'd keep my promise to Sebastian and write him a letter.

Thankfully, the day passed far less eventfully than the previous one. I wasn't sent out with Sebastian, but accompanied Lieutenant Crawley and a cheerful Afghan interpreter called Gawhar, who told me his name meant 'jewel'. He was fascinated by the fact that I wasn't married and didn't have children. He kept asking who was 'in charge' of me. He couldn't comprehend my answer of 'no one'. I wouldn't like to imagine how puzzled he'd be if he ever met a woman officer with men under her command. I hoped my presence gave him another point of view, at the very least.

Gawhar thought women should be educated "up to the age of 11", so that they could be more useful in childrearing. At one time, women in Afghanistan had been able to go to college, but now anyone attempting to educate girls was living very dangerously. Gawhar's attitude was relatively liberal, compared to many.

I sighed. This poor country had a long way to go.

Our patrol was the first one back at the compound. Grant had confirmed that a food drop would be happening soon, so each Marine could have a one-minute shower with what was left from the water ration. Soon, there was an awful lot of naked flesh on display. I was glad I had a pair of sunglasses behind which to hide my blushes—or maybe it was my interest that I was hiding. I'd never used to pay much attention to that sort of thing, even though I lived by a beach. Huh, I blamed Sebastian.

I headed back to my room and started typing up notes and polishing a couple of articles that were almost ready to go. I was pleased with the photographs, too. The ones from the previous day were particularly dramatic, although looking at them brought back some of the knee-trembling terror that I'd felt.

After an hour of typing, I flipped shut the laptop lid, and sat outside to write an old-fashioned pen-and-paper letter to Sebastian. I was determined that if mail did arrive soon, he'd have a letter to open. I spent my time being creative: he said he wanted to get kinky with me, so I roughed out some ideas, to see if any of them were on his 'to do' list. It was a shame our time and space was so limited right now. I wanted to show him what a formerly-sexually-frustrated forty-year-old with a good vocabulary could imagine.

Sebastian's patrol was the last to return to the compound. Even from a distance, I could see that his face was strained. He glanced over to where I was sitting, and shook his head imperceptibly.

A few minutes later he emerged from Grant's makeshift office, and strode over to me.

"Captain Grant would like to see you, ma'am," he said, formally.

I followed him across the compound, feeling anxious as he pressed his lips together in a hard line.

Grant's office seemed gloomy after the punishing sunlight, he waved me to the only other chair in the room and Sebastian stood silently behind me.

"Ms. Venzi, your presence is causing some interest among the local population. Master Sergeant Hunter heard some talk while on patrol that concerned him."

I glanced up at Sebastian who remained resolutely mute.

"And what does this talk say?" I prompted.

"At the moment it's vague, but the news of having a woman with us will spread quickly now. We have a new cook and a new medic arriving in six days, so the heli will be putting down briefly. If you become a person of interest, as I think you will, you'll be at risk and you'll be putting my men at risk, too. I want you on that flight, Ms. Venzi."

I felt like he'd punched me, and all the air left my lungs. But I understood, as well. He was making a strategic decision. He hadn't tried to persuade or softball me, he just told it like it was.

"I see. Well, thank you for being so candid and explaining the situation to me, Captain Grant. I'll ensure that I get as much work done as I can, and I'll be ready to leave when you advise."

The Captain looked relieved. Perhaps he'd expected me to argue, or throw a hissy fit. I may have been a stupid woman who overslept on her first day embedded with his unit, but I wasn't selfish enough to risk the lives of others. Especially not Sebastian's.

The worst part was that I'd be leaving him behind. I'd always known that day would come, I just thought we'd have a little longer first. He was right: we always seemed to be traveling in different directions.

I stood up, and Sebastian escorted me out of the Captain's office.

"Sorry, baby," he murmured.

"That's okay," I replied, quietly. "I don't want to cause more problems out here. Besides, I can get some stories from Leatherneck, so the paper won't be shortchanged."

"If anything happened to you..." he began.

I interrupted him quickly. "I told you, Sebastian, I'm not going to take risks. If you care about me, you won't either."

"*If* I care about you?" he said angrily.

"You know what I mean—and keep your voice down."

He scowled, and looked mutinous.

Great. Sulky Sebastian was back.

Reluctantly, he left me outside my room, and marched off to the other side of the compound where he threw angry glances at me until it was meal time.

I was just drowning my sorrows in some piss-weak coffee, when Lieutenant Crawley emerged from Grant's subterranean office.

"Supply chopper on its way," he announced, then picked out a platoon to retrieve the goodies.

A few minutes later, we all heard the distinctive thrum of the Black Hawk's twin engines chewing up the air around it, and small parachutes began raining down.

Once the swag had been collected and relocated to the compound, everyone gathered around the supplies: ammunition, water and—thank you God—fresh rations. There was also a bag of mail which I volunteered to sort, much to Captain Grant's obvious surprise.

There weren't as many letters as I'd expected. My two shadows, Ben and Larry, helped me, and explained that any parcels from home would be held back until there was room (or spare weight) on the next heli drop.

When they weren't looking, I casually slipped my letter to Sebastian into the pile. It didn't take long to finish sorting, and it was easy to tell which of the guys were family men—they had the most letters, some obviously addressed by their kids.

As he'd said, Sebastian didn't get many letters and that day, mine was the only one addressed to him.

The rest of the unit circled us like sharks, waiting for the moment they heard their name. I saw Sebastian's surprise when Larry called out 'Hunter'.

"You got mail, Sergeant," and he waved the thin envelope at Sebastian.

Of course, I hadn't written a return address, so that should have clued him in, but instead he just looked puzzled. I watched him as he scrolled down the first few lines of my scandalous letter. Then his eyes widened in shock, and a wicked grin crept across his face. He glanced up, and I winked at him.

He read through the whole letter, sitting in the dirt, leaning against the mud wall of the compound. Then he closed his eyes and let his head rock back: he was still smiling.

Yeah, think about those positions, Sarge.

One of the other men, a young guy named Ross from Minneapolis, scrunched up his letter in disgust and dropped it in the dirt.

"What's up man?" said Larry.

"Fucking 'dear John' letter," he said bitterly. "She said she didn't want to spoil my last few days of leave, so she thought she'd wait till I got out here to tell me she was seeing someone else. Bitch."

He got some sympathetic looks. A lot of the men had been there. It could be hard to hold onto relationships in the military.

The sun had sunk behind the mountains and the air was beginning to cool, when there was a sudden flurry of activity.

"Incoming!" came the yell from the sangar.

Suddenly, men were flying everywhere, running for their body armor and weapons. I sprinted for my room, but tripped over an abandoned jacket, and went sprawling in the dust.

The first RPG exploded about 200 yards outside the compound. The noise was horrendous, and the plume of dirt rocketed 90 feet into the air.

I covered my head with my hands, and pushed my face into the loose dirt on the ground. When the dusty shower had subsided, I crawled on my hands and knees into my room, and pulled on my body armor and helmet in double-quick time. Then I grabbed my camera and nervously pointed it out of the tiny window, taking snap after snap of the Marines as they took their positions. Then the *durg-durg* of the heavy machine guns started.

Another RPG exploded, closer this time, and I dropped to the floor, counted to ten, and peered out of my window. After a minute of what seemed like organized chaos, bellows and shouts, silence rippled outwards.

My heart was thundering in my chest, and I realized my hands were shaking. I began to wonder if a nice, safe job in a bank might be a good career move.

Sebastian's head suddenly appeared around my door, and I nearly yelled out in fright.

"You okay, baby?"

"Yes, fine. Don't worry about me," I replied, rather breathlessly.

He nodded, and disappeared.

The Taliban had a new tactic: sleep deprivation. Intermittently throughout the night, they'd fire an RPG randomly toward us. None of them came close enough to cause concern, but it was successful at stopping us resting, not that sleeping in body armor was possible anyway—at least not until complete exhaustion had set in.

Sebastian didn't have another chance to come near me again. I guessed he was in Grant's office to interpret the insurgents' radio chatter and thus help the gunners try to work out targets. At dawn, we were all gritty-eyed and pissed off as we stumbled into line for breakfast.

I don't know why, but an old Beatles song came into my head, and I started humming the opening bars of 'I'm So Tired'—the lines that said his mind is on the blink because he hasn't slept a wink. That was exactly how I felt.

The Marine behind me started singing the tune softly, and I turned around to smile at him and joined in. Then two more started with the harmony. Soon, about 20 burly Marines were singing out of tune and getting their groove on in the breakfast line. It wasn't much, but it was damn funny—and we really needed to laugh.

Captain Grant appeared from his office, unshaven and with dark rings around his eyes, accompanied by Crawley and Sebastian. When Grant saw the kids from 'Glee 'getting funky to the Beatles, his face split with a huge grin. I didn't even know the man had teeth. He gave me an ironic salute, and disappeared back into his den. Crawley laughed out loud, and Sebastian smiled at me proudly.

From that moment on, the men called me 'Yoko', and I laughed happily, seeing their pleasure in something so simple.

It was the last time I laughed for a very long time.

The patrols that day were kept short. Crawley and his team checked out the old marketplace, which seemed to have taken the brunt of most of the RPG activity, two others moved parallel to either side of the main road, Sebastian was gone the longest, disappearing into the foothills with Jankowski and a fast-moving foot patrol.

When they returned, long after everyone else had finished their evening meal, Sebastian looked hot, sweaty, and tired.

He smiled at me wearily, and went to debrief with Grant and Jankowski.

The kitchen reopened, handing out chili-flavored MREs to the dusty crew. Sebastian had just started eating, when Grant called him back into the office. He was in there nearly half-an-hour, and his abandoned food gone cold, when he suddenly re-emerged and headed my way, his face set and grim.

"What is it? What's happened?" I said, scared by the expression on his face.

"Grant wants to see you," he said, ignoring the curious gazes from the other men.

I stood up stiffly, and followed him into the office.

"Please take a seat, Ms. Venzi," said Grant, gently.

My heart rate accelerated. *What the hell was going on?*

"I'm afraid I have some bad news for you ... I told you yesterday that Master Sergeant Hunter picked up some threats to you, well, I'm afraid it's become much more direct. The Taliban have heard that you're with us—and they're viewing you as a prize kill."

I was vaguely aware that Sebastian was scowling at Grant, probably because the information had been so candid, but my brain was in free-fall. *They were targeting me?*

"They're aware of the value of publicity," he said tiredly, "and I'm afraid earlier today, they killed another journalist—a woman—and Hunter has just had confirmed radio chatter that you're a definite target. I'm calling in a heli to evacuate you back to Leatherneck as soon as possible. Ms. Venzi? Ms. Venzi?"

I looked up at him, stunned. "Who?"

"Excuse me?" he said, clearly puzzled.

"Who was the journalist they killed?"

He glanced over to Sebastian questioningly.

"Liz Ashton," said Sebastian, his eyes soft with pity.

No. No no no no no no no.

I dropped my head into my hands.

"I'm sorry," said Grant, uncomfortably. "Of course ... you knew her."

I nodded slowly. "She was my friend."

"I'm sorry," he said again, "but we can't risk our mission here and..."

He bit off what he was going to say, but it didn't matter. I'd guessed that there was some special reason his unit had been sent to Now Zad, and a reason why he didn't want me here in the first place. A remote part of my brain remembered Sebastian had hinted that he'd be traveling to remote villages, out of touch for days or even weeks.

But I was going home.

I looked up into Grant's face, recognizing that this wasn't the first time he'd had to break this sort of news.

"How did she die?"

Grant looked away, and it was Sebastian who answered. "Sniper. She died instantly."

I think Grant tried to say something else to me, but I didn't hear him. I walked out of his office, dry-eyed, my throat aching, vaguely aware that Sebastian had started to reach out for me as I walked past him.

I crossed the compound in a daze, ignoring everyone who spoke to me. I closed the door of my room behind me, and crouched down in the corner.

Not Liz. How could it be Liz? She was indestructible, larger than life. No, not larger than life. She was dead.

Put out the light, then put out the light.

Now her light was gone. One less stuttering candle in the darkness, one less person to tell the truth about this wretched war.

I refused to cry for her: not here, not in this godforsaken outpost.

Wrapping my hands around my knees tightly, I let my head fall forward, pressing my head down, as if to make as small a target as possible.

I don't know how long I hid in the corner, before I heard a soft tap at the door.

I didn't look up—I already knew it would be Sebastian. He shut the door behind him quietly, then sat down next to me and pulled me into his arms.

He didn't speak, just rocked me gently and kissed my hair.

After a while, I let my body relax against him, curling into his chest.

"I'm so sorry, Caro," he murmured. "I know she was your friend."

We sat in silence until night fell, and I took strength from his touch and his unspoken love.

Outside, we heard the sounds of men changing watch, and Sebastian sighed. "I'd better go, or Grant will wonder what the hell we're doing."

He shifted me off his lap and started to stand, but I grabbed hold of his hand.

"Don't go, Sebastian, please. It doesn't matter who knows now—I'm being sent home anyway. Let me spend my last few hours with you."

He sank down again. "I was hoping you'd say that," he admitted, his voice gentle.

We lay on the mattress, fully dressed, our arms and legs tangled together.

"I'm not very good at gardening," I said, thoughtfully.

"What's that, baby?"

"I can't grow things. Plants seem to wither when they see me. Can you grow things?"

I felt him shrug, confused by my question.

"I don't know, Caro. I've never tried."

"I'd like to plant something," I mumbled, "see it live and grow."

He tightened his grip, and stroked my hair.

"Does your place in Long Beach have a backyard?" he asked, gently.

"Yes. It could be pretty. Remember Signora Carello's bougainvillea? Maybe we could grow something like that."

He kissed my hair. "Baby, I can't even spell bougain ... whatever it is." He sighed. "But I guess I could try. Was that the purple stuff?"

I nodded.

"Okay, baby. We can grow purple stuff."

"And pink?"

"Sure, baby, with yellow fucking stripes if you want."

"Okay."

CHAPTER SIXTEEN

I DIDN'T SLEEP THAT NIGHT. I THOUGHT AT ONE POINT SEBASTIAN might have slept, but as I gazed up at his face, I could see that his eyes were open.

When we couldn't put it off any longer, I packed my equipment, and rolled up my deflated mattress, while Sebastian watched in silence.

"I'll miss having you here," he said, at last. "But I'm glad you're getting the fuck out of this shithole."

I wrapped my arms around his waist and leaned into his chest.

"Just come home safe, Sebastian. No heroics, please."

"The only thing you've got to worry about is when I self-combust, especially if you're going to send me more letters like that one you wrote me yesterday."

I tugged on his uniform. "I mean it. Stay safe."

He sighed and nuzzled his face into my hair. "I'll do my best, baby. Promise." Then he lifted up my chin with one, long finger and kissed me softly.

"Fuck, I'm going to miss you, Caro."

"I love you, *tesoro*. So much."

He held my face between his hands and gazed into my eyes. "*Sei tutto per me.*"

Our moment was over, and it was time to go.

Sebastian carried my bag out to the compound, ignoring the open stares of the other men. Captain Grant and Lieutenant Crawley shook hands with me, the latter offering his condolences.

Several of the men I'd been closest to came over and gave me awkward, one-armed hugs.

As soon as we heard the helicopter, eight Marines with M-16s escorted me to the pickup spot, 200 yards outside the compound.

The dust spewed into my eyes, churned up by the rotor blades that didn't stop. Coughing, with my eyes watering, I was yanked inside and had a headset thrust into my hands. We took off immediately, not wishing to offer too easy a target to the unfriendly faces that were sure to be watching from the foothills.

I squinted out of the window, rubbing grit from my eyes, trying to pick out Sebastian from among the small dots of men standing in the compound, but with all of them wearing desert utility uniforms, I couldn't tell which one was him.

My teeth rattled from the helicopter's vibration, and I had to grab onto my seat buckle to stop being thrown around as we banked sharply.

"Excuse me, Miss Venzi." A voice with an English accent reverberated through my earphones. "I'm Flight Lieutenant Reeves, and I'll be escorting you to Bastion."

Oh. I thought I'd be going back to Leatherneck. I guessed it was just a case of who could give me a ride at short notice. In any case— the American and British sections were only a few miles apart.

Camp Bastion, the British base in Helmand, was even larger than Leatherneck. It felt strange to be surrounded by English accents, and I kept expecting Liz's voice to bellow in my ear.

I wasn't sure what they were going to do with me—I assumed they'd transport me over to Leatherneck and let the US decide how to ship me out.

But I was wrong about that. I was bundled into a Land Rover and, instead, escorted to the Field Hospital.

I was greeted by a stocky man in the uniform of the Royal Army Medical Corps.

"Miss Venzi, I'm Major Gibson. I understand you're here to claim the body of Elizabeth Ashton."

I swallowed, my throat suddenly dry, and stared at him.

"No, I..."

He frowned. "I understand you were her next of kin?"

"She was my friend," I said quietly.

"I'm sorry," he said, shortly. "I understand this must be difficult for you. But her employers have given me her death-in-service contact list, and she's named you as next of kin. She was quite specific about that."

"I didn't know," I whispered. "But I don't mind. What did she ... what did she want to happen if...?"

"Her body will be repatriated to the UK. I understand she's requested a cremation and a service at St. Bride's church, Fleet Street."

That made sense. I remembered her telling me that the church's rebuilding after the Second World War had been paid for by journalists —it was their special place. I liked that.

"What do I need to do?"

"There's some paperwork," he said, kindly, "and her personal effects. Her newspaper is arranging for everything else."

I nodded slowly. "Can I see her?"

He looked me in the eye. "I'm sorry, Miss Venzi, that won't be possible."

I could guess the reason.

I signed the forms he gave me, and was given a box with Liz's name on it. Her camera was on top, with her laptop and notebooks at the bottom.

I pulled out her Nikon D4—six-thousand dollars worth of camera. Liz was—had been—serious about her work, she'd always had the best equipment.

"You can take anything you want, Miss Venzi," said the Major.

"Thank you. Did she leave any letters?"

He shook his head. "Not that I know of. She probably filed something with her paper before she flew out."

"Okay, thank you."

We were interrupted by a young woman in scrubs.

"I'm sorry, Major, but we've got three Cat-A wounded coming in."

He stood up, quickly. "I have to go. I'm sorry, Miss Venzi. Your escort will be out front—you're booked on the next flight to Kabul."

He left abruptly. I didn't mind. He couldn't help Liz. Not anymore.

I sat for some minutes, staring at her box. Then I took her camera, stuffed it into my daypack, and headed out.

For the next two hours I sat in a hangar at Camp Bastion, waiting for my flight back to Kabul. I emailed my editor to explain that I needed a flight to the US, and sent the seven features that I'd already written with the photographs from the RPG attacks, as well as life at Leatherneck and from the compound. In other words, I did what Liz would have expected of me: I did my job. I would not let my paper be shortchanged—and I still had a lot to say.

Then, with my laptop balanced on my knee, I wrote Liz's obituary. I wrote about her love of life, her compassion, her curiosity, her fine journalistic sense, her decency and belief in the value of all human life. I remembered her tall stories, her hip-flask—always full of the best Scottish whisky, her sympathy, her stoicism and, most of all, her humanity.

As I wrote, I wondered what would have been said about me, had I died. Would anyone have mentioned Sebastian? Other than Liz, who knew of our affair, our crazy love? Marc knew a little, and Nicole had an inkling, but other than that, would he even have been a footnote?

My insistence on secrecy seemed ridiculous now. Certainly, I wouldn't have been allowed out to Now Zad had our engagement been known, but I could have been sent to another of the US military's remote outposts.

And then I wondered about the two thousand US troops killed in Afghanistan. Who wrote their obituaries? Were their stories carried in small-town papers across the country? Or the 500 British troops, 158 from Canada, 88 from France, 56 from Germany, Italy, Denmark, Australia, Poland, Turkey, Latvia, Finland, Jordan—even Lithuania.

And 37 journalists: now, 38. So many deaths, so much loss.

I took Sebastian's ring off the chain around my neck, and slipped it back onto the third finger of my left hand, where, God willing, it would stay forever.

~

Back in Kabul, I checked into the Mustafa Hotel again. The manager was surprised to see me, but welcomed me and gave me my old room back.

I wished he hadn't. He'd meant to be kind, but staring at the twin bed where Liz had slept—and snored through half the night—I just felt sad.

I worked all night writing a rough draft, then polishing the remainder of the features that I owed the newspaper. All the time I wondered what Sebastian was doing. I hoped he'd finally get some sleep without me being there to distract him.

I sen an email to let him know I was back in Kabul and awaiting a flight home. I didn't know when he'd see it, but it was still important that I sent it. I also hand wrote a letter, telling him how much I loved him and missed him, and then spoke about all the things we could do when he was home with me in Long Beach. It seemed a long way away.

I was ready to pack up and try to sleep when I received an email from my editor. He was doing his best, but warned me it could be three or four days before he managed to get a flight. And he wanted to speak to me.

Just as I was about to call him, the signal on my cell disappeared again. I trudged down to reception to call him from the hotel's landline, which was only slightly more reliable.

When I finally got through, I gave him more information about Liz's death—the things I hadn't been able to put in her obituary. Sounding shocked, he promised he'd get me out as soon as possible.

After that, I didn't feel like sleeping, so, instead, I spent the day wandering the echoing halls of the Afghanistan National Museum. Seventy percent of the artifacts had disappeared during looting over the past three decades, but the museum was slowly coming back to life. I took the opportunity to interview several of the enthusiastic, but poorly-paid, curators. They were hopeful that the long, cultural history had a future in their country.

I hoped they were right, and I was glad that someone felt optimistic about Afghanistan's future.

Wearily, I returned to my hotel room and wrote another letter to Sebastian. This time I told him about the surf spots at Long Beach, up to the Hamptons and as far as Montauk.

I tried hard to make my letter upbeat and cheerful, but it was difficult when I knew I wouldn't see him for at least another five months.

When I'd finished, I kicked off my boots and lay down.

I hadn't eaten and I wasn't hungry. At least I was tired: I curled up under the sheets, in the unbelievable comfort of the narrow bed, and wished that Sebastian's warm body was next to me, with his breath on my neck, and his arms around my waist.

～

A loud knock on the door woke me from a light sleep. I sat up in bed, my heart pounding. I squinted at my wristwatch: 2.45AM.

"Who is it?" I asked loudly and clearly.

"Phone call."

It was a voice I didn't recognize.

"Who's calling me?"

"Phone call."

I couldn't tell if it was simply that the person outside my door didn't speak English, or whether I was in danger. I didn't like it at all, and my anxiety levels shot up to Defcon 1.

Without speaking again, I slipped on my boots, and picked up my evac-grab bag, with my finger one button away from dialing the emergency contact number on my cell.

I looked through the peephole in my door but couldn't see anyone; I listened carefully but couldn't hear anything. I was well aware that someone could easily be waiting for me out of my sightline.

I took a deep breath and yanked the door open: the corridor was empty. Which meant the phone call could very well be genuine and not a ruse. I hurried down the stairs, avoiding the elevator, and made my way to the reception area.

A young man in a heavily embroidered vest over a loose, white shirt was sitting at the desk, half asleep. As I approached, he jerked awake.

"Venzi?"

"Ao," I replied. *Yes.*

"Phone call," he said, pointing at the telephone on his desk.

I picked it up tentatively.

"*As-salaamu' alaykum.* This is Lee Venzi."

"*Caroline. At last! It's David.*"

"David?" What the hell was my ex-husband doing calling me in the middle of the night? Was he drunk? "What's wrong? How did you find me, David? Are you all right?"

"*Caroline, listen, I don't have much time. I'm at the field hospital at Camp Bastion. It's Hunter.*"

"Sebastian?"

Oh no, please God, no.

"*I'm sorry: he was brought in five hours ago. I've been trying to find you.*"

I felt sick and cold, and my knees gave way. I slumped into a chair, clattering the legs against the front desk and making the young man jump.

"What's happened? David, please tell me!"

His voice crackled at the end of the line.

"*They're still trying to establish the facts, but off the record, it was another green-on-blue attack: sniper and a suicide bomber, they think. Caroline, you can't report any of this.*"

"I don't care about that, damn it! How's Sebastian? Is he ... is he hurt? Badly? How badly?"

He hesitated long enough for my world to end.

"*Yes, it's pretty bad.*" He paused briefly, then snapped into doctor mode. "*He has a gunshot injury that has induced a pneumothorax—a collapsed lung. We're not too worried about that as the exit wound is clear and the bullet*" *passed through cleanly, although there may be some nerve damage to his left arm resulting in limited fine motor skills..."*

All the breath left my body.

"But he has a Category A..." he paused again, before continuing slowly. "He has a severe injury to his right thigh with multiple debrided shrapnel wounds. They're taking him into surgery now—they'll decide then if the leg is viable. If not, it will be a trans-femoral amputation..." he paused again, "an above-the-knee amputation."

There was a long silence and all the light in my world poured into a deep, dark hole.

"I'm sorry, Caroline ... I thought you'd want to know."

I held my hand over my mouth, as if I could press back the fear that was threatening to choke me.

"Can I see him?"

He sighed. "At the moment the answer is no. You're not ... look, I'll try and get you access, Caroline, but you'd have to get yourself here and I don't know how easy that will be. I'll see what I can find out ... but it's a long shot. I can't promise anything."

"I see."

Breathe. Breathe.

"Thank you, David. Will you let me know ... if the situation changes."

"Yes, of course. I..."

Whatever he wanted to say died as he tried to speak, and the words remained unspoken.

"I'll be in touch," he said, quietly. "Goodbye, Caroline."

The phone line went dead and I stared at the receiver.

Oh, God, no.

No. NO! They were not going to stop me seeing Sebastian. I didn't care if I'd have to fight the whole damn US Army. My love needed me, and no force of hell on earth could stop me being with him.

And that thought galvanized me into action: now was not the time to go to pieces. I whipped out my phone and scrolled through to find the emergency satcomms number that Sebastian had given me. Emergencies only he'd said—this sure as hell qualified.

The man at reception looked like he wanted to say something about my liberal use of the hotel's telephone, but my ferocious expression stopped him.

I dialed quickly, and it was answered on the second ring.

"Grant."

Oh!

"Captain Grant, this is Lee Venzi. I need a favor: I'm in Kabul but I have to get back to Leatherneck. Can you help me get papers, transport, anything?"

"Miss Venzi?" He sounded surprised and annoyed. "How did you get this number? Look, now isn't a good time."

"I'm sorry, but it's urgent, Captain."

For only the second time since I'd known him, he swore.

"I've just lost three of my men, and a further two are Cat A wounded, and..."

I screamed at him.

"I know that!"

"How the hell do you know that?" he barked back.

"It doesn't matter—I just do."

"The fuck it doesn't! If someone is leaking our movements and..."

I took a deep breath: losing it now was not helping.

"No!" I managed to say, in a more measured tone. "No, it wasn't anything like that: I have a medic friend at Bastion's field hospital, I got the information from him."

"I didn't take you for a ghoul, Lee," he said grimly.

"Fuck you, Grant!" I snarled. "I have a *friend* who is just being operated on and I don't know if he's going to get through alive so just fucking get me there!"

There was a short pause.

"You're talking about Hunter, aren't you?"

"Yes," I said, trying not to let my throat close up.

"Okay, Miss Venzi," he said, in a more even tone. "I'll see if I can pull some strings to get you there. But don't call this number—and don't ask me again."

"I won't," I barked into the phone.

"Where are you staying?"

I gave him the hotel's address and hung up.

I thought he'd try to help me, but he had other men to worry about —other casualties. I chewed on a nail, wondering who else I could call on.

Inspiration struck. There was one more number I could try: Ches Peters—Sebastian's best friend. A man whom I was pretty certain despised me.

I did the math to work out the time difference—it was about seven o'clock in the evening in San Diego. He had two young kids, so I hoped he'd be home.

The phone rang three times before it was answered.

A child's voice trilled down the line.

"Hello, Peters' residence. This is Ben Peters speaking."

"Hi, Ben. Can I talk to your daddy, please?"

"He's making popcorn," said the little boy.

"Could you get him for me? It's important."

There was an angry huff, a short pause where I could hear muffled voices, and then I heard Ches come on the line.

"Hello, who's this?"

"Ches, this is Lee ... this is Caroline Venzi ... I was Caroline Wilson and..."

"I know who you are. What do you want?"

His voice was cool, but full of unspoken contempt.

"I need your help. Well, Mitch's, I guess—I know he's still in the Marines. I'd have called him direct but I don't have his number."

I realized I was babbling. I needed to focus.

"Ches, I'm calling from Afghanistan. Sebastian has been hurt. Pretty badly..."

I had to hold the phone away from my face for a moment, stifling the choking sobs that bubbled up my throat.

"How bad?" Ches whispered.

"Bad. They're taking him into surgery now. They might ... they're talking about amputating his right leg."

I heard Ches's shocked curse.

"He's at the field hospital near Camp Leatherneck, but I'm stuck 300 miles away in Kabul, and without papers. I can't get to him. I know you think I'm a first class bitch and that I ruined his life, but I'm begging you, Ches, begging you..."

I had to pause to catch my breath, forcing the pointless tears away.

"Please," I choked out, "if there's anything you or Mitch can do to get me there. I'm pulling in every favor I can think of, using every contact. I'll do anything. If you know anyone, anyone at all ... please, Ches, please..."

"I'll do what I can, Caroline," he said in a stunned, quiet voice. "Give me the details."

I told him everything I knew, which wasn't much. But it was more than most people would have known in the same circumstances—and it was thanks to David.

I was sorely tempted to call my editor, but I suspected his immediate reaction would be to tell me to stay put until he got me on a flight home. He'd been shocked into silence when I'd told him the reason I was pulled out of Now Zad, and coming on top of what had happened to Liz, I didn't know how much help he'd be.

In fact I was pretty certain he'd try to block me getting back to Kandahar.

Desperate as I was to get to Sebastian, I had to think, I couldn't just charge in. It even crossed my mind to try and speak to Natalie Arnaud: she worked for the UN—she might have contacts. I decided I would wait until morning before I tried my riskier avenues. By then David or Grant might have made some wheels spin, and I was damn sure that Ches and Mitch would pull every string they could.

I went back to my room, and packed up everything, ready to leave at a moment's notice.

When there was nothing left to do, when every last bit of fight and determination had been used up, I lay on the bed clutching Sebastian's ring, and wept.

They say there are no atheists in foxholes. I say there are no atheists when you're begging God to keep alive the person you love.

~

At exactly 5.57AM I woke up and swore.

Damn it! Why hadn't I thought of this last night? *This* was why it was important not to go to pieces in an emergency.

I checked my phone and sent up a silent prayer, thanking the saints of telecommunications.

"Sergeant Benson, this is Lee Venzi—you were my bodyguard last week."

I could tell from his fuzzy voice that he'd been asleep when I rang.

"Miss Venzi?"

"I'm sorry I woke you up, and I'm sorry it's so early, but I need your help. I'm in Kabul..."

"Kabul?"

"Yes, I'm back at the Mustafa Hotel. I got evac-ed from Leatherneck and, well ... it's a long story. Look, I've just found that my ... *fiancé* has been injured and I *have* to get back out there. Can you help me?"

He sounded wide awake now.

"I'm real sorry to hear that, Miss Venzi, but you'll have to go through the usual channels. Have your newspaper contact the Corps' Division of Public Affairs and..."

"I don't have time for that! Listen to me! He's hurt really badly—I don't know if he'll ... I *have* to get there. Please, Sergeant ... he's one of your own—he's a United States Marine."

There was a silence at the end of the line. Then he said, "Give me three hours."

Sergeant Benson was as good as his word.

I called Ches to let him know I was on the move, and promised to get in touch as soon as I had any further news.

A hundred-and-fifty minutes later, I was on my way back to Lashkar Gah. Sergeant Benson had moved heaven and earth to get me where I needed to be. I would never forget his kindness.

To say David was surprised to see me would be a vast understatement. But he didn't waste any time asking me stupid questions either.

As soon as he saw me, he said, "He's still alive, Caroline."

"Thank God."

Those brief words flooded through me, and some of the weight on my chest that had made it hurt to breathe, eased just a little.

He led me through a complex of tents and portable huts, and into what looked like the ICU department of a modern, urban hospital.

"He's in here."

The room was small and brightly lit. Sebastian lay on a hospital bed with a number of tubes and monitors attached to him. His left arm was elevated and he was breathing on a ventilator, his chest rising and falling in time with the machine. It was the only sign he was alive: he was so still and pale.

Below his waist, he was covered with a thin blanket which rose in a mound over the cage that protected his right leg.

Thank God—they'd saved his leg.

A man in desert utilities was standing over Sebastian. At first I thought he was a doctor, but then I heard what he was saying, the rhythmical cadence of words repeated too many times.

"O Father of mercies and God of all comfort, our only help in time of need..."

I recognized the prayer for the sick.

"We humbly beseech thee to behold, visit and relieve thy sick servant Sebastian Hunter, for whom our prayers are desired. Look upon him with the eyes of thy mercy, comfort him with a sense of thy goodness, preserve him from the temptations of the enemy, and give him patience under his affliction. In thy good time, restore him to health, and enable him to lead the residue of his life in thy fear, and to thy glory, and grant that finally Sebastian may dwell with thee in life everlasting, through Jesus Christ our Lord. Amen."

"Amen," I echoed, softly.

The man turned around, and I wasn't surprised to see that he was wearing the white collar of a priest.

I crossed myself.

"Thank you, Padre."

"Is he a friend of yours?"

I nodded. "He's my *fiancé*," I said, quietly.

I couldn't see David's face, but I heard his sudden intake of breath behind me.

The priest patted my arm.

"God hears all prayers, my child. And your young man is very strong."

He gave me a small smile, nodded at David, and left the room.

"You're marrying him?" asked David, his voice oddly strained. "You didn't say that when I saw you before in Kabul. You said you'd only just met again."

I looked up sharply. "I wasn't lying, David. This is ... very new."

"I'm sorry..." he began. Then he cleared his throat and started again.

"They've managed to save the leg for now, but there's still some doubt about whether it's viable. The next few days will be critical. There was dirt in the shrapnel and he's contracted acinetobacter baumannii—it's a common infection out here. We're treating it with antibiotics but..." he sighed. "And he's been put into a medically-induced coma: we were worried about brain swelling as he received a shockwave from the bomb. Well, that's quite typical with these sorts of injuries."

I nodded, unable to speak.

"I'm sorry, Caroline," he said again. "Well, if you need anything..."

Hesitantly, David rested his hand on my shoulder, then turned and left me alone with my grief.

I picked up Sebastian's hand and held it in my own. The fingers felt cold, so I held them to my mouth and blew on them softly, trying to heat them with my breath, just as he had done, only three weeks before in Chamonix.

Dear God—that seemed a lifetime ago. He'd been so alive, so vibrant, so full of hope, and now...

I held his hand to my cheek and closed my eyes.

"Come back to me, Sebastian. Please, *tesoro*, you have to fight. You've always been so strong, don't give up now, don't give up on us. I need you. Come back to me. Please, come back to me."

The ventilator rose and fell, his chest rose and fell, but Sebastian's eyes remained closed.

I talked to him all day: telling him about the bungalow, and the way the ocean trembled with light in the summer sun; how the sky seemed to reach long fingers down to the waves in a storm, spray mingling with rain.

I told him about Alice's kindness and humor, about Jenna's fieriness, and the way Nicole was always trying to set me up on dates—but that I didn't need her to do that anymore. And I told him what Ches had said to me on the telephone.

"He told me to kick your butt right out of this hospital bed, Sebastian. You promised him you'd go surfing in California after this tour, a fact that you completely forgot to mention to me, I might add. Do you want to have our honeymoon in California, *tesoro*? Because I don't care where we have it. Anywhere you like, my love. Sebastian, can you hear me? I love you so much—we have our whole lives ahead of us. I'll go anywhere, do anything to be with you. Just please wake up, *tesoro*."

A medic came past and checked the machine's readouts, before methodically pushing some more meds into the IV bag that was suspended next to the bed.

"You a friend of his, ma'am?"

"Yes, I am."

"Perhaps you can help me then? We found a letter on him when he was brought in, but the name isn't anyone on his emergency contact list. We just held onto it, kinda hoping we could find someone to give it to. Do you know a 'Carolina Hunter' ma'am? We figured it was some relative of his, but so far we can't trace her."

I gasped slightly, then nodded. "Yes, I know her. I'll make sure she gets it."

"Thank you, ma'am."

He reached into a locker next to Sebastian's bed and pulled out a muddy envelope.

When he handed it to me, I realized it wasn't covered in dirt, but blood—Sebastian's blood. The medic shrugged his apology, and walked away to check on his next patient.

My hands shook as I tore open the envelope.

There was a single sheet of lined paper with a ragged edge inside, probably torn from a notebook. One side contained a short message in Sebastian's careful handwriting.

> *Caro, my love,*
>   *Just writing these words makes me happier than I can remember being for a very long time—ten years, in fact.*
>   *I'm not one for words—I leave that to you—my beautiful, talented Caro. But we've had the news we were waiting for and soon we'll be heading out. I hope you never read this letter, but if you do, it means I've gone on to the next big adventure.*
>   *Knowing that you are in the world and wearing my ring, makes me the happiest man alive, and the last few weeks have been the best and happiest of my whole life.*
>   *Be happy, Caro, because that's what you deserve.*
>   *I love you, I have always loved you, and wherever I go after this world, I will always love you. Sempre e per sempre.*
>   *Sebastian*

I clutched his letter to my chest, trying to find a way to fill the aching void. I couldn't understand why my heart was still beating.

I gave up trying to be strong. I lay my head next to his hand, and my tears soaked into the crisp, white sheet.

My love was slipping away from me, and there was nothing I could do.

~

The night passed and I sat staring at Sebastian's face, memorizing every line and angle: the softness of his cheeks, now covered with a fine, light brown stubble, the full, sensual lips, distorted by the breathing tube that had been placed into his throat, the strong, straight nose, the wide forehead, the beautiful symmetry of his cheekbones. But his lovely eyes, the windows to his sweet soul, were hidden.

I whispered my secrets to him, all my desires and fears, hoping that in some way he knew that I was with him. I ran my fingers along the back of his hand and up his forearm, tracing the faint veins, knowing that they were still pumping blood through his body, and that the fight wasn't over.

David returned at some point, although whether it was day or night by then, I couldn't tell.

"Caroline, perhaps you should try and get some sleep. I've arranged for you to have a cot-bed in the doctors' lounge. Well, it's not much of a lounge, more of a shed really."

"Thank you, David. That's very kind of you. Maybe later."

He looked at me thoughtfully.

"He's holding on, Caroline. He's strong, but ... they're trying to decide whether to medivac him to Germany. It just depends on ... whether he's stable enough to make the journey."

I stared up at him.

"Why are you being so nice to me, David? I always thought you must hate me after ... everything that happened."

He looked surprised, then rubbed a hand tiredly across his cheeks.

"I tried to hate you. I thought I did, for a while, but I couldn't really. I knew it was my fault."

I blinked with surprise, amazed by his words.

"Why did you think that? I was the one who ... had the affair."

His eyes closed briefly and when he opened them again, he seemed to have made a decision.

"You were so full of life, Caroline, and I loved you so much. I tried so hard to hold onto you, but the harder I tried to hold on, the more you slipped away from me. I ended up crushing you. I was so terrified you'd see through me ... I did everything I could to stifle you. I knew it was wrong, but I couldn't stop myself. I will regret that to my dying day."

Then he gestured toward Sebastian. "He brought you back to life."

I hung my head, humbled by his admission and his apology, remembering all his cruelty and bullying. And remembering, too, his new kindness in my hour of need.

"I'm so sorry, David. For everything that happened between us. For what I did to you. I never meant to hurt you. But ... I fell in love."

"I know," he said, softly. "I just wish it had been with me."

He smiled sadly, and walked away.

The days and nights began to blur together. If it hadn't been for David, bringing me food or insisting that I slept, I don't know how I would have coped.

I called Ches each day, but there wasn't much I could tell him. I heard the hope in his voice every time I called, and every time I could only repeat the same words, "There's no change."

The chaplain visited us daily, and told me not to give up hope. Sometimes he prayed with me, sometimes he brought me a sandwich. Both were equally welcome.

I'd been there four or five days, the colorless hours merging together, when David told me that Sebastian was stable enough to be moved. Some news, at last.

"We're going to bring him out of the coma, then he'll be sent to the Landstuhl Regional Medical Center in Germany. From there, on to Bethesda in Maryland or Walter Reed in DC. I'm not sure which."

"Will I be able to go with him?"

He sighed. "Normally, I'd say that was highly unlikely. But, off the record, Caroline, if you can use your Press connections, then maybe."

"Thank you," I said, quietly, touching his hand.

He smiled briefly.

That was all the encouragement I needed. I was on the phone to my editor within 20 minutes and I refused to take no for an answer. I promised as many articles as he wanted, exclusive interviews and photographs of life in a military medical center. In the end, he agreed to help. I don't know how many strings he pulled in Washington, but he promised me he'd get me on the same flight as Sebastian.

When I returned to Sebastian's room, I couldn't work out what was different—and then I realized it was too quiet. The ventilator had stopped working. I panicked, looking around wildly for help, but then … I saw that Sebastian's eyes were open, and he was looking at me.

He spoke, and his voice was so soft and hoarse that I could barely hear him.

"I *knew* you wouldn't give up on us," he said.

We were flown out that evening, and arrived at the medical center in Germany at dawn. The critical cases were taken off first—those with brain injuries and missing limbs. We waited on the chilly tarmac for 15 minutes before the rest of us were loaded onto a fleet of blue buses.

We were met by the Head of the Critical Care Team, and the army chaplain.

"You're here at the US army hospital. We're going to take good care of you. We're praying for you. You're here at the US army hospital. We're going to take good care of you. We're praying for you."

Over and over again, the tired-looking chaplain repeated the words, as stretcher after stretcher passed him, the syllables blurring and becoming meaningless.

Sebastian held my hand tightly but didn't speak.

We were there for just two nights while Sebastian was 'processed'.

The harried but sympathetic staff gave me a small, cell-like room in the women's quarters. Day and night the injured arrived: there wasn't time to learn the names of the soldiers with so many identical injuries who streamed through the hospital, some from Iraq, most from Afghanistan. They were treated and moved on. Treated and moved on. An endless flow of mutilated flesh and tortured minds.

Sebastian had the option to go back to San Diego or to an East Coast facility. We decided it would be easier if we were near home— my home—our home, and we flew out to Walter Reed in Maryland on a Thursday at the start of May.

The journey from Germany was long and painful for Sebastian, he didn't complain once, even though I could tell he was in agony, his body covered in an unhealthy sheen of sweat. But he didn't speak to me either, and that scared me.

There were many who were far worse off. One young man I spoke quietly with during those dreary hours was named Lance. He'd lost both legs and one arm. He told me that he was 'glad' it had happened to him, because he wouldn't have wanted it to happen to any of his buddies in his platoon.

He was 22.

~

Our arrival back on US soil was without fanfare. I traveled with Sebastian the whole time and saw him settled into a unit, before I found myself accommodation nearby in a cheap motel. There were other wives and family members staying there and we became close, sharing our hopes and dreams—or rather, forging new dreams that were far more limited in their scope than formerly.

Liz's memorial service came and went. I sent a letter to her editor, asking him to read it out for me, and I asked him to recite the poem 'High Flight' by Pilot Officer Gillespie Magee. I knew it had always been a favorite of Liz's.

> *Oh! I have slipped the surly bonds of earth*
> *And danced the skies on laughter-silvered wings,*
> *Sunward I've climbed, and joined the tumbling mirth*
> *Of sun-split clouds—and done a hundred things*
> *You have not dreamed of—wheeled and soared and swung*
> *High in the sunlit silence. Hov'ring there*
> *I've chased the shouting wind along, and flung*

My eager craft through footless halls of air.
Up, up the long delirious, burning blue,
I've topped the windswept heights with easy grace
Where never lark, or even eagle flew –
And, while with silent lifting mind I've trod
The high untresspassed sanctity of space,
Put out my hand and touched the face of God.

Alone in my motel room, I said a prayer for her, too.

For nine weeks, I waited and watched with anxious eyes as Sebastian slowly began to heal.

He was given intensive physiotherapy to help him use his left arm and to walk again. He became breathless and tired quickly, but, in the face of so many with worse injuries, he hid his true feelings. I think I was the only one who could see the simmering anger beneath the surface.

To other soldiers and to the staff, he seemed cheerful and worked hard at whatever exercises he was given. But to me, he was closed and distant. He'd always been so honest and open with me, I felt lost and alone—more truly lonely in his company than when I was by myself.

It soon became obvious that the extent of his injuries would render him unfit for duty. One of the prerequisites of being a Marine was the ability to run without a limp. The doctors thought it extremely unlikely that Sebastian would ever be able to walk without using a crutches, let alone run. A medical discharge was the most likely scenario.

The military was generous to those wounded in combat, and although Sebastian wouldn't qualify for a medical pension, not having served his 20 years, he was told he could still expect to receive between a third and half of his current salary. He would be a disabled veteran.

Those words sent him into a fury. He ranted at me for nearly half an hour.

"I won't take it," he growled.

"What? Why not?"

"I just won't," he said, with finality.

"Sebastian, you deserve that—after everything you've been through…"

"I'm not fucking taking it, Caro. I'm 27. I don't fucking want disability pay!"

"Okay, *tesoro*. That's your choice."

I think the fact that I wouldn't fight with him just made it worse. He had vast reserves of pent-up anger, and I was the nearest target—and probably the only one he felt he could take it out on.

The military also offered him the chance to take college courses through the GI Bill, but he wouldn't discuss that either. The list of unmentionable topics became longer each day.

The tense silence between us was exhausting. At a loss, I thought it might help if I gave him some space and let him come to terms with everything that had happened without my constant presence—and without what he seemed to feel was my constant interference.

I decided we needed a break from each other and I wanted to go and check on my house, too. Alice had been going over there regularly, but I longed to be in my own home. I really thought it might help our tenuous relationship if I just visited Sebastian on the weekends. It was also getting expensive staying in the motel, although I didn't mention that to him.

We were resting on a bench in the grounds after Sebastian had managed to walk almost 200 yards, leaning heavily on a crutch. It was hard for me to see him struggle when he had always been so strong and vigorous, but how much harder it was for him, I could only imagine.

"You did well today, Sebastian."

He grunted an answer, and I couldn't tell if he was agreeing with me or not.

I sighed, then took a deep breath.

"I've been thinking I should go back to Long Beach. Just to make sure everything is okay at home. I want to try and start working a little more..."

My words died away as he looked at me with something like loathing.

"You're leaving me."

It was a statement, not a question.

"No, *tesoro!* Why would you say that? No, never!"

"Don't fucking lie to me, Caro," he shouted. "You've made it pretty fucking obvious you don't want to be here. Well, fine. Just fucking go."

And he turned away from me.

I tried to speak, but I choked on the sounds.

"Please, Sebastian," I said, touching his arm. "That's not what I'm saying. I just wanted to ... try and get some ... some normalcy. I'd visit on weekends."

He shrugged me off.

"Don't fucking drag it out, Caro," he said, bitterly. "I'm not completely fucking dumb."

I stood suddenly, and the movement made him look up.

"Damn you, Sebastian!" I yelled. "I'm not leaving you! You'll never get rid of me, so you can just stop trying. Right now."

He looked away again.

"Whatever," he said.

That was a bad, bad day. I wondered how much further we had to fall—and I dreaded finding out. But I also realized that although Sebastian sniped and snarled at me day after day, he needed me to be with him. I decided to stay in Maryland: Alice would be able to continue looking after the bungalow.

We'd manage—somehow.

Seven days later, the Physical Evaluation Board Liaison Officer, a friendly but efficient woman whom I knew as Joan, told Sebastian that the PEB would, 'authorize his disability separation, with disability benefits, as he had been found unfit and his condition was incompatible with continued military service'.

Sebastian was no longer a US Marine.

CHAPTER SEVENTEEN

THE DAY SEBASTIAN CAME HOME SHOULD HAVE BEEN THE HAPPIEST of our lives, but my love was broken in body and spirit.

I arranged for a taxi to pick us up from the airport. Nicole and Jenna had both offered to drive us, but I thought it would be better for him to have a quiet return. Sebastian was in no shape to meet my friends, no matter how well-meaning.

Alice had been to the bungalow to clean and air it, and had also promised to stock up the fridge.

I'd arranged for a wheelchair to take Sebastian from the plane to the airport's entrance, but he refused to even consider it.

"I'm not fucking using it, Caro, so just drop it," he snapped at me.

I quietly acquiesced, and watched his slow and painful struggle through the terminal building, using the crutch to support his right leg, which still couldn't bear his weight.

The taxi driver chatted away during the journey back to Long Beach, and I tried to keep up a desultory conversation while Sebastian stared out of the window.

I thought I detected a slight change in him when he saw the ocean, today a sharp, slate-blue under the August sunshine, but then he closed up and the shutters on his emotions came crashing down again.

When we arrived at my bungalow, the driver collected our bags from the trunk and deposited them on the porch. I stood back while Sebastian struggled from the car, desperate to help him, but knowing he'd hate it and resent the interference.

"Dude, what happened to your leg?" the driver suddenly asked him.

"Bomb."

"Say what?"

"Bomb: got blown up."

"Cool!"

I thought Sebastian would smile or roll his eyes or give some indication of the callousness of the driver's comment, but he didn't. The light had gone out of his eyes and I didn't know what it would take to rekindle it.

We'd find a way. We'd always find a way.

But it was hard.

Sebastian was exhausted and in pain. He made his way to my couch and lowered himself carefully, biting back the groan that rose to his lips.

"Do you want to lie down, *tesoro*?"

I badly wanted him to make a joke, to say something about me wanting to get him into bed as soon as possible, but he didn't. He just shook his head.

"I'll stay here for a while."

"Okay." I hesitated. "Well, I'll put your bags in the spare room for now. We can go through them later."

He didn't answer.

I shoved his duffel bag and backpack under the bed. I decided I'd unpack these when he was asleep. He didn't need to see his uniforms now. I didn't even know if he'd want to keep them.

When I walked back into the living room, he was staring into space.

"Are you hungry? Would you like some pasta?"

He shook his head. "No."

I bit back my words, which would have insisted that he eat something.

He'd lost weight, a lot of weight, his face gaunt, and his beauty, which had always seemed so tangible, had become ethereal.

"Maybe later," I said, softly.

He didn't answer.

I felt odd and ill at ease being home after such an extended absence and Sebastian's silent, volcanic presence intimidated me.

"This wasn't what I'd planned," he said.

"It's not what either of us had in mind, but we'll deal, won't we?"

"I thought I'd be carrying you over the fucking threshold," he said, his face twisted with disgust.

"That doesn't matter, Sebastian. We..."

"Yes, it does fucking matter, Caro!" he shouted, making me jump. "It really fucking matters! Christ, can't you understand something as fucking simple as that?"

I blanched, his anger cutting me to the core.

"I'm sorry, Sebastian, I just…"

"Just what, Caro?"

"Nothing," I muttered, walking into the kitchen, and holding onto the sink.

I will not cry. I will not cry.

I needed something to do with my hands to stop them from shaking. I hunted through the fridge, trying to think of something he might like to eat. In the end I kept it simple—a cheese sandwich with lettuce and tomato. It wasn't really the sort of thing I enjoyed eating, but I hoped if I had the same food, it might tempt him.

I took two plates into the living room and set one down next to him. He didn't even look at the food, just continued staring into space, as if his outburst had never happened.

I tried not to panic: he'd been through a lot. How trivial that sounded—he'd nearly died and he was a long way from recovering—even the doctors still failed to agree on how full that recovery would be.

I couldn't stand the silence. Eventually, I turned on the TV, something I rarely did when I was by myself. I had to change channel several times before I found something that didn't have news programs or anything to do with Afghanistan. We ended up watching something about meerkats in Africa: very educational—neither of us heard more than half a dozen words, and Sebastian didn't touch his food.

"Do you have any beer?"

"Oh, no, sorry," I stuttered. "I could open some wine?"

He nodded. "Yeah, that'll do."

I opened a bottle Chianti and watched him drink three glasses, one after the other. He would have finished the bottle if I hadn't taken it into the kitchen.

"Caro, what are you doing with the fucking wine?"

No. I wasn't having this. He wasn't going to drown his sorrows in a bottle.

"You haven't eaten anything, and you have to take your pain killers, Sebastian. So, no, the wine stays in the kitchen."

He exploded. Swearing at me, shouting and yelling. Who the fuck did I think I was? Who was I to tell him how to live his life? And on and on.

I hoped that when he'd finished, he'd have gotten some of the poison out of him, but he soon reverted to the cold silence that hurt the most.

By 9PM, his face was gray with tiredness.

"Should I show you where the bedroom is?"

"It's a fucking bungalow, Caro," he said, "how fucking difficult do you think it's going to be? I'm not a fucking moron, even if I am a cripple."

"Sebastian..."

But he didn't want to listen. He pulled himself off the couch, gasping as pain lanced through him, and he clenched his teeth.

After a false start, where he crashed into the spare room, he found his way to the bedroom. I gave him a few minutes, then followed. He was lying on his good side, facing away from my side of the bed.

I brushed my teeth and slipped in next to him, carefully curling my body into his and enjoying the moment when my arm rested across his waist, feeling his bare skin again after nearly three months.

He shifted minutely.

"Don't," he said.

I pulled my hand back as if stung.

He didn't want me to touch him? He didn't want me to touch him.

I'd learned during my first marriage that it is possible to cry without making a sound, I didn't think Sebastian would take me back to those years. And that was more painful than anything. I lay next to him as the tears slipped silently down my cheeks.

Over the next few days, things became worse. He had no interest in anything; I had to nag to get him to shower or change his clothes, and he refused point blank to shave, so his beautiful face was covered in a light-brown stubble that was unfamiliar and unwelcome.

He ate little, preferring instead to work his way through my small collection of wine, and cut off any attempt of mine to stop him.

He barely spoke to me. His usual responses included shouting and yelling, or just ignoring me. He didn't read, he didn't watch TV, he didn't do anything except drink.

My friends wanted to come and visit. Tentatively, I suggested it to him, thinking he might be persuaded into making an effort for them, if not for me.

"Yeah, they want to come see the fucking war cripple," he sneered, "make them feel good, like fucking charity. What's the matter with you, Caro? Do I look like I'm ready to see anyone?"

"Sebastian, they're my friends. They want to meet you, and they

want to see me. You don't have to put on a performance for them."
Even though that was exactly what I'd hoped.

He shrugged, and said that if they came, he'd stay in the bedroom.

I decided to ask them to postpone their visit.

Before I'd returned from Afghanistan, I'd telephoned each of them, explaining everything about Sebastian: how we'd met, why we'd been forced apart. It had been deeply uncomfortable, and I was afraid of their censure. Instead, they'd been supportive, although I could tell that they were hurt that I'd never been completely candid with them before. I hoped they understood my reasons. I hadn't told them we were engaged, although I wasn't sure why.

I took my phone and walked down to the beach alone.

"Nic, it's Lee."

"Hey, honey! What time do you want us tomorrow?"

"Look, it's not good timing. Sebastian is ... struggling. He's not ready to meet anyone."

She could hear the tremor in my voice.

"Fuck that, Lee! I want to see *you*. This isn't something you have to do by yourself."

"I know that, Nic, but now just isn't good. Maybe in a few weeks."

There was a short silence.

"How bad is it, Lee?"

"Bad," I said. "Really bad."

And then I started crying, and couldn't stop.

Nicole listened to me sobbing into the phone for several minutes. When I finally began to calm down, she spoke to me firmly.

"Lee, you need professional help on this, Sebastian needs professional help. Can't the VA hospital do something? I mean, the military has programs to help with exactly this problem."

I shook my head wearily, wishing she was there to throw a comforting arm around me.

"He refuses to talk to anyone, Nic. He barely talks to me. I don't know what to do—he says he's had enough of hospitals and never wants to see another doctor. I get that, and I feel the same in some ways, but I'm at the end of my rope here. And he's drinking, he hardly eats. He doesn't touch me, and won't let me touch him. I don't know what to do."

She hesitated for a moment.

"Are you sure you want to do this at all, Lee?"

I took a sharp intake of breath.

Out of everything I thought she'd say, that had been furthest from my thoughts. And I had considered that I might not be what he needed, but I'd always assumed that he'd be the one to walk away.

"I can't abandon him now, Nic. He needs me, more than ever."

"I'm sure he does, but unless he accepts your help, you can't do anything. He has to want to get better."

I knew she was right, I just wasn't sure what to do about it.

By then the nightmares had started, too. Or rather, I hadn't realized how bad they had become, but now we were sharing a bed, it became clear to me how traumatic they really were. Sebastian would have intense dreams and wake up screaming. Once, I thought he was going to attack me, his flashback was so vivid. He held back at the last second, his eyes wild and black with terror. I think it was seeing my fear that stopped him from ... from hurting me.

He started checking that the windows and doors were locked two or three times a night before we went to bed, and he became paranoid about people coming to the house, whether it was the mailman or one of our neighbors dropping a leaflet through the door.

He refused to leave the house, but hated me going out, too. We became virtual recluses. I tried to carry on working, but there was only so much I could do from home, and I began to resent his attempts to control me.

One day, he yelled at me because there was no alcohol in the house and I'd refused to buy any more.

I yelled back.

"If you want a fucking drink, then get your fucking ass off that couch and go get it yourself, Sebastian!"

I marched out of the bungalow, my blood boiling.

I felt horribly guilty the moment I slammed the door behind me, but I wasn't backing down. We'd reached an impasse: something had to change.

When I'd calmed enough to go home, a place that was no longer a refuge, Sebastian had gone to bed. He didn't even acknowledge me as I climbed in beside him. Our bed had become another battleground.

And he wouldn't touch me: he barely looked at me, shunned any embrace, and we didn't make love. We were strangers to each other, but sharing a bed.

In the morning, I wearily dragged myself awake, both of us having slept badly. He'd had another terrifying nightmare, screaming out in fear. I longed to hold him, but he wouldn't even look at me. When I touched him, he flinched.

I didn't know how much longer we could go on like this. And he still refused to speak to any doctors.

"What the fuck do they know about it, Caro?"

"A lot: you're not the first Marine who's been injured."

"Former Marine, former fucking Marine, Caro. I'm nothing now. Maybe you can try and fucking remember that."

His words cracked my heart.

He'd been my lover, he'd been a Marine, and now he was neither. The past was another country and the future was ... well, he couldn't see that he had a future. We lived from each slow hour to the next.

And he felt guilty—so guilty for having been the one who had survived. No one would tell me exactly what had happened but from what I'd pieced together, and from what David had told me during that first phone call, someone on the inside, an ally, had started shooting and then detonated a bomb. Three other Marines had died and two more were injured, although not as badly as Sebastian. Surviving wasn't about skill, it was about luck.

During those long, dark days, two things kept me going. The first was his letter, the one he'd written before his last mission. The paper had become soft and fragile with the number of times I'd read it. I looked at it often when I was alone for a few seconds, even though I'd long memorized the words.

The second was a small thing, ridiculous really, but it signified a lot to me, and I think to Sebastian, too.

I'd been sorting through a pile of dirty clothes: one of those joyless, thankless jobs that we all have to do, but never get finished because they're never-ending.

I was making sure buttons were done up, and shirts were turned inside out before I threw them into the washer, tedious but necessary, when I picked up Sebastian's jeans. As usual, he'd tossed them into the hamper unbuttoned and unzipped. I thought I'd better check the pockets, too ... and that's when I found it.

I felt a hard lump in the hip pocket. I pushed my hand inside and pulled out a small, white pebble. It was the little piece of quartz that I'd found on the beach, that silly sentimental gift that I'd given to Sebastian the day he'd flown out to Afghanistan. And he'd kept it. More than that, he kept it with him even now.

My throat started to ache with tears but I refused to let myself cry, because they would have been hopeful tears. If Sebastian cared enough to keep that little pebble, surely it meant he still cared for me? That he was still capable of caring for me?

～

A loud crash brought me running to the living room.

Sebastian was thrashing around on the floor, swearing up and down, cursing like it was going out of fashion, and surrounded by books.

"What happened?" I asked breathlessly.

"I fucking fell! What does it look like?" he snarled.

I guessed that he'd lost his balance and tried to hold onto the bookshelf, but pulled the whole thing down instead.

I bent down to help him up.

"Leave me alone! I'm not a complete fucking cripple."

I bit my lip and watched as he struggled to his feet. His frustration at what he perceived as his helplessness boiled over several times a day. I had to remind myself that he wasn't mad at me, but sometimes it was hard. It hurt to see him fight so hard: fight his own body as it continued to heal, fight me, fight everyone.

He was sinking deeper into depression each day, and I didn't know how to help him.

He even refused to talk about getting married or anything that involved planning for our future.

"I'm not going to let you marry a useless, fucking cripple," he roared, when I'd been foolish enough to press the subject. "If I can't even walk down the fucking aisle without a fucking crutch..."

I bit back my angry retort that there wouldn't be an aisle at City Hall, and left him alone to stew in his own black anger.

My own hopes and dreams drifted further away.

In silence, I bent down and started picking up the books that had tumbled down around him—the ones out of his reach. He watched me sullenly for a moment, then reached out to collect the volumes nearest to him. As he picked up my copy of 'Lolita' by its cover, an envelope fell out, fluttering to the ground. I knew at once what it was and leaned over to pick it up. Sebastian was faster.

"What's this?" he asked, his voice puzzled. "It has my name on it."

He looked up at me. "The date on it ... that's the day we first..."

"Yes, I know," I said, quietly.

The small envelope did indeed have Sebastian's name scrawled across one corner in my untidy handwriting. The date was ten years ago: the day I'd found him alone in the park, bruised and bloodied after yet another fight with his father. The bastard had hit him several times and then hacked off chunks of Sebastian's long, surfer hair. I'd taken him to my house, patched him up, and shaved the rest of his hair into an elegant buzz cut, trying to mask the evidence of his father's assault. It was also the night we'd first made love.

"What's in it, Caro?" he asked, fingering the small, paper package.

It was the only time he'd shown a spark of interest in anything in weeks.

I shrugged. "Open it."

He propped himself up against the couch then heaved himself up so he was leaning against the cushions. He fumbled, trying to open the sealed envelope, the motor skills of his left hand still limited.

He was probably expecting to find some sort of letter inside, but he was wrong.

A lock of long, blond hair fell out.

I saw the shock of recognition on his face.

"This is mine: my hair. You kept it—all these years?"

"Yes, *tesoro*. It was all I had of you."

He closed his eyes, holding the lock in his hand.

"Caro, I don't understand. Why do you love me?"

"Just because ... because the sky is blue and the sea is green."

And then he started to cry. He fisted his hands over his eyes and sobbed into my arms. And, at last, I could hold him. I wrapped my arms around him and held him tightly, willing the darkness away, trying to heal him with my body, with my touch.

"I love you, Sebastian, please don't push me away. I love you."

"Oh God, Caro. I just don't know what I'm doing any more, I'm so fucked up—I feel like I can't fucking breathe. Don't give up on me, Caro. Please don't give up on me. I need you, baby. I love you so much. I'm so sorry."

I could forgive anything now that he'd let me touch him.

I held him for an hour, just stroking his hair, as he rested his head in my lap, my fingers running over his rough beard. I realized he'd taken one small step toward me, toward living again—I needed him to take another.

"It's time to go out now, Sebastian," I said, softly.

He closed his eyes and swallowed.

"I don't know if I can do that, Caro."

"You don't have to do this by yourself, Sebastian. We go together. Come on, *tesoro*. Together."

I could tell he was nervous, so we took it slowly. I gave him my Yankees baseball cap, which he pulled down over his eyes, and he wore his old biker jacket, which hung loosely from his shoulders, emphasizing how thin he'd become.

I took his hand, and, with Sebastian leaning heavily on his walking cane, we made our way slowly along West Beech Street. Sebastian kept looking over his shoulder, checking the windows of buildings along the road, and I knew he was unconsciously looking for snipers. I didn't hurry him, we went at his pace, but the feeling that flowed through me from being with him outdoors at last was almost overwhelming.

"There's a café over there, Sebastian. Why don't we go have a coffee?"

"I don't know, Caro ... sitting outside? I wouldn't feel ... safe."

"Sebastian, you know rationally that there's nothing to worry about. Let's just try it for a couple of minutes: if you really can't handle it, we'll leave."

He twitched unhappily, but didn't argue.

The waiter came toward us and Sebastian flinched away from him.

"I'll have an espresso. Sebastian?"

His eyes were wide with fear, constantly flicking nervously about him.

"And a Bud Light," I answered for him.

The waiter wandered away, he was used to crazy among his customers.

I couldn't say that Sebastian truly relaxed, but he sipped his beer and began to look a fraction less anxious.

He seemed happier once we were moving again. I could tell he was tired, but I wanted him to see the ocean up close, and not just from the windows of our small home.

The boardwalk was busy, full of people strolling in the sunshine. A teenager on a skateboard swept past and my poor, wounded man trembled with terror at the sudden noise.

"It's okay, *tesoro*. You'll be okay."

"Fuck, Caro," he said, his face white with fear.

We carried on walking, Sebastian clinging onto my hand and trying to control his rapid breathing.

It hurt badly to see him so scared when he'd always been so strong, but I knew the only way to help him was to force him to face his fears. We'd face them together.

When we reached the end of the Boardwalk, we found an empty bench and sat looking at the ocean. He breathed in deeply, and I saw that it calmed him. The waves tumbled across the sand and the repeated, rhythmical motion soothed us both. A couple of kids were playing on body boards, shouting out happily. Sebastian leaned forward to watch them, his face alight with interest. The ocean had always been his place of refuge, somewhere his parents couldn't touch him, and the beach had always had a special significance for us. I became determined that we'd walk here every day, because I believed it would help Sebastian to get stronger. And it would bring us together.

"The ocean always reminds me of you, *tesoro*. It's the same color as your eyes today."

He looked at me in surprise, then lifted my hand to his lips, kissing it gently.

"Caro."

He breathed my name softly, like a prayer.

As we sat in the sunshine, a light breeze ruffling my hair, I felt life flowing back into his body. He closed his eyes, relaxing in the summer warmth, his face held up toward the light like a young plant that had been kept in the dark.

"Thank you for this, Caro," he whispered.

I leaned against him and he wrapped his good arm around my shoulder, pulling me in.

"Ready to go home, *tesoro*?"

He nodded, and we stood up to walk back to our home.

I led us back by a different route to the bungalow, and we strolled past a café that I'd not seen before. It must have opened while we were living as hermits. Three men with black hair, olive skin and dark eyes, seemed to be arguing loudly. I wanted to take the long way around in case they reminded him of Afghanistan, but something about them intrigued Sebastian. He looked up, and I could tell he was listening to what they were saying. I realized they must be speaking a language he recognized, which could mean they were Afghans.

I was really worried, wondering what to do for the best. I glanced around, seeing if there were any taxis nearby. And then I was astonished to see a small smile lift Sebastian's lips.

My heart soared. I hadn't seen him smile like that since he'd come home.

As we walked past, Sebastian threw in a comment. The men stared at him in amazement. One called out something else and Sebastian replied. Suddenly all the men started shouting at once. They came toward him, and I was worried it might be too much, but soon they were deep in conversation and I could tell they were asking him questions. Then Sebastian grinned at them. It was like seeing the sun after a month of rain, and I dared to feel hope.

They talked a little longer and then Sebastian introduced me. The men greeted me respectfully but with little interest, and eventually, after several more minutes where I didn't understand a single word, but stood happily as Sebastian stroked my hand, watching him chat away, he said goodbye and we carried on walking.

"What on earth were you talking about for so long?"

"Baseball," he said.

I stared at him doubtfully.

"You're kidding me?"

He smiled again, "Universal language, Caro."

And just like that, the world began to turn again.

The first change was that Sebastian started doing the exercises that the therapist had given him: exercises to help build up dexterity in the fingers of his left hand, and leg stretches to help the damaged muscles of his right thigh, and he even used the exercise bike that I'd ordered for him—although he'd shouted at me the day it had been delivered. He also began doing sit-ups and push-ups with a vengeance.

The second change came a week after meeting the Afghan men. It was evening, and I was standing in the kitchen, cooking pasta *arrabiata* for our supper, when Sebastian poked his head around the door, a quizzical expression on his face.

I stared at him for a moment before I realized what was different.

"You've shaved!"

"Well, you didn't like the beard, did you?"

"That's putting it mildly, Sebastian."

He looked so beautiful, my heart gave another, small, hopeful lurch.

The third, and most startling change, was that he slipped his hands around my waist and nuzzled my neck. I was so shocked, I froze. His smile fell away and he let go of me.

"No, *tesoro*, no!" and I pulled his arms back around my waist, laying my head on his chest. I couldn't help the tears spilling down my cheeks, soaking into his t-shirt.

"I'm so sorry, baby," he said, stroking my hair.

"Oh, God, I've missed you, Sebastian."

"I know, baby," he said, gently, "but I'm here now."

It felt so good to have his arms around me after months of his numb coldness and distance.

I lifted my head to look at him, and he wiped my tears away with his thumbs.

"I'm sorry I made you cry, baby," he said, softly. "I never meant to hurt you. I know that I did."

I locked my arms around his neck and pulled his head down, kissing his lips, gently at first, and then with increasing hunger and need.

He hesitated for a fraction of a second, then his lips parted and I felt his tongue sweep into my mouth, and sudden, hot, unexpected arousal flooded through me.

I moaned into his mouth, the intensity of my desire taking me by surprise. Sebastian gasped and stepped back half a pace, gazing down at me.

Inside, I was begging him not to reject me again, but I felt strongly that the next step needed to come from him.

"I want to make love to you, Caro."

His voice was so quiet I could hardly hear him.

"You do?" I breathed.

"God, yes, baby. Only if you want to."

I stared at his face, and found the love in his eyes that seemed to have been hidden for so long.

"I've waited and waited to hear you say that, *tesoro*."

I turned off the gas stove, abandoning the pasta.

He held my hand, gazing into my eyes as we walked into the bedroom.

CHAPTER EIGHTEEN

THE LAST TIME WE'D MADE LOVE IT HAD BEEN IN A SMALL, STINKING mud-built room, in a former police compound in Now Zad, now it was very different.

He stood hesitantly next to the bed, and it reminded me so much of our very first time together. He'd been broken then, too.

I pulled the curtains, but the sun was still high in the sky and the room was filled with a soft, muted light.

I walked back over to him and reached up to stroke his face. He leaned into my hand and his eyes closed.

"I don't know if I can..."

"Shh, *tesoro*. I just want to feel your skin next to mine. Anything else, well, that's a bonus."

I kissed him slowly and tenderly, remembering, relearning, starting again. He returned my kisses, carefully to begin with, and I felt the first small flames of passion heat his blood. He swept my hair off my neck and ran his tongue up to my jaw. His hands massaged my waist, kneading my flesh. Then his right hand crept up my body and I felt his touch hover over my bra strap, before his left hand slowly descended to cup my behind.

It felt so good to have his hands on me again and, despite what I'd said to him, I was desperate for him to know me as a man could know a woman, but I also knew I couldn't rush this.

I pushed my hands up under his t-shirt and stroked his warm, silky skin. Carefully, I traced my finger across the small, round scar, where the bullet that punctured his lung had exited his body. I needed him to know that it didn't make any difference to me, that I loved him regardless.

He tensed slightly, so I moved my hand away, instead letting my fingers drift down his spine, stroking his back and shoulders.

He continued to kiss me, his touch slowly becoming more assured. He weaved his fingers into my hair, tightening his grip.

I could taste his desire and need, but I could feel his anxiety, too. It had been so long since we'd touched each other that there was an additional pressure and weight of expectation.

Gently, I reached for his t-shirt, feeling his slight resistance before he let me pull it over his head.

I could see his ribs plainly, but his muscle tone was beginning to recover. Plenty of love and home-cooking: that's what he needed. And time—a whole lifetime of love.

I wondered, briefly, where he'd put his dog tags, they'd disappeared shortly after he'd come home. I hoped he hadn't done anything hasty, like destroying them or throwing them away, because I knew he'd regret that one day.

I reached for his belt, cinched in two more holes because of his weight loss, but he caught my hands and shook his head.

"I don't think I'm ready for this, Caro. What if...?"

My frustration was ready to boil over, but then I was struck with sudden inspiration.

"Want me to show you how I reminded myself of you when you were in the hospital?" I said, looking directly into his eyes.

He nodded, his pupils dilating in a way that filled me with confidence, because it showed that he still desired me.

"I will, if you take off your pants."

"Caro..."

"That's the deal, Sebastian. Non-negotiable."

He hesitated for a moment, then unbuckled his belt and dropped his jeans to the floor. He angled his right leg away from me, and I knew it was because he was trying to hide the ugly scar that ran the length of his thigh. But it didn't hide the slight bulge in his briefs—it wasn't a full erection by any means, but it was a start.

"Sit in the chair, make yourself comfortable—I could be some time."

I was rewarded with a slight smile.

"First, I'd draw the curtains," I said, pointing toward the windows like a flight attendant. "Then, I'd pull back the duvet and arrange the pillows."

As I spoke, I flicked back the sheets and piled up the pillows near the headboard.

"Then I'd put on a little mood music..."

I pointed the remote control at my CD player, and the sounds of *Martha's Harbour* swirled softly from the speakers.

You are an ocean wave, my love
Crashing at my bow...

"I'd kick off my sneakers, because, well, I'm really not a Manolo sort of girl ... that's high heels to you, Hunter."

He rolled his eyes. "I lived in Paris for six months, Caro. I have heard of Manolo Blahnik."

"Yes, well, he's from Spain, so there's no need to look so superior, Sebastian."

Secretly, I was thrilled he was playing along and had relaxed enough to be able to tease me.

"Besides," I went on, "I can't walk in high-heels unless I have you to hang onto ... but I'm not averse to wearing them in the bedroom."

His breath caught in his throat, and his hands gripped the edge of his chair. I tried not to stare at his briefs, but that was the area I really wanted to affect. I hoped our banter would help him to relax, because I longed to feel his body—next to mine, inside mine.

I kept the smile plastered on my face and tried to sound natural and cheerful—maybe even a little bit sensual, if I could remember how.

"So, after I've kicked off my sneakers, I'd peel off my socks, because leaving them on just isn't sexy, and if you ever do that, Hunter, I'll be justified in filing for divorce—after we're married, of course, which *you* keep putting off."

He frowned slightly, so I decided to concentrate on the mission in hand, so to speak.

"I'd imagine your fingers teasing me around my waistband," I said, mimicking my words. "And then I'd think about you unzipping my jeans and standing back while I shimmy out of them."

His eyes followed my pants, as I slid them down my legs to the floor.

"And I'd pull off my t-shirt because I'd be feeling hot, just thinking about you touching me."

My t-shirt followed my jeans, making a small pile.

"And then I'd touch my breasts like this, Sebastian," I said, squeezing my breasts together and throwing my head back, "like you asked me to once before, and I'd imagine you running your hands over me and unhooking my bra, and you'd torment my nipples with your hands and your hot, sweet mouth, your tongue moving around and around me like this."

I glanced at him, and saw that his eyes were transfixed by my breasts and—yes! There was a significant bulge in his briefs—my plan was working.

I unhooked my bra, dropped it to the floor, and then turned my back on him.

"And I'd have to climb onto the bed, just like this, Sebastian," I said, provocatively wiggling my ass at him, as I slunk up toward the pillows.

Then I knelt up and turned around to face him. "And I'd think about how you'd toy with the lace on my panties, just like this, and how your fingers would tease me, sliding inside me, finding me all hot and wet and wanting."

I rubbed myself inside my panties, and closed my eyes as sensation began to pulse through me, making me moan softly.

"And I'd think what it was like to feel your mouth on me, and your tongue inside me, tantalizing and torturing me, bringing on an orgasm with a flick of your tongue."

"Fuck!" I heard him hiss.

"And I'd lie back on the bed and imagine your long, hard cock, sliding inside me, thrusting fast—really fast—and bringing on another orgasm, just like this."

I lay back on the bed and shimmied out of my panties, then propped myself up on the pillows, pulled my knees up slightly and opened my legs.

I gazed up at him from beneath my eyelashes as I continued to touch myself. I saw him lick his lips and shift on the chair.

"And I'd wish you were with me, Sebastian, because although I have a damn good imagination, I'd rather have the real thing any day."

I closed my eyes for a moment, then looked up to meet his.

"I'm so wet for you, Sebastian. Do you want to touch me?"

He swallowed and I saw some of his anxiety return, so I closed my eyes and rubbed myself harder.

Then I heard the floorboards creak as he stood up, and felt the mattress shift as he climbed onto the bed. He hesitated for a second, and then I felt him nudge my hand out of the way, as he circled his fingers around, then pushed two inside me.

I groaned loudly when he fastened his mouth over my breast and started to tease the nipple out, sucking hard. I ran my hands over his shoulders and felt a slight tremor ripple through him. He moved over to my other breast, swirling his tongue around and over me, pulling lightly with his teeth, filling me with need.

Then his kisses trailed down my body, and I held my breath as I felt his tongue sliding inside me.

I called out his name, and he pushed my legs further apart, really working me, and I orgasmed loudly, watching as he moved up to kiss my thigh.

"Much, much better than my imagination, Sebastian!" I gasped.

He chuckled quietly.

I brushed my hands over his briefs, unable to help myself.

"Oh, you're so hard, *tesoro* ... I want you inside me."

"Where are the fucking condoms, Caro," he said, in a tight voice.

"Don't need them: I've been taking the pill. Just you, Sebastian, now."

I pushed his briefs over his hips, and fastened both hands over his erection and guided him inside me.

He groaned, a long, drawn-out sigh of pleasure.

It felt so good, stretching and filling, deep inside me. I clenched around him.

"Fuck, Caro!" he gasped.

"Don't try and control it," I begged him, "Just love me. Love me, Sebastian."

He flexed his hips and began to thrust into me.

It felt so intense, we were so intimately connected, joined together, man and woman, moving as one body, one soul, one purpose.

He cried out and shuddered, pouring himself inside me, filling me with his love and trust, bringing us together again.

When he'd finished, he rested between my thighs, his face buried in my neck, his breath still coming in gasps. I stroked his back and told him I loved him.

Eventually he pulled out and curled up next to me: I could feel his cheeks were wet with tears.

"Are you okay?" I asked quietly.

He nodded without speaking, and then he opened his eyes and smiled at me.

"Very okay, Caro. I'm very okay."

And we held each other without the need to speak again.

~

After that, the dam holding back our intimacy had been breached, and Sebastian's mind started to heal as well as his body.

There was something I had to ask him, and I didn't know if it was going to be a good idea or not.

We were slumped together on the sofa, drinking herbal tea just before going to bed. I didn't really enjoy the thin, bitter liquid, but caffeine made Sebastian jumpy.

"Sebastian, can I ask you something?"

"Sure, baby," he said, running his hand down my arm, and twining his fingers with mine.

"Well, I was wondering ... what are your nightmares about?"

I felt him tense immediately, and regretted my question.

"It's hard to talk about, Caro," he said, his voice low and quiet.

"It's okay—you don't have to tell me."

"I just don't want you to have that shit in your head."

"Sebastian, you wake up screaming every night—it doesn't have to be me, but I think you need to tell someone."

"I'm not seeing a fucking shrink," he said testily.

I didn't reply.

We sat silently, staring out of the windows, watching the horizon growing paler as the sun sank behind the sea.

And then he began to speak.

"I can't tell you everything, Caro, because it's classified, and you can't report any of this."

"Of course not!"

I was hurt that he'd even think that.

"Sorry, baby, I had to say it." He sighed. "We were in Now Zad in the first place to make contact with someone—a local guy—who was going to get us to one of the Taliban leaders—so we could take him out. That's why they wanted me there, because they were worried about using local interpreters for a sensitive op. It was supposed to be a small patrol, just the 14 of us, with Jankowski in charge. At the last minute, Grant was told we had to take these two guys from the Afghan National Army with us. He wasn't happy, but he was overruled. We headed out into the mountains for what we thought would be three or four days, but we didn't get that far. When we arrived at the village for the meet, we knew right away that something was wrong—it was just too damn quiet. There was nobody in the fields, no one sitting outside their houses. We were all on edge.

"I went ahead with the ANA guys and they were calling out for the man we were supposed to meet. Then this guy came out from behind one of the buildings and he was talking really fast, and he looked fucking terrified. I realized he was quoting from the Koran and I knew then he'd been turned into a human fucking bomb. I yelled at everyone to get back, but then I felt like I'd been punched in the shoulder and I realized I'd been shot. One of the ANA guys had tried to take me out, then shot his colleague and turned his rifle on the rest of the squad. The firefight started, and I could hear Jankowski yelling at the contact to get down. Mark and Jez came running over to help me—and that's when the bomb was detonated."

Sebastian swallowed and closed his eyes.

"The Afghan contact was just pink mist: Jankowski, Mark and Jez were caught in the blast. If Jez hadn't been so close to me, I'd have been killed, too, but he took it for me."

Sebastian's voice dropped to a whisper.

"I had pieces of Jez all over me. That's what I dream about."

His hands were shaking and his breathing had become shallow.

"I understand, I do, *tesoro*," I murmured, gently stroking his cheek. "When I was in Iraq ... it was the sound of the helicopters, they were bringing in wounded and I saw ... I saw. But I don't have that nightmare anymore, Sebastian, because my worst nightmare is losing you."

I held him tightly, because that was all I could do.

Two days later, just as he was finishing his exercises, a sheen of sweat making his body glisten in a way that made my mouth water, I decided it was time to take a further step into the world.

"How do you feel about another challenge, Sebastian?"

He glanced over at me and smiled. "Sounds interesting. Does this one involve leaving the bedroom?"

I grinned at him. "Yes, it does, but now you've got me thinking other things, Hunter, and my once pristine thoughts are getting a little dirty."

"How dirty?" he said, his eyes heating under my gaze.

I stood with my hands on my hips and looked him in the eye.

"*Very* dirty."

He groaned. "Why didn't you say that *before* I did that damn workout, Caro?"

I laughed. "Rain check until tonight, Hunter. It's a beautiful day, we should be outside."

He nodded his agreement, then lifted my hand to his lips, brushing soft, sweet kisses over the tip of each finger.

"Yeah, okay. I need to see Atash anyway. He's got some problem with immigration that he wants me to look into."

Atash was the name of one of the Afghan men from the café and, against the odds, he and Sebastian had become friends. Atash's family had been forced to leave their village near Lashkar Gah in Helmand province and were lost and alone in a new country. Being useful to them brought Sebastian back to life, day by day. And day by day, it brought him back to me.

I wasn't sure if Sebastian and Atash had bonded over baseball, or simply because Sebastian was probably the only other person in all of Long Beach who spoke his language. But most days they found an excuse to meet up. And once Sebastian had started helping Atash and his family with their legal status, they spent even more time together.

Atash was shy about coming to our home so, mostly, Sebastian walked over to see him. I was glad he had a reason to leave the bungalow, and one that was completely separate from our life together. He needed it, and I think he knew that.

"So, if you're not talking about sex, Caro," he prompted me, "what's this challenge that you're on about?"

"I want you to meet my friends. I miss them, and they really want to meet you."

His gaze dropped to the floor.

"Okay, I guess it's time."

He didn't look thrilled by the idea, but he didn't object either.

I spoke to Nicole first.

"He's doing much better now, and I'd like you to meet him. We want to invite you over this weekend."

"Oh, he's finally going to let you see the light of day, is he, Lee?"

I was taken aback.

"That's ... harsh. He's been ill, Nic."

I could sense her indignant and judgmental silence on the other end of the line.

"Okay," she said, rather reluctantly. "Yes, of course I'll be there. Do you want me to talk to Jenna and Alice?"

"No, that's fine," I said, trying to keep my tone neutral and the hurt I felt out of my voice. "I should make the calls. Come for lunch?"

As Saturday approached, I threw myself into a frenzy of cooking.

I'd dragged Sebastian all over Long Beach to find the ingredients I wanted. He was beginning to look much more like himself. Although he was still very slender, he was beginning to pile the muscle weight back on. His hair was longer than I was used to seeing it, turning into a crazy, blond mop.

"Thought I'd grow it for a while," he said, casually.

"Fine by me," I grinned, tugging a lock in my hand.

Day by day, he was looking more like the surfer boy I'd fallen in love with. He still had bad days and some very bad nights, and he was still in a considerable amount of pain from the shrapnel wounds in his thigh. But on good days he was able to walk without a cane, although he still had a significant limp.

"I spoke to Ches while you were out," he said casually.

"You did?"

I was pleased that he'd finally gotten around to talking to his friend—but nervous about what had been said: particularly about me.

"And?"

"He said he and Amy would fly out for our wedding."

I caught my breath and stared at him.

"If you still want to marry me, Caro?"

The small stone of grief that I'd been carrying in my heart melted away.

"Of course I do, Sebastian. I ... I thought you'd changed your mind."

He shook his head slowly, his eyes full of love.

"Never that, Caro, but I didn't want to marry you if ... if I couldn't be a man ... with you. And I promised myself I wouldn't be using a fucking cane when I walked down the aisle."

"They don't have aisles in City Hall," I said, somewhere between a laugh and a sob.

He gathered me into his arms and rocked me slowly, repeatedly kissing my hair.

"So what else did Ches say?" I mumbled into his chest.

I was pleased that I'd managed to get the words out without sounding too pathetically shaky.

"He said that he'd decided if he still hadn't heard from me by Labor Day, he was going to come out here and kick my ass himself."

"Good idea," I agreed with a murmur, "he should do that anyway. Did he say anything about me?"

Sebastian smiled.

"I guess he was surprised—and pleased, I think—that you hadn't kicked me out. He's cool, Caro, don't worry about him."

"And Amy?"

"Oh, she just wants to kick my ass, period."

I smiled. "I think I'll get along with her."

"That's what I'm afraid of," muttered Sebastian.

He was only half joking.

He held my face gently and looked into my eyes.

"Just promise me you won't turn into one of those bat-shit crazy women about the whole wedding thing, Caro."

"Such sweet nothings you whisper," I teased him. "Don't worry, Sebastian, that's not my style." I slapped his chest. "I don't care if I get married in jeans."

"Jeans?" he said, raising his eyebrows.

"Well, my favorite jeans," I replied, with a challenging stare.

"Okay, jeans. Cool."

Sebastian was nervous about meeting my friends, understandably, perhaps. I tried to reassure him, but he felt they'd be judging him: he was undoubtedly right.

He looked delicious in a white t-shirt and blue jeans, and, with his bare feet jammed into a pair of flip-flops, he looked like he'd just strolled off the beach. Except for the fact that when he walked, he still had a pronounced limp.

I heard Nicole's car pull up and I leaned out of the window, waving excitedly. I pretended not to hear Sebastian murmur, "Incoming."

I ran out of the door, and Alice leapt on me first, hugging me tightly.

"Oh my God! It's so good to see you, Lee!"

"You've lost weight, beotch!" yelled Nicole, grappling me around the waist, and smearing a lipstick kiss onto my cheek.

"I've brought chocolate and champagne," sang Jenna, flinging her arms around me.

And then Nicole shrieked.

"Omigod! Omigod! Is that what I think it is?"

She grabbed my left hand and stared at my engagement ring. There were loud gasps and shocked looks from Alice and Jenna.

I nodded.

"You guys are all invited to a wedding in the fall," I said quietly.

At that, there were loud shrieks and cries of congratulations, plus a few tears. They all hugged me again but I was growing uncomfortable, aware that Sebastian would be watching, and waiting for us to come in.

"When did this happen?" asked Alice, grabbing my hand again to look at the ring.

"That's a nice piece of rock, Venzi," murmured Nicole. "But are you sure about this? I mean right now, the way everything is..."

"I'll tell you all about it later. Just be ... cool, okay?"

"Well, come on," said Nicole, rather tersely, "let's meet the paragon."

"Nic!" I said, my voice warning.

She held up her hands. "I'll be good."

Which didn't fill me with hope.

Sebastian was standing in the middle of the living room when my friends walked inside. I could tell he was nervous, but to anyone who didn't know him, he would have merely appeared arrogant.

I introduced everyone, and Nicole couldn't help herself, running her eyes up and down Sebastian's body: it was practically a Pavlovian response with her when she saw a cute guy. Jenna and Alice had taken sneaky peeks, too, they were just more subtle about it.

The girls settled themselves around the room, and then an uncomfortable silence descended, with everyone's eyes fixed on me. I could tell Sebastian was feeling overwhelmed at having so many people in our small home, so I smiled at him, took his hand, and led him back to his favorite chair.

I could see the pitying faces of my friends as they watched Sebastian limp painfully across the room. I wished they wouldn't—Sebastian loathed being pitied—but their reaction was understandable.

I perched on the arm of his chair, and he rested his hand on my knee. It was as if he needed physical contact with me to get him through what he clearly saw as an ordeal.

"Well, you know what I've been doing," I said, calmly. "I want to know what all of you've been up to."

Gradually the conversation began to flow. Sebastian was silent at first, but slowly Alice began to draw him out, asking about his plans to go back to school.

"I was going to study Italian and English Lit," he admitted, "but that kinda got interrupted." He glanced at me and I squeezed his hand. "But I don't know now."

"Lee says you speak several Arab languages, too."

"Plus Italian and French," I added.

Sebastian looked slightly embarrassed. "Well, yeah, I can speak Arabic, but I don't read it well."

"Could that be something for you?" she asked.

He shrugged. "I thought maybe I'd look into some paralegal studies. I've kinda been helping out a neighbor who's got immigration problems."

"You didn't tell me about that idea, Sebastian?" I said, delighted that he was planning ahead.

"I haven't decided anything yet, Caro, I'm still thinking about it."

"Well, there's plenty of time—you don't have to decide now."

"No, I can just continue sponging off you," he said, quietly.

He was still refusing to touch his disability pay checks, and the money was collecting dust in his bank account.

The conversation died away, my friends staring everywhere but at us.

"Sebastian, no," I whispered, really upset.

"It's what all your friends are thinking, Caro," he said, heatedly. "I can see it in their eyes."

"Don't assume you know what I'm thinking," snapped Jenna.

"I agree," said Nicole, evenly. "Because I was actually thinking that nearly dying in the service of your country earns you the right to time off—and if my friend is having as many orgasms as she says she is, you must be doing something right."

Sebastian looked startled, then amused.

"Is that what she said?" he murmured, glancing over to me, before fixing his gaze on Nicole.

"I'm paraphrasing, of course," replied Nicole, meeting his eyes.

Sebastian shrugged. "She taught me everything I know."

Jenna chuckled, and Alice laughed out loud.

"Don't mind me," I said, my face glowing beet red.

"Later, baby," said Sebastian, taking my hand and grazing my knuckles with a kiss.

There was a knock at the door, which was a welcome interruption to my public embarrassment.

"I'll get it," said Sebastian, pulling himself out of the chair.

Nicole's eyes followed him across the room, then she turned to smile at me and winked.

"You and I will be having words," I hissed at her.

"Just telling him the way it is, Lee. He didn't seem to mind. I don't know, is he the kind of guy who keeps score, because I dated a musician once who used to make a note of my orgasms in his diary, not that he could even tell which ones were faked."

"I've never faked one," I batted back at her.

"God, I hate you!" she said.

I was half-listening for Sebastian's voice at the front door. When he switched from English, I guessed who our new visitor must be.

Nervously, Atash made his way into the room, smiling at my friends, while they turned to stare, giving brief, puzzled smiles back.

"Hi, Atash," I said, and quickly introduced them to him.

He smiled again and nodded politely, but looked uncomfortable.

"We'll be next door," Sebastian said to me.

Then he steered Atash into the kitchen, where I heard him filling the kettle to make the horribly sweet tea that was traditional in Afghanistan, while they chatted away.

"What language is that, Lee?" said Alice. "Is that Arabic?"

"No, that's Dari. Sebastian says it's related to Persian not Arabic. He speaks Pashto, too," I added, proudly.

They looked suitably surprised, and I was pleased that Sebastian had had a chance to impress them with something other than his looks —or his hot temper. I knew that had been bothering him.

"With those language skills, I'm surprised Military Intelligence didn't snap him up," continued Alice.

I didn't answer, but couldn't meet her eyes.

"Oh," she said, knowingly, and swapped a significant look with the others.

And then I heard Sebastian's laughter coming from the kitchen—a long, loud, joyous laugh. I thought my heart would stop.

"Lee, are you okay?" said Jenna anxiously. "You look..."

"Sebastian's laughing." I could hear the tremor in my own voice.

"Oh, honey," said Alice, giving my arm a squeeze.

"You're doing okay, Venzi," said Nicole, formerly Sebastian's harshest critic. "I think you're both doing okay."

Atash left soon after, hurrying out of the door, smiling shyly.

"What was all that about?" I said, thrilled to see that Sebastian was grinning broadly.

"Atash wanted to know if I needed some hashish," he said, casually.

Jenna and Alice looked slightly shocked, and Nicole frowned.

"Excuse me?" I said, sharply. "I hope you said no."

Sebastian shrugged. "He said it's good for pain."

I noticed Sebastian hadn't answered me directly, and he *so* wasn't getting away with an excuse like that—but it was a conversation to have in private.

"And what else?" I asked, eyeing him curiously. "What aren't you telling me, Hunter?"

Sebastian's grin became wider.

"He was wondering why I'm making the tea when I have four wives to do it."

My mouth dropped open, and Nicole snorted with laughter.

"Well, I hope you put him straight! Sebastian?"

He grinned wickedly.

God, I'd missed that smile.

"I'll put him straight, Caro. Eventually."

Jenna started to laugh and then Nicole joined in. Soon we were all laughing our asses off. Damn, it felt good.

"You and I will have words later, Hunter," I said, in a threatening voice.

"Looking forward to it, baby," he said, still grinning at me.

After Atash's visit, we moved outside to sit in my yard, enjoying the nice weather. I'd dug out an old sundress to wear, and had the pleasure of watching Sebastian's eyes drift up and down my legs. I hitched my skirt slightly higher and raised an eyebrow at him, as his eyes followed my movement and he ran the tip of his tongue over his lips.

"Oh, just stop it, you two," Nicole groaned. "I haven't been laid in months and you're wafting all this sexual tension around. It's so unfair."

Alice laughed at her. "Lee got lucky—and it isn't like she hasn't put in more than her fair share of waiting over the years," she pointed out. "Besides, I've decided to give up on men: I'm going down the B.O.B. route."

I could see Sebastian was puzzled.

"Battery-operated boyfriend," I whispered in his ear.

He smirked at me and sat back to listen. I could see he was intrigued, watching me with my friends, seeing a different side to me.

Alice nodded.

"No offense, Sebastian, but men just take up too much energy. Or maybe it's just the men I meet. I can't tell you how many times I've been to dinner parties and listened to them droning on about football, or fishing, or how damn important they are at work. One even gave me a blow-by-blow description of building a model airplane. I mean, come on!"

Jenna agreed.

"Although maybe it's just men our age. We should do what Lee has done and find ourselves some younger guys."

"I'd definitely recommend it," I said, winking at Sebastian, whose eyes were flicking between Alice and Jenna so quickly, he looked as if he was watching a table tennis match.

He grinned at me, while Alice continued.

"Well, I'm a little out of practice now, I admit it, but food has some serious advantages over sex."

I laughed out loud, and Nicole told her she was talking bullshit.

"I'm serious!" she said, ticking off the points on her fingers. "Eating: you can do it every day, at least three times a day, with snacks in between; you can do it with as many people as you want, of any gender, and you don't have to worry about their sexual orientation; there are more good recipes and restaurants than hot, available men around—and believe me, I've done some research on this; I'm not going to get pregnant or STDs by eating ice cream; and, best of all, even if you gorge yourself with different people every time, no one calls you a slut."

"You're just a food slut!" yelled Jenna.

"We should ask Sebastian's opinion," said Nicole. "Where do you stand on the whole food versus sex thing?"

"Nic," I said, knowing she was deliberately baiting him.

But Sebastian didn't need my help.

"Caro's a great cook," he said, smiling at me. Then he whispered in my ear so no one else could hear him, "but I think you feed me well because you know I'll need my energy later."

"Ugh!" shouted Jenna. "I *know* you just said something really hot," she accused Sebastian. "It's so mean of him, Lee! Come on, you could at least tell us what he said."

I shook my head. "Need to know basis, Jenna, and you don't need to know."

Sebastian grinned, not looking the least embarrassed. I was relieved: sometimes my friends could be a real handful.

After a couple of hours, I could tell he was getting tired. He was moving awkwardly, and I knew that sitting so long was hurting him.

"Why don't you go take a nap, *tesoro*," I said, quietly. "We'll just be chatting out here for a while. You've more than done your part."

"You don't mind?"

"Of course not. Just take care of yourself and rest."

He smiled. "Okay, but wake me up before they go?"

"You really want some more?" I said, pretending to be shocked.

"They're okay," he said, smiling. "They really care about you, Caro. That's all that matters."

He made his apologies and left us alone outside. I knew their evaluation of him would be offered up any second.

Nicole weighed in first.

"Well, he's even hotter in the flesh, Lee, hot-tempered, too."

"Both are equally true," I agreed.

"You guys look good together," said Jenna, thoughtfully. "I must admit I had my doubts, but it's obvious he adores you. Hell, that's as good a start as any."

Alice nodded. "He needs to find a new direction, Lee. He's not the kind of man who can just sit around."

"I know, but it's still new. I'm not going to rush him. I'm just enjoying having him home and seeing him getting stronger."

"So when do you think you'll be getting married?" asked Alice

"No, don't encourage her!" whined Nicole. "This is baaaad. Where are we going to go to ogle hot surfer guys?"

"You can still come here," I said, laughing.

"What? And ogle your hot husband? That's just plain weird!"

"That's not what I meant at all, and you know it, Nicole! Look, you guys are my friends—you'll always be welcome here."

Nicole rubbed her hands together. "Well, I'm going to enjoy making you shop, Lee—get you out of your damn jeans for a change, although I see you've made an effort today."

I smiled at her. "Nope, no shopping."

"What?"

"I'm not turning into one of those Bridezillas: it'll just be you three and Sebastian's friends from San Diego. My friend Marc said he'd try and fly in, depending on the date. We're going to see if we can get October 2nd—it'll be Sebastian's 28th birthday."

"Oh, God! Twenty-eight," sighed Alice. "That sounds so young! Oh well, at least he won't be able to forget your anniversary."

The girls were just getting ready to leave, and I was wondering whether or not to let Sebastian carry on sleeping, when he screamed loudly again and again, a chilling, heart-rending sound.

Alice jumped and Nicole swore, but I was already on my feet and running.

Sebastian was thrashing around, his face contorted, his body covered in sweat. I shook him awake urgently.

"It's okay, it's okay, I'm here."

He clung to me, his breath shuddering in his chest.

"It's all right, Sebastian, it's going to be all right, *tesoro*."

"Fuck, Caro," he gasped. "I keep seeing..."

"I know, baby, I know."

He covered his eyes with trembling hands. "I can't go out there, Caro. I can't see *them* like this."

"You don't have to. Stay here, I'll see them off. Two minutes, *tesoro*."

In the yard, my friends were sitting staring at the backdoor as I came out.

"Jesus, Lee! What the hell was that?" Nicole asked for them all.

"He was blown up, Nic—three people died in front of him, men he worked with. He gets nightmares."

"Are you sure you know what you're taking on?" Jenna asked quietly.

I shrugged. "I love him."

I could see the concern in their eyes and Alice offered to stay, but I needed to be alone with Sebastian.

They said goodbye, and I promised that I'd be in touch.

When I went back to our room, the bed was empty and I could hear the shower running. Sebastian was leaning against the tiles, his hands outstretched, and the water pouring down over his head.

I pulled off my clothes, and walked into the shower behind him. He turned, and wrapped his arms around me, and we stood together, letting his fear wash away.

The next day Sebastian was in a foul mood. He was embarrassed that my friends had seen, or rather heard him, at his most vulnerable, and he blamed me. When I'd had enough of his sulking, I went for a long walk on the beach, and took my time sipping an espresso at a café on the boardwalk.

After a couple of hours to myself, I felt ready to go home and face whatever emotional grenades he'd be tossing at me today.

I think he must have been watching out of the window, because when I walked in, he was waiting by the door.

"I'm sorry, baby," he said, pulling me in for a hug and kissing my hair. "I know I'm being a dumb-ass."

"That's one of the words I had in mind."

He smiled. "Yeah, I bet. Hey, I have something to show you."

He took my hand and tugged me into the living room.

"What's that?"

A beautiful, red cedar Spanish guitar was lying on the coffee table.

"Your friend Nicole dropped by."

"Really?"

"Yeah, apparently you told her I wanted to learn guitar. She said she didn't need this, so she's given it to me. We talked for quite a long time —seeing as I'd pissed you off and you weren't here..."

He arched an eyebrow.

I decided to ignore that comment.

"Nicole isn't quite the ball-breaker you thought she was?"

"I didn't say that ... but she was ... okay."

"Praise indeed."

"Yeah," he said, with a smile. Then he paused. "Baby, when did I tell you I wanted to play guitar?"

"A long time ago," I said, softly. "Ten years ago."

He stared down at me, his eyes filled with love.

"You take my breath away, Caro."

He pulled me into a tight hug and I stood there drinking him in. He kissed my hair, nuzzling me softly.

"Oh, hey. You got mail."

He let go of me and reached over to pass me an envelope that had been tossed onto the table.

"On a Sunday?"

"Yeah, it went to Mrs. Levenson's house by mistake, she just came back from her grandson's today and she brought it over."

I turned the envelope over, looking at the sender's address.

"It's from England."

I frowned. I didn't know anyone in England—not any more.

I tore open the thick, parchment-type envelope and read the typewritten letter. As I took in the meaning, I couldn't help gasping with surprise.

Sebastian looked concerned. "What is it, baby?"

I slumped down onto the couch, and handed him the letter without speaking.

"Lawyers?"

He sat down next to me and read through the pages.

When he'd finished, he set the letter down and wrapped his good arm around me, pulling me against his chest.

"I didn't know," I whispered. "She never said anything. I knew Liz didn't have any family, but I never thought..."

"It's a lot of money, baby. What are you going to do with it?"

I shook my head. I was still trying to process the information.

The letter was from Dougal and Bright, Liz's lawyers. She'd named me in her Will and had left me everything—her entire estate. She hadn't owned much, but her small apartment in north London was worth over $550,000.

"Why did she leave it to me? We were friends, but … I don't understand."

"What don't you understand, Caro? She loved you. Why do you always have a hard time realizing that, baby?"

I shrugged.

"This is good news," he said, stroking my hair. "Out of all of this shit, it's something good."

"I know. It's just … so unexpected."

He hesitated before he spoke again. "It'll pay off your mortgage. You wouldn't have to work overseas … if you didn't want to…"

I knew what he was trying to say, but I couldn't make a decision like that here and now.

"Anyway, it's *our* money," I said quietly.

Sebastian shook his head angrily.

"I'm not going to take your fucking money, Caro!"

I placed my hand over his mouth, cutting off his stormy words.

"I mean it, Sebastian. Either we're in this together, or we're not. If you won't accept it, then I won't accept it. I'll give it to the Journalism Without Borders charity before I let this money come between us. You said yourself we deserved some good luck."

He ran his hand through his hair in frustration.

"She didn't even like me, Caro. There's no way she'd want me to have anything to do with your inheritance. Hell, as far as she was concerned, I was just fucking you for something to do and…"

"You're wrong. She knew all about us."

His rant ground to a halt, he looked stunned.

"She did?"

"Of course. I told her everything—and I told her we were going to get married."

Sebastian leaned back and stared at me. "You told her? Everything?"

"Yes, *tesoro*."

He scratched his eyebrow thoughtfully. "What did she say?"

I gave him a small smile. "She wanted to know if you were as good in bed as she'd heard."

I thought he was going to choke, but then I saw a wicked gleam in his eye. "And what did you say?"

I gave him a prim look. "Nothing, of course … although…"

"Although what?"

"I may have winked at her."

He smirked at me.

"Sebastian," I said, my voice serious, "if it hadn't been for me, you would have gone to college, gotten your degree..."

I waved away his denial.

"We both know that's true. Well, here we are—I can pay off the mortgage, you can use the GI bill, go to college, get your degree, if that's what you want."

He shifted uncomfortably. "It doesn't feel right, Caro. Let me think about it."

He was so frustrating, I wanted to hit him. Or kiss him. Probably both.

And, as we were on a roll, I decided to tackle one more task that we'd both been putting off.

I took a deep breath.

"Sebastian," I said, gently, "it's time you decided what you want to do with your uniforms—and your medals."

His sudden, sharp intake of breath showed how hard he found this, but he nodded slowly, staring at the floor. Then he squared his shoulders and met my steady gaze.

"Okay. Let's do it."

We stood up and I took him by the hand, leading him into the spare room. He leaned against the door frame, his arms folded tightly across his chest. I gave him a quick, encouraging smile, then pulled out his duffel bag and backpack from under the bed.

His Dress Blues and khaki Service Uniform were crumpled and rather sad when I dragged them out. There was no sign of his desert utility uniform, I didn't want to think about the reason why—I assumed the doctors would have had to cut him out of it when...

He stared at the clothes coldly, keeping all his emotions tightly contained.

"Get rid of them, Caro. I don't want to see them again."

"And the medals?"

His Service Uniform was festooned with an array of colorful ribbons and medals. I ran through them in my mind, as I touched them one by one: his Afghanistan Campaign Medal, Marine Commendation Medal, Meritorious Service Medal, Navy and Marine Corps Overseas Service Ribbon, National Defense Service Medal, Defense Meritorious Service Medal, and a Navy and Marine Corps Medal. And, still in its presentation box at the bottom of his backpack, his Purple Heart, for being wounded in action.

As Sebastian watched, I opened the box, stroking the ridges of silky ribbon, and ran my finger over the embossed words, 'For military merit'.

"Do what you want with them," he said, his face creasing with pain. "I don't want to see them. Ever."

I took another deep breath.

"You don't want to save them to ... maybe ... show our children ... if..."

He looked up suddenly, a smile hovering around his lips. "You ... you'd try?"

"Yes, Sebastian ... *we* will try."

He let out a shout of pure happiness and scooped me up, twirling me around.

"Let's start trying right now," he breathed out onto my skin.

"I'm still on the Pill!" I laughed.

"Doesn't matter," he murmured into my neck. "I want to practice."

I kissed him hard, as he walked me backward into our bedroom.

As Sebastian had once said, if children happened, we'd welcome them, if not, well, that was okay, too.

We had our whole lives ahead of us.

EPILOGUE

When a woman reaches forty, she is no longer young, but not yet old. My friends had offered this piece of wisdom on my birthday seven months ago.

And yet, it seemed that my life was starting again, or, perhaps I should say, entering a new phase.

Surrounded by love, my beautiful 28 year old husband stood at my side, and in front of our friends, we were joined together by the sacred vows of marriage.

Marc, between assignments, had flown in from France and we'd had an evening drinking to Liz's memory, recalling her humor and craziness, her warmth and strength—crying just a little. And the day before, Ches and his family had arrived from San Diego. His children had peered at me shyly until they spotted Sebastian, and then they'd tried to throw themselves at him, their mother gently restraining them, afraid they'd hurt him. He waved away her concerns and let them climb all over him. It was a wonderful thing to see and my spirits soared, full of hope for the future.

Mitch and Shirley had arrived from South Carolina, and Shirley wept copiously, apologizing over and over. I finally realized that she was apologizing for not having received my letter seven years earlier. We cried together and hugged each other, and agreed to leave the past in the past. Even Donna had flown up for our special day, although Johan had been too ill to travel. Donna had written to us with their congratulations as soon as Shirley had given them the good news. It was strange to see her after all those years, but having her there—

smiling with maternal pride—somehow everything had come full circle.

Nicole, Jenna and Alice were there to support me: Nicole determinedly arguing until the last second that I should go on at least one shopping spree to find a bridal outfit, and me stating with equal determination that it would never happen.

My friends' initial wariness of Sebastian had long since worn off, and they treated him something like a younger brother, much to his irritation and my amusement.

Sebastian stood by my side in front of the deputy clerk at City Hall and promised to love me every day for the rest of his life. I cried tears of joy, and said I would never again let anything separate us.

The day was cold and clear, and the crystal sun shone on our small party as we celebrated the life that Sebastian and I were, at last, going to have.

Despite the difficulties we had been through, despite the difficulties we had yet to face, I had never been happier in my whole life, full of hope and gazing through tears at the man I loved. We were beginning again, or, perhaps, adding a new chapter to our story.

The bride wore jeans.

THE END

And that is Seb and Caro's story—what a ride it's been. These characters mean so much to me, and I just haven't been able to say goodbye to them completely.

I wrote 'Semper Fi' which is the retelling of this book, 'The Education of Caroline', but this time from Sebastian's POV. Proceeds from Semper Fi book are donated to the UK bomb disposal charity Felix Fund.

You'll also be able to read 12 bonus chapters which cover parts of the missing years, as well as the next ten years of their life from the end of this story.

I told you I loved them!

*Oh, and **three bonus epilogues** in this book—click here*

AUTHOR'S NOTE

Sebastian's battle with PTSD was a difficult part of the story to write, and I tried to make this as accurate as possible to do justice those who live with it on a daily basis.

While I was researching the subject, and talking to friends who have been in the military, I was inspired by a number of websites whose organizations seek to help those men and women who are or were serving military personnel.

If you're interested in finding out more, please go to:

www.woundedwarriorproject.org

www.woundedwarriors.ca

www.soldieron.org.au

www.helpforheroes.org.uk

www.felixfund.org.uk

Thank you.

JHB

REVIEWS

and my newsletter

I love reviews! Other readers do, too, because it helps them decide that our book is as awesome as you say it is (I hope!). So please leave a review on Amazon or Goodreads – it would be truly appreciated. Thank you!

Want a free book?!

This one here <<

Of course you do! My acclaimed novella PLAYING IN THE RAIN was featured in Huffington Post's list of Top Ugly Cry Reads! Click here to see the whole list.

You'll receive it for **free** when you sign up to my **monthly short story mailing**. Easy peasy!

You'll also get a chance to read ARCs of my new books and other offers **exclusive** to **VIP newsletter readers** and completely **free**. Best of all, you'll receive a new and original short story *every* month.

Sign up here --> http://janeharveyberrick.co.uk/shortstory-signup/

MORE BOOKS BY JHB

Series Titles
*The Education Series
An epic love story spanning the years, through war zones and more...
*The Education of Sebastian (Education series #1)
*The Education of Caroline (Education series #2)
*The Education of Sebastian & Caroline (combined edition, books 1 &
2 plus bonus chapters)
Semper Fi: The Education of Caroline (Education series #3, from
Sebastian's POV)

The Traveling Series
All the fun of the fair...
*The Traveling Man (Traveling series #1)
*The Traveling Woman (Traveling series #2)
*Roustabout (Traveling series #3)
*Carnival (Traveling series #4)
*Gypsy (Traveling series #5)

* The EOD Series
Blood, bombs and heartbreak
*Tick Tock (EOD series #1)
* Bombshell (EOD series #2)
* The Tick Tock duet (EOD #1 and EOD #2)

*The Rhythm Series

Blood, sweat, tears and dance
*Slave to the Rhythm (Rhythm series #1)
*Luka (Rhythm series #2)

The Justin Trainer Series
The bodyguard and the billionaire
Guarding the Billionaire (Justin Trainer series #1)
Saving the Billionaire (Justin Trainer series #2)

Standalone Titles
Historical Romance
The Lilac Cadillac (dual timeline, WW2 & contemporary)

Contemporary Romance
Battle Scars
One Careful Owner
*Lifers
At Your Beck & Call
The New Samurai
Exposure

New Adult
*Dangerous to Know & Love
Dazzled
Summer of Seventeen
Paranormal
*The Dark Detective: Venator (Book #1, summer 2022)
*The Dark Detective: Paukúnnum (Book #2, autumn 2022)

Novellas
Playing in the Rain
*Behind the Walls
* The Year Book (a short story for every month of the year)

Audio Books
One Careful Owner
(*narrated by Seth Clayton*)

On the Stage
Later, After: Playscript
Trailer

Books with Stu Reardon & me

Two book series – contemporary romance
*Undefeated (Undefeated series #1)
*Model Boyfriend (Undefeated series #2)

Three book series – RomCom
*Gym Or Chocolate? (Gym or Chocolate series #1)
*The World According to Vince (Gym or Chocolate series #2)
*The Baby Game (Gym or Chocolate series #3)

Standalone
*Touch My Soul (novella)

Books with Alana Albertson & me

Father Figure
* These titles are published in languages other than English. Please check Jane's website for details.

BONUS EPILOGUE 1

Christmas at Long Beach

Three months later

Sebastian

"For fuck's sake, Caro! How many people have you invited?"

I'm staring at a fucking Himalaya of food covering our coffee table, our kitchen table, and across every surface in the kitchen.

She's slumped on our couch, looking so fucking sexy, hair all mussed up.

She glares at me, but I can see the amusement in her eyes, too.

"Huh! We both know you'll eat at least half of this, Hunter." *Which is true.* "You know that I've only invited the girls, Atash and his family." *Which is also true.* "I feel like I've been standing in the kitchen all day— my feet are killing me."

I have married a fucking wonderful cook. Hell, she's just a fucking wonderful woman, period.

"Want me to rub your feet, baby?"

"Oh, please, Sebastian."

"Scoot over."

I sit on the couch and pull off her sneakers and socks. She moans softly as I massage her feet—fuck, that sound turns me on. And she has beautiful feet: kinda reminds me of some of those fucking boring statues she dragged me to see when we were in Italy.

She closes her eyes, then says, sleepily, "That's not my foot, Sebastian."

"I know, baby. What can I say, if a job's worth doing..."

I lie on the couch and press myself into her. I can't help it: I get hard just looking at her, but touching her. Yeah ... definitely her fault.

"Ugh, you're all sweaty, Sebastian!"

True. I've been out for a run. Well, more of a slow, fucking limping jog along the boardwalk. I hate being so fucking feeble, but it's getting better. The doc says I'll always have a limp—well, what the fuck does he know?

It's already dark outside, but the boardwalk is buzzing, everyone drinking, having a good time, celebrating Christmas Eve.

I'm beginning to feel part of it, like this really is my home. But the truth is, home could be anywhere, as long as I'm with Caro. I am one lucky bastard. Even with a bullet hole through my damn shoulder and a chunk of muscle missing from my right thigh.

She pushes me off.

"Hold that thought, Hunter. I'm going for a shower."

She slides out from underneath me and heads for the bathroom. I wait until I can hear the water running and then I follow. Although I may have just taken a slight strategic detour to taste some of that amazing fucking food along the way.

I peel off my sweatshirt and t-shirt in one go and somewhere between the living room and the bathroom, I kick off my sneakers and socks. I know she'll be mad at me for that later, as I leave a trail of clothes through the house, but I fucking love it when she chews me out: the way her dark eyes flash, and her nostrils give that little flare. My sweatpants and briefs make it as far as the bathroom door before I lose them. She keeps reminding me we have elderly neighbors and thin curtains. Whatever.

I slide into the shower behind her and she gives a little gasp.

Her hair is all lathered up so I run my hands through it, massaging her scalp, and she gives a groan of pleasure. Yep, definitely feeling that in my dick.

Then I take the shower gel and wash her all over, sliding my hands over her gorgeous, soft skin, over her fantastic ass, and, my favorite, her beautiful breasts.

I bend down to kiss her and the water from the shower pours over us both, but I don't need the warmth of the water—I'm fucking on fire just touching her.

I'd like to crouch down to taste her delicious, wet pussy, but the truth is it's fucking agony stretching out my thigh muscles like that. The thought pisses me off. Whatever. There's other stuff I want to do. *A lot* of other stuff.

"Sebastian, I'm slipping!"

I pick her up around her waist and carry her out into the bathroom, sitting her on the edge of the tub.

Yeah, kneeling—that'll work!

I fall to the floor in front of her and spread her knees out wide. She gasps as I go down on her and that sound alone is enough to make me come. *Hold it in, Hunter, you fucking lightweight.*

I work her some with my tongue and some with my finger, but then she comes suddenly and unexpectedly. *Jeez, that was quick.*

"Fuck, Caro! You okay, baby?"

I look up at her and I love that hot, abandoned look. Her hair is hanging down her back, almost to her waist, and those beautiful breasts are rising and falling rapidly with her *very* fast breathing.

She nods but doesn't seem capable of speaking, and that makes me smile. I pull her up and half-carry her to the bedroom.

She sprawls out on her back and then holds up her arms and wiggles her fingers at me. That means she wants me to lie down with her. I fucking love that we have this unspoken language between us. I've done a lot of shit with a lot of women, but I've never had this level of intimacy with any of them. Only Caro. It's only ever been Caro.

I lie down and kiss her throat, feeling her hot, sweet skin next to mine, as she stretches out like a cat, arching her back and smiling.

"You want to go from behind, Sebastian?" she says, looking up at me, with that wicked gleam in her eye that really fucking turns me on.

"No, baby, I want to *come* from behind."

She slaps my chest but rolls onto her front, and lifts her ass in the air.

"Come and get it, big boy!"

I can't help laughing out loud.

"What movies have you been watching, Caro? *Come and get it, big boy?*"

She smiles over her shoulder at me.

"I made that one up. Original, huh?"

"Yeah, baby. It turns me on."

She smirks.

"Sebastian, according to you, you get turned on when I ask you to do the dishes!"

"I know, baby, I think it's the hot water and foam—gets me thinking stuff."

"I've noticed," she says, drily. "Now am I going to have to wave my ass in the air forever, or are you going to do something about it?"

I'm too much of a fucking gentleman to keep her waiting any longer.

"You want it hard or soft, baby?"

"Both."

Yeah, I can do that.

I slide myself into her gently, feeling that fucking amazing slight resistance that turns into hot, sweet flesh closing all around me.

"Fuck, Caro!"

She pushes back into me.

Fuck, if she does that again, there ain't gonna be much chance of 'soft'.

I slide all the way out, then push into her again, rolling my hips so I can feel her all around me, massaging her inside.

I manage one more slow action before I feel her quiver again and that tips me over the fucking edge. I grip her hips and start pounding into her, the headboard is banging so hard, I think it's going to go through the fucking wall. Again, I'm surprised when she comes really quickly: normally we have better timing than that. Not that I care, because feeling her clenching around me just brings me on faster. Fuck, that woman can milk me!

I wonder, briefly, if it's possible to run out of cum. *Yeah, well, not so far.*

She clenches around me again and I spill into her, pressing her body into the mattress. I pull out carefully and roll onto my back, breathing hard.

Fuck, that felt good!

I didn't know Christmas Eve could be so much fun—it never has been before, although some of the Christmases I spent with Ches, or Shirley and Mitch were pretty good. Nothing like this, though, obviously.

And I fucking love the fact that we've given up condoms. No matter what anyone says, the sensation just isn't the same. And as for being spontaneous, forget that. I mean, have you ever tried to have shower sex when you're using condoms? Yeah, well, see what I mean?

But more than that, I love that Caro has given up taking the Pill. It's like there are no barriers between us. I know she's worried about being an older mom, but she'll be so fucking amazing at it. Hell, she's so fucking patient with me, and I know I've given her a really shitty time since I got back from Afghan. But things feel like they're really on track now.

And she's promised she'll give up the war reporting stuff. I know I should feel guilty about that, but I just can't. I'm relieved that she's not going to put herself in danger like that anymore. And after what happened to Liz Ashton, I'd fucking burn Caro's passport and chain her to the bed before I let her get anywhere near an airplane.

But she's had another offer, one I'm much happier about. She wrote a piece about us biking through Italy. I didn't even know she'd done it, but one day she came in with this travel magazine and a photograph of me next to my Kawasaki ZZ-R1400 somewhere above Amalfi. That was a great bike. Might have to get another of those.

Turns out the travel mag people have offered her a couple of features, including some motorcycle rides in the US. I'm *definitely* up for that. But they're talking about Spain, too. Oh yeah, I'll carry her bags on that job. Yes, ma'am!

I'm still not sure what I want to do, but sorting out Atash's immigration shit has been really interesting. Caro thinks I could make a good attorney but I'm not sure I'd have the patience for that. I'd have to do a degree then a Master's degree. And even if I could take all that studying, which would be enough dry words to choke a camel, I'd probably end up mouthing off to the judge and getting thrown in jail for contempt of court or some shit. I've had some work doing interpreting, but until I get my reading of Arabic and Persian up to speed, it'll remain limited. Guess I'm just kinda looking around.

But one thing that does interest me is doing fitness training with people who have disabilities. I've worked with some great therapists who helped me get my shit together—and some fucking useless ones who shouldn't be let near a real live human being. I'd always thought I might do something along the lines of a personal trainer—I can't imagine being stuck in some rabbit hutch of an office all day—but this kind of appeals. At least I'd know what the fuck I'm talking about.

Alice got me a pass to use the NYU cardio room and weight room. One day, there was this British woman doing one of those motivational talks. I was going to skip it but I heard her say that she'd broken her back paragliding and the doctors told her she probably wouldn't walk again. So she told them all to shove it, ignored all medical advice and, three months later, took her first steps. Now she runs those ultra long-distance marathons*.

I'm not interested in that, but I really like the idea that the doctors didn't know everything. They've told me I'll always have a limp and I'll never get my full fitness back. Well, fuck that. They don't know *me*. Caro told me she doesn't care if I have a limp, so long as I haven't got a limp dick. No way, baby! No chance of that with her. Fuck! She's so sexy and she really doesn't know it.

Shit! I can't keep my mind off sex for two fucking minutes.

Focus, Hunter!

I also heard that the Wounded Warriors Project takes vets on surfing vacations. Although I'm not sure about getting involved with anything military again ... being on the outside now. But I'll find out about that—maybe I could teach or something. Not that I've been back on a board since ... but next year, definitely. We'll both go. That would be cool.

It's been weird getting used to doing stuff together. I don't mean all the relationship stuff, because I fucking love that. But all the day-to-day stuff that I never thought about: joint bank accounts, for one. I really love that we have a checking account that says 'Mr. and Mrs. Hunter' but I hate using it because most of the money is hers. Well, given to her by Liz Ashton. I have quite a lot of savings from the Marines because I only ever spent my money on drinking and fucking around, oh, and a couple of motorcycles, but it's not like I ever had a home to pay for before, so it's a chunk of cash.

I talked to Ches about it and he kinda put things in perspective for me. He said I should stop thinking about *my* money and *her* money and try and think about it as *our* money. I get what he's saying, but it's not easy. Caro says we'll get used to it, and she's not really wrong about this shit. I guess I'm the one who's fucked in the head about it.

It was fucking amazing seeing Ches and the kids when Caro and I got married. I really love those little bugs: they're so fucking honest and open—you know, not afraid to love. I don't ever remember being like that when I was a kid, but when you've had assholes for parents, you learn that if you're going to cry, you do it alone in your room. I think I stopped crying when I was about six. The only person who can make me cry now is Caro. I think she knows that, but it's not something we talk about.

She hasn't mentioned the kids thing since she stopped taking the Pill and I'm not going to push it. I meant what I said: if it happens that would be fucking awesome, but if it doesn't, our lives are really rich already. I just don't want her to miss out on anything because of me.

"Hey, where did you go just now, Sebastian?" she says, her eyes all soft and full of love.

The way she looks at me just cracks my heart wide open. It's like I've answered all her questions, just by being alive—I can't get enough of that look.

"Been right here, baby. Just thinking how cute you're going to look in your Christmas stockings."

She twines her hand through mine.

"Sebastian, you do realize that it's *a stocking* as in noun: singular—and that you're supposed to hang it up by the chimney for Santa to fill *if* you've been a good boy—which, of course, you haven't."

"Yeah, well, I think we should start a new tradition. Caro in stockings for Christmas. Hey, that alliterates, too."

"Gosh, you do know some big words, Sebastian," she says, laughing.

"You taught me everything I know, baby," and I fasten my teeth around her nipple and tug gently.

She gasps. "Although I never had to teach you that move, did I?"

"Mmm," I say, in agreement, "guess I'm a natural."

I tug slightly harder and my right hand moves down to her thighs.

"Again?" she says, in amazement.

"Yeah, it's Christmas, baby, and I want my presents early."

Waking up next to Caro is my favorite fucking thing in the world. I mean, yeah, I fucking love being buried inside her and I love seeing her face when she comes, but the absolute best thing is that moment when I watch her wake up. She's soft and sweet when she's asleep and then her eyelids blink open and there's that wicked gleam in the depths of her dark brown eyes. She stretches out and I feel her arms and legs and body brushing my skin. And I know she's all mine—forever.

And I really fucking love wake-up sex. Since she told me that trick about her orgasm being more intense if she hasn't been to the bathroom, I always try and get a quickie in before breakfast. It's a great way to start the day. She comes like a fucking train—yeah.

"Merry Christmas, Sebastian," she says softly.

God, I love hearing those words. This is the best fucking Christmas ever—and it's still only 7AM.

"Merry Christmas, Caro. I love you so much, baby."

She leans over to kiss me, sighing into my mouth. And Christmas Day starts really, really well.

Two hours later, she starts to get up.

"Uh-uh, baby. I'm going to make you breakfast in bed."

She smiles, that lovely sexy, sleepy smile.

"You can't cook, Sebastian, despite my best efforts to teach you."

Wow, that hurts. I'm a really good cook: I can make coffee and ... espresso.

"You want coffee in bed, baby?"

She laughs and nods.

My real reason for getting up is to go fetch her present. I found a really cool hiding place at the back of the closet in the spare bedroom. It's high up and, being such a shrimp, she'd need to stand on a chair to find it. I'm pretty fucking pleased with myself.

And I remember to make the coffee. Yeah, she's got me tamed—and I fucking love it.

I carry the coffee in two mugs, with the parcel under my left arm. The coffee is in danger of slopping over the sides because I've overfilled *again*, but also because my fucking leg is so damn useless first thing in the morning and my limp is a lot worse. Caro never says anything, but she knows it bothers me.

I put the coffee down and toss her the gift.

"For me?"

"Yeah, kind of."

She raises her eyebrows and then pulls on the ribbon holding it together. A riot of colorful silk spills out onto the bed. She gazes up, a slow smile spreading across her face.

"Colors, Hunter?"

She's teasing me: my entire wardrobe consists of white, gray, black, and blue jeans. Oh, and a pair of crazily-bright boardshorts that I bought in Italy.

She holds up one of the pieces of flimsy silk and lace.

"Yes, ma'am. A different color for every day of the week."

"What color would you like me to wear today?"

"Red: it's Christmas."

She laughs. "Ok, I'll wear the red. Are we saving black for Saturday nights?"

Fuck! That sounds hot.

"Whatever you like, baby."

She knows I'm lying and she smirks at me.

"Your present is under the bed, Sebastian."

What? I go to all that trouble to hide her gift properly, and mine is under the fucking bed?

She laughs at my expression.

"I learned being sneaky from this hot Marine I used to know..."

She stops mid-sentence.

"It's okay, baby," I say, quietly.

Her hands are on her mouth. "I didn't mean it like that, Sebastian."

And her eyes fill with tears.

"I know, baby. Don't cry, Caro. It's okay. I'm not ... it's okay."

Fuck. Will I ever get used to this? Being a 'former' Marine? Sometimes it just hits me like a fucking sledgehammer.

"Where's that damn present that you've hidden so stealthily?"

She smiles, wiping a tear away, and I feel so fucking bad that I made her cry—on Christmas.

I hang off the bed and look underneath.

That is a fucking big present!

I pull it out and even though I know exactly what it is—because she couldn't exactly hide it—she's gift-wrapped it in Christmas paper.

"I hope you like it," she says, nervously.

"Baby, I love it already."

She's bought me a surfboard. It's a thruster in style, pointed at the nose, but I can see that it's slightly longer and wider than someone of my height and weight would usually have. The extra width and length will give it more buoyancy—it's going to make it easier for me to surf on, because my balance is still fucked.

But when I unwrap it...

"Do you like it?" she says, chewing on her lip.

The design is clean and simple: a single blue-green stripe trimming the edge, and across the middle are the words, *Semper Fidelis*.

"Baby, I love it."

And I do. I really do.

She looks relieved.

I kiss her, showing her without words how much she means to me.

She kisses me back, weaving her magic around me, and the world disappears.

When she pulls away from me, I'm hard again, and I try to tug her back, but she laughs and shakes her head.

"Our guests will be here in 45 minutes and neither of us are showered, let alone dressed. And unless you want Nic, Alice and Jenna to see you in your shorts—which I suspect they'd be thrilled at, by the way—I think you should put some pants on.

Ah, crap. The three witches.

Okay, they're not that bad, but they can be really fucking patronizing. Sometimes I just feel like a piece of meat, the way they look at me when they think I'm not watching. I mean, fuck! They're my *wife's* friends. That's so fucking uncool.

Caro just laughs and reminds me I'm the one who married an older woman with older friends, so I should just suck it up.

The other day we were in a store buying groceries and were lining up to pay. Caro realized she'd forgotten some weird cheese she wanted, so she went off to find it. Then this woman in a pant-suit who was standing behind us in the line starts chatting to me. I'd like to believe she was just being friendly, but then she reached over and laid her hand on my chest in this flirty little move. I mean, she'd just seen me with *my wife*, for fuck's sake! What is with these women? Caro thought it was pretty damn funny.

I haven't told Caro the real reason it pisses me off, because it would upset her, but they're exactly the kind of women I used to hit on when I was single—tough, career women who told themselves they'd never fall for me—older women who reminded me of Caro.

I push the thought away because this is our first Christmas together and I don't want to spoil it.

Caro won't let me shower with her: she knows me too well. So I make the bed while she's in the bathroom and tidy up the kitchen where I spilt the coffee when I was making it. She never says anything when I clear up, but I know she loves it, because she gets this look on her face like she can't believe I do stuff around the house. She just doesn't get that I want to take care of her in whatever way I can. Because I fucking love her.

When I go back into the bedroom, she's just slipping her cute, black cocktail dress over the red, silk underwear I bought her.

Fuck! I was too late.

"Rain check, Hunter," she says, in a firm voice.

Ah hell. I'll just have to walk around with a boner all day, knowing she's wearing that fucking sexy bra and panties under her dress.

I take a shower—a cold one.

I'm just pulling on a t-shirt when a car pulls up outside. I open the front door for Caro's friends, and she runs out and takes the lion share of the hugging and kissing, thank fuck. I'm relieved when I see Atash's family walking up the street.

"*As-salaamu' alaykum!*"

They come in, looking a little nervous, but soon everyone is sitting on cushions on the floor—because we don't have enough chairs—and chatting away. Atash and his brother Kambiz are the only ones in their family who speak any English but it all works out pretty well.

And, I'm not going to tell Caro, but Kambiz knows where to get the best hash. I don't do it very often, but sometimes I just need to chill.

Caro's food is fucking amazing, which is a real ice-breaker. She's made Italian dishes: some weird salted cod thing, baked pasta, capon, fish salad and a whole bunch of stuff I can't even pronounce, let alone recognize.

Kambiz's eyes are popping out of his head when he sees the Afghan food that she's made, as well: *Qabli Pulao* of rice, raisins and carrot with lamb, *mantu* dumplings with minced beef and onions, spicy vegetables, and two *chalow* rice dishes.

Atash just smiles because he's had Caro's cooking before.

I feel so fucking proud of her. She did most of it herself: okay, well, all of it. I tried to help but she nearly fucking lynched me when I managed to let the rice burn dry ... um ... the first lot of rice. I'll do my part later—all the fucking washing up. Thank fuck she insisted on getting paper plates to eat off.

And during the day, I have a revelation. I fucking love Christmas!

It was a nightmare when I was a kid: lots of drunken arguments, and most of the time I'd try and hide in my room. It was better when Ches and his folks moved to San Diego because they'd invite me over and I'd spend as much time as I could with them. Yeah, those were pretty good. Got to surf on Christmas Day a few times, although Shirley tore a strip off Mitch if he brought us back late for the food.

I've had four Christmas's overseas: one in Iraq with my unit, which was kind of okay, although a lot of the guys were going on about missing their families, and I never had anyone to miss; one in Afghanistan, where we got the fuck shelled out of us on Christmas Day, which kind of put a damper on things; and one where it was just the chaplain going on about some shit or other. Last Christmas I was in Switzerland and I spent it screwing some rich German woman in a fucking amazing hotel in Klosters. Something else I haven't mentioned to Caro. Did some snowboarding, too.

Caro knows I've done this shit, but she never asks and she never uses it as a weapon when we're fighting, which is pretty fucking cool of her.

I could have flown back to spend Christmas with Ches last year, but since I'd fucked Amy's friend *and* her friend's friend, she's been kinda pissed at me. Not that I cared about that, but I didn't want to screw things up for Ches, so I stayed away.

Amy was kind of okay with me when Caro and I married. It really helped that they got along so well. I think Amy was in a state of shock that I was 'settling down' as she put it (several times, for fuck's sake).

But I wasn't surprised that she got along with Caro: everyone loves Caro. She's just so positive, energetic, kind, generous, and no one is capable of hating her for it, she's so beautiful but she's even lovelier on the inside. She doesn't see it—but everyone else does. And she's so fucking sexy.

This Christmas was perfect, so full of fun and love and laughter. I am a lucky bastard. I don't know what I've done to deserve such ... such happiness.

I have one more gift for her, but I'll wait until everyone has gone home.

Finally, *finally*, we get the place to ourselves. Caro made everyone take food home with them so at least we don't have to wrap up a load of leftovers. Atash's family were really pleased with that. Probably enough to last them a few days.

"I'm just glad to see it gone," says Caro, groaning. "I can't eat another thing. Never, *never* show me another mince pie."

"You did amazing, Caro. Now sit down and let me do the dishes."

Of course, she doesn't.

"Don't be silly, Sebastian. I can tell your leg is hurting you. Just let me take care of it all."

"Damn it, woman!" I half yell at her. "Aren't you ever going to take a fucking order?"

"Sure," she says, laughing at me, "when you tell me to get my ass in your bed."

I groan. How the hell am I going to be able to concentrate on anything else now?

We clear up together and when we're done, we collapse onto the couch and she snuggles up on my chest.

"Today was fun," she sighs. "It felt ... right."

"I know what you mean, baby."

"Let's go to bed, Sebastian. I'm beat."

"Yeah, okay, baby ... I have another gift for you first."

"Does it involve getting naked in a variety of new and interesting positions?"

Fuck! She's a mind-reader!

"Well, yeah, that, too, but ... um ... there's something else. I don't know ... you might think it's lame."

She sits up and looks at me.

"Sebastian, I'd never think *anything* you gave me was lame. *Not ever.*"

"Yeah, well ... you might when you've heard it."

"Heard it?"

"I ... um ... I ... I wrote a song for you, Caro."

She looks stunned.

"For me?"

I've been trying to learn guitar. It's really fucking hard—my left hand won't do shit since I got shot in the shoulder, but it turns out that most songs only have about four chords anyway. I don't think I'll ever play a diminished seventh. Fuck it.

And I stand up to go get the guitar before I lose my nerve.

I've been practicing while Caro has been out. Sometimes it sounds okay, sometimes it sounds like crap.

I walk back into the living room, but I can't meet her eyes.

I position my fingers over the strings and take a deep breath. *Fuck. My mouth has gone dry.*

Here goes.

> Just when I'd seen it all
> Just when I'd heard it all
> And the road got weary
> I heard you call.
>
> I thought I knew it all
> I thought I called the shots
> No colors in my life
> So far to fall.
>
> *Filled with sunshine*
> *That's in your smile*
> *Always loving*
> *I'll walk that extra mile.*
>
> No place to call my home
> No woman of my own
> But then you rescued me
> And your love is the key.
>
> *Filled with sunshine*
> *That's in your smile*
> *Always loving*
> *We'll go that extra mile.*

The last note dies away and I still can't look up.

The silence hangs in the air.

She stands up and takes the guitar from me, and lays it carefully on the table. Then she sits on my knee and my arms automatically curl around her waist.

"You made me cry," she says, softly.

"Oh no, baby. Was it that bad?"

"Idiot!" she sniffs, between her tears. "It was beautiful. Oh, Sebastian, it was just wonderful. I love it. And I love you. So much, *tesoro*."

Relief floods through me and all the tension drains away. *She loved it*.

I stand up with her still in my arms.

"Good, let's go to bed."

She snuggles into my chest, and lets me carry her into the bedroom.

I'm *really* looking forward to unwrapping my next present and seeing her in all that fucking sexy red underwear.

I put her down on the bed and yank my t-shirt over my head.

Oh, crap! I think I heard the seam rip again.

"Wait!" she says, loudly.

I stare at her, puzzled.

"I have another present for you yet, Sebastian."

"I know, baby, and I'm looking forward to unwrapping it."

She rolls her eyes.

"A *different* present."

"You got me something else?"

I can't help smiling.

Fuck. I love getting presents—I've never had that many before. I kinda get why people like Christmas now.

She opens the drawer of her bedside cabinet and pulls out a small envelope, and hands it to me.

"What is it?"

"Sebastian, the whole point is that you open it," she says, with a smile twitching at her lips.

I toss the pillows behind me and sit propped up against the headboard.

I tear open the envelope and pull out a small photograph. I have no fucking idea what I'm looking at. It's a weird black and white, swirly picture. For all I know it could be a Klingon vessel attacking the Starship Enterprise.

One.

Two.

Three.

"Oh fuck!"

Four.

Five.

Six.

"Caro?"

Seven.

Eight.

"Is this?"

Nine.

Ten.

"Yes," she says. "We're going to have a baby—you'll be a father. Merry Christmas, Sebastian."

My wife is the only person in the whole fucking world who can make me cry. And tonight, for the first time in my miserable fucking existence, I cry tears of joy.

BONUS EPILOGUE 2

Three Years Later

Caroline

Marco really is a beautiful little boy. I know every mother says that or at least thinks it about their own child, but in Marco's case it's true. Just last week, I was approached by a woman who said she was a scout from a modeling agency, and that she was sure she could find plenty of work for him: catalogues, magazines, even TV commercials.

She was pretty pushy, and couldn't believe that I wasn't interested in making money out of my two-year-old son. I took her card out of politeness, but I really wanted to tell her to shove it where the sun don't necessarily shine.

My language skills have plummeted since my marriage to a certain potty-mouthed former-Marine named Sebastian Hunter. Two and three-quarter years of marriage haven't managed to curtail the habits picked up from his ten years in the United States Marine Corps. He swears like a drunken sailor on shore leave—and he doesn't even notice he's doing it.

But I think the fact that Marco is starting to talk and understand whole sentences, might have a more salutary effect than all of my nagging. But I'm not holding my breath: if Marco drops the f-bomb at Kindergarten, I'm blaming his father.

My eyes must have glazed over because the model agency woman was staring at me like I was simple. But then she spotted something behind me, and I saw her suck in her stomach and stick out her boobs.

I could almost predict what she'd seen. Right on cue, I heard Marco's happy whoop as Sebastian scooped him into his arms.

"Papa! Papa!"

Hearing my son using those words was a bittersweet experience. Now I was a mother, I missed my own dear father so much more. We named our son after him.

"Hey, little man!"

And I turned around as Sebastian plastered a loud, squishy kiss on the top of Marco's head, causing him to laugh and squeal.

"I can see where your son gets his looks," said the agency woman, her gaze ravaging Sebastian's body.

I couldn't blame her for looking. I'd long suspected that half of the mothers in the park came here at this hour to enjoy the scenery: and I wasn't talking about the wonderful view across the beach toward the ocean. I was talking about 6'2" of solid muscle, sculpted abs, broad firm pecs, an ass you could bounce a quarter off (which I knew for a fact, having spent an enjoyable pre-baby afternoon doing exactly that), all topped by a face so beautiful that I was used to people stopping to do a double-take. I'm biased, of course, but it was no exaggeration that men and women were drawn to Sebastian's ridiculous good looks.

But the best thing, the absolute best thing, was that he was always smiling. Happiness radiated from him. And because there was a time when it seemed like he'd never be happy again, each smile was a small miracle, a special gift, and I treasured every one of them.

The agency woman was still eye-fucking my husband.

"Have you ever done any modeling?" she purred, one hand raised as if she wanted to stroke his stomach. "Because I was just telling the nanny—clients would pay a lot of money to use photographs of you and your son in an advertising campaign." She laughed lightly. "Obviously the apple didn't fall too far from the tree."

The nanny? Good to know that my son's looks had absolutely nothing to do with me. Although, to be fair, he did look far more like Sebastian than me. Except for his eyes. Marco had my eyes: brown. Well, I called them brown, Sebastian called them hot chocolate, which always made me laugh. His own eyes were a remarkable shade of blue-green that seemed to change like the color of the ocean.

Sebastian shot me an amused glance as he balanced Marco on his hip, transferring his weight to his good leg.

Even though he'd worked hard to retain a high level of fitness, his injuries from Afghanistan still bothered him, more so when he was tired, or when the weather was particularly cold.

But today it was hot and sunny, and all he was wearing was a small pair of running shorts, his chest and shoulders glowing with sweat. Delicious.

"Yeah, I do modeling," he said, looking straight at the agency woman as she started to drool. "But only in private ... for my wife. Hey, baby."

Then he leaned down to kiss me, and the agency woman looked as if she had been wading through dog poop in her $600 Louboutins.

"Oh. You're the mother."

I raised my eyebrows at her but she didn't even have the courtesy to blush. She shoved another business card at Sebastian and threw the words, "Call me!" over her shoulder.

"You gonna bitch-slap her, Caro?" he asked, nuzzling my ear, "'cause you really look like you want to right now."

"Not at all," I said, primly. "I'm modeling good behavior for our son."

He smirked at me. "I love it when you're good, baby, but I love it even more when you're bad."

After that encounter, it was nap time. Marco slept soundly while I was thoroughly fucked by 190 pounds of prime manhood.

Sebastian called it 'practice'. What he meant was that we were hoping to conceive baby number two. He didn't say it, but I knew that he hoped Marco wasn't going to be an only child. Sebastian had grown up alone and he didn't want that for his son. Thank goodness he'd met Ches and the Peters' family when he was 13. It was the only time he'd known what a real home was like—until now.

But unlike my impossible-to-wear-out 30-year-old husband, I was 43—having a toddler running around who was learning how to get into everything, was exhausting enough. We'd been trying for another baby for the last year. I was beginning to think it would never happen.

It wouldn't be so bad if it didn't, but still, I hoped.

Every month I'd be disappointed when my period started. Even this morning, my heart pounding like a subway train in rush hour, I'd peed on a little plastic stick. I was two days late, and I had my fingers crossed, my eyes crossed, although not my legs crossed—obviously.

Not Pregnant.

The words on that little piece of white plastic haunted me. I wanted to cry but then a little golden-haired bundle of cuteness tugged on my leg.

"Beach, mommy!"

I'm instantly smiling.

I was supposed to be working on an article for one of the nationals about wounded service men and women learning to surf. But the sun was shining, and my walking, talking, loving son wanted to go to the beach. I shut down my laptop, and was a willing accomplice to his desire to sit on sun-warmed sand and paddle in the ocean.

Besides, my deadline was still several days away. And over the past three years since Sebastian and I had met again, I'd learned not to take these precious moments for granted. Work could wait, even work I greatly enjoyed.

I picked up my beach bag that was waiting by the front door, ready for action. It was a sort of mommy's version of my journalist's grab bag for emergency evac. But instead of passport, solar-powered phone charger, first aid supplies, dried food, water, flashlight, and pocket knife, I now carried baby wipes, mints, sun screen, cell phone, swim diapers, pail and shovel, a towel, some water and a snack, wallet and three baseball caps. Today we'd only need two because Sebastian was in the city working at the gym, although only for the morning. He didn't usually work on a Sunday, but he was doing it as a favor for one of his clients.

Over the last two years, he'd really started to build his business as a personal fitness trainer, specializing in people who'd suffered traumatic injury, including loss of limbs. Not all of his clients were ex-military. One 19-year-old he worked with had lost a leg in a motorcycle accident, and another was born without the lower portion of his left arm.

Sebastian had lost 17% of the muscle from his right thigh, and was left with femoral nerve dysfunction, which could be very painful at times. He'd also been shot in his shoulder and had diminished motor skills in his left hand. You'd hardly know it to look at him, although when he wore his running shorts, the ugly scar covering the upper portion of his right leg was hard to miss.

He'd been very self-conscious of it at one time, but now it didn't bother him when people openly stared. I was more likely to be annoyed by their curiosity than he was.

A couple of months ago he'd starting volunteering as one of the instructors for the Wave Warriors Surf Camp at Virginia Beach. So every other weekend throughout the summer, we were making the seven hour drive south and joining in with the other ex-services families. I'd gotten to know some really amazing people, some of whom were the focus of my article.

And Marco loved it. He was turning into a little surf rat, taking after his father in so many ways. They even shared the same crazy mop of blond hair, although Sebastian was threatening to shave his off again, saying it was getting too long. I'd begged him to keep it, but I wasn't sure how much longer I'd win that battle.

As far as the surfing went, the long-term plan was for Sebastian to start a similar surf camp for veterans nearer to home.

But right now, we were waiting on even more exciting news. His work with disabled people had been noticed, and the gym manager had put Sebastian's name forward to be a personal trainer at Rio in 2016 for the US Paralympics team. Essentially, he'd be helping athletes to use the on-site equipment, although it was a job that was more about kudos than pay. He'd been learning Portuguese via an interactive online program in the hope that this would help his application, even though it wasn't a requirement. He was picking it up easily, which was very annoying, as my own language skills were severely limited, but damn, I was proud of him, too.

If he got the job, I was planning to join him for at least one of the three weeks he'd be there. At first, I'd been reluctant to agree to go, not wanting to be a distraction while he was focusing on something so important. But then he said he'd been away from me long enough during the ten years we were apart—a comment that filled me with guilt, almost as much as it made me swoon. We were undecided on whether Marco would come with us. If not, Ches and Amy had offered to take him. But Sebastian wanted his son with him, and I suspected he'd get his way. I found it hard to say no to him, a fact which he exploited shamelessly at times.

Once a year, we made a point of traveling out to San Diego to spend time with Sebastian's best friend, Ches, and his family. Not only that, but Ches's parents now lived on the west coast and I thought it was good for Marco to have a chance to experience what it was like to have grandparents. Sebastian was estranged from both his mother and father, and I hadn't heard a word from my mom in 13 years. We'd never got along, and my divorce from David gave her the excuse she'd wanted to cut me out of her life. I knew she was still alive, but that was all.

I didn't want Marco to miss out on anything, and Ches's parents, Shirley and Mitch, treated him as part of their family, and Sebastian had always been a second son to them. I wanted to make sure we kept as much connection as was possible even though we lived 3,000 miles apart.

I loved living at Long Beach. It was near enough to urban life, but also had a real small town community vibe about it. And very importantly as far as Sebastian was concerned, it had a good-size surf, with waves coming off the Atlantic that provided long, workable rides.

While Marco and I were strolling toward the beach, I texted my girlfriends to see if they wanted to come and join us. They enjoyed driving out from the city, leaving behind the frantic bustle to have some quality beach time. They also enjoyed ogling the local surfers as they dove through the blue-gray waves, their perfectly toned bodies rippling in the summer sun. Let's just say they enjoyed the window-dressing.

Things were changing in my group of friends. Nicole had started dating some high-powered Swiss banker, so they only saw each other every couple of weeks. It wouldn't have suited everyone, but it seemed to work for them. Jenna was still happily single, but Alice had recently become engaged to a fellow professor at NYU, an archeologist who was currently away on a field trip in Peru.

It was rare that the four of us got together these days, so it was almost like old times, except for the fact that Marco was making sandcastles next to us.

Sebastian joined us an hour later, thankful to be back from the madness that was NYC. He scooped up Marco to go for a swim, which meant having Marco's chubby arms fastened around Sebastian's neck as he swam up and down.

"It's almost indecent how hot your husband is," sighed Nicole. "And seeing him with Marco, I swear my ovaries start doing salsa moves."

I laughed. "Thinking of joining the club, Nic?"

"God, no! I'll leave motherhood to you, Lee. You're a natural—you make everyone else look bad."

I snorted. "Hardly. It's an uphill struggle sometimes, and I'm not getting any younger."

Alice looked at me sympathetically. "Still feeling broody?"

I sighed. "I don't know. Yes, no, maybe. Sometimes I think ... well, if it's meant to be, it will happen."

Jenna patted my arm. "Whatever happens, Lee, you've got Sebastian behind you. That man completely adores you."

"Yes," agreed Nicole. "Actually, it's rather nauseating."

We all laughed, and the subject was dropped.

～

The following Monday, Sebastian texted me to say he'd be late home. His Afghan friend, Atash, had asked him to drop by after work.

Atash was a near neighbor. He and his family were refugees from Lashkar Gah in the south of Afghanistan, one of the few Shi'a Muslims in Helmand Province, a largely Sunni area.

Some people thought it strange that Sebastian was friends with Afghans, when it was people from that nation who'd caused his life-changing injury and killed two of his colleagues in front of him. But Sebastian never blamed individuals, his hatred was saved for the politicians who'd let it happen.

But I'd been waiting for hours, watching the lasagna I made slowly desiccating in the oven, and Marco had to go to bed without Daddy's goodnight kiss. He was very grumpy about that, and I thought it might be tantrum time. I had to promise that Daddy would sneak in and kiss him when he came home. Marco was satisfied with that. Just about.

When I finally heard the front door open and close again quietly, it was nearly 11PM.

"Hey, baby," Sebastian said, tiredly.

He slumped down next to me on the couch, his limp more pronounced than usual, and I curled up into his side.

"Is everything okay?"

He sighed heavily.

"Yeah, I guess. I've been with Atash and his family for the last four, God, five hours."

He rubbed his forehead, and I started to pull away, meaning to go to the kitchen and get him something to eat.

"Later," he said, tightening his arms around me. "There's something I need to talk to you about."

"Okay," I said, cautiously.

His serious tone was making me nervous, but then Sebastian's smile quirked up one side of his beautiful lips.

"It's nothing bad," he said. "Not really."

"So what's up?"

He leaned back and closed his eyes, settling me onto his chest. As I felt the steady rise and fall of his warm body, I began to relax again.

"Atash has a cousin—some sort of second cousin 37 times removed," he began.

I had to smile. Working out Atash's family relations was an impossible task.

"He's arrived in the US and landed on Atash. They're kind of cramped there already ... and he has this kid with him ... another distant cousin or something, I don't think he even knows how they're related. Anyway, her parents were killed during an IED explosion in the market at Now Zad. Caro, she doesn't have anyone really, and she's only three. Her name is Sofia."

"Sebastian, what are you trying to tell me?"

He opened his eyes and gazed down at me.

"We have room here," he said, softly.

"What? You didn't! You didn't make any promises, did you?" I said, pulling away from him.

"Not exactly..." he muttered.

"Then exactly what, Hunter?" I snapped.

"I just thought ... well, it would be good for Marco to have a big sister, wouldn't it? I mean, I know that you could still ... but she needs a home *now*, Caro. You should see her: she's so cute, with all this long, brown hair and big brown eyes. She kinda reminds me of you."

His smile was wistful and I felt my heart miss a beat.

"So ... what does that mean? What do you think is going to happen? That'd she'll come and live with us for a while? What happens when Marco becomes attached to her and then she just leaves? There are laws in this country, Sebastian. You can't just go around taking children from their families!"

"I know that, Caro," he said calmly as my voice began to rise. "We could ... help ... maybe ... adopt her? She needs someone, baby. Sure, she's got Atash's family, but they're busting at the seams there, and she needs something secure. Fuck knows what she's been through already. She lost her parents ... she saw them die."

My heart went out to that lost little girl, but I had to be practical here, because God knows Sebastian wasn't going to be.

"Do you even know if they've entered the country legally? And Child Services need to be informed so..."

"Fuck that! I have no idea and I don't care. Rules aren't for us, baby. They never were—not when it really matters, not when the law is shit and makes no fucking sense."

His words stung me. I wanted to cry out and yell and say, *No! There are consequences. Look what happened last time—we lost 10 years!* But I didn't. I couldn't.

"She needs us *now*," he stressed, gripping my shoulders. "Baby, you've got so much love to give. You're an awesome mom. You're amazing with Marco, so fucking patient. We can do this, Caro. We can give her the home she needs."

"Does she even understand English?"

"No, but that won't be a problem. She's Pashtun—I can talk to her."

"There are rules! We'd have to apply to be her adoptive parents and that could take a couple of years and..."

His eyes sparkled. "So that's a yes?"

"It's a maybe," I said tentatively, feeling angry at being bulldozed and guilty about being the sensible one. "This isn't something we can go into without really thinking it through."

"So we'll go see her tomorrow," he said, pulling me into another hug.

"I said *maybe!*"

But I knew I was losing the battle. The truth was, I didn't want to win it, but I *had* to be sensible. Taking on another woman's child—I didn't know if I could do it.

That night, Sebastian made slow, sweet love to me, whispering hot, dirty, passionate words in my ear, worshipping me with his body. At times like this, it felt like life had a greater meaning than the two of us, than our small family. It was hard to explain, and I wasn't sure I wanted to try and see how the magic worked.

Sebastian fell asleep quickly that night, but I lay awake for hours, thinking, wondering. I tried hard to keep the practical problems in front of me: lack of space in our little bungalow for one, adoption procedures for another. Maybe I was too old to be approved as an adoptive mother. I just didn't know. And there was a good chance that Child Services would think Sofia would be better off with another Afghan family, people who shared her culture and religion. But if we did go ahead, it would undoubtedly help that Sebastian spoke Pashto, but still ... were we the right family for her? And how would Marco react? The only child, suddenly presented with a ready-made sister?

My eyes widened as I realized that I'd already thought of Sofia as his sister.

I watched Sebastian sleeping for a long time.

Moving as quietly as I could, I rolled out of bed.

"Where're you going?" he murmured, sleepily.

Darn Marine! He slept like a cat.

"Bathroom," I whispered.

He grunted something inaudible and rolled onto his side.

Instead, I headed for my laptop, stopping briefly to look in on Marco.

He looked like a tiny angel, a cherub, his face flushed from sleep, one arm flung over his head. My heart skittered, and I closed the door quietly, then decided to leave it slightly ajar.

I flipped up the laptop's lid, and switched it on.

I was journalist and I needed facts: they were my bread and butter.

The bottom line was that in order to even have a child see a doctor it would need to be under our insurance or else pay out of pocket. If we wanted to add Sofia to our insurance, we would need a birth certificate or court documents. The same held true for going to school. We would need to have proof of custody or guardianship or a birth certificate in order to register her. So technically, Sofia could live with us for months, but not long term. We would need to make arrangements to adopt her and start the process immediately.

I batted the idea back and forwards for hours, unsure what to do, finally crawling back to bed and falling asleep a couple of hours before dawn.

I was woken too early by some small person yanking on my arm, wanting pancakes and a glass of milk.

Sebastian sat up yawning, and exhausted as I was, I couldn't help but appreciate the beauty of his hard body, tousled hair, face sleep-softened.

"Let mommy rest, buddy. She's real tired."

He pulled on his running shorts and a t-shirt, discreetly tucking his morning wood away, before taking Marco by the hand, their voices disappearing in a quiet murmur.

Of course, I couldn't get back to sleep, and in the end I got up and showered, my body still half asleep, my mind whirring.

When I staggered into the kitchen, Sebastian was halfway through burning a batch of pancakes. Okay, they weren't completely burned, but perhaps just a little darker than I would have made them. His cooking skills had only improved slightly. Very slightly.

I took over while he poured milk into a sippy cup for Marco, and made us coffee. I felt his warm hands circle my waist as I stacked the pancakes.

"So, any thoughts?"

"Lots of them, and all confused."

"Oh, okay."

There was a world of disappointment in those two words.

"But I think we should go and see her—see Sofia—as a family."

"Really?"

I turned to face him and his eyes were lit up with surprise and pleasure.

"Really? You'll go see her?"

"Yes, but it's just to say hello. Nothing more."

I said the words, but inside it felt like that once we'd seen her, there'd be no going back.

Marco picked up on Sebastian's excitement, and went running around the kitchen yelling and shrieking at a piercing level. He laughed even louder when Sebastian pretended to chase him, and I left them playing hide and seek with the kitchen furniture.

Dear God! If Sofia did join our family, I was in danger of having two toddlers, and one grown-up kid who was more work than the rest of them combined. I couldn't help smiling at the thought.

A sister for Marco. *Our daughter.*

I gave myself a good talking to for jumping the gun, but the nervous excitement was bubbling up inside me, too, as we reached Atash's house.

Two men I didn't recognize were sitting on the steps, but they seemed to know Sebastian, calling out a greeting. He replied, "*As-salaamu' alaykum,*" and I smiled and nodded as we walked inside.

As usual, organized chaos flowed through the small house. Children ran screaming happily, and the babble of voices filled every room. Sebastian hadn't been joking when he said the house was splitting at the seams. Atash's house had become an informal community center for the local Afghan population. A good number of them seemed to use it as a staging post to start their journey to other family members spread across the country.

Atash came to greet us, offering the ubiquitous sweet tea. We both accepted, even though I couldn't stand the stuff, my teeth aching just from looking at it. Sebastian tolerated it better, but had perfected the practice of making one small cup last as long as his visit entailed.

Marco ran out into the tiny backyard, completely at home, mingling happily with the other children, uncaring that they spoke a different language. Maybe when you're a child, that's the only language you need.

Sebastian nudged me.

"That's her. The one sitting by the fence."

A small girl in a dowdy brown shalwar kameez was pushing her hands in the sandy soil and making a dusty pile in front of her. Her hair was long and loose and her feet were bare, a pair of tattered flip-flops lying next to her. Even though she was a year older than Marco, she didn't appear much bigger.

She glanced up suddenly, and her huge brown eyes made me catch my breath. She looked so lost and alone, such an adult expression of suffering on her small face.

I could help myself. I went over and sat next to her, kicking off my sandals and making my own mud pie next to hers. She watched me seriously, then continued to make her pile grow, her hands and nails filthy, like mine.

"Sofia," I said quietly, not looking at her. "That's a pretty name."

There was the tiniest pause, when she heard her own name.

I talked quietly, chattering about nothing in particular, until Marco came and plopped himself in my lap.

Sofia's eyes widened, and after a moment's thought, she reached out to touch his gold-colored hair.

Marco squirmed and blinked with one eye scrunched up. Without warning, he launched himself at her, squashing her mud pie completely flat then laughing like a small hyena.

And that was it. They were up and running around the garden together, squawking and chattering, each with their own childish babble.

Sebastian came and sat down in the dirt next to me.

"What do you think?"

I shook my head slowly. "I think I'm in a lot of trouble."

He put his arm around my shoulder and pulled me in for a hug.

"Guess we'll be in trouble together then."

"Guess we will."

～

Of course, it wasn't as simple as that, no matter how much we might have wished it. For one thing, Child Services were horrified by the informal way everything had happened, and threatened to take Sofia away. But by then, she'd been living with us for six weeks and had settled incredibly well. And yes, I admit it, we'd deliberately dragged our feet informing them.

They continued to be quite threatening for a while, but I played the journalism card, and then the refugee card on Sofia's behalf. Sebastian threw in the vet card as well as the work he'd done in the local refugee community, and in the end, they had to admit that they didn't have any better alternatives to offer her. A fact that we already knew.

Her formal adoption would take much longer, but to us that was merely a thin strip of red-tape.

Marco loved his new ready-made sister and she seemed happy, as well, although there were times when she was too quiet and we wondered what heavy thoughts and memories troubled her.

She had night terrors sometimes, but that was something we understood, having lived through Sebastian's PTSD as well as my own grim, clouded souvenirs of war.

We'd decided that it was important for Sofia to know as much about her own culture as possible, so we spent even more time with Atash and his extensive family. Not only that, but Sebastian spoke to her in Pashto, so she wouldn't lose her language. I spoke to her in English, and she seemed to grasp that distinction very easily.

Soon, she was chattering away in both languages. Marco took it all in his stride, but surprised us one day by calling Sebastian 'baba'—the Pashto version of 'daddy'. It seemed likely that we'd have two bi-lingual children on our hands.

Sofia had been with us for three months and I couldn't have been happier, but then something else happened that sent my well ordered world spinning on a different axis. Again.

And I blamed Sebastian.

That man had always been trouble. God, I loved that about him. One of the many things.

Marco and Sofia were safely corralled, playing in the backyard. Sebastian was in the living room doing sit-ups, a sight that very nearly distracted me from what I had to say.

I sat down on the edge of the couch, more than a little anxious.

He grinned at me as he caught me checking out his abs. Alright, I was counting them—and possibly imaging running my tongue over them.

He winked and did another ten crunches before I finally got up the nerve to speak.

"Sebastian, we need to talk about your ... about your disability money."

He stopped immediately and scowled.

The money he'd been given for his injuries had been gathering dust in a bank account, untouched for three years.

"For fuck's sake, Caro! You know I don't want anything to do with that shit. It feels ... I just can't."

"I know, but we're going to need it. Now we have Sofia."

He sighed.

"They're just kids, Caro. They can share a room for a few years."

"Yes, but I think we'll need somewhere bigger than the bungalow before that."

"You need an office, baby. I know. Maybe I could build something in the yard and..."

"No, Sebastian. We'll need another bedroom."

His eyebrows drew together in a frown. "Why? What did you do?"

I took his hands in mine and smiled at him. "It's more what *you* did." Nope, the penny wasn't dropping. He continued to look at me blankly, I was going to have to spell it out. "I'm pregnant."

His eyes widened. "Holy fuck!"

"Quite. And if I remember correctly, that's what I said at the time."

He gave a happy shout of laughter and picked me up in his arms, whirling me around. Then he put me down as carefully as if he were handling glass.

"Fuck me, you're amazing!"

"You're pretty amazing yourself, Sebastian. You're so great with Marco and Sofia. You think you can handle another one?" I laughed a little anxiously. "Three kids under the age of five."

"Yeah, that's really something."

He shook his head disbelievingly. "Everything's changing so fast."

My heart clenched painfully.

"Too fast?"

"Fuck, no! It's just more ... more than I ever dared dream of. You, Marco, and then Sofia. Now this. It's so fucking amazing, it scares me. I feel like I don't deserve to be such a lucky bastard."

That was so typical of him, and I was going to spend the rest of my life proving that he deserved every good thing that happened to him —to us.

"You're everything I ever wanted, Sebastian. Thank you for giving me this wonderful life."

His eyes became glassy, and his arms tightened around me.

"I love you, Caro."

"And I love you, Sebastian. *Sempre e per sempre.*"

It was time to begin the next chapter in our lives.

BONUS EPILOGUE 3

Tenth Wedding Anniversary

Sebastian

"Hey, hot mama!"

I take a moment to appreciate the beautiful woman who's my baby mama. Well, the kids are not so much babies now. Marco is nine-going-on-nineteen, if the way he notices girls is anything to go by—little dude has all the moves. Our baby girl, Shirley, is nearly six, named for the woman I think of as my mom. And Sofia, our adopted daughter is 11 and such a beautiful soul. She loves being a big sister and shows it in everything she does—the way she looks after her brother and sister, the way she talks to them and tells them stories. Cutest fucking thing ever. Sometimes it's hard to believe that her life started in the stark mountain ranges of Afghanistan. I talk to her in her own language every day so she has some connection with her homeland, but in all other ways, she's an American girl, just starting junior high. And I will personally FUBAR any teenage boy who lays eyeballs on either of my daughters. EVER.

I look at my family and wonder how I got to be such a lucky mofo. It's not all been smooth sailing, not by a long shot, but life is good right now, we're good.

Caro had her 50th birthday a few months back. I know it bothers her, although she doesn't say much, but I caught her coloring her grays in the bathroom with a home dye kit.

"Grays show up more when you've got dark hair, Sebastian," she snapped at me when I asked her why she was doing it, although her eyes were glassy with unshed tears when she said it.

"Baby, I don't care. If you want to color your hair pink, green and purple, then go ahead. You'll always be beautiful to me."

"It's alright for you," she snorted, torn between tears and laughter. "You're blond—no one will ever notice."

And although she didn't say it, sometimes the fact that I'm 13 years younger still bothers her.

Things had gotten a little tense between us for a while, and it was for the dumbest of reasons.

Since I was medically discharged from the Marines, I work as a personal trainer at an upscale Manhattan gym four days a week. That sounds fucked up, but when I was discharged, the docs thought I'd never walk well again, and the bullet that went through my shoulder left me with poor motor skills in that arm. But I've worked really hard to get as much function back as possible. I'm fitter than most guys in their thirties.

So now I work with people like me—I mean guys who've been injured. I even had to go back to school to learn all the biology shit to be a personal trainer, but it was worth it in the end. When I first started out, I used my USMC connections to cut a deal with a gym owner, Connor Gibson, a guy who has a chain of gyms across the East Coast. He wanted to do something for ex-servicemen and women, so I persuaded him to let me do rehabilitation work with guys who'd lost limbs in Iraq and Afghan. When he saw that it was good marketing, good for business, and highly fucking motivating for the able-bodied in his gym, he made it a core concept for the whole chain. But part of the deal was that he wanted me working more on the marketing side, as a kind of poster-boy for people recovering from injuries. What-the-fuck-ever if it helped my guys.

I definitely had injuries: as well as being shot, I'd lost 17% of muscle mass from my right thigh after getting caught in a suicide bombing in Afghan.

But then Gibsy had the bright idea of putting me on the front of a fucking calendar that he sold for the charity Wounded Warriors. That was bad enough, but it got worse. Because that's when I was approached by a model agency to do underwear modeling for them. I'm not kidding! How fucking embarrassing is that? A bunch of strangers staring at my junk! But the killer in the contract was that they'd fundraise on behalf of Wounded Warriors—a deal that would net hundreds of thousands of dollars for the charity. How could I say no to that? And Caro talked me into it, as well.

So seven or eight times a year, I'm flown off to some beach or photo studio, and paid crazy amounts of money to strut around in skivvies. Too fucking funny. Except that I started getting stopped in the street by strange women, or even groped in public.

At first Caro thought it was kind of amusing, but the way these women treated her wasn't. Yeah, it caused some tension for a while. I said I'd stop the dumb modeling, but she pointed out how much money the charity would lose, and the publicity meant that Gibsy gave extra free memberships to rehab guys to use his facilities. I guess you could say I was locked into it.

I'd just gotten back from a shoot in Florida and surprised Caro and the kids by turning up three hours earlier than they'd expected.

Caro is sitting on the deck in the backyard reading a book. She jumps when I whisper in her ear.

"Hey, hot mama."

"Sebastian!" she manages to breathe out, before I give her the long, hot kiss that I've been imagining for days.

Then Marco looks up from where he's been kicking a soccer ball and a huge smile spreads across his face.

I never had that as a kid. The only emotions my dad invoked in me were fear and hatred. My kids would never know what that was like. Never.

"Dad!" yells Marco. "It's Dad!"

Shirley runs out of the house, shrieking at an ear-splitting volume, and she and Marco start using me like a jungle gym. Then Sofia joins in and it becomes a group hug-a-thon, and we crumple onto the deck while they climb all over me. I fuckin' love it.

"Hey, can we have a BBQ tonight?" yells Marco.

"Sure, bud—at Atash's place. Me and my girl are having a date night."

Marco kicks at a dandelion growing in the cracked paving, sending the seeds floating into the air.

"That means you're going to have sex," he grimaces. "That's gross."

What the fuck? I mouth to Caro.

She shrugs, as if to say, *You're his dad—you fix it.*

"Don't disrespect your mom," I say to Marco seriously. "I've missed her and we just want to spend some time together."

"I think it's romantic," giggles Sofia, and I can't help rolling my eyes.

Fuck knows what books she's reading these days. I leave that shit up to Caro.

"Sorry, Mom," Marco mutters when I give him another hard stare.

"Did ya miss me, too, Daddy?" asks Shirley.

"Yeah, I missed all my babies!" I say pulling her into a hug.

But she wriggles away looking annoyed. "I'm *not* a baby anymore, Daddy!"

"Aw, you'll always be my baby," I laugh.

Sofia takes Shirley's hand and herds Marco toward the door.

"Come on, we're going to Uncle Atash."

"I'll pick you guys up at twenty-hundred hours!" I call after them, and laugh as Marco salutes.

Kid wants to be a Marine and is forever asking Caro about my medals and where I served. He knows I don't like talking about it, so he asks her. She's gently trying to dissuade him from enlisting and figures that she might be successful with another nine years of persuading him to go to college instead, but I'm not so sure. He reminds me a lot of me at that age—stubborn and single-minded, just a lot happier.

Besides, the only thing I ever really wanted was Caro.

They wave goodbye and I stare at my wife. "Bed, woman. Now."

She sucks her teeth and looks down. "Can we talk first?"

That doesn't sound good. I sit next to her and hold her hand. "Sure, baby, what's up?"

She's silent, just staring down at our joined hands until she lets go and rakes her fingers through her hair.

"I feel like we're drifting apart," she says, and the words threaten to shatter me. She hasn't finished talking and I'm trying not to freak out. "You have gym and your modeling work. The kids are in school now. I'm bored with covering local events for community news-sites. And you and I..."

My heart clenches. *What the fuck is she trying to say?*

"Well, frankly, Sebastian, the only time we see each other is in bed and we're..."

"Fucking like it's the end of the world?"

She laughs suddenly and I feel my shoulders relax for the first time since she told me she wanted 'to talk'.

"Something like that," she smiles, shaking her head. "I just meant we don't have much time to talk about 'us'."

"What's worrying you, baby?" I pick up her left hand and start playing with her wedding rings. "This isn't like you."

Her lips twist in a wry smile that fades quickly.

"I suppose it's a lot of things, Sebastian. You're this super-hot model and doing all these photo shoots..."

"Which you know I'd stop quicker than ass on ice..."

"I know, but you're jetting off to exotic locations with all these young models..."

"You think I give a fuck about them? Seriously?"

She looks down.

"No, not really."

"Then what? Because you know that you're the only woman I've ever looked at. For fuck's sake, Caro! You think I'm screwing around on you?"

My heart is starting to race. How did we get here? How did we get to be one of *those* couples?

She sits up straighter. "No, I don't think that. I didn't mean it to come out like that. You've never given me a moment's concern in that direction. It's just that..."

"Then what is it, baby?"

"I feel old."

There's a beat as I stare at her in surprise. My reply is as dumb as it sounds. "No, you're not."

She gives a small smile. "I feel it sometimes. You're so fit and..."

"Caro, when the winter storms roll in, I'm the one limping around like a fucking retiree!"

She rests her hand on my right thigh, over the ugly scars that there're always so fucking anxious to show in photo shoots.

"I know, *tesoro*. But..." she huffs out in frustration. "My periods have stopped."

She looks up and stares at me.

"You're pregnant?!"

"No!" Her voice cuts across my happy thoughts.

Now I'm just freakin' confused. "Um, okay?"

Her lips thin slightly and she crosses her arms. Not sure how I'm pissing her off...

"It's menopause, Sebastian," she explains, her voice brittle. "It's a big deal. A very big deal. I can't ... I'm not..."

Now I'm getting it. Okay, so not always the sharpest pencil in the box when it comes to this shit, but I know what to do.

I pull her into my arms.

"Caro, I get that this, um, change of life, is a big deal, I do. But I love you, baby, and nothing else matters."

"I just feel so *old* compared to you. You're a model, for God's sake. I feel old and frumpy and I'm just so *bored*."

She pulls away from me and I'm wary now. I swallow several times.

"Bored with me?"

Her head whips around so fast, her hair fans out around her.

"No, *tesoro!* God, no! Never that! But I need to be challenged—and not just athletically in the bedroom."

I can't help a small smirk at that comment, but I reel it back in because her eyes are flashing with annoyance.

"So what sort of challenge do you want?"

"Well, there was that assignment in Syria that came up and..."

"No! No fucking way! We talked about that!"

"Actually, we didn't talk about that, Sebastian. You lost your temper and stormed out of the house."

True.

"Caro, it's fucking dangerous out there. No more war zones. No more places you have to wear body armor. Don't tell me we didn't discuss *that*, because we fucking did. You're not going."

"Stop telling me what to do!"

"Stop being so fucking selfish!"

She gasps and her eyes glitter dangerously, but I'm not backing down.

"I mean it, Caro. We've got three kids. What the fuck do you think would happen to us if something happened to you? I couldn't..."

I can't finish the sentence, so we sit there glaring at each other. Caro takes a deep breath and I can tell that she's trying to talk calmly.

"All I was going to say is that since I turned down the Syria assignment, I've felt ... adrift. I need a good story to get my teeth into." She pauses. "And I had an offer this morning."

"Not a war zone."

She rolls her eyes. "No, not a war zone."

"Okay, then."

"Okay, what?"

"You've gotten a new assignment. It's not a warzone. How long will you be away for?"

I hate this bit. I hate her going away, but she hates it when I leave, as well. And this is a partnership.

She smiles slightly. "Well, it would be about a month ... or two..."

That's a lot longer than I was expecting, but I can see the excitement inside her. I'll miss her like fuck, but we'll deal. Somehow.

"Fuck, Caro, two months ... that's a long time," I say quietly. "But if it's what you need..."

My words trail off. I'm already imagining what it will be like to be without her for so long. Fucking grim.

She runs her warm hands down my arm. "Don't you want to know what the assignment is?"

"Sure, baby," I say, trying to smile.

"I'll be sailing to Hawaii from San Diego. They want me to write an article about the challenges ... for a family."

I look up, wanting confirmation for what I've heard. "A family? What?"

"It's a series of articles about alternative ways of family life. You know, families who go backpacking around the world, families who live in eco communities and grow their own food. Well, the editor is following a family at the start of their sailing-around-the-world trip. I've been asked to go and report on it ... and then I suggested to the editor that we all go for the first month, so I get a real flavor of what it's like. All of us."

Her words run together rapidly and I'm not sure who she's trying to persuade—me or herself.

"It would be an amazing learning opportunity for the kids: geography, sailing, navigation, cooking in a galley, fishing ... I don't know! Lots of things. It would be good for us, as well, Sebastian, to spend time together."

She's pretty much convinced me, and I can see how amazing it would be to do something like that. But one thing worries me.

"It sounds great, Caro, but I don't know ... Sofia has only just started at her new school and she really likes it. It could fuck things up if we take her out for a couple of months now."

Caro smiles at me. "You're such a good father, Sebastian. So responsible."

I know she's teasing me, because I used to be kind of wild, but this shit is important.

"I'll have to ask permission to take the children out of school for so long, but if the school goes for it, do you have any other objections?"

"No, baby. Not even one."

Caro smiles at me in a way that has my dick hardening immediately. That's something that's never changed—no other woman has ever gotten me so hot so quickly. And she knows it.

"We'd be away for your birthday and our tenth wedding anniversary," she says, as if I could forget that.

"Baby, all that matters is you being happy."

"So, you think I should take the assignment?" she asks.

I roll my eyes. "Caro, you made up your mind before I walked through the door."

She thinks about this. "No, I hadn't made up my mind, but I'd have been disappointed if you thought it was a bad idea. So, I'll tell the editor yes?"

"Yeah, baby."

She kisses my lips softly. "I love you, *tesoro*." Then she runs her hand over my straining zipper. "Now, I think you need to be thanked properly."

I scoop her up and carry her into the bedroom. I know *exactly* how she can thank me.

~

We start making plans the next day. Gibsy is pissed until I throw him a bone and promise I'll do some shots for his fuckin' calendar while I'm in Hawaii. Then he starts getting excited about doing a shoot at the Marine Corps Base in Kaneohe Bay. He doesn't care that I'll get the piss ripped out of me. Whatever. It raises money.

One of the best parts of the plan is that we'll be able to spend some time with my brother Ches in San Diego. We try to meet up twice a year but it's not always possible with family commitments as well as work.

Caro is glowing. It hurts somewhere deep inside my chest because I can see now the difference in her. I'd stopped noticing—hadn't realized she wasn't happy—and that is un-fucking-forgivable. I won't let shit like this happen again.

Marco is ecstatic that he'll be getting time off school, until Caro points out that he'll lose his place in Little League. I take him to one side and promise that we'll do a load of surfing and all his friends will be jealous as shit.

Then I have to get him to promise that he won't tell his mom I said 'shit'. Little dude worked me for five bucks.

The schools aren't very happy with us, but Caro talked the Principals into it somehow. I was left behind for that discussion. She says the male teachers get defensive around me, and the female teachers are too busy checking me out to make sensible decisions. Yeah, whatever.

We have to pack light because there won't be a lot of room on the boat. Shirley is in tears when Caro tells her that she can only take one Barbie doll with her. I promise that I'll buy her a Hawaii Barbie when we get there. I've no idea if there is such a thing, so Caro might have to figure out how to make a grass skirt and a lei for a doll. And then I start wondering how Caro would look in just a grass skirt and a lei, but because the kids are eating their supper, I have to shake that thought and take a cold shower instead.

It's a long flight to San Diego. All the kids have done it before, but it doesn't mean it gets any easier. Thank fuck for laptops and DVDs. We're taking one with us on the boat, but that's strictly for Caro's use. No one is allowed to touch her laptop—that would be like another Marine touching your M16. That shit is just wrong.

Ches is waiting for us at the airport with his Suburban.

I'm shocked by how fat he's become. It's been nine months since I've seen him and if he wasn't a guy, I'd swear the fat fucker was pregnant. Caro elbows me in the ribs, which means I must have been staring. But come on! I grew up with this guy—he was as fit as me. I mean yeah, I know that he has an office job and I work in a gym, but that's no excuse. I'm going to have words with my best friend.

His wife Amy meets us at the front door and even manages to hug me without pulling a face. She's never been a fan of mine, and she has her reasons. Well, two friends who won't talk to her because of me. But that was a long time ago now. Women sure have long memories—or maybe the sex was just that good. What? I'm a guy—that's how we think.

Caro goes with Amy to get the kids situated, and I go with Ches to get take-out.

I can't hold it back any longer.

"What's with the beer gut, man?"

"Fuck you, Seb! You spend all your day at the gym. It's hard to find time to work-out. You don't know what it's like."

"I'm calling bullshit on that. I see plenty of guys who have families and office jobs. What's really going on?"

He looks at me sideways then glances back to the road.

"You wouldn't understand."

That pisses me off.

"I see guys every day with their legs blown off. Yeah, they have great prosthetics, but the best equipment in the world isn't as good as a real leg, and you're not using yours. It's just frustrating, man!"

Ches blows out a breath. "Just life, I guess. Kids are growing up. I'm in the same freakin' job I was ten years ago, jeez, Seb, the same place where we bussed tables when we were 17. I just feel like life is passing me by. And look at you and Caro, doing all this crazy stuff. Amy has her friends, her job, her book club—she doesn't need me. I just..."

His words trail off.

"I think you're wrong," I say seriously. "But maybe you need to think about what you want for you. Spend some time at the beach, go surfing. We always used to go there to figure things out." He nods slowly. "And I'll draw you up an exercise schedule, something to get you fine and fuckable, my friend."

He gives me the finger and we both laugh.

We eat pizza and I can't help smiling as Ches tries to force down some salad instead of a fourth slice. It's a start.

I get the kids bathed and into bed, and then collapse onto the sofa with Caro curled up next to me.

Ches and Amy are filling the dishwasher, so I take the opportunity to slide my hands under Caro's shirt, running my hands across her ribs and brushing the underside of her breasts.

"Sebastian," she chides in a breathy voice before kissing the hell out of me.

Amy interrupts us. I knew she hated me.

"OMG, you guys! Don't you ever stop? You're like a couple of horny teenagers!"

Caro looks embarrassed, but I just grin at Amy and raise my eyebrows. I always did know how to piss her off.

We spend three days with Ches and Amy before we head to the Harbor Yacht Club to find our host family and the boat we'll be sailing on.

The Falcon looks like something out of a pirate movie with two tall masts and a web of rigging, the sails stored for now.

It's a beautiful, sleek boat, and I know from the research we did that she's 74 feet and can sleep 12 people. I did a lot of sailing when I was a Marine, but never in anything this upscale. I can't wait to be on board. The kids are just as excited, and Caro's eyes are shining with happiness.

Our host family come out to meet us. We've skyped with Ken and Ellen so we know what to expect. But all the same, I make sure that Ken keeps his eyes off of Caro. He seems cool, but you never know.

But his enthusiasm is contagious. And soon we're clambering all over the yacht, admiring when Ken tells us about it ... her.

"She was originally built in Genoa in 1948," says Ken.

I can't help turning to grin at Caro. We had some good times there before we were married. She smirks at me and I have to look away before there's an uprising below decks. Yeah, totally getting into a nautical mood.

Ken is oblivious, but Ellen is smiling at me and Caro. I like her already.

"*Falcon* was completely restored and rebuilt in the nineties," Ken continues, "and converted to a twin screw gaff rigged schooner with six cabins—all with AC."

The polished oak and mahogany gleams in the sunshine.

"Fuck me, she's a beauty," I say, still grinning at Caro.

She shakes her head at my language, but smiles back.

Caro

My man has a serious potty-mouth—the habit of ten years in the Marines that he never could break, although I'm not sure how hard he's tried.

He's so excited about this trip. I think it'll be good for both of us. There was something about turning 50 that really got to me. I can't even find the words to explain, but I suppose it's the feeling that I'm truly in middle-age and the signs are obvious, not just the grays in my hair. Whereas Sebastian, he seems to get even more handsome with age, something I didn't think was possible.

He has women falling all over him, but he barely notices, or if he does notice, he doesn't do anything about it. I've never had to worry about him like that.

My beautiful boy.

I watch as his muscles ripple under his silky skin—the blue of the sky, the green of the sea in his expressive eyes, the sun forever fixed in his golden hair. The kindness and goodness that matches his beauty on the outside.

He turns to smile at me, his eyes asking why I'm staring at him so intently. The answer? Because I know I'm loved. My skin will wrinkle and my hair will go gray, my body will bend with age—and I will be loved. In this life and in the next. I will be loved. Whatever the world throws at us, wherever the next adventure leads, I will be loved.

Sempre e per sempre.

THE END

Don't forget to check out the additional bonus chapters on my website

Printed in Great Britain
by Amazon